CLAUDIA *Returns*

January 1st 2019

CLAUDIA *Returns*

To Carrie
Happy Reading!

D.H. Wright

D.H. Wright

ISBN 978-1-7750002-2-8 (softcover)
ISBN 978-1-775-002-3-5 (ebook)

Editing by Glenda Emerson
Cover and interior design, layout and typesetting by
Jan Westendorp (www.katodesignandphoto.com)
Front cover image: © Subbotina Anna/Bigstock
Back cover image: © Katja Gerasimova/Bigstock

Create Space

Prologue

2000

THE WHIZZING SOUND of the helicopter blades deafened me as I stood near the yacht's landing pad. Behind me, the medical attendants were waiting to get Mikhail safely inside for the trip back to Dubai. These past few months with him were sheer joy. Even with all the psychological preparation, and knowing this day would eventually come, I was losing the purest love God had given me: my son.

Chapter 1

1973: 18 YEARS OLD

PUNGENT AROMAS, of the not so fragrant kind, were escaping the newly vacated lockers in the hallways of Burnaby South Senior Secondary. I, Claudia, just realized that the five-minute warning bell wouldn't be ringing today. Reality set in. I wasn't coming back in September; all of my best friends and me were going in different directions. It was a sobering thought.

My destination is Cairo. My Uncle Ashif arranged a great opportunity for me to work with him at the University of Cairo. I enrolled in some university courses as well. Throughout my childhood, and growing up, I had been strongly encouraged by both my parents to experience the creative arts as they had. My early life was filled with all types of culture, music, and literature. I excelled at pretty much anything that pertained to languages and by fifteen. I was already fluent in Arabic, Hebrew, Turkish and Persian. Galib, my father, a chartered accountant and my mother, Jada, had a doctorate in music; thus, I had an endless amount of support and I attributed that from being the only child.

"Claudia Samara!" Papa stated. "Cairo, is far away, far away from your mom and me, but if this is something you're sure you're ready for, we will understand." He had his way of getting my attention.

At twelve I learned about my adoption and thankful to share the same Arabic ancestry as my adoptive parents. Not knowing the exact African heritage of my biological mother has left a void and a deeper curiosity for me to discover.

The school year ended quickly and the excitement and unknown of living in a foreign country were conflicting. The whole idea of leaving my family and worst of all, leaving my dear "guy friend" Kelly; however, living in the culture of my ancestry was drawing me more.

Today was the last day to return our textbooks and to clean out our lockers. I shared mine with my best friend Daina. The only remaining piece of evidence that we shared a locker was a photo of us taken on a field trip to Lillooet standing on the back of the BC Rail caboose. I smiled wondering if Daina left it on purpose so I wouldn't forget our times together.

Our graduating class of 1973 had planned a big campout to celebrate our final school year. Everyone, along with my six close friends were going to Porteau Cove, just north of Vancouver, this weekend. it was going to be fun yet a little sad too.

I'm leaving for Cairo in eight days and my list of things to do is shrinking, but not as quickly as it should be. Thankfully everything from school was completed. I closed my locker door and as I headed down the hallway, Kelly and another friend Daniel approached me.

Kelly asked, "Hey Claudia, looks like you have your arms full, are you walking home?"

"Hi Kel, yes, I should have taken some of this home before now, it's all light stuff, not a big deal." I noticed Kelly glanced over at Daniel who by now was searching through his locker and not paying any attention to us.

He answered, "I've got my car if you wait I'll drive you, I have to talk to you, I have an idea."

"Okay, that would be great," I answered. I leaned against the wall to watch my two guy friends hastily grab their belongings from their lockers.

Daniel seemed preoccupied in what he was doing, which seemed odd for him, I wondered if he was sharing my somber thoughts.

And then there was Kelly, wearing a totally different expression as his eyes met mine. He was smiling.

"Hey Young," he called out to Daniel. "Catch ya later hey?"

"Yeah for sure, see you guys later," he said.

Kelly asked, "Oh hey, when are you leaving for Porteau?"

"Not sure, call me before you leave we'll follow you guys up." With that, he slammed the locker door, waved and walked away.

"I sure wish I could hold your hand Claudia, we have only a few days left before you leave," Kelly said brushed up against my shoulder. "It's not going to be the same with you gone. I'm going to find it hard not seeing you every day."

"I know Kel. At least at school, we were able to sneak some time alone. I'm sure going to miss those times in the library. I hope time goes by fast, being so far away will probably make me homesick. Can you imagine what it's going to be like in Cairo?"

Kelly looked down at his feet, sliding one foot across the other, "I guess it will be interesting for sure. Claudia, do you realize four years is a long time to be apart? But by then we'll have finished our education, have our degrees, then we can be together. We can do it, just focus on learning, at least we can write letters."

"You better write back MacAskill," I teased him knowing full well he would probably write more letters than me.

We had less than a ten-minute drive home, so Kelly detoured to the back lot of the A&W Restaurant. He suggested, "Let's sneak off together and go camping on our own, we'll tell everyone you're sick and I'll offer to drive you home. Better still, I'll tell everyone my grandparents are coming, that way no one will suspect anything and our parents won't know any different. They'll think we're at Porteau right? I want to spend time alone with you Claudia. What do you think?"

"What if we get caught? Kelly, you'd be in so much trouble, your dad would kill you. My parents would be out of their minds." I reached over and squeezed his hand.

"We're not going to get caught Claudia, I don't care, I'll risk it. I want to spend time alone with you, what do you say? It's our only chance to spend time alone."

I nodded and agreed, "Yes, okay. I want that too, but we have to be careful."

A few hours later the six of us had our tents set up at Porteau. Daina, Cindy and I shared Sherry's big tent and Kelly and Daniel each had their own two-man tents. As it turned out, there were only forty or so of the hundred and twenty graduating class that came out. Of course, some brought alcohol, which we knew if the cops came would be confiscated and our parents notified.

Friday night, with the bonfires going and music playing, I watched Cindy hitting on Kelly very discretely and he seemed oblivious to it. It was obvious she liked him; even though I was pretty sure she knew where Kelly's heart was, but she did it anyway. Pangs of jealousy shot through me. I cared deeply for my friends, but Cindy had better stop flirting with him. I knew I had to stay stoic and get through this one day and night.

I hated having to keep our relationship a secret, especially now that I was leaving. Soon I wouldn't have any knowledge of how Cindy would be acting around my boyfriend. Our pretense of not dating wasn't our choice; it was because of Kelly's bigoted dad. There would be hell to pay if he ever found out about us. I never understood why all of a sudden, he saw me differently, my light chocolate skin had always been darker than Kelly's and when we were little kids it never bothered him.

Two volleyball nets were set up on opposite ends of the beach and the four teams decided. The six of us were all split up. The team at the other end of the beach picked Sherry and me; while Kelly and Cindy played opposite of Daniel. I found it difficult not to look over at Kelly. I didn't want to share the last few days I had with anyone else but him. It was somewhat tolerable knowing I'd have him all to myself tomorrow and Sunday.

I worried all evening about how I would convince my friends that I was sick; perhaps I should just pretend to have the flu, bad cramps, or a migraine. For the rest of the evening, while everyone gathered around the bonfire, I worked on fabricating my story. It needed to be an illness that started now. Well, I thought, here it goes and I made a run for the washrooms.

At first, no one commented, I didn't get any attention and on my way back Kelly grabbed my waist and pulled me out of sight. "Are you okay?" He sounded concerned.

"Yes, it's part of the plan, I didn't know what else to do."

"Oh good, you're smart Claudia," he said as he snuck a kiss, while his finger gathered my hair. We never got too many kissing opportunities and actually, I wasn't even sure I was any good at kissing. Come to think of it, Kelly stole kisses every opportunity he got and I never objected.

His fingers hooked in the loops of my cut offs, he was using them as an anchor to draw me closer to him. I was glad for those few moments together, "Kelly, you know Cindy has a crush on you, you do know that? I see her staring at you."

"Yes, I know, she asked me if I wanted to go for a walk down the other end of the beach, I just shrugged and said maybe later. You're not jealous, are you?" He took my chin in his fingers.

"I guess I am, a little, maybe. It's worse because when I'm gone she's going to try to get you, Kelly."

"What do I tell her Claudia?"

"I don't know, nothing I guess, maybe she'll get the hint. Do you think she's cute Kelly?"

"She's cute, but not pretty like you, you're my girl Clauds and I'm only into you," he smiled as his arm slid over my shoulder.

"Come on, we better get back before we're missed."

"Don't worry about me and Cindy that won't ever happen. Wait a minute Claudia . . . " Kelly's lips took mine and this time he swept the inside of my mouth with his tongue; I was surprised and soon caught up in his energy. I wanted to do it again, but it would have to wait.

"Come on Kelly let's go back," I encouraged him before freeing his hand from mine.

The next morning, I woke up sick to my stomach and figured it must be from nerves and the lie I was about to tell my best friends.

I nudged Daina, "Dai, I don't feel good, I'm sick and I threw up a couple of times during the night. I have to go home and I'm going to ask Kelly if he'll drop off when he leaves."

"No Claudia you can't be sick, we are having so much fun. Wait and see how you feel later okay, Kelly's not going home until this afternoon." Daina was upset and so was I for lying to my best friend.

After holding my stomach, and running back and forth to the washrooms, I hoped I was putting on a good act. Everyone in our group, except a pouting Cindy, agreed that Kelly should take me home. Both Kelly and I were relieved once we were driving north along on Highway 99 towards Squamish.

"Move over here, come and sit beside me, we don't have to hide out now Claudia, I know a great place where nobody goes we don't have to worry about other people."

I didn't wait a second before inching my way over to get as close as I could to him; immediately Kelly rested his hand over mine. We stopped long enough to buy hotdogs and stuff for the whole campfire routine. From there it was less than a twenty-minute drive where Kelly parked at a great spot by a creek.

A canopy of cedar trees formed a perfect enclosure for our tent. It couldn't have been more serene and private. We pitched our tent amongst the trees, Kelly gathered some wood and got the fire pit ready, then we threw a baseball back and forth as we hiked and followed the creek. We didn't have to refrain from holding hands and flirting any longer

We found a couple of flat rocks and I took off my shorts and T-shirt; all of a sudden, I was very aware of how Kelly's eyes navigated my body. My bikini wasn't as revealing as the other girls, my parents forbid me from wearing anything too skimpy.

Kelly spoke up, "We have to tell someone Claudia because you can't use my address when you write to me. I trust Daniel, I know he will keep our secret."

I agreed, "We can trust Daniel, I know we can Kelly. What will his parents think though, won't they ask?"

"Just address it to him; he'll know it's for me Clauds, that's the only safe thing to do." Kelly put my hand in his; I turned onto my stomach to face him.

"I trust Daniel as long as he swears he won't tell anyone . . . what if your brothers find out and say something to your parents? They'll disown you, then your parents will hate me forever."

"I'll be careful Claudia I promise. I have a confession, Daniel already knows, he's known a long time. He's our friend, right?"

Kelly reached over, took a strand of my hair that was hanging in front of my face, pushed it over my shoulder and kissed me softly. I asked, "How did you learn to kiss Kelly?"

"I've watched TV and I really like kissing you, you have nice lips."

"Kelly, teach me how." I watched as a grin crossed his lips.

"Okay, we can do that right now."

He was being funny but I was very serious. He pressed the tip of his nose to mine and I closed my eyes.

"Claudia, you are so beautiful I think my heart is going to beat out of my chest."

"I know Kelly, mine too you make me happy."

Once again, he slipped his tongue gently and slowly between the crease of my lips, parting them slightly, just enough to nibble my bottom lip before repeating his actions to my upper one. I concentrated on the sensations that were filling my mind, but when he pulled away I was disappointed and desired more.

"I love you, Claudia, I have waited so long to say it. I'm going to marry you, Claudia. I don't want to wait, as soon as you come home, even if it means eloping."

This gaze was different then the looks I'd seen in his eyes before. My stomach felt full of butterflies, it wasn't a familiar sensation. I rested my arms on his hips, put my face on his chest and whispered, "I love you too Kelly, so much I think I'm going to die. You really want to marry me? I want that too Kelly." My heart was racing after he confirmed what I'd hoped he'd say, "Kiss me again please."

"You can kiss me; you don't have to ask you know?" Kelly responded. I didn't wait. I tried to be soft, but Kelly took control, oh wow I didn't want to open my eyes. My heart was jumping out of my chest. I had never felt anything like this before, everything was just perfect in that moment; we were alone on the rock without a care in the world.

A couple of hours later, with the sun setting, Kelly lit the campfire. We roasted hotdogs and marshmallows and sat side-by-side sharing kisses. I liked the new sensations settling in my chest. My body was reacting in ways I didn't understand; all I knew was how good it felt.

Having the comfort of Kelly's arm around me as we played with the fire couldn't have been better. Each kiss lingered just a bit longer as the passion exploded between us. Kelly took my hand and pulled me into the tent, "This is much more comfortable, on the air mattress."

When we were on our sides facing each other once again I reached up to meet his mouth, each kiss became more intense something urging pressed inside my being.

"Claudia, will you have sex with me? I promise you I won't hurt you."

"Kelly, I'm scared, Mom said I should wait until I got married to do that. I need to be a good girl, for my husband." I felt embarrassed and excited all at the same time.

"I know, Claudia I know that I am going to marry you one day, but I won't do anything you don't want to do." Kelly kissed my head. I weaved my fingers between his.

"Would that make me a bad girl Kelly?"

You could never be bad Claudia, not ever."

This was the first time we had ever talked about sex. I hadn't even given it a thought, all I knew was he was the right one for me, and ever since we were little children he had always been my protector.

"I want to try it, but if it hurts will you stop?"

"Are you sure Claudia? We can wait; it's okay. Don't do it because you think you have to. I know I love you and I don't want to have sex with anyone else but you."

"I want to, I want to know what it's like and four years is going to be a long time Kelly."

"You're sure? Really sure?" He asked.

I nodded confidently.

"Okay," he suggested, "let's zip up our sleeping bags together, it will be more comfortable and that way we can hold each other when we go to sleep."

I knew looking at him it was right, we made a commitment to each other back in elementary school. I never doubted for a moment that we shared something special. I slipped off my cut-offs and T-shirt again, I wasn't quite ready to take off my bikini, not quite yet. Kelly scrambled out of his shorts and T-shirt as well and moved under the protection of the sleeping bag.

I sat on the soles of my feet in a kneeling position feeling a little shy.

"I want to look at you naked, I can't help it if I stare at you Claudia, you are so pretty."

Keeping my eyes on his, he reached behind me and undid the clasp of the bikini top and then untied the string at the back of my neck. I trembled. I drew in a deep breath as it fell away. My timid and shy nature took over and I attempted to cover myself with my hands.

"You're beautiful Claudia, please don't hide from me, it's okay," as he sat up and put his arms around me.

"I love you, Kelly, I'm okay, I just want you to like me."

"I like you, everything about you, shh . . . come here." He pushed me slowly down onto my back while pressing his lips firmly on mine; it felt amazing. For the first time, I experienced the sensation of his naked flesh against mine.

"I love you, Claudia, I will love you forever."

Kelly rested his palms on my ripe trembling flesh.

"Do you know what to do Kelly?"

Kelly didn't reply, he kissed me harder and deeper and I gasped as his finger slid my last piece of clothing off the secret place. "What are you going to do?"

"Can I touch you there?" Kelly rested the tip of his finger on my pelvis before sliding his finger to the entrance; I shuddered and nodded. "Claudia, you don't have to if you're scared. Are you okay?"

"A little scared, but Kelly, I'm okay. I want to, I want to know what it's like, I want to lose my virginity to you." I felt anxious when his hand started moving amongst my pubic hair and down to my labia.

"You won't do this with anyone else, promise me, Claudia."

"I promise Kelly . . . just you . . . "

I must have made a strange expression because he asked, "Does it feel okay? Am I hurting you?" Closing my eyes, I concentrated on how his fingers were touching me, my stomach tightened, it was strange how my body was responding, "Ooo . . . Kelly, what was that?"

"I heard Sebastian talking to his buddy about what he and Tammy do. He said the girl needs to get wet, to be gentle and stroke the clitoris, he said it could take a while."

"That feels good Kelly, strange good." His finger rubbed an unfamiliar place I wasn't prepared for and unexplained sounds escaped from my mouth. He positioned himself over me, parting my legs with one knee.

"Claudia, I'm going to put him in, you're wet, is that okay?"

I shuddered in an awkward state of expectation, "Yes, yes, it's okay."

Kelly entered me cautiously until he couldn't wait. I didn't know what to do, should I move? It felt uncomfortable at first until something happened, Kelly began thrusting in and out when my own natural rhythm caught up with Kelly's thrusts. It was a strange and overwhelming sensation coming from inside of me, and then I felt Kelly pulsating inside me. He gasped and I shuddered.

"Now you really are my girl Claudia, you belong to me." Kelly pulled out and noticed my eyes must have been closed. "Are you all right Claudia, did I hurt you?"

"No, it didn't hurt, but I feel different somehow, can't explain it." As he slid beside me on his side Kelly traced down my forehead, the brim of my nose and over my lips.

"I couldn't imagine not loving you." He kissed me again and then traced my body with his fingers sending goose bumps through me.

"I could only love you Kel." I studied him for a moment and snuggled close to him. "We'll be okay, right Kelly?"

"Yes, but we have to be careful Claudia, we'll write to each other all the time and I'll wait for you to come home, I promise"

"I'm happy Kelly, this is how it is supposed to be, and I am really your girl, you belong to me. Please don't let Cindy come between us, she's going to try, I can tell."

"I wish I was going with you, Claudia!" He pulled the sleeping bag around us and held me in his arms, tight against him.

Chapter 2

1977: 22 YEARS OLD

FOUR YEARS LATER my life in Cairo was coming to an end. In a couple of months, I was going home to Canada. My happy thoughts would soon change to sadness and despair.

The cause for this was an enigmatic, larger than life Middle Eastern man: Jasim Kassis al-Masri. The moment I set eyes on him my body reacted with shivers of caution at his presence. He had a stately appearance; his tall, lean body and a head full of thick, black, wavy hair with matching ebony eyes raised my curiosity. I was instantly caught up in his aura I quivered as his eyes connected with mine, a possessive nature seemed to illuminate from them. He didn't break eye contact; causing me to turn in the opposite direction and head to the conference room where the talks were being given by Palestinian Arab scholars.

The room was buzzing with Arabic voices. I was eagerly looking into the crowd for my protégé, Pascha. I had been teaching him English for the past four years. He was one of the speakers, yet only a couple of years older than me and already becoming an established author who was depicting the life he'd lived in the streets of The West Bank as an orphan. Pascha was nowhere in sight. I scanned the room and spotted what looked like a perfect seat close enough to the stage where I could acknowledge him.

I proceeded in that direction and sitting down I smoothed out my camel colored suede mini skirt and placed the matching suede jacket across my lap. I was excited about the lectures and ready to take notes for the university.

The lights dimmed and everyone settled in for the introduction when an unfamiliar hand appeared on my right knee. "Please, this is my business card. I would like it if you would call me at your convenience okay?"

He removed his hand leaving the crisp white card resting in its place. I released a breath of air; there was such a dramatic manner in his touch. It was him, the man with the ebony eyes. I fumbled with the card before responding. I read a name etched in gold leaf, Jasim Kassis al-Masri, President & CEO, Kassis, Hussein & Co.

"Mr. al-Masri, how can I help you?" I whispered, all the while exploring the depth in his eyes and the smooth full lips that moved in rhythm with his Arabic accent which sounded Cairene.

In a low voice, he answered, "You're a very stunning young woman, I am curious about you. Your name, tell me, what is your name?"

The room had become silent as the emcee made his way to the microphone.

"Claudia, my name is Claudia." I wasn't sure if he had heard my reply.

Several weeks passed before I came across the crisp white business card that had concealed itself between the pages of my notebook. I had no idea that the decision to follow up would change everything I had planned for my life.

"I thought I'd lost you," I said aloud as I waved the little card in the air, holding it upright in order to read the gold etched words.

Curiosity led me to my telephone.

"Good afternoon Kassis, Hussein and Company, how may I direct your call?" the monotone voice asked from the other end of the line.

"I'd like to speak with Mr. al-Masri, please."

"May I tell him who's calling?" the woman asked.

"Oh yes, of course, this is Claudia Samara, we spoke at the Palestine Lecture Series."

How many years ago was that? I wondered. The late afternoon breeze off the Aegean Sea brought pungent scents combined with fragrances from the gardens below. Those scents and the glass of wine on the table beside me brought me back to the present.

After taking a large mouthful of dry white wine, I placed the glass back on the table and drew my knees up to my chest. Those long-ago memories flooded my mind as the words fell from my mouth, "What would my life be like if I had lost that business card and never phoned him?"

The permanent knot inside me expanded like an elastic band, stubborn tears waited to form, but there was no way I would succumb to them, not now, not ever: that would signal he had shattered me.

All those years ago at the moment when I entered his Cairo office, I had a direct view of the Giza Pyramids, which wasn't what I expected, to say the least, but then he wasn't like any man I had come across at my age. He exuded power and an overbearing arrogant attitude. I soon learned that Jasim could say more with his eyes at any given moment than any words.

"Claudia, please have a seat. My assistant will bring you a refreshment, what may she bring you?" He sat across from me, not at a desk but on an ottoman.

"Thank you, Mr. Kassis, I will pass on a refreshment. What did you want to meet with me about sir? I'm not sure I understand why you asked me to come."

Jasim tapped his finger gently on my right knee; he didn't speak for a few seconds. I was incensed at his overconfidence and froze in my spot.

"You are the English tutor from the University of Cairo, am I right? I'm aware of your accomplishments with the Palestinian people Claudia."

"What do you know about me exactly Mr. al-Masri?" A slight chill touched the back of my neck.

"The time you spent working with Pascha Elmisri sure changed that street boy's life." Jasim's English and Arabic accent was charming and I foolishly allowed myself to be captivated by him. He chuckled, "Such nice work Claudia, and maybe you could tutor my bad accent."

That was the first time I felt at ease with his energy. Jasim stood up and walked towards one of the office windows; three identical full paneled glass windows that encompassed the most amazing views of Cairo. Jasim scratched the side of his face, "Pascha Elmisri is my son, but he doesn't know who I am."

A chill covered my body, and it wasn't coming from the Mediterranean evening air, but from those first underhanded and cruel memories with Jasim.

After pouring the remainder of the wine bottle into my glass, I submerged into a fragrant bubble bath with Asalah Nasri's songs playing in the background. Her sultry robust words buried every other thought as I soaked in the fragrance of the perfumed water. My empty wine glass signaled my soak had come to an end and my hungry stomach was rousing another sense. It took an unexpected sensation of the towel's brisk exchange across my throbbing nipple to trigger another memory.

Back to our first meeting, Jasim's insistence and the fat check he offered was very alluring. I had to meet my financial obligations, so it was too good to resist. Pascha's best interest was the catalyst that sealed my fate. But Jasim's scheme to clean up his broken accent, as he so put it, was a bit over the top. However, I agreed to be the go-between with him and Pascha as long as it didn't interfere with my return to Canada. Jasim guaranteed profusely that wouldn't be a problem.

A few days had passed and I was supposed to be on a fact-finding dinner meeting when I found myself back at his office to discuss the ways I would approach the subject of Pascha's paternity with him. There was a strange energy in the room; I shrugged it off. I often noticed the subtle way Jasim's eyes scanned every part of my body, but I wouldn't acknowledge that it bothered me. Casually I moved towards the window to study the view. The city lights were visible from three different angles in the room and I used it as a deterrent for his behavior and stood as close as I could to the glass.

"This is such an amazing place Jasim, how long have you been here?" When I turned I was taken by surprise with his nearness. It was that moment he slipped his hand between the buttons of my blouse: so rapidly that my breast was exposed and he was massaging my nipple with his thick thumb. I froze, shuddering, no one but Kelly had ever touched me in such an intimate way. I jerked in an attempt to get away.

Jasim shook his head and spoke, "I'm not going to fuck you, Claudia, at least not tonight." His fingers gripped my soft young flesh. "Have you a lover, does he enjoy your breasts, Claudia?"

He questioned before bending forward to lick my nipple. I froze; caught off guard by the erotic sensation. I froze in my spot, right there in front of the window while his fingers violated my breasts. I wanted to bolt from the room, from his unsolicited action. My mind reeled and panic set in.

"Your body is alluring Claudia and it could be even better." He removed his hand and slowly closed the buttons of my blouse. "Have you have ever had a man's hands on your breasts? Are mine the first ones to have felt them? Is that true Claudia?"

I didn't respond, it was private and he didn't need to know. He walked back to the table, picked up both glasses of the sweet, red wine and handed me my glass. I stayed silent, feeling violated and nervous. I needed to think. I needed to escape, but unknowing at that moment that my freedom would be short lived, a week later I'd become his wife.

The towel on my nipple brought me back to 1982 . . . I let it go and studied the oversized flesh in front of me. The two, perfect, natural-feeling tits, that he gifted me, as he called it. Yeah, your unwanted gift Jasim, you son-of-a-bitch. It was the beginning of many forced acquisitions. I studied my fingers, watching them as they moved over both nipples, taking hold of both of them, the way he had, pressing the palm of each hand firm against both nipples. It was a sharp rippling sensation that hit each nipple. Something was different with my breasts, they had never been this sensitive, but that could be because my period was due. The perfect form of rebellion entered my mind. What would he think if I returned home without these?

My plotted revenge would be so sweet in such a defiant way. My fit and healthy body had been achieved with hard work, exercise, massage and lavish spa treatments from Jasim's money. Keeping it perfect had become a religion, and he demanded it. I have to admit, I have grown fond of how my body changed; it had never been so perfect. Even now, no matter where I go, I keep up the rigorous hours of body care, as time-consuming as it was, and I love lavishing wonderful rewards on myself.

1985: Age 30

The cool Aegean Sea air was welcoming; it gives me such an intimate sensation as it collects the last drops of moisture my towel missed.

How erotic it feels as the breeze licks the remaining moisture off my skin. With an empty wine glass in one hand and my silk robe in the other, I took the few steps into the kitchen to refill my glass.

Then, I heard someone else in the room. It was Pascha, our eyes connected; then his focus on my firm erect breasts.

"Oh, shit Clauds! Or should I say Wow Claudia, I keep forgetting how fucking hot your body is, and that sure is one hell of a body, oh, but fuck!" His eyes still fixed on me as they did a full scan. Shyness had escaped me since life began with Jasim, I allowed his eyes to drink me up as I slowly put on the luxury silk robe and tied it up. "Well that was the best welcome I've had in a long time Claudia," he chuckled playfully.

"Really Pascha what the hell are you doing here anyway and how do you know about this place?"

"I just happened to stumble across it."

My eyes moved from him to the refrigerator while he kept talking, "I talked to the old man the other day and he told me about this house, he didn't say anything about you being here."

I changed the subject, "Have you had anything to eat, are you hungry? I've drunk a bottle of wine and I think I should get some food in me."

Pascha moved in behind me, just a little too close for comfort. "What do you have to eat in there? Let me give you a hand, I have a meeting in Athens next week and need to prepare for a presentation so I need an English lesson. I didn't expect this kind of a welcome though! So, where's the old man anyway?" Pascha questioned as he studied my expression while still standing too close, I could feel his breath on my neck.

I avoided his question. "Make yourself useful Pascha and uncork that bottle of red wine over there, so it can breathe," I ordered, directing him to the wine bottle. To myself, I thought, so I also can breathe . . . shit, I didn't need Jasim knowing I'd found this place, and now that Pascha had access to this villa, a strong father and son relationship must be developing, I would play the game, Pasch had no reason to think my being here was out of the norm.

"Sure thing, am I making you uncomfortable Claudia? You still haven't answered my question, where's Jasim?"

I shook my head; it was an easy response since I really didn't have any idea. "He's probably off on that new island he just acquired." I could trust Pascha, but I chose to give him only a snippet of information; he was too good at dissecting my answers. "You can't tell anyone I'm here Pascha, let alone that I'm even aware that Villa Phoenicia exists," I stated and swirled the wine in my glass.

He raised his eyebrow up at me. "Interesting!"

He grinned and I knew exactly where his mind was. Damn him! Pascha knew he had me. It was almost two years into the marriage when I began a sexual relationship with Pascha, having sex with him was only to have revenge. He was a younger man and Jasim's son. I did it all because Jasim forced me to use my body to benefit him I retaliated, giving myself to whomever I chose and however I chose to. It was all I had, my only control, whenever I could. I carried that secret and it was sweet, but that sweetness would sour.

Picking up my plate of food and glass of wine I headed to the patio. "Pasch, are you going to join me out here?" I nodded in the direction of the terrace. I sat down wondering how much of his father's life he knew about. Pascha had been cautious and standoffish at learning his paternity, he had never trusted Jasim. Now exactly how much had changed, it had been three years since he learned he was Jasim's son. 1977 had seen a change in both our lives, especially when I spoke those five words to Pascha. Jasim is your biological father! He went silent, it was not the reaction I had expected. I'd listened to Pascha and he never had a problem revealing his feelings to me, this time was much different.

I remember the mocking expression that appeared on his face, how disconcerted he'd become. But Pascha never commented. His hand shook my shoulder and he left the coffee shop. All I got was his reminder of our meeting that night with the group.

Would Jasim confide anything to his son? Probably not, he was too shrewd and secretive.

Pascha became aware of my scrutinizing, now motioning his fork in my direction, "What has Jasim been holding over you for all these years Claudia? He didn't knock you up for you to marry him. You are too hot and too young of a woman to be in a marriage with a man like him. He's a first-class asshole and figures his money will get him what he wants. Yeah, he's loaded and all, but Claud I know you're not that kind of woman. I haven't seen any longing for him in your eyes."

His eyes penetrated mine, his longing was apparent. Placing the napkin on my lap and the fork beside the plate I sat back carefully chewing on his question before answering. "You think my husband is holding something over me. I don't know what that could be Pascha, do you know something I should?" I lowered my eyes then swept them up to find his.

He eyeballed me and said, "I thought it was strange how quickly you married him, only a week after you guys met. Jasim bragged about it to me, he figured out I was sweet on you. If he only knew just how bad I have it for you. Hmm, and yes, just how many ways I've had you."

Pascha ran his hand across the back of his neck. "If that's not the case then could it be a business arrangement?"

I shook my head and smiled at the inquisition. It was the catalyst that brought my thoughts to that other time. I took a sip of wine and said, "Pascha why all these questions? And why is it so important to you?"

"I'm curious Claudia, back at the University in Cairo you ignored my sexual advances, then, what happened? We were close and I thought it was going to go somewhere, hell Clauds look at the things we did together. The chances we took, together."

I had to redirect him, "Maybe he bores me, lacks libido . . . hey, I'm a nympho what can I say?" I wished I could confide in him, tell him that I loved Kelly and that's why I'd ignored his advances at the time. I continued, "Pasch you should let it go okay, we agreed no strings, no emotions, and definitely no questions, right?" But Pascha continued to share his feelings towards me. I was gravely concerned that he might accidentally say something about my secrets to Jasim. My thoughts went back to Cairo, 1977. . . .

The rain fell uncontrollably that winter afternoon as I crossed the university campus in Cairo. I had just completed my portfolio and apply for a teaching position with the Vancouver British Columbia school district and anxious to get it mailed off. I was confident I would find the perfect teaching position back in Canada, home again with my family. It had been a long week and I had an upcoming trip to the West Bank to meet with Pascha to explain his paternity to him. Jasim wanted to build a relationship with Pascha and thought it wouldn't be a good idea for him to tell him, he felt I should be the one.

Having just crossed the street from the campus I hoped there would be a cab coming in my direction. After scanning the street, a white Bentley pulled up and I knew immediately who the passenger was.

Jasim opened the back door. "Come in and get out of the rain Claudia." His smile was intimidating in an erotic kind of way. What is this man about? What am I doing agreeing to this plan of his, the dollar signs popped into my mind, especially since I was last in his office?

I got inside and he said, "Let's get that wet coat off of you," and he attempted to undo my coat buttons.

"I'm fine, thank you." I wouldn't comply to his quest this time.

Then, the same intimidating smile appeared on his face as before. Jasim used his thick wide fingers as a squeegee sliding the water down the top of my forehead through my hair and then through my long ponytail.

His dark eyes burned into mine, "Claudia I just made a purchase and I would like your thoughts about it."

It seemed strange that someone as industrious as Jasim would be interested in my input, but maybe it had something to do with Pascha. "Jasim, I have maybe an hour before I have to meet a student." He poured a clear liquid into two glasses and placed one in my hand. As he downed his I could smell the contents, it was an unfamiliar, "What is this?"

"Only a little something to warm you up," he said and winked.

Taking a sip, I knew immediately what is was, "It's Arak, and I don't drink before meeting a student." Strange, I thought, why would Jasim insist I drink arak? What was I up against today? He must have ulterior motives and I was becoming nervous.

The driver drove into an underground parking lot and pulled up to a steel door elevator with the word "PRIVATE" written in dark bold letters. Jasim opened the car door, not waiting for his driver and before I knew it was escorted inside. The elevator door closed and ascended without any commands. Feelings of uneasiness crept over me, what was happening? It was like I wasn't present in my own mind and he had an invisible control over me.

"Is this a new office you're showing me Jasim?" He only grinned. This was his playful, devious side, His dark ebony eyes were unreadable, but his body language was whispering caution. It took seconds before the elevator reached its destination, but when the door opened, the flickering light of candles glowed against the gray afternoon sky.

Jasim took my hand as we stepped into the room, "First of all, it's not finished, but I guarantee it will be by the end of the week."

Wall-to-wall glass panels looked over a 180 degree view of the city of Cairo. "Jasim this is stunning." I had never seen anything so exquisite. He walked me from room to room and pointed out the unique features of each: his entertainment room, a massage room, a gym, the master suite and three guest rooms. In the kitchen, he pointed out the staff quarters. What was he saying? Everything was roughed in, and I had no problem imagining its completion.

"Claudia what do you think?" he asked as we completed the tour. He led me to the middle of the room, which was dancing with candlelight.

"What could I be thinking Jasim? It will be fabulous and you will probably enjoy living here immensely." I walked over to the windows and Jasim reached out for my shoulder.

He stated calmly, "You're going to marry me and this is where we are going to live Claudia,"

My heart stopped, what did he say? "I don't think I heard you right Jasim, you said . . . " I couldn't get the words out.

"Yes, Claudia, you heard me right." He pulled me to face him. I must have looked stunned. How could he think I would? "I'm not marrying anyone. No, I don't even know you Jasim. I'm going home to Canada soon."

"You will marry me Claudia and this is why!"

The panic set in, I couldn't comprehend his words, but my eyes followed his movement. He walked over to the counter and handed me a large manila envelope. I soon discovered why he was so insistent on the Arak.

Chapter 3

1977: Age 22

JASIM PINCHED MY CHIN and pulled my mouth to his for our first kiss as husband and wife. The ceremony was a blur and before I comprehended it all I was seated beside him in the Bentley driving to sights unknown. My mind journeyed back to my camping trip with Kelly, over four years ago now. The plans he'd shared with me in all the letters he'd written. The commitment we made to each other, the delicious love that was undeniable through the words in his letters. These last ten days and now a marriage to that man is absolute insanity; it has to be a terrible nightmare. It just can't be my reality.

"Soon I will be removing every stitch of your clothing Claudia!" he whispered masochistically and he kissed along my jawline. I cringed at the thoughts of him touching my body. "But that will have to wait. We have to celebrate first!" Jasim slid his hand between my legs, stroking my upper thigh.

The emotional pain was horrendous. Two days ago, I was making plans to go home to Vancouver, to Kelly, and we would finally start our lives together as a couple. Everything was in order, our educational goals had been reached and I had applied for several teaching positions through the city, but now that wouldn't happen.

"You will fulfill yourself as my wife Claudia, besides, you and I will be doing lots of traveling." He whispered, "I have so many plans for you Claudia, you will bring me so many rewards." There was something cynical about the look he gave me as his eyes moved across my face. "I will make you like it, Claudia, you'll see, you won't want me to leave our bed." Jasim's fingers moved up to my jawline, keeping his eyes steady on mine.

He controlled everything. He'd even chosen the white full-length bridal dress for me to wear, the virginal look, the pure untouched Claudia. He will be disappointed when he gets his grubby hands on me; I felt a sick ache inside.

We drove to a mosque where the Katb el-Kitab, the official marriage ceremony would be performed. The imam gave a short speech to Jasim about how the Prophet honored his wives and how to honor women, I would later realize that part was not meant for Jasim. While I was told how women should treat their husbands and honor them. Then the imam told Jasim to heed the speech that was just given. The ceremony was the reading of the Fatiha, considered a more official ceremony in front of God. Jasim had two male witnesses and by signing their names to the marriage contract: we were officially married.

Our wedding dinner was at the Shepheard's Hotel in the Nefertiti Ballroom where we dined on an elaborate cuisine that Jasim had arranged, but I consumed as much champagne as Jasim allowed. It dulled my ache. I hardly spoke to him; I gave yes and no answers to his questions. It seemed so surreal, my head was spinning and it wasn't the fault of the alcohol, not quite yet. How could this have happened; how did he find out?

The group I had belonged to, was so secretive. How did he know I worked for them at university?

It was not the wedding day I imagined, void of family and friends to support me. No Papa, to hand me to my groom with a tender kiss to my forehead, my papa will never understand. And my mom, she wasn't there to make sure every little detail was in place, her heart will be broken. They had spoken about my special day: their only daughter's wedding. It would be dreadful telling them about this, I have to tell them that I just married a man twenty year older than myself. A man I've known for a week, a man who will control every aspect of my life. My heart, my life was broken; and worst of all, what would Kelly think? Would he think I'd betrayed our love? My insides twisted. There's Daina, Daniel, Sherry, and Cindy, all my best friends. My Kelly, my one and only, he will never forgive me, he won't understand. How could I ever pretend Jasim is the love of my life, they'll all see something is wrong. I'll have to convince them, or as he promised: it will be bad for me.

Afterward, in his apartment, I watched as he removed his jacket and hung it on the back of the chair. Then he undid and removed his tie. He kept his eyes on me the whole time as I poured the remainder of the champagne into my glass. What plans did he have for me? Taking the champagne flute, Jasim pulled me into his arms and carried me to his bed allowing my head to rest on the pillow. I waited, with a clamped jaw. I wasn't going willingly and he could do whatever he wanted. He would never have me the way he wanted me, it would be under protest and contempt. I would never, ever submit to him willingly, or would I?

"Look at me, Claudia!" He demanded, gripping my face in his hands. "This night could be enjoyable, or not! You make the choice!"

My heart sunk deep into the abyss of my being.

"Oh yes Claudia, I like that, the sight of your blazing eyes. Give me your fire Claudia!"

Jasim's lips possessed mine; I tasted him as he swept his tongue thoroughly through my mouth before briskly sucking on my tongue. I wanted to spit the vile taste of him in his face. His hands pulled out the strands of my hair that had been tucked in a tight knot at the base of my skull. My long black waist length hair was now falling out of control like my will. I felt his hands move to the base of my spine as he slid his fingers up into the buttons that held me prisoner in the white silk. Both fingers maneuvered behind the buttons and with one quick jerk, I heard and felt the material disintegrate at his touch. His one hand rested on my shoulder, he kept his eyes focused on me, while his thick fingers dealt with the remainder of the dress. I was filled with fear and hatred; hatred I hoped he was privy to. When he finished with the dress, one hand was climbing up the back of my head grabbing a handful of my hair before yanking my head back.

My eyes fell back and covered the scene. In a slow sweep, his wet tongue was at the base of my neck then up to my chin, his teeth gently caressed along the jawline. As he released my hair he plunged his tongue into my mouth again. I could feel his movements as he undid his shirt buttons, still holding my mouth possessively he raked his teeth across my lip slowly. I was going to surrender and he was sure of that. All I could feel next was two big palms flattened against my breasts, he pulled my firm young flesh, plucking my nipples, and then his fingers rubbed each one briskly before closing his thumb and forefinger on the stub. He pulled at them, rubbed them until they became extended and hard. Afraid, but unwilling to let him see my fear even when I became weak, I wished I could slither onto the floor. I was too afraid to breathe, I was petrified knowing what was coming next.

"It's time Claudia, to explore this virginal place," his two fingers inched their way beneath my panties and rested before the labia. Out from within me an unexpected guttural groan.

"No, no please, please you can't do this to me," I cried out.

"Shh . . . Claudia, I will be gentle, you'll see. Shh!" I felt his whispers at my throat before the ripping sounds as the last piece of flimsy material left my body exposed to a snake.

I heard the sound of his zipper anxiously unzipped with one hand while the other clutched my aching breast. He quickly moved his leg between mine, just enough to run his palm flat against my pubic bone. It was seconds before the tip of his index finger connected with the tip of my clitoris. My body tightened, I waited for his next act of violation. It wasn't happening, it was only when he had the cheeks of my ass in his hands moving me around the luxurious king size bed, I didn't know how to prepare myself for something that was supposed to be so wonderful and loving like I had with . . . oooh . . . He had me positioned in place, but it was the sight of what hung between his legs that set panic in motion. Jasim's equipment was almost as large as a stallion. He reached down and took it between his hands and began jerking himself. I shuddered, knowing he would impale me with his tool. He grabbed my hand as he stood over me.

"Grip a hold on him, feel the strength of him, Claudia, stroke it woman. Get familiar with him, imagine how I'm going to feel deep in there." He murmured as he moved in closer, reaching for my pubic area.

I was about to get some retribution, "You're not my first Jasim, you can fuck me but know as you're doing it how much I loathe you." I seethed the words. Just then his arm flew up coming down with a thundering force against my face. This would be the first of many more times I would feel the impact of his self-humiliation. It stung and I glared. "Hit me again you coward! But you will never have me the way you want me, ever!"

I challenged him as my tears formed, stinging my eyes and panic settled in, but worst of all he was witnessing it all.

Within seconds his whole presence and demeanor changed. "I will not hurt you, Claudia, I promise, I will use him gently until you get comfortable with his girth," he spoke while his body straddled over me. "You belong to me my beauty, I will train you, I will train you for so many things, and you will do as I say . . . won't you? You'll make my deals."

Deal-maker? Then once again his seduction began he was sliding his wet tongue down between my breasts towards my navel, while his tongue swirled inside it. He moved slower and slower until he reached my pubic hair. He forced my legs apart and rested himself on his knees. I felt his thumbs separating my vaginal lips as my sweet place opened. I couldn't be prepared for something I wasn't familiar with, a fright formed a cloud in my brain, but it wasn't what I expected.

Jasim's warm breath was washing the area around the clitoris, he continued to blow lightly and the coolness alerted my desire. Placing his lips gently near the tip he sucked softly before greeting it with his wet tongue, he encircled it, he stroked underneath, and then he pulled the flap in between his lips. I encompassed his sex, his exploration, then responded exactly as he knew I would, he carefully raked his teeth lightly through it . . . m body was peaking and attempting to arch my back in preparation to receive him. He ignored my signals. It was when he began pulling it between his lips and shaking it aggressively that I felt an unwanted sensation gripping me, deeply, and the plunging of his tongue into my vagina caused an eruption. It was alarming and intrusive, it was overtaking me, how I wanted out of my skin, as my body began to convulse. I gasped, released and through the sensation of it all Jasim's mouth secured me in place.

"Oo . . . Ooo . . . www . . . " I wailed in sheer panic at how my body defied me. Not looking up at him, I kept my eyes closed, hating him but hating my body even more for betraying me. How could it be possible for me to be so excited with what he'd created in me? My place of pleasure was being invaded by two thick fingers moving in and out, I froze, not wanting to acknowledge the pleasure I was receiving from his movements. My body was reacting at the sensation of his fingers tapping inside the wall of my vagina.

"Oo . . . hh," I panted, "what's happening to me? I feel as though I'm bursting inside."

Jasim growled lowly, and he continued the tapping. I trembled as the liquid left my body—I was I urinating. He moved up my body, sliding his hands to pull my arms up over my head, as soon as he had them in place his mouth imprisoned mine, but the kiss was soft and gentle, it was stirring something innocent within my heart.

The kiss got deeper and hotter; I pushed his tongue away in protest. My sex was awakened and I was caught up in the natural rhythms, without any warning Jasim plunged himself slowly but aggressively deeply and snuggly inside me. I winced and cried out loud in terror, the burning. I left my mind while he pushed harder and deeper, pushing harder, deeper each stroke until I couldn't breathe, wincing once more, he pulled out then eased back in again, repeating his actions, until I realized he would continue until I participated, he filled me deeper and deeper. The shattering explosion took my body, the sounds of guttural groans as I exploded and vibrated, feeling so confused and sexually satisfied at the same time.

"How much do you loathe me now Claudia huh, should I stop now?" He quickly pulled his cock out of me, I shuddered grateful he was done. "Say it, Claudia, tell me what you want me to do." He moved over so his eyes were near mine. He spoke before running his wet tongue over my upper lip then down along the bottom lip before parting them and sliding in to find mine. His kiss hard and cruel, "What do you want to say to me now Claudia?" His eyes danced around as he grinned at me. "What do you want?"

I hesitated, "Leave me alone."

He provoked me, "What did you say, Claudia? I didn't quite hear you."

"Fuck you Jasim, fuck you!" I hollered up at him.

"Now that's much better my dear, show me what you can do for me, darling." His words were swooning from his lips I bent my head back against the silk tufted headboard, praying he would leave me alone now. That wasn't his plan; he wasn't finished. His cool breath was once again arousing my desire, his finger rubbing the entrance and up to meet the waiting clitoris, he continued in that method slowly and relentlessly. I felt an urge as my body winced.

"Not yet darling, no, no, not yet." He whispered then flicked the tip of my clitoris; I winced in an erotic sharp pain. He squeezed the tip tight between his teeth, my body lurched forward, and that was when he speared himself abruptly and quickly harder and deeper into me. Jasim drew my legs up placing my ankles around his neck; his hands gripped my ass; he banged almost violently. It wasn't long before the rippling sensation filled my body I was woozy, now caught up in his actions. When the orgasm happened, I couldn't have imagined the extremity. It was when the sting and fire that exploded across my ass that was startling. His slap was so hard and so unexpected I wailed as waves of another orgasm filled me, my panting breaths made it almost impossible for me to catch my breath; convulsions took over. I felt his body vibrating and knew he was ejaculating deep inside of me. It was seconds until I heard his throaty sounds against my ears. Jasim rolled off, but not before trailing his finger up my navel in between my lips.

"See Claudia, you came willingly, I will continue to satisfy the beautiful Claudia." He kissed each side of my mouth. For a moment my feelings were conflicting, a connection, a deep desire, something wonderful had happened from someone I loathed.

Jasim rolled over onto his back and I rolled to look at him, "Why me? Why like this Jasim?" My head was perched on my elbow, my hair falling all around me, in an attempt at moving it from my face, his hands gathered it into his palms. He pushed it exposing my breast. He captured my breast into the palm of his hand. His thumb rubbed gently across my skin sending desire through me.

"You are exquisite Claudia, and I know you don't have any idea just how. I have plans, first of all, breast implants. I have arranged for you to have surgery tomorrow and you will like them, with the help of some special people you will have the body every man will be enthralled by. Your natural beauty and your grace will steal their souls Claudia." His thumb circled my nipple as he spoke. I blocked his words, my body mesmerized by his touch. "Oh, my dear, you want something?" He grinned with bright white teeth piercing through his lips. The reality set in and so did the panic.

"You could have made me pregnant Jasim! I don't want babies I don't! What are you thinking?" I cried profusely.

"Hey Claudia, don't, stop it, I will take care of it in the morning. I won't let you get pregnant. Stop crying." He gently rolled up against me, covering me protectively with his arm. "Shh . . . now, sleep, Beautiful, I will fix everything, you 'll see." He stroked my hair after violating me. I hated him, but what I had just experienced: I liked a lot. It didn't feel like that with Kelly, it wasn't like that, but then we only did it once. God, I asked myself, how could I like those kinds of feelings from a man I loathe? I could still feel the sharp pain high in my womb, the numbness. I was so embarrassed as I thought back to how I'd reacted, oh my God, what's wrong with me? I loathed him.

I woke up alone the next morning in the big king-sized bed. It wasn't a dream and that was obvious from the solid gold band on my left hand. I slept on an off all night. The raw numbness between my legs was a painful reminder of what my life would now be like. I was afraid to move all night long, he slept too close to me. As I shifted I saw a small pool of blood underneath me, the evidence of his brutality. It was becoming more concrete there was no way out of this for me, not now, not ever, unless one of us was dead. I was his slave, his wife. The bedroom door opened and it was Jasim carrying a breakfast tray.

"Jasim if you brought breakfast I don't want it, I'm not hungry!" I waved it away and slung my legs over the side of the bed. Jasim placed it on the ottoman at the end of the bed. He handed me a glass of orange juice and he was holding something else in between his fingers. "Of course, Claudia. If you're not hungry, I understand, but take this. It's the morning after pill, no baby for you Claudia."

I took a deep breath, a deep breath of relief and quickly swallowed it with the full glass of juice. Jasim sat down, preventing me from moving. I shook my head, “Please no more my body hurts Jasim.” I dropped my eyes to my hands as I spoke.

“Shh . . . shh . . . Claudia,” he whispered before placing his hands over my breasts. “Now Claudia, these, it’s time, but we won’t make them too big, but fuller, yeah? I have already arranged everything.”

I shook my head, “No, I’m not going to let you do that to me!” My voice spilled objection, his eyes exerted supremacy. “I won’t do it Jasim, I won’t rearrange my body because you are blackmailing me, never!” I jerked back and pulled myself off the bed.

Jasim reached out, grabbed my arm and pulled me back onto the bed. I froze. “No is not in your vocabulary with me Claudia, do you understand?” Within an instant, I felt the familiar sting of a slap across my cheek, which would be a regular routine in my life now. I would also learn as quickly as the violence came with one hand, the speed of his other hand would sweep up my hair while his mouth covered mine.

In that moment, all I felt was the sting. I was unprepared for the invasion of his tongue as it lurched deep into my mouth and his one hand slid up my leg. Forcefully, his fingers were penetrating and filling me with shame, his unwanted fingers stretched my young body. He kept me pressed hard on my back and slid his fingers in and out of me rhythmically until they were deeply positioned.

“Oh yes . . . Claudia, feel that, nice and spongy the g-spot. Oh, good girl!” He growled. Using his legs, he pinned me even harder against the bed. With one hand, he kept my belly flat. “Don’t try to move, I’m not going to let you.” Jasim continued his mission.

It wasn’t long before I responded exactly the way he had intended. Something was spewing out of me again. I thought I was urinating, my head felt the same convulsions the rest of my body was experiencing. I didn’t understand what was happening, so much fear filled me. I heard the words he was saying, I didn’t comprehend them, what had just happened? What he was saying? I wanted to curl up in a ball, but I was shivering in fear, gasping for air and totally aroused all at the same time. It was painful and cruel I lay there with my arm crossed over my face, a prisoner to his desires.

When it was over he ordered, "Go shower Claudia, I will be in the den." He massaged my belly gently. "Yes, you are going to make me a very happy man Claudia."

He left the room. I lay still, trying to comprehend what had just happened to me, my body . . . the body I would never own again. How much I loathed him and thought of ways to kill him. I am capable of killing: I had done so before, with the group and it came easy for me.

There would be new sensations I would soon learn about. After weeks of holding in my pain, it would take something so unexplainable to cause me to submit gracefully and accept the role my body had to surrender to. My new appetite for the orgasmic sensations erupted within me, but the cost would nearly destroy me. While the currents of ecstasy surfaced, my body's betrayal would create an addiction that he could only relieve. What a despicable man: my jailor.

1980: Age 25

Something was different that day. Jasim phoned and insisted I put something pretty on, nothing over the top, but pretty. Wondering what he meant by that, I chose a layered cobalt blue organza knee length dress with a pair of red heels and a pair of drop halo earrings, featuring the 2.33 carat antique cushion diamonds that Jasim had bought as a reward for services rendered. They were my favorites and I chose to wear them.

Jasim stood in his closet choosing something to wear for whatever the occasion was. I asked, "Are you preparing me for one of your assignments? Is that what tonight is all about?

"No Claudia, you and I are going out for the evening, for dinner, I want to take my wife dancing. You and I need to be seen a lot more in public." He spoke in his Cairene Arabic dialogue without even turning around to look at me. "I would like your help in choosing something for me to wear Claudia." He finally turned his head and when he actually looked at me the look of approval crossed his eyes. "Yes, that is very pretty Claudia, you're very beautiful and everyone needs to remember who your husband is."

His out-reached hand encouraged my presence in front of his rack of clothes. Jasim wore a lot of suits so I chose a pair of linen trousers and a jacket in silver gray with a darker gray shirt. I perused his eyes and he seemed pleased with my choice. As I turned to leave his dressing room, Jasim's hand caught mine and he rested his lips on my shoulder. I pulled away quickly. He said nothing, he just walked through to his bathroom and soon the sound of water slapping loudly in the shower stall.

I crossed to my side of the bedroom, to the floor-to-ceiling drawers that housed bags and shoes. I chose a Judith Leiber "slide lock minaudiere hyacinth bag" with matching shoes and added a few items as Jasim's towel-clad body greeted me. The man was sharp looking; his jet-black wavy hair was already lying perfectly off of his face. Even at his age he was very self-conscious about his body and kept it well groomed, he even kept his chest and back free of hair.

A few minutes later he called out "Claudia come here and adjust my tie please?" I did as I was asked while he finished zipping up his trousers and all the while I felt his eyes burning into my face. "Thank you, darling." He removed the jacket from the hanger and I abstained from making eye contact with him as he finished settling into his clothes. How I loathed him beyond loathing.

In the next second, he was holding something between his fingers. "I want you to have this Claudia, please wear it." He handed me a large red diamond ring.

"What are you doing Jasim? What is this?" I asked disgusted at what it represented. I had no desire to slip it on my finger.

"Just accept it, it's flawless, it's a perfect 10.5 karat blood, red diamond. The diamond is almost as elegant as you Claudia." Jasim tipped back my chin detaining it for his purposes. I knew exactly what was coming and when his lips touched mine, it wasn't the demanding aggressive kiss like usual. It was a kiss that was soft and sensual, something I seldom experienced with him; that left me even more uncomfortable and cautious. What the hell was he up to? His fingers were lightly stroking my upper arms sending unsettling shivers through me. What is he up to?

"Come, Claudia, let's go and have a nice evening together."

Something grand was happening in Abu Dhabi in the Etihad Ballroom of the Emirates Palace. Jasim led me through the entrance with his hand at the base of my spine. It was some kind of a supper club atmosphere. He had his reasons for everything he did and I couldn't help wondering if this was a lead up to another one of his assignments.

The golden candlelit room had tables arranged from groups to couples and we were directed to a table for two in a very secluded part of the room. It was definitely an evening for the elite. The vast number of security personnel made that statement as I casually glanced around the banquet room. In between the labored conversations, Jasim was greeted by a number of people I recognized. During these three years, I'd met some of these people at previous functions and even during the assignments he forced on me. This time it was an engagement party.

I felt the urge to do something to embarrass him, perhaps a dress malfunction where one of my surgically formed breasts would slide into view. What difference would it make? I didn't know just how many people in the room had already scrutinized my naked body. Thoughts of the repercussions changed my mind and I decided to behave.

Jasim pre-ordered our meal. He always made it very special when we dined out. I wasn't at all surprised when the priciest champagne and a decadent meal arrived. He was all about the show, all about power and prestige.

"Claudia, we need to spend some time totally alone by ourselves. I want you to see the side of me you don't know, maybe then you wouldn't detest me. I see that hateful look in your eyes." His fingers moved quickly to meet mine.

"Don't Jasim, this is about all I can stomach of you. You can't do anything to make me change my mind about you." Smugly I took a sip of champagne, smiled brightly and looked at my food.

Jasim said nothing more and his conversation turned to travel and he began to describe Bali and the things we'd be experiencing. That was the clue to my next assignment. When the blues and jazz music started to fill the room, I was feeling light headed from all the champagne. Without giving it a second thought, he escorted me to the dance floor. Knowing from the placement of his hand and the way he held me, I was on display. While we danced his fingers moved lightly over the naked skin along the lowest part of my back sending more of the same unsettling shivers through me. He swirled me and as he did, I caught a split-second glance of his. There it was, I knew he had a motive that brought us there tonight.

Another woman, a beautiful blonde woman appeared. She appeared young like me, so I decided to play his game. Jasim gave me a questioning look as my left hand roamed up his back slowly and seductively. I rested the tip of my nose on his temple. Jasim then took over the moves; he must have thought I was seducing him. With each turn, my eyes captured the scenes in the background, the beautiful blonde, and her obvious discomfort. It was apparent Jasim was involved with her. I was getting all the information I needed and what could I do with it? Jasim kept me on the dance floor and I suspected something was definitely playing out between him and the blonde. After the dance, we returned to our seats and the champagne kept coming and I kept drinking. It was the elixir of the "let's forget reality and let go" and let go I did. A short while later his hands were at the back of my head, his fingers removed the diamond clip from my curls and they fell down the length of my back.

"Oh, you are lovely, and the rest of the room sees it too Claudia. You belong to me; don't you ever forget it!"

I wanted to clamp my teeth around the finger that was caressing my bottom lip. The champagne was still plentiful, even when we got home and so did the dancing. Jasim was seducing me in the way I dreamt a husband would; for me as his willing partner. He removed his jacket and necktie, undid the top three buttons of his shirt and I kicked off my heels.

His seduction was slow and deliberate and soon every inch of my body and every nerve ending seemed to tingle at the sensations his kisses were having on me. I was trained to dance; erotic and crude, just as he ordered. I could be seductive and alluring in the most innocent ways, but that was something he would never experience with me. Jasim moved me around the room in a tango. I figured he had hoped the sexy Argentine movements would contribute to my sexual appetite. He was handsome and at that moment I felt the pangs of jealousy towards the blonde woman, but why? Love was a void between us, there was no love filled nights of sex. So, why was I feeling this way? Envious maybe? That was it, that blonde woman was in love with Jasim, I could see it in her eyes. It was seconds when the bedroom door appeared in front of me; the heady aroma of his cologne filled my champagne mind, encouraging the sensuality his fingers and his lips were creating. The heat from his every touch spread through my body, his passion, our passion exploded. I was on fire for his sex. The times when Jasim could be loving and gentle, just like now, he brought me the most exquisite orgasms I longed for.

Was I imagining his whispers? "I love you, Claudia. Oh God, Claudia, I love you, I need you to love me back." Jasim nibbled along the curve of my neck as his deep steady thrusts brought me to orgasm again . . . I thrashed from his pleasuring, it was uncontrollable.

"Jasim, oh Jasim, fuck oh . . . yes," I growled and panted, as I saw the enjoyment in his eyes. He would never get the response he was hoping for.

His breath on my neck woke me up in the morning. His leg weaved between mine. The swirling in my head confirmed I was going to vomit. I didn't want to move a muscle. Jasim's leg shifted between mine, a signal that he wasn't finished with me, it was his morning enjoyment that I hated. You fucking moron, just leave me alone I thought. That wasn't going to happen as he began massaging that orifice.

"Does the beautiful blonde that couldn't keep her eyes off of you let you fuck her in the ass Jasim? Because you should run right over there now and do her instead of me." My voice stayed calm. Jasim got agitated.

"What the hell are you talking about?" I felt the tip of his penis moving into me.

"Stop, stop it, leave me alone! You hurt me Jasim!"

He ignored me and inched in further, spreading one hand firm against my stomach and massaged the area and slowly I felt the thickness of a lubed thumb moving into me vaginally, stretching me. "Relax, baby I will pleasure you if you just relax, if you fight of course it will be painful."

My head was spinning and so was my stomach. How convenient it would be if the contents of my stomach escaped at that precise moment when his forceful desire took hold.

"Please Jasim, my head hurts, I don't want this, please stop."

"Don't ever tell me to stop Claudia, why do we always have to have this conversation? Relax, one more time Claudia, I need this, I need you."

He eased in slowly, while his fingers were moving rapidly inside me vaginally. "Yes, see, you want it, you can't deny it you're slick and creamy in there, oh yes." Jasim pushed his hard cock abruptly into me, while my head continued spinning and my stomach churning. He continued deep and hard, thrusting himself over and over harder and deeper, just as his arm wrenched me back and hard against him, I couldn't hold the stomach contents any longer, pulling the sheet to my face, and after the initial expulsion, he removed himself and I ran into the bathroom.

Hope you enjoyed that, you sick fuck I thought to myself. And when I returned to the room; not a word came from his mouth. I collected my robe and tied the sash tightly around me. Jasim must have requested a staff member to change the bed linens because a knock came at the door and young Simi entered.

Alone now in my bathroom, I listened to the running water in his adjacent bathroom and his voice singing an Arabic song. I began tuning him out and concentrated on my body, the tingles, and reactions that were still emanating from inside me.

He walked in and saw me, "Now that is sexy my darling! Make yourself cum for me, I want to watch you!" Jasim's voice interrupted my momentum. The pleasure I was giving myself was over and I attempted to move away from the mirror, but Jasim was quick to prevent me from moving.

"Do you want more? You are insatiable, that's good Claudia, right?" He stood beside me.

I answered, "Not with you, I don't understand why you have to do this to me. How can you be with someone who dislikes you so much Jasim? That blonde woman, she wants you, it's so obvious. Please Jasim, please let me go back to my life." I begged and watched, but he only shook his head.

"No, that's enough talk, I forbid you to continue with such nonsense. We are married and that is how it's going to be. Do you understand?" His tone escalated and I was aware of his anger, and if I didn't back off, I would feel his wrath.

But my anger was uncontrollable. "I detest everything about you Jasim, you're a disgusting pig!" I waited for something vile to happen. His eyes met mine and I couldn't look away, I waited for his words.

Then finally, "Claudia you can make things a lot easier on yourself. You know what you have to do. I can make you very happy, let me." His fingers began moving over my breast. He backed me onto the bed and continued, "You also know I can also make you very unhappy, the choice is yours. Now darling, about that blonde, don't give her any thought. Be my wife one hundred percent and she will go away."

"Jasim, why don't you make both our lives better and let me go? Go be with her, she obviously has feelings for you. I don't and I never will."

"Claudia, she is not you darling. You are my wife and that will never change, trust me, you don't have a choice, look at all the treasures you bring me. Don't anger me and you will have the world and good fucking."

His lips like his fingers were once again teasing my genitals, but he stopped the closer I got to an orgasm. "Claudia, think about what I said, it would be so easy for you if you really took the role of my wife seriously."

"Never Jasim, not ever!" I was at his mercy and now he was taking his position and claiming that orifice and I would only benefit from the pain of his punishment for being disrespectful.

Chapter 4

1981 Age 26

Jasim's treasured 1963 Cobra MKII grazed the cliffs of Corfu as I wrestled with the steering wheel. He'd pushed me way too far this time. I was devastated. I didn't have any tears of frustration; there was only rage fermenting inside my soul. Maybe a little revenge would feed my disgust. I even thought about sailing through the air over the cliff with his prized Cobra. With all the other vehicles he had accumulated, what was so special about this one? But killing myself, I couldn't do that. I would be leaving my family and friends without any knowledge of my truth. I also knew I would face consequences, serious consequences if anything was the slightest out of place with the Cobra. At that moment, it didn't matter. There couldn't be any other pain as hurtful and comparable to what I was experiencing now: after Aswad. There was nothing Jasim could do that would measure up to my loathing heart.

The villa was only minutes away. The sight of the turquoise blue water was so welcoming; knowing there would be solitude and a place to meditate and purge my body and soul was starting to soothe those thoughts of revenge from the throngs of my pain. It didn't matter where my thoughts took me; to replace the treachery of his dirty deeds the last pieces of that situation had to be destroyed. Greece would be the last place Jasim would think to look for me; it was the perfect hideout. The gates of Villa Phoenicia opened as I approached; it was ingenious how the electronics sensor sensed their arrival as the sports car approached the gates allowing it to proceed without slowing down.

With the Cobra now secured inside the secluded parking garage, I reached into the passenger seat grabbing the purchases I needed for the next few days. Sliding open the floor-to-ceiling glass doors, the vanilla scent of white heliotrope filled my senses and flooded my mind. I wandered onto the large patio off the main living room taking in the splendid views around me, the beauty of the white and pink oleanders were in full bloom, it was splendid. Sipping a glass of white wine, I found myself staring out to the end of the sea. What a remarkable place, I wondered, how many other spectacular places like this does he own? If he only knew how I found this place. My throat gurgled with satisfaction, what other things does Jasim keep private?

One of the dozen plush, cushioned, wicker loungers lined up around the natural stone Infiniti pool just meters from the sea invited me after the many hours in the air. Traveling on a commercial airline and a local bus from Athens wasn't the service I was familiar with when traveling with Jasim; however, that was the only way to cover my tracks.

Stretching out, I tilted my head slightly back, closed my eyes, and felt the warm sun bathing my cold numb body. I was desperate for some kind of comfort. I ached. Every cell in my body felt pain. This would be the last time he would put me in a situation like that: it stops now. However, I needed it to end, it would end.

If it wasn't for Slade, Jasim's pilot, having figured out Jasim's control on me, I wouldn't have known he was having me watched. So, with Slade's betrayal, I could now protect myself from some of Jasim's abuse. I was grateful he helped make this happen, I needed to hide away.

The disturbance of my foot being adjusted unsuspectingly brought my attention back to the present moment. My eyes took an irritable sweep over to Pascha's face catching him off guard.

"Where did you go to Claudia? Did I say something that took you out of the present? Hey, you can, trust me, Claudia, if you need to talk. I am all ears."

"Please, let me put your mind at ease. I don't know where you got the impression there is something wrong in our marriage." I tried using a convincing voice, which I had learned to master exceptionally well.

Not convinced he stated, "When you fall apart at my touch Claudia, that's how I know. I just wish I knew the reasons you come to me." Pascha held his glass to his lips and kept his toe near mine.

"Please don't Pascha, you and I shouldn't even be here alone. We've got to stop I don't want it to happen anymore, we both know what can happen. I got caught up in you, I made a mistake, I don't have feelings for you . . . and you're his son. Lord, if he ever found out what we've done." Sitting deep in the lounge chair I reached over for the last mouthful of wine.

"So, if that's the case then this shouldn't bother you."

He pulled me out of my chair and took off his shirt. He wasn't ripped, but he had a younger virile and a sexual energy that I wanted. "Don't touch me then Claudia! If that's the truth, and if you don't feel the heat anymore, you're a liar!"

I moved out of his presence and into my bedroom, Pascha was my safe place, a place where I had comfort and control. I could take that control with him. Now that I knew Jasim tracked my moves, and God only knows what would happen if he ever found out that Pascha and I were here alone, I knew someone would get seriously hurt and I would be that someone.

I studied every detail on my face, perusing any traces of lines or oncoming imperfections and taking stock of any slight changes in my body. So far, so good, plastic surgery wasn't needed. It had been a few days since I had been to a spa and my body was becoming aware of it. Tomorrow I would go into the village and check the area for a day spa. If there wasn't one, it would mean driving into Athens for the day and spending a night in town.

I removed my robe, slowly around in a circle examining my neck; my eyes rested on the recreated breasts, it had been four years since they were surgically altered. It looked like some changes were occurring when I touched both nipples. They shouldn't be this sensitive, it usually took a few days after the nipple clamps before the sensitivity would subside, but they were unfamiliarly sensitive to anything coming in close contact with them. I decided to make an appointment with the plastic surgeon when I returned home to Abu Dhabi. Standing closer to the full-length mirror, it was becoming obvious a total body exfoliation was needed. Yes, body care tomorrow and deep massage, possibly a Rolfing tune up to release the remnants of what had happened during Jasim's last assignment.

I was unable to sleep, especially because I knew Pascha was somewhere in the house. It was crucial that I pushed the insanity of Aswan out of my mind and body. I could do that with Pascha, my reward to myself, and it was a pure pleasure with him, tenderness and climaxing was never the objective, it was his touch and safety and the wonderful sense of comfort he gave me.

Oh God, if I could only tell someone about the blackmail and everything Jasim was making me do; how wonderful it would be to release it all. I don't have a life of my own. My life consisted of Jasim's oppressive decisions that he made for me. Pascha, maybe one more time . . . I would have to convince him that this had to be the last time. That voice inside of me was screaming loudly. One last time, go to him and then never see each other this way again.

Grabbing a robe, I wandered through the massive villa into each bedroom hoping he hadn't gone into town. I was pleased to find him stretched out, clad only in boxers on top of the sheets. I sat down on the bed beside him. His massive head of long, tight ringlets hid his face as he slept, his breathing was subtle. I found a lone ringlet that was resting on one nostril and brushed it away. Pascha wiggled and his hand moved up in search of the object tickling him.

When his eyes opened and he was able to focus he spoke. "Hey is something wrong? What time is it?"

Sometime after two, nothing's wrong Pasch, I, we need to talk." I reached over to adjust his other curls.

"Can't it wait until the morning? I really am too tired to talk." He wiped the back of his hand over his eyes. I momentarily regretted having woken him. I picked myself up off the bed, but not soon enough, his hand caught me.

"You didn't come to talk did you, Claudia?"

I turned towards him, "But I did, I guess I did want . . . " I stopped myself.

"Stop lying to me and yourself, you were just as happy to see me as I was you, enough bullshit Claudia." I sat down again. "Talk then, if that's all you want." He knew as well as I did talking wasn't what brought me there. He reached around my waist where I tied the robe, his fingers pulled the loop and he yanked the sash separating the material. "What do you have to say?"

He was sitting so close but didn't touch me. I looked back over my shoulder and our eyes met. "If I could tell you I would, you have to know I didn't choose him. That's all I can tell you, so please don't ask me any more questions!"

His fingers clasped over the opened lapel and he pulled it from my shoulders. "Leave him, Claudia, you don't have to stay." Pascha's hand adjusted my hair moving it from my right shoulder; he pressed his face against my neck while his hands squeezed the top sides of my arms.

"I can't, if it was only that easy I would have left a long time ago." I was becoming intoxicated by his touch, his mouth moving oh so slow up my neck.

"Feel good Claudia?"

"Yes . . . " I whispered as I turned for his lips. He slid an arm around the front of me pushing his nose against mine. He whispered into my mouth, "Kiss me Claudia give me your tongue."

I shuddered as his suction aroused every part of me. He maneuvered me onto my back, his hands clasped my rib cage as he slid me in place, and then once again his lips were gliding all the way to the top of my chest.

"I could stay here all night with my face between these, sucking your tits Clauds, man their so big, I like it when you squeeze my cock in them, letting me cum all over each one. Fuck I'm getting hard." Pascha continued to roam across each breast kneading them deeper in between little bites between the hollow. When he sucked an erect nipple between his lips and gently bit down I howled in pain, "Ow, they are so sore."

"Wow, that was gentle compared to other times, but hey I'll be careful." Then he licked and sucked each one gently before his mouth returned to mine. My hair weaved through his fingers as he took his place over top of me. "What do you need Claudia? You haven't asked me yet. Should I suck your clit until you are as hard as I am or do I just fuck you?" He pulled my hair taunt.

"Fuck me, take me, make me forget!" I screamed.

He rose up and met my stare. "Make you forget what?"

"My life, please Pascha, touch my body make it come alive."

"What the hell, this isn't you Claudia, tell me what is going on." He raised himself over my body resting on the palms of his hands to straddle me. " Will you ever trust me enough to let me help you? I care about you, you know that."

I grabbed each side of his back and attempted to pull him onto me. "If that's true Pasch then you have to take me at my word, I just need you right now. I'll figure the rest out myself."

Taking me at my word, he didn't wait, he took control and moved deep, into me. With him nothing was taboo, it was a total turn on for him while using very explicit language, he followed my commands. Pascha's deep thrusts continued slowly and deliberate. With the next stroke he took, with deliberate intentions, and then his hands reached under my body rolling me on top of him. He knew my desires like no one else. He knew when and how to please, he gave me exactly what I wanted. He waited. I murmured and rotated while my vaginal muscles captured his erection. Pascha's hands rested on the base of my hips, gripping firmly. My breathing accelerated and he propelled himself harder into me. My body twisted as the sweetest sensation pulsated through me. I gasped and swallowed hard before opening my eyes to see him smiling up at me.

"So now what do you want a baby?" He looked up at me with love as he requisitioned. I felt his hands lifting my ass cheeks.

"Just your touch right now Pasch, please, your hands all over me." Pascha kissed my mouth tenderly and possessively and the back of his finger brushed along my cheek. "Don't go back to him Claudia, stay with me, you know how I feel about you. He's a bastard Claudia, if he's doing something to you, I'll kill him myself. You know I can."

I closed my eyes and shook my head while my fingers grazed his cheek. "Please Pasch, it has to be this way right now." Slowly drawing his finger across my jaw, his lips moved under my throat. I was purring and accepting of his delightful acts. Pascha's wonderful gentle fingers seemed to heal the horrific pain in each cell in my body. I didn't need to instruct him when it came to making love: he taught me the lessons of being loved. I received a gift that night, unconditional love and support.

When his last kiss left the arch of my foot and my breathing had calmed, like my being, Pascha moved up alongside me. I found his face and cradled it between my fingers and thumb. "You seem to find me at the most significant times in my life. If I could share the truth with anyone, it would be you, please know that. There are no words to express what you mean to me. But you have to understand, I'm not in love with you and that will never happen, one day you will understand why. We have to end this, tonight, this can't ever happen again." I knew with time Jasim would find out about us. I couldn't take the risk any longer. Not having Pascha like this again saddened and pissed me off because we shared a journey together and more than one secret.

"Claudia, we can always go to Palestine, he wouldn't dare follow us there, he is not very popular and I'm almost positive they would love to get their hands on him." "Pascha, no, it is the way it is right now, I can't risk this anymore, either can you. This has to be the last time Pascha, it really does." I left his bed and went in search of another bottle of wine. Damn it, I knew this would happen, he's going to push it.

There is something kinky and hot that turned me on when I check myself out after sex, especially after experiencing sex on my terms, seeing traces of our orgasms in the folds of my vagina was a turn on. Was I crazy? What Jasim and his cohorts were doing to my mind and body must be making me mental and for sure immoral. I stood there with my foot perched on the settee, running a finger around my labia, watching my own expressions in the bathroom mirror. I didn't realize the show I was putting on for Pascha until he pressed up against me.

"What do you see in the mirror when you look at your cunt after I fucked it Clauds?" He grinned and his hands roamed over my breasts.

"A very happy pussy, I like seeing my clit throbbing."

He reached down and under, sliding his finger hard and fast against it. I gasped at the quick firm action his finger took. "Watch, while I pleasure you. Then I'll fuck your ass while you continue watching."

"Oh, shit Pascha, you are making me wet."

"Mmm . . . yes, I am, this is a perfect, nice tight ass, Clauds."

Anal sex with Pascha was exceptional, he took it carefully and slowly, before penetration he slathered a thick coat of lube over his index finger, massaging and relaxing the muscle before inserting his well-proportioned cock. Pascha made anal sex safe and sensual, my orgasms took longer, he knew exactly what it took to please me and release his load.

"Christ, I wish my mouth could be down there lapping your juices up as I fuck your ass."

My breasts filled his hands and just the heightened sensation in my nipples felt like static electricity at his touch. I growled and watched myself move while he controlled my sex. Taking my hand he placed my index finger against my clit making me rub firmly around it, insisting I pleasure myself, his thrusts were becoming quicker and firmer. I struggled to lift my leg enough to slide my own fingers inside. "Wow look at you, fuck you're hot. Claudia your nipples are rock hard baby."

His finger flicked the end of one nipple, sending me over the edge. It was a good kind of hurt, as the electricity shot through me. "You and I are good together Claudia, shit, this is so good. Why would you ever want this to stop?"

"Don't Pach, don't ruin this, it's wonderful right now." I uttered as I leaned my head against his neck. He continued banging hard into me, pushing his hand hard against the one I was masturbating with, I quaked and shuddered as the orgasm took over my body. An excruciating sweet moan erupted loudly from my lungs as I felt him jerking inside of me. A big smile crossed my lips at the sight of him, just to see the sensual expression on Pascha's face as he climaxed.

"Wow, that was wickedly hot! Pasch open your mouth, I have something for you." I touched his lip with an index finger and his tongue took charge and sucked on them."

"Mmm yes, nice let's not let any of that go to waste." I enjoyed him and the freedom and led him into the shower before taking him into my bed for what I decided had to be the very last time.

When I woke up alone I found a note Pascha left on the bedside table.

I'm outta here beauty, you know how to find me if you change your mind. Tweak those nipples once and awhile for me . . . Later! Pasch

He sure had a way of making an exit memorable. Everything was light and un-pretentious with him and that was why I felt safe and found comfort with him. Shutting my eyes again, with thoughts of more sleep, suddenly a feeling of nausea was stirring inside my stomach. It must have been because I hadn't eaten much before drinking all that wine. The freshness of intercourse and my throbbing body parts reminded me that my body was trying to tell me something. It was when a finger found my still pert nipples and the sensitivity was still present that I had other ideas.

Chapter 5

It was like yesterday, that day in 1977 when I stood in front of the mirror in the plastic surgeon's office after he'd removed the bandages. "Well, Claudia, what do you think?" The doctor's fingers pressed at the side of my left tit. "There is mall amount of swelling but that should soon go away."

I perused my size D's and knew Jasim was going to go ballistic. He distinctly said, "A nice full C-cup." I let a large smile escape, deciding then I would find as many ways to be defiant and have some kind of control of my own body. There wasn't any readable expression on his face when he entered the examining room. Jasim eyes moved over my new mammal glands, then up into my eyes.

He turned to the doctor. "What cup size did you make her? I don't think it looks like any C-cup!"

"No, Mr. al-Masri, that's correct, we used 450 ccs to increase your wife to a D-cup as my patient requested." Jasim stood beside me as he rested his fingers lightly on my shoulder. I knew I would definitely get an earful once we left the office, but for me, that was caused to smile, even if it was just an inner smile of what I pulled over him. The only problem was, I grieved my natural comfortable breasts.

In 1978 I turned twenty-three, that was when we went to Pezenas, France. After a day of shopping, fine dining and enjoying all the special things I loved to do: the reins of freedom were severed. I became his prisoner. Jasim confined me to the property, no trips into town, no shopping, all services were brought to me.

Jasim escorted me into his study the next day where a movie screen and a projector were ready to go at his nod. I watched as the evidence of my involvement with the Palestine Liberation Organization played out just like a movie. I shivered as I watched how clearly my image was captured by the camera. I could easily be picked out of the crowd during that day's attack. Every movement was exposed in front of my eyes; my voice would be identified easily in the recorded conversations.

I faced Jasim, who was comfortably perched beside me, wearing a look of contentment. My whole being went numb; my bones felt like jelly. I felt dizzy and light headed as the fog covered my eyes. I realized I truly was his prisoner. Jasim turned to face me, cradling my face against his hand. I wanted to spit in his face.

"As your husband Claudia, it is my duty to teach you obedience, to be submissive and honor your husband's requests, all requests. A respectful wife does not question her husband's orders." Jasim waved his finger back and forth. "When your husband enters a room, you will refrain from anything, anything you are doing in the moment and you will greet me with, 'Yes, my husband how can I serve you?' Then you fall onto your knees and wait for my response."

I closed my eyes before swallowing hard. "No Jasim, no I refuse!" My voice filled with terror. His eyes seared mine and the look of his evil filled them. Jasim grasped hold of what flesh filled my cheeks, gripping them so hard they brought tears to my eyes.

"You will never ever use that word in my presence again Claudia. There will never be any more 'Nos' coming from these lips. Do you hear me?" He gripped me tighter as he shook me. I tried to speak, but could only nod my head. He pushed me down to the floor. "Get on your knees, Claudia."

I conformed, and in doing so rolled my head into my chest. I could hear his footsteps as he moved around me. "We will stay here, in this place, for as long as it takes until it becomes the normal way for you, my wife."

"Stand up Claudia!" He ordered. Slowly I pulled myself up. "Take your dress off, leave your panties on Claudia." I brought my fingers up to my face, begging the pain away. "Now Claudia, do it now." I unzipped the zipper on the back of my summer dress and stepped out of it, unclasped my bra and slipped my arms out of the straps. Stepping out of my shoes, I stood to face him exactly how he demanded. His eyes inspected me. He poured a drink, sat himself down, crossed his legs and caressed his bottom lip. He didn't speak. He just sat there roaming his eyes over me. It seemed like hours he kept me standing. "Be off with you, go to your bed, Claudia." He ordered. I reached down for my clothing. "Leave them, the staff will deal with them. Go, Claudia, get out of my sight."

I couldn't get away quick enough. I tried to hide my over-sized chest behind my hands from the staffs' curious eyes as I left the room and moved up the long staircase. I reached what I hoped was the safety of my room, pulled the bed covers tightly around me and lost all control of my emotions. Jasim must have given me what he figured enough time to deal with the residual effects of my new life-style when I heard the door open. I was about to jump out of the bed and act on his demands when he spoke.

"No Claudia, not here, this is our sanctuary . . . our bedroom where your natural response to my desires will take place. Right my darling wife?" Jasim began undoing the buttons of his shirt and moved towards my side of the bed.

"Aren't you going to welcome your husband into his bed, Claudia? I am waiting now." He grinned. I pulled the covers back then laid curled up in the fetal position. "Come, come, Claudia, it's not all that bad."

Jasim's naked body was forming against mine. His fingers found the soft nubs and he ran his fingers over my entire breast while his leg was busy separating mine. "Darling . . . " he whispered, "I am going to be such a happy man. You'll see how happy you will make me." He pushed his erection deep into my anus, not responding to my painful cries. My body turned hot and clammy as sweat beads formed, and pain shot through me. I was choking, my only relief was knowing I would have a few days to recover from the damage he was doing before he would repeat the act and others again.

I cringed every time a door opened or heard footsteps. "Yes, my husband, how can I serve you?" It was all about sex and being submissive. He made me perform deplorable acts in front of him and even our staff members. When I hesitated, he'd punish me. On one of my darkest times, when my monthly was causing me painful cramps, I begged him to give me a break from his sexual demands that day. When I was finally allowed to look up after falling to my knees, after being ordered to strip off my clothing, one of his bodyguards was in the room with us and Jasim was stroking his swollen cock.

"On your knees, and come here."

"Please, Jasim I'm not well, please not today."

"Do it now Nazmi!" Jasim shrieked, grabbed me by my hair and yanked me up onto my feet, quick enough to see the flash of the bodyguard's gun before feeling the barrel being rammed into my vagina. "Show her Nazmi . . . my punishment for her disobedience." The room went black.

The trials and tribulations that took away my innocence made the timing perfect for Jasim introduction of me to Kenji, a practitioner of sadomasochism. I guessed Kenji was Japanese, very soft spoken with a militant attitude. Before our introductions, Jasim prepared me for the types of lessons I'd learn, and accept. During the first few weeks, Jasim was present as I succumbed to what Kenji was training me for. Kenji was to be obeyed exactly as I obeyed Jasim.

Claudia Samara disappeared somewhere inside my mind. The

shell remained, empty and void of all ego. My body became lean and firm, my skin radiant and flawless, even my diet was directed by Jasim. Kenji and Jasim's blueprint was taking shape. Kenji began a regiment with Geisha sex training and Asian bondage. I learned quickly how severely Kenji could discipline me, in order for me to void myself of any remaining inhibitions. Kenji taught me to walk, to carry myself proudly, to hold my breath in order to keep my body in a certain position. I learned exotic and erotic dance. Jasim ordered that my body to be clear and free of all body hair as if I were a porcelain doll. Then Kenji introduced me to tools: nipple and clitoris clamps, suction cups, anal plugs, and beads. Kenji was an androgyny, something I didn't understand because I was never introduced to people like that before in my life.

After months of Kenji connecting different types of body restraints to the most intimate places of my body, and using different methods of arousal, Jasim would make intimate contact with me just before my orgasm. After several months into the training, Jasim had my first assignment waiting and Kenji prepared me for the introduction.

It began with my nipples being pumped until the whole areola was erect, then my clitoris was pumped until it was hard and protruding and then the clamps were attached. I was to wear them until I was ready to perform. I was wrapped in two or three yards of white silk, just like a mummy.

I had no idea what or who I would be dancing for until the time came. There wouldn't be any music to guide me through the steps. I had to be perfect; no mistakes allowed. I was under the impression I would be dancing and performing those erotic moves for my husband, and I wondered if Jasim would be taking part in the final erotic piece.

My light chocolate skin was sleek and glowing from the expensive oils; my jet-black hair was tight against the back of my head, and the mummy dress was perfectly arranged on my athletic hard body.

I heard the bells chime and it was time to make my appearance. My well-trained walk brought me into the room. I was taken by surprise when I saw another man at the opposite side of the room from my husband. There weren't any introductions, only a soft kiss when Jasim took the end of the fabric out of my hand. That was the signal for me to begin.

"Keep your eyes focused directly on his," Jasim whispered in an authoritative tone.

The dance began and I did exactly what was ordered. With every turn, I locked my eyes on the stranger's eyes as he watched. The fabric fell from my body after each turn; Jasim rolled it up exactly how Kenji had done. The fabric's end was nearing, so my nakedness would be exposed: as would the nipple clamp that was holding the end of the material. Jasim jerked the material and the clamps released. I danced naked before the stranger and moved close without touching him. Then I turned around, bent over, rolled my ass in the air and released the clamp exposing my swollen sex.

I had built up so much hatred for Jasim that I did the unthinkable. Strutting near enough I was able to wiggle my nipples near his lips, just close enough, but hopefully out of Jasim's vision. Before turning in Jasim's direction, I met his eyes and I smiled brightly before leaving the room, but not before I saw that familiar look of my upcoming punishment on his face. He didn't miss my movement after all. I loved being defiant, and I would grow more defiant as the years past and his punishment would match my acts of defiance.

The punishment I was faced with after that dance, was being suspended in the air in body cuffs with my legs wide open and he whipped my genitals. As he escorted me to the room, he announced that his punishment matched my crime. He wouldn't leave any marks on my exposed body; instead, he punished me by using many unpleasant methods and tools from gagging to hours of bondage.

I was not, at any time to have any physical contact with men. I was only to perform indecent sexual acts. Then, the day came when Jasim made the decision to let anyone he saw fit have me, but only he selected the acts that would follow and he remained present: until Aswad, then it all came to end.

The gold lame' tube dress formed to my body like a second skin, as one of the staff dressers smoothed any wrinkled spots where the material didn't sit smoothly. The make-up artist and hair stylist created accents that added to my exotic looks; my hair was straightened and pulled back from my face in an elaborate ponytail. I slid gold bracelets up my arms just before my biceps.

When Jasim appeared in the mirror, looking up I caught his smile, but it was a different smile, a smile I hadn't seen before. He approached me from behind and rested against the chair I sat in, his hands gripped my shoulders as his flat palms he moved down to my nipples. "I'm so proud of my wife. You are perfect Claudia, beautiful, graceful and so so sexy." My eyes stayed focused on his. "You made a very good choice making these so big Claudia, better than I could have imagined." His nails pinched the nubs, in a way that would have made me shudder, but this time nothing he did got the results he expected. I knew the staff was well aware of his cruelty to me, they knew not to react in any way. "It is still only my right to touch what is lawfully mine. I will now choose who will touch you, you have given me no choice remember that Claudia." His words burned her ears like the nipples between his fingers he kept hostage. Before releasing me, he trailed kisses up along my neck pausing at my ear. He said, "I will never ever let you go my beauty," before leaving the room.

I sprayed on one of the exquisite fragrances he'd brought back from one of his excursions (as my reward), each one had a unique scent, so delicious and arousing. I studied myself in front of the mirror and graciously smiled at Suki, a very young girl, was the daughter of another staff member. Her eyes lit up and she carefully smiled at me, she had been disciplined to keep a neutral expression at all times. Suki helped me with my shoes and assessed the dress before she left the room. It was time to join him.

I approached the formal stateroom in the manner he expected of me. My eyes scanned the room and rested on a tall, very handsome Middle Eastern man. He was dressed in his customary attire, a thawb and on his head a white matching ghutra an iqal. He stood taunt and orderly.

"Aswad this is my wife Claudia." Jasim grinned like the cat that swallowed the canary. Aswad nodded, I watched as his eyes met Jasim's and avoided mine.

I said, "Scotch please Bernard," without looking at my husband, I carefully perused the man speaking in a dialect that I wasn't familiar with. I felt an ice-cold uneasiness around him. I was prepared for the evening, praying that he wasn't there for me. Fuck you Jasim, fuck you! My silent voice spewed.

One of the house staff advised Jasim that our meal was ready and we could be seated. Jasim directed Aswad into the formal dining room and placed one of his hands at the base of my spine. Jasim's fingers moved in a scratching manner and it was as though he was uncomfortable. The two men spoke Arabic throughout dinner and they kept their voices low during their conversation. Sitting respectfully, as I'd been taught, I was curious about what my role would be with Aswad.

Kenji hadn't prepared me for the evening, maybe this was different and just a dinner meeting. The two men consumed their food with great pleasure. I didn't have an interest in the food what so ever, Jasim noticed, but not before I requested one of the servers to bring me scotch neat. Jasim waved him away. That didn't go over well, I politely excused myself, pushing my chair back from the table and located the scotch bottle on the bar and poured myself another. Jasim glared at me. I gave him one of my newly found sensuous grins and took a long sip. It was a matter of seconds before I received the, "I'm going to deal with you later" look. Then I returned to my place at the table at my husband's side. What's new I thought.

Jasim summoned the staff, "Please bring the after-dinner spirits to the lounge." And he invited Aswad to join him, making sure he was comfortable before excusing himself.

Taking my hand, Jasim led me towards the guest bedroom. Instantly, I became uneasy. He attempted to kiss me my temple but was unsuccessful because of my quick shifting motion.

Jasim opened the door and pulled me into him. "Don't push me away from you Claudia, you know you don't want to do that." He whispered in his threatening voice. My eyes spotted a gold box tied up in silver ribbons placed on the guestroom bed. What's this? I wondered, Jasim's face was now nuzzling into my hair and his lips began the journey to mine. Once he'd released my mouth he motioned over at the box, "Claudia you can open the box please?" I did as he asked and found the most luxurious black piece of lingerie I had ever seen. "Baby, do you like it?" He murmured as his hands caressed my backside.

"Yes, of course, it's beautiful Jasim," I replied obediently as I held up the sexy piece of material.

"Put it on Claudia, I need you wearing it." At that moment, I became aware of something dark and devious in his eyes. It was all starting to make sense, he was about to hand me over to Aswad. "You will do everything he asks of you Claudia; do you understand me? Jasim demanded, grabbing my arm.

I dropped to my knees "Yes, my husband how can I serve you?"

"Get up Claudia, listen to me and I mean listen to me. You must make this deal happen, if it doesn't you will regret it. You will do this for your husband." Again, the decision was made for me. I had no choice and began the process of going to that void space in my mind. My blood turned cold and the feeling of evil was creeping into the dimly lit room.

Soothing Arabic music was playing in the background, it was what I saw laying out in the open that made me panic: the tools Jasim used for my punishments, wrist and ankle restraints and a gag and blindfold. I had no sooner scanned over the articles when the door opened and Aswad appeared. His face was expression free, but his eyes were dancing, I knew he was already devouring my body with his eyes. Claudia Al-Masri took over as I watched the person with the cold expression in his eyes closing in on me, all the while twisting his hands in excitement.

The quietness in the bedroom that mid-morning was soothing for me, for many reasons. I was actually very much alone and very much void of unwanted or regulated interruptions. The weeks I moved from place to place to find solace from the Aswad nightmare and to keep my distance from Jasim were treasured times of freedom. I didn't have to submit to any more of Jasim's assignments, nor be his object for sexual gratification. It was exactly what I needed, celibacy from him and from the life he inflicted on me, but most of all from his assignments. After four years, I was comfortable in my body for the first time since marrying him.

The times I spent with Pascha was pure pleasure, fulfilling sexual enjoyment with a young virile body such as his. I had begun hating my body for deceiving me. He was so tender, my body loved the gratification I figured it was what my body was made for, Claudia Samara slowly returned while I was with Pascha.

The first time I succumbed to Pascha was after he'd learned that Jasim was his biological father and he had insisted that he come and live with us. That was before he whisked me off to France when he started transforming me for his devious assignments. Jasim thought he could willingly convert me by showering me with luxurious things such as fine clothes, jewelry and travel. Pascha and I continued with his studies, I continued to tutor him in English Literature and art.

One day, the two of us sat opposite each other when the conversation took an unexpected change when Pascha asked, "I've been wondering about them, Claudia." His eyes shifted to my chest. I sat back lowered my head and scanned the area his eyes were resting.

"I gather you're talking about my breasts?"

He nodded, "Whose idea was that?"

I didn't respond.

"I thought so, why did you do that? You want to be a stripper for the old man or something else Claudia?"

I met his eyes, "It was my idea, I think they look great. Don't you?" I lied. I hated the lie. Before even realizing what, I was doing, my fingers had the buttons of my top undone, exposing perfectly formed flesh.

I watched the words form on his lips . . . "Wow, they're unbelievable." He grinned and his face flushed.

I reached for both of his hands and placed them on each one, closed my eyes, "Do they feel real to you Pasch?"

He sat there stunned for seconds before accepting my blatant offer. "They're amazing Claud, I shouldn't be doing this. What do you want me to do?"

Letting my head fall to the side. "Appreciate them, Pasch, show me." I closed my eyes in anticipation of a tender touch.

"Claudia the old man, what about him? Are you sure this is what you want?"

I replied without even opening my eyes. "Shh. . . , don't break the magic. Please show me how you appreciate big boobs!"

There was silence, only the movement of the air in the room was audible. It was the heel of his hand slowly descending above my heart that brought air into my lungs. I felt his fingers as he softly traced around the dark areola several times before connecting with an evolving nipple. Pascha's other hand stroked the same breast softly as he watched how quickly my puckered nipple responded to his touch. Running his finger down the valley between them and over to the other, he stroked that nipple in the same pace as the first, before bending forward quickly sliding it between his lips. My hands found a place amongst his curls and I moaned softly at the sensations he was creating. Lowering my face into his hair must have been the signal. It took seconds until he had me by the waist placing me on his lap before his mouth reached up to take mine. I greeted his lips; the kiss was nothing less than what I knew it would be; eager sensuous and playful.

My longing for sweet passion, tenderness, and his youth had been welling up inside me. My fingers followed his sides to the waistband of his pants, quickly finding the zipper, he gasped pulled back from me. His eyes darted to mine. I closed mine and shook my head, continuing with the task at hand. There was no disappointment when I released his hardness before I attempted to bend down to taste him. Show him my appreciation for the hard flesh. He stopped me. "This is what I want Pasch, I know you do too. Please let me."

He stared into my eyes, "Really, this is really what you want? What if he finds out?" He was serious.

I grinned, "Oh . . . he'll just kill me." I said flippantly knowing full well I'd suffer, but at that moment it would be well worth it.

We examined each other's bodies. I savored his tenderness, his touch, his strength, his sex drive. Sitting back on his heels, Pascha, ordered me to stand up. Standing naked in front of him, he encouraged me closer, close enough for him to separate my knees and bury his face up into me. It was seconds before he had my body responding in the most delectable way. He nibbled gently, feeling my growing desire. I pressed myself tightly against him. "Not yet beautiful, you can't cum yet, sit on me. I want inside of you now." He placed his face between my breasts and pressed both hands against them. Together our young bodies did pirouettes.

My memory of Pascha conflicted with the one with Aswad. Even after six weeks, I was unable to repair the memory of the Aswad's assault. My mind held too many of those memories to block them from the forefront of my mind. The extreme pain Aswad inflicted on my body, with my husband's consent was unfathomable. I rarely disobeyed what Jasim demanded and as a result, I barely lived through Aswad's punishment. So why would Jasim allow someone to torture me when I had obeyed him to the last letter? But most disturbing was how distant Jasim had become when he found me bound, gagged, shivering and sobbing. Aswad left my body covered in welts and there had been a large bloody discharge from my vagina. Jasim had carried me into my bathroom and still held me while drawing the bathwater. He had tucked my head into his chest almost in protection mode. When the tub was ready he slowly placed me into it. I flinched as the water found its way to my wounds.

"Claudia, don't think I'm going to let him get away with what he did to you, he is going to wish he was a dead man, once I destroy his empire, I will have revenge for you, Claudia." Jasim's words were as clear right then as if he'd spoken them that day.

I hissed, "Your revenge is for you Jasim, not me. Your only concern is that you won't be able to send me on your assignments until I heal, that's your only concern, you pig." I didn't care how hard his fist retaliated against my numb body, but he was silent and didn't even twitch at my comment.

I sat up straight as though a lightning bolt penetrated my body. "I can't be . . . how could it have happened? How could I be pregnant? I can't be, I just can't be. I've been using birth control." I counted back trying to remember my last period, "Oh shit, shit I missed it!" I had totally overlooked it, put it out of my mind, "I must have missed it. I don't remember when I last had one."

I dragged my body to the bed and crawled under the covers. I knew it was time to go back home, after being away for six weeks, I knew Jasim would be even more furious and threatening if he didn't hear from me soon. I was probably already walking a thin line. It was also possible that he had the documents ready to turn me to the Israeli's. These were the times I wished he'd kill me and get it over with. My life was not worth it anymore.

Chapter 6

THE DRIVER PULLED UP in front of the private elevator, which was open and ready for me to enter. I checked the time, hoping Jasim would either be sleeping or away somewhere, I prayed for the later. The calming music flowing into the elevator acknowledged I was home, back to prison. Dropping my coat on a chair, I walked towards the master suite, hoping all the way, that he wouldn't be home. In case he was, I would be careful not to disturb him. I quietly opened the door and he was there. Feeling disappointed, I closed the door as quietly as I had opened it and headed through to the bathroom, removed my clothes and found a nightgown to change into.

I was careful sliding beneath the covers, not to wake him or get anywhere near him, preventing his touch and his sexual advances. I wanted to sleep and knowing if I moved to quickly and carelessly he would wake up and expect me to perform my wifely duties.

Once he knew I was carrying a child any hope of freedom would be out of reach. I positioned myself as close to the edge of the mattress as possible with my head on the pillow. Had I been careful enough? Could I close my eyes and sleep? Tonight, was the same as every other night, I wait for sleep with an ache in my heart to be back in Canada, leading the simplistic life I'd once known.

For over ten years I longed to wake up in the innocence of my own bed with Mom and Dad just down the hallway. Those days had passed long ago and even the relationships with my friends have been seriously reshaped, there were still threads of familiarity and still, the friendships were somewhat intact at least where Daina was concerned, somehow Jasim endorsed her and seemed not threatened by our close ties.

The one friend that remained strong in my heart was Kelly and our secret; a secret that began in high school only because of his father's racist attitude. Kelly's father was a bigot in every form and definition. He hated Negro's or anyone whose skin wasn't the same shade as his. My Arabic and African ancestry wasn't welcomed in their house once we started high school together; everything changed from our early childhood playtimes when we ran in and out of each other's houses. Once Kelly invited their group home for a barbecue after a soccer tournament and the first time I was made aware that I was different, a "dirty nigger" were his father's exact words. Everyone was stunned especially Kelly at his father's comment to Kelly, "Get that dirty nigger out of my house!" He hollered at a horrified Kelly. Our friends just stood there with mouths open leaving shocked expressions, everyone left the MacAskill residence including Kelly. We all knew Mr. MacAskill liked to drink and generally under the influence. Kelly tried to convince everyone that it was the booze talking, but I knew different. I saw his eyes, the hate, and resentment that came through his bold and blatant stare. From that day on Kelly and I couldn't be seen alone together in public, but that didn't extinguish the feelings that had been brewing within both of us ever since we were children

All the MacAskill children would attend the University of British Columbia with funds their grandfather had set up for them. Kelly had planned out his future to every last detail and he wouldn't let anything come between him and his dreams. Kelly was determined to make it happen. Once we became established in our professions, it would be the perfect time to make a life together even if it meant compromising his family relationships. Kelly had talked about walking away from them and taking me far away from his family, but that would mean I would be forsaking my own family. I couldn't even think about something like that happening, little did I know my worst fears would come to fruition. My journey took a different route. It brought me to this life because I was willing to stand up for a cause, a political cause, one that I hadn't any idea would turn out so destructively and that one stupid error destroyed all my hopes and dreams forever. Jasim's blackmail ruined everything for Kelly and I. As long as I was owned by Jasim, I could never disclose the circumstances that got me there to anyone. . . .and that included Kelly. Our letters back and forth had been weekly not always wordy, and Kelly kept the conversation light and humorous. I wondered what would be going through Kelly's mind when my letters stopped, without any explanation. Jasim goons that packed up my belongings had been ordered to get rid of anything from home. I was left with nothing to keep me strong, no loving words, but Jasim couldn't erase the words that were chiseled in my memory.

I lay there, next to Jasim, but remembering a day in 1982 . . . after being married for three years, I was heading to one more of Jasim's assignments when I couldn't have received a better gift. It was Kelly and it was like magic to see that wonderful face in the crowd. The boy I'd promised my future to so long ago. Kelly hadn't noticed me until I caught up to him and slipped my hand into his. Shocked at the sudden contact, he jerked his hand away before turning and recognizing me. A smile appeared on his face and it said everything I could have ever hoped for. He reached his arms around my waist and I nuzzled into his neck, the place I had thought about in every dream while seeking comfort from the sick reality I was living.

"Are you arriving, or departing Kel?" I ran my hand down his forearm. Kelly was absorbed in me as he grazed my face with his eyes.

"I'm actually heading home, back to Canada. You wouldn't happen to be heading there, too would you?"

"Oh how I wish I was going home, home to Canada, "Actually Kelly I'm meeting Jasim in Monaco, there is some mechanical problem with Jasim's jet so now I have to fly commercial." I studied his face scrutinized his eyes for something, something I really wasn't sure of. "When is your flight Kel?" As his lips moved I became almost desperate to have his kiss once more. He drew me back into his arms. "Three hours and twenty-three minutes. About yours?" He paused, "You know Claud, I didn't believe it when Daina told us you married Jasim. I need an explanation, I really do." His arms tightened around me. "You owe me, Claudia."

"I don't have a flight booked when we landed to refuel the pilot alerted me there were some major issues with the plane, Jasim told me to arrange a charter." I relished in the idea of having three hours with Kelly and would make good use of every second.

"I'm changing my flight Claudia; will you stay the rest of the day and spend the night here? We can fly out tomorrow, please Claud we need to talk."

I didn't need convincing. I would have the flight to Monaco to come up with an excuse for Jasim, it was my only opportunity to connect with the man I still loved dearly.

"Come on let's find a place to stay." Kelly paused, looking at me "Getting a room with you doesn't imply anything sexual Claudia, I promise. I just want to spend time with you." He placed is hands on my shoulders, sending heat through my body.

"I didn't even go there Kel, we've been friends for so long, I respect your marriage, we're both married now." My stomach was forming knots. His frown spoke volumes.

"The Great Fosters Hotel is only a couple of kilometers away. I passed it on the way in. I'm going to reserve a room and change my flight."

"I'll get a limo after I book a charter out tomorrow Kelly." Oh my God here we were, after ten minutes heading to a hotel, this is crazy. Kelly changed his flight and after we had everything in place we left the airport.

It was unbelievable the sight of the hotel, "I registered us as Mr. and Mrs. I hope you don't mind me doing that."

"It's all right Kelly."

Kelly checked in and we stood in a room done up in mint green, it was the big king size bed was what caught my eye. Kelly and I were alone for the first te since we were teenagers. We decided to tour the gardens and chat about whatever came to mind; we avoided talking about our marriages.

It was Kelly's question that set the stage for my emotions. "When did I lose you, Claudia? I believed you when you promised me that no one else would ever come between us. It killed me Clauds. I stayed true to you until I heard you got married right after meeting him! He must have swept you off your feet huh Claudia?"

The gardens offered a stunning and an idyllic place to relax in privacy. Seeing the void in his eyes, I was unable to contain my emotions. I could only shake my head.

"It wasn't like that Kelly. You never lost me. I didn't have a choice; he forced me to marry him. I can't get into the details . . . just know I didn't have a choice, you have to trust me and know that you are my only love, only you Kelly. No matter what happens to us, I have only ever loved you. I still do, so much. Please, please don't ask me any questions." I watched the expression on his face.

"Why haven't you talked to me before now Claudia, hell it's been nine years, we could have figured all this out?"

I could only shake my head. "You have to trust me with this Kelly, I couldn't and I still can't, I have already said too much." I looked down at my feet.

"So now what am I supposed to do with that statement Claud? You expect me to get on a flight tomorrow and forget everything you've said?" He sounded angry and confused.

I nodded, "Yes I do, you have to, but now, know you never ever lost me."

"Come on let's go check the rest of the hotel's estate if I can't ask any questions I have to get my mind on other things." Kelly was having difficulty looking at me.

"Of course, I'd love to check it out . . . Kelly hey it's me, talk to me, I understand what I'm asking you to do. I promise you one day you will know everything. I promise." How I wanted to reach out for him and hold him but that couldn't happen. I watched Kelly's face and knew he was still digesting what I had said, how do I leave it tomorrow? I knew he needed some sort of an explanation.

When we returned to the hotel room it was late in the afternoon, so we decided to visit the cocktail bar. I quickly showered and changed into a soft pink shift dress and left my hair loose in curls. I opened the bathroom door and spotted Kelly, he was half sitting on the window seat looking out to the gardens.

"Why is it that a shower does a body so good?" I tried to lighten up the energy in the room.

"You look great Claudia, about that shower I really don't know. But I agree it does do a body good."

I folded the clothes I'd worn and placed them back in the bag and then searched for the sandals I'd brought with me specially to wear with that dress. I was well aware of his movement and thought he was going to shower, but he stopped, reached over and took my hand. I knew what was coming. He gently pulled me into his arms. "I don't give a damn if you get mad at me, I'm not going to pretend what you said hasn't stirred my insides, Claudia."

Taking me by the shoulders, I made eye contact knowing what was about to happen. I was anxious for the feelings his lips used to give me. This was not the eighteen-year-old I remembered: this was Kelly the adult. I knew I would be in trouble and of course, I would risk it. As my eyes fell shut, it was seconds before his lips softly held my upper lip, and his tongue ran between them opening them gently enough to slide his tongue eagerly in search of mine. This was not the way I remembered his kiss to be, this was Kelly the man and these kisses were very possessive and urgent movements, sucking each lip gently and lovingly. I followed suit, returning the sensations to him.

"You love me, Claudia, those are the most beautiful words I've heard ever! I couldn't let an opportunity get away. I have always been in love with you, there has never been a time when that has changed. I love you too Claudia. I promise if you don't want me to kiss you again I won't, we'll have a great evening and I will go home with this knowledge, maybe even a little happier."

I hugged him tightly and whispered, "Oh yes, oh always, forever I love you too." Then I pulled away.

"Still the poet Ms. Samara, aren't you?" He left me and walked into the bathroom to take a shower.

We managed to keep our conversation light and even shared some memories as we drank wine and ordered dinner. We both chose the same meal; slow cooked cannon of lamb, confit lamb breast, kohl-rabi, pod peas, pistachio, and madeira.

It was like old times again. Even while we were alone in the room, it was comfortable, and no one broke the rules. Falling asleep was difficult, because of my re-occurring nightmares of Aswad. I wouldn't expose him to that. How wonderful I felt spooning with him. I couldn't help but feel the kisses he managed to sneak into my hair. My only thoughts were . . . I love you too Kelly!

Jasim's body shifted and he was moving closer to me. I began to pray he wouldn't sense my presence. No sooner had the thoughts of Kelly left me when an accidental brush of his outstretched leg touched mine and woke him.

"Claudia, you're home?" He yawned through his words. "Where have you been? I've been worried, no communication Claudia. I was beginning to think you were trying to leave me, but I knew you are smarter than that, aren't you darling?" Jasim words were as direct as they always were.

"I had no intentions of leaving you, not ever Jasim, I needed to get away, to think and allow my body time to heal. You must understand that?" I tried to appease him while remaining still and hoping he wouldn't touch me. But Jasim still had an outrageous appetite to punish me, to keep me in line, to bully me into believing I could love him. I listened to his breathing, hoping his rhythm was settling him back to sleep, but those thoughts were quickly distinguished with his reaching fingers.

"Jasim, I've had a long day." I pleaded.

"Yes, I understand Claudia, I really do." He responded sarcastically. "But you didn't have to go, you chose too." Jasim turned onto his side and it was seconds before his unwanted gestures began. I couldn't stop the victimization. The words "No" and "Stop" weren't a part of my vocabulary, I had no choice but to accept what was happening. Jasim began massaging my abdomen slowly before sliding his hand onto my pelvis, without any warning he inserted his index finger deep inside of me, harshly rubbing my clit with his thumb. I stayed motionless as he did what he wanted to.

"No play Claudia? All right baby let's not then." He conceded. I exhaled. It took him seconds to move his leg over me to straddle my body. Throwing back the covers, Jasim began masturbating and moving upwards towards me, He ordered, "Open your beautiful mouth, Claudia." Moving onto his knees, he positioned himself for an easy access to my mouth, then slid his rock-hard cock into my mouth and ordered, "Suck me off Claudia!"

I followed orders and opened my mouth mechanically. He pushed himself deep to the back of my throat, it was all I could do to stop myself from gagging. I did my duty, my wifely duty by working him as fast and as thorough as I could to get it over with. His release came quickly as the warm salty liquid filled my throat. Jasim shivered and I released his limp shaft from my mouth. I swallowed the remainder of what hadn't seeped down my throat and he lay back on his side of the bed. To myself I said, when will you get it Jasim! You can 't get to me through pain, I will have my revenge, I promise.

I wanted to get some sleep and turned on my side away from him. When the sound of the bedside drawer opened, I didn't give it much thought. Then, he reached over, ordering me to lie on my stomach. You rotten bastard! "Please Jasim, I can't take that right now! Please, please Jasim." I pleaded and begged.

"Get on your knees, come on Claudia, don't force me, and please honey I don't want to hurt you, you know I don't. We can do this easy or you know . . . " He spoke softly and controlling. Reaching underneath me, his thumb hooked inside my vagina, his other hand squeezing cold lube between the cheeks of my ass, he proceeded to massage the entrance of my rectum while he stroked his cock. All I could do was breathe shallow enough to force relaxation; then leave for that void place in my mind. I felt the tip of Jasim cock firmly pressed against the entrance to my rectum. Reaching underneath me, grabbing at my breasts, he pushed into me and pinched my nipples with his fingernails: I screamed out in pain. It felt as though he had pierced my nipples with straight pins.

"I'm pregnant you bastard, let go of me!"

Jasim let me go, immediately. "Pregnant, how the hell did that happen? Claudia, you're lying. You can't be pregnant. Did you stop taking your pill?" He looked terrified.

"Of course not! Jasim, you'd be the last person I'd want as a father for my child. I glared and held my breasts . . . I spoke to a doctor and he told me it happens quite often."

"How far along are you?" Jasim questioned. I recognized the look of horror on his face and knew just what he was thinking.

"Yes Jasim, this baby could be that bastard Aswad's, how about that, I'm almost two months along?" I gave a snarky reply. There was silence, Jasim pulled the covers over my body and left the room.

Several days had passed before he came home, he was a different person, but the anger was still present in those dark eyes. He motioned with his finger for me to sit. "What are you going to do about the pregnancy Claudia?" He asked, before standing up and moving to the opposite end of the room.

"What do you think I'm going to do? Exactly what I'm expected to do, give birth to my child. Don't think for a moment you will force me to abort this baby Jasim, I won't. You can torture me, or better yet, kill me before I would kill my child. You could be killing your own child."

"Don't be so melodramatic Claudia. It would be for your own damn good. What if he impregnated you, you could still want a baby after what happened to you?"

"How hypocritical you are Jasim, you're worse than him. I loathe you both." The memory of his weapon, his hand had not crossed my mind as I blurted out my hatred. Why hadn't he hit me? It was at that moment I realized why he asked the question, I would no longer be able to fulfill his assignments. The pregnancy was my out, something to be thankful for, a small miracle in a contemptible way.

Those next few months I spent most of my time doing good things for my body and the baby I was carrying. Jasim's surveillance was less and I was able to come and go. I took charge of my existence and had the chefs research the right foods for my pregnancy. I sought out prenatal care and created a peaceful environment in my bedroom. It took all the courage I had to move my belongings out of our bedroom and into one of the spare rooms. Then, I had to inform Jasim he would no longer use my body any way he chose. It was all over now. That conversation happened after a morning speed walk when I returned to find Jasim waiting to have breakfast with me. He seemed like a different man, he spoke to me with an air of respect, and decency. I stayed skeptical, to say the least, I wouldn't trust him ever.

"Claudia, we need to find out the paternity of this baby, don't you think?" He reached out across the table to touch my hand. I retracted mine immediately. "No Jasim, you are going to accept this baby whether or not it is yours. Or you're going to give me my freedom! The choice is yours." That was when it clicked! Oh, my maybe that was his intent, if it's Aswad's he'll let me go, he doesn't want someone else's baby with me. Fuck I'm his wife whore.

"Claudia, you can walk away from all this if you're not carrying my child. Isn't that a good initiative to have a test done?"

"If this is your baby Jasim, then what?"

"Nothing changes Claudia, we raise our child together as a family. You've served your purpose for now Claudia. I won't touch you if that's what you want. We will remain in separate beds if that's what you decide." Jasim said as he crossed his legs and turned sideways. "I did what I did to make myself the wealthiest man in Egypt, and because of you I succeeded. I could never have gotten you to go along with my plan. I orchestrated it all Claudia, my arrangement with the PLO, you were young and very impressionable and I used my resources to get what I wanted and I wanted you. I have given you everything you could ever want Claudia, you could have the world with me, now, especially now, if you give us a chance, you could love me, just as much as I love you." He spoke quietly and calmly.

I sat back, swirling the fork in my omelet, "Are you kidding me? Love you, look at what you've done to me. I'm a prisoner. You're my abuser, you've abused me every way imaginable Jasim. There are no words to describe how much I detest you." The anger erupted inside of me after hearing his confessions, I should have figured that out. Of course, only he would do something so evil, setting me up was perfect. "You make me sick, love you like you love me, you sick fuck. I bet you do, you adore me all right. Well Jasim, I abhor you with every iota in my body. I would love to see you dead Jasim!" I grinned at him as I spoke and then returned to eating my omelet.

Jasim was quiet for a few moments. "I know Claudia, I know." He said pulling himself out of the chair. "Let me know your decision about the paternity test?"

"They're going to want Aswad's DNA, how are you prepared to get it? He can't suspect anything Jasim." I replied.

"Don't you worry, I will get it." He stated surly and headed towards his office. I pushed the plate away, after that I couldn't eat anymore. I realized I was fortunate, to have avoided morning sickness. I was actually enjoying the pregnancy, placing my hands on a rounding belly, thinking about the child I am carrying. "Little one, I love you already you know." How satirical when I loathed both potential fathers.

Pushing myself out of the chair, I followed Jasim into his office and without knocking I walked in. His back was to the door and he was embroiled in a conversation. I didn't care if he thought I was eavesdropping. "Jasim . . . " He motioned for me to sit. Interesting, I was sure he said, "Find that bastard" but I wasn't going to assume anything. His telephone conversation ended quickly and he sat back in his soft lambskin chair.

"You can arrange for the DNA test, and I will let my doctor know to expect a call from you Jasim."

"You made a good decision Claudia. I already have put things in motion to find him. We both need to know, don't you think?" Again, how uncanny, to have my freedom and carry the other rapists' child, and to raise it would be glorious. Sadly, there was a huge part of me praying that Aswad would be the father.

I was at the end of the second trimester before the paternity test happened. The week dragged and by now the baby was really expanding my belly. I was having so many confused thoughts. At one point, I considered a strenuous workout to miscarry but rethought that after feeling the miracle of his or her movements inside me. This is my baby, the child would be mine, innocent and mine, I would not recognize its father, or even acknowledge one if Jasim wasn't the dad only because I was still his prisoner. But still, I prayed that whole week for my freedom, that Jasim hadn't impregnated me.

I made so many promises to God! Please, Lord, I served my prison time and I deserve to be free. "Right God?" I spoke out loud. My thoughts took me to Canada, back home, oh how I wanted to share the news about my pregnancy. But I couldn't, I wanted to talk to Daina and just let go of everything. I hated pretending Jasim and I was happily in love like I had that first New Year's Eve he'd agreed to spend in Kelowna, British Columbia. It was a long-awaited reward for being an obedient wife.

Chapter 7

1982 Age: 27

It was New Years and Jasim and I had been married for three years, and I hadn't seen my family or friends since1973. He agreed, but only if I agreed to his terms. I would have done anything at that point; so, to portray the wife that adored her husband was a minor trade off.

We landed in Kelowna two days before New Year's Eve and Jasim treated it like our honeymoon get-a-way. He'd arranged for an opulent suite at Kelowna's Eldorado, he lavished me with spa treatments and fine dining and then one-day skiing at Big White.

It was the trip to Big White that caught me off guard, how I needed love and my fucked up brainwashed mind was like a sponge sopping up something that resembled my desire. It must have been because we were away from the Middle East and I hoped he might release me if I tried to love him. I saw a different side of Jasim, those days alone together. He seemed genuinely attentive and romantic like I had never experienced before.

By day we skied, we arrived at the summit just as the sun broke through. For us to see the spectacular view. He embraced me from behind and rested his head against mine. "I am very happy Claudia, you give me happiness. I want it like this always. Let me make you happy?" He spoke quietly and as his lips moved along my neck and I felt the energy of a different man. My heart wasn't softening. It was just curious, maybe hopeful of normalcy in life. I kept the terms he set for me, willing myself to weaken and genuinely give into him.

He stood in front of me and I studied his eyes and hoped he was sincere. I kissed my husband for the first time with passion and acceptance. He pulled me close and showed me the loving side of himself. We skied and stopped long enough to try another kiss or two. Soon we were sharing laughter and acting exactly as a loving couple did. Even our dinner conversation was interesting and at that instance, I felt his equal. At that moment, I wanted to fall in love with him and I felt I might be able to if this version was real. We hadn't quite finished our meal when his napkin rested on his plate and his hand reached out for mine.

"One moment Claudia, I will call the waiter over." He changed his mind. "Wait, wait here, I will be right back." And left the table.

I felt something strange stirring inside of me, a longing for something, maybe it was the longing to be loved and appreciated, to love and appreciate the man, my husband. Could it happen? He returned and helped me out of my chair and then weaved his fingers into mine. He stood in front of me; his fingers escorted the strand of loose hair back behind my ear then kissed my forehead, "Beautiful woman, yes this is being happy." I looked up at him unsure and conflicted, but at the same time curious to explore this further.

When we entered our suite, the room was flooded with white pillars of candlelight and colorful roses sat in vases, "Jasim, you did this . . . for me? I'm touched by how beautiful it looks." Not once in three years had he bought me flowers? I was surprised.

"It may seem strange to you Claudia, but you are the closest I ever come to feeling love." Jasim removed the already loose cork from the chilled champagne and poured. I took a sip then placed my hand against his chest. He swallowed hard at my touch. His eyes moved with my fingers as I maneuvered them under the lapel of his jacket, before helping him out of it. I kept my eyes focused on his, watching them soften and his breathing rising up and down on my hand. Slowly I undid his tie and let it fall off his neck before unbuttoning the row of buttons of his linen shirt. Jasim placed his palm was flat against my cheek, and his thumb swept across my lips. The hand that often left my skin burning after outrageous and offensive beatings was now soft and sensuously moving over my skin. I felt goose bumps form all the way down my back, almost as if it was a warning. I chose to kiss each one of his fingers before making my way to his face, while my other hand slipped the zipper of his fly down and unloosed the button from its hole. Hooking my fingers into his shorts and trousers I had him standing naked before me. When he attempted to undress me, I pulled away.

"No . . . wait, I'm not finished yet," I whispered and returned to the spot under his ear lobe, placing kisses up and over them, while feeling his breathing exhilarate and he swallowed hard again as I continued my seduction. His chest was vibrating. I could sense how relaxed he was becoming. I continued running my fingers slowly and sensuously getting closer to his manhood. "Claudia, let me!" He attempted to pull me closer.

"Shh . . . not yet, I'm not finished yet." I saw a grin, not that devious one he wore before administrating his punishment. My fingers found his growing erection, I stroked it and attempted to shift to my knees to perform an uncomfortable act, one that pleased him, but he stopped me.

"No . . . Claudia, not now, let me show you what's the proper ..." He paused, "Let me be right with you Claudia, please if I can just make one thing right." Jasim took my waist and steadied me. He pushed my hair back over my shoulders and his smooth lips kissed my brow, all the way along my jawline. His finger hooked the zipper and brought it slowly down my back, before bringing the bottom of the dress up and over my head. Jasim's hands roamed my sides, hips then up to the thigh pulling one leg up onto his shoulder. Watching my face, his fingers trailed the length of my leg to the top of my silk stocking, slowly and with intent he rolled it just far enough to trail soft kisses under my kneecap. Then he floated a finger to trace the shape of my calf and along the sole of my foot before replacing it with the other, again tantalizing my desires. The next second, the sound of the fabric from my panties being ripped from my body increased my breathing.

I sucked in a deep breath when his hand slid under my bra, finger splayed like the teeth of a comb capturing a nipple between his digits. Jasim collected the full areola closing his fingers together he stretched and plucked it before his thumb gyrated the growing nipple. Jasim and I were both on fire, the passion had ignited and I threw back my head when his hands pushed my large breasts together as he began licking and sucking each nipple in unison. He was savoring me almost as if he had never tasted my skin before. Keeping my nipple between his lips, he hoisted me up off my feet. His teeth firmly gripping it and I squirmed in delight. I felt the pillow meet the back of my head and he quickly captured my legs, throwing them over his shoulders. His tongue moved around the entrance of my vagina, and then around my clitoris slowly and deliberately. I could almost make out the shape of kisses around the opening. Then it happened, I went to the void, this time to the place where I felt safe.

I fell asleep in Jasim's arms for the first time, knowing he'd entered me and brought me to orgasm. We slept close, something I'd never experienced before with him and the realization came when I awoke to the sensation of his hands moving around the small of my back. Panic set in, he was getting ready to I was sure of it. Quickly I shifted onto my back, my heart was pounding so hard I was sure he could see it coming out of my chest. "Morning Jasim! Did you get any sleep? God, what time is it?"

"It's only six, go back to sleep, I'm sorry for waking you, but I am enjoying you." I yawned and tried to move in close, but Jasim pulled back.

"What now Claudia? I see your fear and felt it just then. You are playing me aren't you, aren't you Claudia?"

I shook my head," No, not at all Jasim, I can't forget everything you've done to me so quickly at the drop of a dime." I felt him retreat into his old self again.

"Jasim, I'm willing to try, but you have to stop hurting me and making me do those things I deplore. I want it all to stop, please destroy what you have to me. I promise you, I will try to find what you want from me." My hand reached smoothing over his chest.

No . . . not yet Claudia, I need you to continue, I have plans for you, big plans. You're my sure thing, I will have it all Claudia and you will see to that. Don't ever try anything like this again Claudia. If you think you can play me, it's not going to happen." Jasim turned over and my heart sunk.

"I meant everything I said Jasim, I will try, you have to meet me halfway."

"There's no half Claudia, you are my wife and you will do it my way!"

I reached over to him, running my fingers through his jet-black, wavy hair. I moved up to find his lips, hoping that would reassure him in a small way. I sucked softly on each side of his mouth before closing softly over his lips. "Jasim, give me a chance, please."

He glared at me and didn't speak. The cruel hurtful Jasim returned. "All right, it's New Year's Eve and I will continue the agreement we made." I rolled over and wondered, who are you really Jasim? What happened to make you like this?

A few hours later, having just showered, I walked back into the bedroom to find something casual to wear. Jasim was on the bed stroking his cock and it was obvious the coldness had returned into his black eyes. I shivered at the sight of him and suspected he was about to make demands once again.

"Come here Claudia and leave the towel behind."

"Jasim, I was just about to leave for the massage you scheduled for me, can you wait until I get back?" I turned to walk to the closet.

"Now Claudia, or you'll be really late."

"Jasim come on." I let the towel fall to the floor and did as I was told. I attempted to swing a leg onto the bed in front of him and was about to perform oral sex.

"That's not what I want Claudia, turn around on your knees and bend over."

"No, please no . . . you hurt me when you're like this."

"Stop your whining, and do as you're told."

I surrendered, feeling humiliated and once again at his mercy. I attempted some relaxation techniques to ease my muscles and waited. His warm breath moved over the cheeks of my ass and his tongue was slide between them. That was when the unexpected happened. "Such a pretty little cunt you've got Claudia, perfect lips, pink and plump. So kissable, how nicely they respond to all the pleasures I give them." His hands came down hard across the flesh on my ass as he grabbed each cheek tightly and separated the folds. Panic set in at the unknown. Jasim sucked and chewed, I responded and throbbed gyrating against him. He pulled me back against his face, and then raised himself over me, before ramming his thick cock.

"Oh . . . Jasim, yes please, more, don't stop." I begged and he pounded, I was fulfilled, satisfied before he sat back against the headboard and pulled me down and pushed himself into my rectum and released his load. I closed down and went away.

It was now later on New Year's Eve as the limousine pulled up to Sherry & Daniels address on the east side of Kelowna/ It seemed to me that more than seven years had passed since I'd seen my best friends. How would I come face-to-face with Kelly and Cindy; who became his wife after all? How am I going to get through that? I would never doubt Kelly would keep the secret of our meeting at

Heathrow Airport.

There were several cars parked on the street. I hoped the house would be full of people, that way it would be simpler to keep my distance from Kelly and stay calm, especially because Jasim would be watching my every move. We hadn't spoken a word to each other since I'd returned from the massage. He'd taken my chin between his fingers and said, "Remember the deal Claudia, you screw up and you know what the consequences will be."

He reverberated before kissing me in his possessive manner. All I wanted was the hurt to stop. In an attempt to reach out to him, I raised my hand to his face, pulling him to meet my eyes, "Please Jasim, we can try." He pulled back and walked away. There was nothing more to do to regain what we'd had the day before.

I pulled the black fur tightly around me as I got out of the car. Jasim took my hand and escorted me into the house. A doorman greeted and led us through to the living room. Had we been the last to arrive? As soon as we walked into the room, I was bombarded by everyone but Kelly.

I was aware that Daina and Sherry were uncomfortable because Jasim wouldn't leave my side. He was only gone long enough to take a piss or refill our glasses. It was an alert Daniel who'd coerced him away, giving me the time I longed to have alone with my friends. The four of us women wandered into the kitchen and it was all I could do to put on a happy face for Cindy, who had the role meant for me as Kelly's wife. I was coming apart internally. I ached for the love of my life. Kelly was avoiding me, it broke my heart after being so close and almost intimate during our time in Britain.

Daina threw her arms around me, "Geez Claudia, why don't we ever hear from you? He's being greedy and keeping you to himself, I must have a word with him!"

I forced a giggle, "Yeah, he does, it has been incredible, the life I have with him. My life with Jasim is one I could never have imagined, the places we've been, let alone the experiences are out of this world Daina. What a life, let me tell ya! I love him in a way." I stopped mid-sentence, "Yes, in a way I could never love another." I thought I was going to get sick over my own lies. I glanced over at Cindy, she glowed with happiness, and it was obvious she was having Kelly's baby. The resentment burned deep in my belly like molten lava. Jasim had taken so much from me, not just my soul, and the happiness I waited so long for. I searched inside my toolbox for another act and the right emotions, a way to put on the right expression. I could tell Cindy was eager to show off her diamond wedding ring to me when she caught sight of my gaudy red diamond she pulled back and I said, "Oh Cindy, it's beautiful, did you and Kelly pick it out together?" I wanted to act happy for her.

"No Claudia, he picked it out and pretended it was a birthday present, can you believe how romantic he is, proposing on my birthday."

"He must adore you Cin, I'm so happy for you two." I listened to their wedding day stories and just as Cindy was finishing, Kelly made his entrance. I didn't know where to direct my eyes. Even though I had learned about his marriage, at that moment I didn't want him to see how hurt I was.

"I heard that you and Jasim arrived, Claudia, you've been hiding out." Kelly walked towards me and with a quick motion, I experienced a careful hug. His mouth against my ear, he whispered, "I'm so sorry this is such an awkward situation."

That was the most difficult moment of my life. "Congratulations, I'm so happy for you and Cin, now you have a baby coming. I'm so happy for you." I stroked his arm carefully, keeping myself in check. I needed an escape. "So where is my husband anyway?"

"I just left him and Daniel, I think Daniel has him deep in conversation." Kelly kept his eyes on me. I had to excuse myself to locate the bar, but it was Daina's hand on my arm that interrupted that idea.

"Not so fast Claudia, wait for me, I'm going to keep you as close to me, 'cause soon you'll be gone again." Daina rested her head against mine, instantly melancholy emotions surfaced. I had to fight back the tears.

"Dai, where is the washroom?" I asked hoping she would point it out, so I would have a few minutes to catch my breath and shift into the role of Mrs. Al-Masari again, but instead, she pulled me in the direction.

"You have to meet Eric, Claudia," she stated.

"Bathroom first girlfriend!"

When midnight arrived, I made sure I was by Jasim's side, playing the role, portraying his adoring wife. His embrace and kiss reminded me of the night before, the passion and heat was there, he was once again putting on a show for whomever was watching and groped my ass while his mouth moved over my ear, "Your dress is really short darling, too bad you're wearing panties I'd love to get in there."

"Later baby, you're going to have to wait." Claudia allowed the range of her voice to raise an octave above normal so those around could hear. Unfortunately, Kelly was in earshot distance. I caught his expression and thought, one-day Kelly, one day you will know the whole truth.

After the toasts to welcome in the New Year, Sherry pulled me into the kitchen when Daina and Eric joined us. I knew who Eric was, and it surprised me that Daina chose him for a husband. He was wild and got into trouble all the time. He used to drink a lot and I wondered if he still did. When Eric shook my hand it was a little too long and he was a bit too close for comfort.

"Wow, you sure look good Claudia, what a hot babe you turned into. Hell Daina, you should have told me just how good looking she is."

I became even more uncomfortable, Sherry was aware and stood between the two of us, "Good God Claudia, that engagement ring of yours is wicked. It's such a deep red, that's crazy girl." She smiled a safe smile, I knew full well why and mouthed a "Thanks."

It was time to track Jasim down; the acting was not working. It was safer for me to be at his side than to slip and let my dear friends see a minuscule of my angst. Jasim must have recognized my distress because his questioning look said it all. I mouthed, "We need to go," I noticed he seemed to be relaxed and enjoying himself which made it more difficult because I, should be the one in comfort with my friends.

I knew it had been a mistake going there for New Year's Eve, it only caused my heart to ache even more for Kelly. Kelly always so respectful and that evening he had been very observant. I knew Kelly was aware of the awkward relationship between Jasim and me. He kept a respectful distance, as best he could without alerting suspicion of our obvious feeling for each other. It was too painful knowing he and Cindy were having a life together as well as a family. I held on to the words he spoke to me when we in Britain . . . "I have always been in love with you; there has never been a time when that changed."

Kelly is not the, "I'm going to sweep you off your feet" kind of man. He's a good-looking man, but he doesn't have Jasim's looks. He's a wholesome looking man and that was extremely alluring to me. My heart raced at the sight of his six-foot stocky frame. As a kid, he had the goofiest sense of humor and that grew on me. Unlike our other friends, Kelly didn't eat and breathe sports, we were both active, but we also enjoyed literature, fine arts, and music. There were times when we'd be hiding out in the back of the library. The place where I learned Kelly's secrets: the place I fell in love. The library was our place, at the very back sitting on the floor with our backs up against the wall. It was during one of those times when a bag of peanuts and some play fighting resulted in our first real intimate kiss. We were two fifteen-year-olds experiencing what was considered to be puppy love, but even back then I knew Kelly was who I was meant to spend my life with.

Chapter 8

RETURNING TO THE REALITY of my growing pregnancy and the life I was living in Dubai, I opened my eyes, as the morning sun warmed my face. I sat on the lounge chair hiding from reality with the characters in the novel I was reading. The very last thing I wanted was to have someone join me, and that bubble burst with the sound of Jasim's voice.

"Claudia the courier has just dropped off the envelope with the lab report. Do you want to open it?" Jasim held the package out to me.

I sat quietly for a moment. "Maybe you should read it. No, it's my child. I should see the results first." I took the envelope, carefully ripped it open, took a deep breath, scanned it quickly and shrieked, "Fuck, oh my fucking God!" I handed him the results and left the patio.

I retreated to our bedroom, locking the door behind me. I sobbed for hours. There went my freedom out the window. The test was 99.3 percent certain that Jasim Kasim al Masari was the biological father to the male child inside me. Resting a hand on my belly, I thought, "So my little son, there is no escape for us." It was imperative that I change my emotion because depression and anxiety would only manifest in the fetus and cause it to experience the same anxiety as me. I had worked so hard programming myself into believing the baby was the only mine, that there was nothing of Jasim in him. I thought of my child with love and joy, this child would have the best beginning I could give him. Settling into the facts, that there wouldn't be any other life for me, but at least now I had something worthwhile to live for.

I choose to call him Mikhail and he was busting out of me, my body looked like I was carrying twins. That little boy was always busy inside of me and I tired easily sooner. Jasim would never allow me to go anywhere alone, which kept me aware of my prisoner status. That alone would set me off emotionally; however, on one occasion I was actually thankful for his interference.

It happened during an outing to find some special little items for the baby's arrival when Saad, my driver, slash bodyguard, announced we had to immediately leave the plaza. I wasn't pleased with being told what to do until I looked and saw Aswad. "Oh my God Saad, he must not see me." I must have sounded as horrified as I felt. Taking my scarf, I quickly wrapped it securely over my hair and adjusted my sunglasses while Saad led me away. "Come ma'am let's get you home!"

He spoke calmly and reached for my arm. It was difficult moving at the speed my feet wanted to take me and even supporting my large belly in my hands didn't help. I was never so relieved to get into any vehicle as at that moment. When Saad had me safely home, Mikhail decided it was the time to do somersaults. I didn't even notice Jasim standing in the doorway watching me as I giggled and sang to my son in Arabic and English. Jasim carefully reached over and for the first time placed his hand on my belly, it came as such a surprise. For the first time, I was extremely happy carrying my child.

Soon I'd be cradling this little love in my arms. I covered Jasim's hands with mine, and something happened in that moment as he looked over at me. The reality was he is the daddy, and it would be wrong and doing our child a big misfortune if I didn't allow him the joys I was experiencing.

"Jasim," I whispered, "isn't that amazing? Feeling a life inside me, so innocent and with God's grace unscathed from the trauma that produced him. He's safe and strong and letting us know he is in here."

At first, he didn't respond or even react to me. "Yes, Claudia we did that, you and I, he will be perfect." Jasim looked up. I didn't trust him and he didn't trust me. How I hated him, just maybe there could be some kind of reprieve and we could take one small step at a time.

"You're about to be a father again, our son needs to sense his father's presence and hear his voice."

That night Jasim slept beside me again, it wasn't our marital bed, it was my room and my bed. I made him promise not to make any sexual contact with me. "I understand Claudia." Jasim was or never could show humility, it was all a pretentious attitude.

September 22, 1983, Mikhail arrived and I did it naturally, he was serene and I had never seen anything more beautiful than my baby son. I never thought I could be filled with so much joy and love. How I cherished every moment alone with him and watching him suckle my breast. His dark curly hair and lovely skin tone was the same color as mine, but "Mik" as Jasim called him looked like his dad. I saw the love he had for him and wished I could forgive him, but there would never be forgiveness, and I had no intention to go soul searching for it either. Jasim took his role as daddy extremely well, bringing him to bed for me to nurse and making sure he had a clean, dry diaper before returning him to the cradle, he even rocked him to sleep at times.

As the months went by our relationship seemed to improve to the point he would share small parts of his everyday problems, one day we were actually laughing and enjoying each other's company.

On the first night that Mikhail didn't wake up for his early morning feeding, I woke up like an alarm clock. I panicked, bailed out of bed and ran to his bed. Jasim sat up. "Claudia, it's okay, he's fine, I just checked on him not too long ago, come back to bed.

I ran my fingers through my sons' hair, "Oh, my sleepy boy."

When I crawled back into bed, Jasim was sitting up watching me with a strange look in his eyes. I didn't want to know, I was afraid. His hand was resting on top of the covers beside him.

"Could this be the beginning of full night sleep for us Jasim?" I smiled at the thought. He pulled his fingers through the strands of my hair and I tried not to react in a negative way.

"You were even more beautiful when you were pregnant Claudia, did you know that?"

I turned in his direction and joked, "I'm surprised you took notice, I thought my belly was all that was in your sights."

A cautious Jasim took a moment before replying. "Claudia your beauty has an observer. I saw every change that took place in you. I really am falling in love with you . . . please don't make a remark about what I just said. I know how you abhor me. I understand." I couldn't look at him. I focused on my hands as I reached over for some hand cream. I did loathe him and I sensed that I was being set up.

Mikhail's schedule was becoming consistent, I tried to have some kind of normalcy in my life, how could I, I might as well have had a leg monitor, Jasim still controlled my comings and goings. Rarely was there an instance when I could sneak out without house staff and guards watching my every move. I chalked it up to Jasim knowing my motherly instincts and the knowledge I wouldn't chance him taking me away from my child so it was a bit like an electric fence. But this day the weather was perfect for a run.

Mikhail was down for his nap and the staff was on duty, so things were as good as they could be. I headed out and ditched my bodyguard. I was so tired of him following me. I was feeling stronger and my body was back in shape. I increased my pace and felt my muscles burn, it felt invigorating and I was once again in charge of my body. My mind was focused on a schedule of weight training and cardio and I was also getting back to kickboxing. I had to fight tooth and nail to get Jasim to agree on allowing me to participate in a so-called man's sport, but finally, he gave in.

I was on the last leg of my fast-paced workout, half walk, half jog, I felt uneasy. Something wasn't right, turning around I didn't see a thing. My eyes darted up and down the street, but nothing appeared out of the ordinary. Then, just as I turned the corner a man darted out of the building, grabbed me by the arm, and he pulled me into the darkness amongst some parked vehicles. I couldn't scream as his hand firmly covered my mouth. I recognized him immediately: it was Aswad. He didn't even try to hide his identity. He said nothing, but I saw the glow of the steel in his hand and gasped, Oh no, no he's going to kill me! Oh my God Mikhail, "No, no please!" His knife pointed towards my crotch and with a sudden flick of the knife, he exposed my genitals. His hand gripped the remainder of the material and he ripped it off, then he exposed himself. I knew what he was going to do, and I began to shake.

"Oh God, you can't let this happen to me again." He showed me no mercy, his violation was cruel it was the knife slicing at my vagina before the quick hard blows to my face and head that threw me out of my mind as my body disintegrated and I fell to the pavement. I refused to pass out. I would not go into the abyss: my child needed me. He worked swiftly and left that way. I was alone and prayed someone would find me. I was in horrible pain, with an oozy head and the sensation of my flesh burning I saw blood streaming from the wound.

I fought to get up and found my clothing, it was all I could do to re-dress myself, I pressed my head scarf between my legs to stop the bleeding. It took every bit of strength I had in me to get myself off the ground. I staggered, searching for someone, and with some luck, saw a shadow and called out for help. I heard noise and prayed it was help coming for me, I called out. When I woke I was being questioned by the ambulance attendants. "Please, my husband is Jasim Kassis al-Masri. He needs to know what has happened to me.". By the expression on one of the paramedic's face, he knew immediately who I was asking for. This was the first and only time I prayed that Jasim was at home.

Jasim entered the hospital room less than an hour later, I shook at the sight of him, his eyes were enlarged with an emptiness I'd seen once before; I didn't know how to read the situation or him.

I left the hospital with my genitals still intact. Aswad missed his target. His intent I was to circumcise me, but why? Was he trying to punish Jasim through me? What else could it have been?

Jasim and his bodyguards moved us quickly from the hospital to Jasim waiting jet at the Dubai airport and soon we were in the air my son Jasim and me.

"Where are you taking us Jasim? I would really like go home to Canada, please Jasim.".

"Geneva, you'll be safe there until I deal with the situation. We're not going to Canada. You can get over that idea Claudia.""

Once again, I was reunited with the old version of my husband. I had hoped that maybe the brutal stage in our marriage had come to an end, and I had no choice but to do what I was told.

I turned to face him and stroked his face. "Okay Jasim, okay, I will trust you this time. Mikhail is too important I would die if anyone tried to hurt him."

Jasim kissed my fingers, "I need to keep both of you safe, it's not our Mikhail he's after Claudia, and it's you he wants. I took everything from him, he thinks he can retaliate by getting to you. Don't worry Claudia were keeping track of his movements, you should have never gone on that run without security Claudia. He will be taking his last breath very soon I promise you." Jasim's stern expression spoke darker than his words.

I needed to hold my son, undoing his safety harness, I pulled my sweet boy into me, it was awful having to bring him to the hospital for feedings. He would soon be nine months old I planned to nurse him until I knew it wasn't necessary for him. I smiled seeing how excited he became at the sight of my naked breast, his little mouth shaking to get to it.

"Oh Mikhail, you are so much your mommy's boy," Jasim said as he watched our son snuggling into me. I covered his little fingers with mine as they rested on my flesh. "Yes because Mommy has what Mikhail likes, warm sweet milk." I knew I would never have had this experience if things hadn't happened the way they had. I never would have chosen to have a child with Jasim. I bent in close enough to inhale my boy, before kissing that little head.

"His mother is loved, she needs to know that too," Jasim said confidently.

I nodded, "Not the type of love I need Jasim, please don't say speak like that anymore, things are comfortable between us now and I wouldn't want that to deteriorate." I knew where his thoughts were going, he needed to be clear what my feelings for him were, that they hadn't changed. He was still my jailor and yet my child's father. "Jasim, right now your and I are in a comfortable place. You have your hold on me, and we're raising our son together. That's all, that's all there will ever be Jasim. Don't forget that, I will never ever forgive you, I could or would never love you Jasim." My words were deliberate and calm.

Chapter 9

FROM 1983 TO 1989 WE LIVED in Geneva for the first six years of Mikhail's life. I had the freedom to come and go as I liked. Aswad had been disposed of and I was definitely not interested in any of the details. Knowing Jasim as well as I did, there was no doubt he suffered ten times more than what he had caused me. Mik and I explored all the museums, everything and anything that has to do with arts and music in Geneva.

Occasionally we ran into the same woman at the same venues. I took the first step and invited her for coffee and we hit it off immediately. It turned out Sofie was single, a few years younger than me and we shared many of the same interests. During the times Jasim was out of the country, I spent time with Sofie which made my life happier. We became close and the three of us ended up spending hours together as Mikhail took to her immediately.

Sofie was an incredible sculptress and convinced me to be a model. I didn't hesitate, it excited me even when she asked me to pose naked in very risky positions. I laughed at Sofie's hesitation if she had an inkling of half the things I did. Working from her photographs she created many different observations in her work. During a photo shoot, she had gentler ideas than what I was prepared for, yet I totally surprised when I began removing my clothes without any reluctance. I knew I had caught her off guard.

"You are definitely going to be one easy model to work with Claudia. Wow, you are incredibly beautiful especially after having a baby not that long ago. Tight skin, even your muscle tone is perfectly sculpted, Claudia how did you do it?" She questioned in a very curious stare. "I have had a privileged lifestyle and the best health advantages, Sofie, you know us trophy wives?" I laughed to shift the topic of conversation into another direction. "Sofie, what kind of pose are you visualizing?" She put her camera on the floor and moved in to arrange my body. She took one leg and extended it out to the side while I held a knee to my chest, letting a cheek rest on the same knee. Sofie pointed my profile to the left; she had all my hair falling to the right of my nude body. It was the most erotic picture I'd ever seen of myself. But the surprise came months later when Sofie unveiled the sculpture, for my eyes only. It was as though she had been there to witness those times my nipples had been extended to their limits, my reddened swollen clitoris that was so hard I was afraid to walk. Sofie had brought that knowledge to view. I gasped, "Sofie what have you done?" I turned to meet her eyes.

"Claudia do you think it is too much? I just copied the photo of you, erotic art is such a part of our world now and this is spectacular, even if I do say so myself."

I was very aware of that, but this was me, and was Sofie aware of my past? I guessed Sofie wanted to create other pieces and I was right.

"I would love to do a series of you in some of the most provocative poses, but we need to talk more. I know you will need time to think about it." Sofie said suggestively.

My insides woke up, as did my sexuality. Excitement oozed in me, especially after all this time. I loved the things I was able to do with my body. Little did I know what the effects of the sculpture would have on me.

"I want to do it Sofie, yes without a doubt, this piece is so delicious, and how could I not want to do it?" I replied eagerly.

Sofie stood back studying me, "If I didn't know better, I would think this isn't new to you Claudia." She replied with a slight grin.

"Don't we all have a bit of pent up sexual extroversion in us?" I chuckled, if you only knew, to myself.

Sofie started what she believed was my education. I played her game and pretended by asking all the right questions. The sight of the body harness made me shiver, the memories of Kenji's punishment came rushing back like a movie reel in my memory as I took a discretionary deep breath and looked over at Sofie.

"Claudia, you are free to use my bedroom to get familiar with it, but you may need my help with tightening the straps. Are you okay with it?"

"Of course, I am really curious about this for sure, I'm sure you will need to do the buckles up for me. But yeah, I'm in," and I grinned even wider inside.

Sofie had so many ideas for different photo shoots; ideas for posing and I was all in, but then I made my first mistake: I hadn't given any thought to what Jasim would think. When Sofie approached me about the copyright, I realized I would be giving her permission to use my images as she saw fit for the primary purpose of sales and distribution. It hadn't crossed my mind that Sofie would want to sell the images and they would definitely be going to buyers throughout the world.

"Ohh . . . Sofie, I don't think so, I could be recognized. I have to talk to Jasim before I agree to this." I knew he wouldn't agree with any of it.

"I will give you the time you need to think about it, but I can adjust your expressions in order to conceal your identity if you would feel better about it."

A week later I showed up at Sofie's studio to find her in the middle of the floor with pictures of me scattered everywhere. Sitting down beside Sofie I began looking at each photo very carefully and after a while something occurred to me; something that had always been in the back of my mind, I suspected Sofie was a lesbian.

Sofie's expression, as she looked at my photos, was obvious. She must have sensed my thoughts because she reached across, picked up a photo that looked as though I was masturbating.

"Claudia these photos are my next project! What do you think?"

Without even really thinking about it, I ran my tongue over my upper lip, "I don't know Sofie." I felt her presence so near.

"Claudia!" She whispered softly. "I am totally taken with you."

Turning to look over at her, Sofie's mouth moved to mine and for some reason I waited, just letting the kiss to happen. It was soft and sexy, especially when she parted my lips with her tongue. Slowly resting my head on the floor, I kept my eyes closed as Sofie's tongue tantalized me. Her lips gently sucked and pulled at my lower lip. She never broke the kiss, as she moved to my upper lip and repeated it again on the lower lip.

The dormant part of me was aroused and I didn't pull away. I was curious to see where Sofie was going to take it; then she slid her hand up onto my breast. As her fingers explored my firm flesh, I kissed her back; it was pure lust. Her hand moved over to my other breast as she continued with her movements without any attempt to locate my nipple. She just ran her finger and palms up and across; she broke the kiss when her lips traveled down and over my chin under and towards the base of my neck.

Sofie's kisses turned into soft biting and sucking. She ignited my fire; I was full of desire. She created a different frenzy in me and I definitely did not object. As Sofie drew away from my neck, the tip of her tongue was moving very slowly, arousing the sensitivity to every nerve ending in my body. I was so aroused when her mouth sucked in my full nipple; she nibbled the long bud. Then she let it go, the coolness washed over the hardened bud and once more she brought it into her mouth and sucked my nipple deep into her mouth.

I relished the sensation and the sounds I was making verified it. I lay there, in awe of the gentleness of another woman's touch. She continued her seduction and when she reached my sweet spot and her mouth was controlling my sex with the nibbling of my clitoris, I gasped and reached an incredible orgasm. Sofie held me gently in place as she lapped up the evidence of my pleasure.

"Sofie, oh this can't happen again! It really can't! It shouldn't have come to this."

She smiled sweetly at me, "I know you liked it, Claudia, I taste it on my lips."

I blushed, "No Sofie, I'm not saying I didn't enjoy that, I did! Too much . . . I'm not a lesbian Sofie and I'm only attracted to you as a friend. I really enjoyed the experience; I won't lie. Please don't put me in that situation again."

She challenged me by reaching and capturing my nipple again. She held my eyes as she rolled it again so gently between her fingers. Without breaking eye contact, I reached over and removed her hand.

"I had to try Claudia, you know, give it one more shot. But then who knows how you will feel later when you think about this."

I knew this was going to be a battle of strengths and I had to cut it off. I dressed and left, but not before giving her a warm hug.

The house was filled with laughter, Jasim's mixed with his son's. Jasim had been gone for nearly three months and I never questioned his whereabouts. I didn't care. For all I knew he was with the blonde woman, but that was more than fine with her.

My three-year-old Mikhail spotted me "Mommy, mommy!" His little arms reached out for me. Sweeping him into my arms, I planted kiss after kiss all over his face as he attempted to push my mouth away. Then I kissed his little fingers, but that only lasted for seconds before he insisted on being put down. Then Mikhail turned and ran towards his daddy. I watched and waited because I was anxious to talk to Jasim and it wouldn't be the kind of conversation he would be pleased about. I knew it wouldn't go over well if I tried to hide anything from him. I had learned a lot during the seven years with Jasim, but having a woman making love to me was definitely not something he would look favorably on; however, that experience with Sofie was unbelievably erotic for me. It was sweet, feminine and so very hot, but I clearly knew my own sexual orientation.

My long braid hung loose and I was about to brush it out when I felt Jasim's presence. He placed his hands on both sides of my hips and I could feel the warmth of his hands through the silk robe. Slowly his hands moved up the sides of my body reaching my waist, then a hand crossed over onto my belly, gently pulling me up against him. He closed his hands over me and turned me to face him. Jasim took my mouth in his.

Tenderly, his kisses filled me. "I missed you, Claudia, you have no idea how much!" He pulled me with him onto the bed, pulling me in close, his lips moving passionately over my face. I felt a lust for him, down to the deepest part of my soul. I was drunk and high in the desire of what he created in me.

"Fuck me Jasim, please!" I spoke into his kisses.

Jasim pulled back and looked into her eyes and smiled. "I like it when you ask me that, Claudia say it again please." He ran his finger over my bottom lip. "You are so beautiful Claudia!" He moaned.

I searched out his eyes and smiled, "Jasim, fuck me please!" I repeated, before wrapping my arms around his neck and legs around his waist. When he was incapable of bringing me over the edge, like I was accustomed to, frustration took over. He couldn't satisfy me any longer, it took extreme devices to send me over the edge now. I turned in his arms as he continued his exploration of my genitals. I played the one card I hoped would be the catalyst to get me what I needed. "Jasim," I whispered, "I have done something you won't approve of, but you know me." I announced and then turned onto my stomach, "I posed for an artist Jasim, it was rather erotic." I watched his face carefully, very aware that he would turn on me again.

"Okay, tell me, sweetheart."

"One of the poses is now a sculpture Jasim. I made a mistake, I don't want you to fix it for me, I am capable of doing that . . . "

Jasim interrupted, "How erotic Claudia?"

"Very, but there is more, she seduced me Jasim and I enjoyed it, but it was a one-time experience I don't want it to happen again." I waited for a negative response. This was the perfect opportunity to incite his anger, I knew just enough would cause him to make me pay for my bad behavior, just the right amount of pain to relieve my frustrated and yearning body.

"Wish I could have watched the two of you, I would like to watch your expressions all through the seduction and see your eyes when you climaxed. Did you climax Claudia?" His body language changed.

"Jasim about the sculpture, it is very obvious who the model is. It is going to be sold, but I need to know, do I need legal protection."

"Would you like my opinion, Claudia? I can also help if you need it."

I nodded, "Yes, I think I would, the piece is on display in her studio." I whispered feeling frustrated at his response.

"Give me the address and I will take a look at it tomorrow."

I closed my eyes, "She has also taken hundreds of pictures too. That's the problem."

"Not a big one, we can get a seizure order, I really think now you should leave this to me, Claudia." He rubbed my shoulder. I didn't want to end the friendship with Sofie, but I was becoming aware that I wouldn't have a choice. I shivered at the memory of Sofie's touch. Jasim remained calm. That was what worried me the most.

I walked over to Sofie's studio with Mikhail and decided to stop and pick up something for lunch. I couldn't leave things the way they were with Sofie, maybe I could salvage the friendship. I had just crossed the street when I thought I was seeing things, could it be? Yes, it was, it was Kelly, and he was coming out of the Four Seasons Hotel-Des-Bergues. He spotted me immediately and the look on his face said it all, his eyes moved from me to Mikhail then back to me. I put the stroller brakes on making sure Mikhail was safe, then quickly reaching up to wrap my arms around him. Kelly's body felt so good and how wonderful he felt against me. I sure didn't want to let him go.

"I'm just as surprised to see you, Claud, maybe even more, who's this little guy?" I reached down and undid Mik's safety harness and picked up my three-year-old'

"This little sweetheart is Mikhail, my son! Can you say, 'Hi Kelly', Mikhail?"

Kelly touched his little foot. "He's like you Claudia, he's a beautiful boy. How are you?"

My mind was screaming, take me out of here, I'm much better now that you are here. It was obvious he'd been caught off guard. "Do you have time for coffee Kelly? Or are you in a hurry? I know a great little spot, just down the street here."

"Of course I have time for coffee. I would make time for you."

I tried not to stare too much as we walked towards the bistro. I wanted to touch him, hold him and tell him everything. We found a table and sat opposite each other. Mikhail was content with his crackers.

"I am confused Claudia, why are you keeping your life a secret? Why haven't you shared your little guy with all of us? Do your parents know they have a grandson?" Kelly asked as he reached to touch my fingers. I shuddered at his touch. "Are you cold?" he asked. I shook my head, "No Kel, I'm not cold, it's, it's just so good to have you here in front of me. No one knows about my son Kelly and you have to promise me it will stay like this for now. Please?"

He squeezed my hands, "What has happened to you to be surrounded by so much secrecy, Claudia? You've changed so much."

I thought I was going to cry. "No Kel, l really I haven't, it's me it really is." I lost a few tears and bit my lip. "Kelly, one day I will tell you everything, I promise. Please, can we change the subject? Tell me everything that's going on at home, I haven't spoken with Daina for a while, or the rest of the group. I miss everyone so much."

"Do you have regrets, Claudia? Every day I regret one decision, I should have taken you far away with me. We would have figured it out. I've never been happy since you left and I never will be."

I had to stay strong. How many regrets? Well if I blurted everything out, neither of us would be safe and it would make my plan all the harder to follow through. "Knowing how you feeling Kelly makes me sad and I don't want that for you. Find your passion in life and live for it." I caught myself before adding, "until I get back to you."

Mikhail started to fuss and I knew it wasn't wise to stay too much longer. Jasim was home and I had to be careful. He had eyes everywhere. "I must go Kelly . . . I should go, I'm supposed to meet a friend."

He stood up and waited for me to gather up my belongings. His hand rested on my forearm. I reached in for one last hug and it sent shivers through me. His hand moved almost to the top of my head and he pulled me to his chest, kissing my head.

"I hope you come home for a visit soon!" Sadness and longing filled me. I had to keep going. I knew I would have to tell Jasim that I saw Kelly. I didn't need him having any ammunition to use against me.

I couldn't carry on to Sofie's studio, I was rattled after my time with Kelly, besides Mik was fussy and wanted to move around, he was at the age where sitting in one place for any amount of time frustrated him.

Jasim had kept his word. The evidence greeted me in a crate when I entered the foyer. "Claudia, you're home, good, when you can, come to my office, please."

"I will be right up, Mik needs a nap, I will put him down and be right there." One thing I knew, as I looked at my son, he had the best and that was because Jasim was a good father. I held him for a few moments even after he'd fallen asleep. He looked like his father. As his mom, I had to teach him to honor women, but most of all himself. Resting my head on his, I folded my arms protectively around him. I was about ready to lay him in his bed when Jasim entered the room. He seemed a little anxious.

When we were in his office, behind closed doors, he handed me a thick envelope. "You were right, they are definitely very erotic Claudia. She has an eye for you doesn't she?"

I raised my eyes up to him but didn't comment. "My lawyer has handled all the legalities and I am hoping you will keep away from her." He sat on the corner of his desk watching while I looked through the pictures to see if they were all there. "Thank you, this must of cost you big Jasim. I'm sorry. I appreciate you going to the trouble. I think these are all of them."

I laid them on his desk and followed through with what I knew he expected. Taking his face in mine, I kissed him deeply and fully then undid his zipper . . . I had learned to be good at that but hated every bit of it as I knelt at his feet in that obedient manner. I licked the underside of him, working on an erection.

"I have to go back to Dubai tonight, I don't know for how long I will be gone for. You and Mik will join me there in a few weeks." He said getting throaty. I continued the task that was growing in my mouth, feeling him getting closer and closer to climaxing. What surprised me the most was when he pulled himself out of my mouth and undid my skirt, Jasim always got a thrill at ripping my panties off. He positioned me over the desk and I was unsure where he would enter, he hoisted me up off the ground and I become excited as he approached me vaginally.

He pushed himself quickly and deep inside me. I gasped, as the delicious pain touched my needs, "Harder," I screamed out. I needed desperately to release. I hadn't climaxed in such a long time. He rested his head on my back while wrapping his arms around me. Nothing happened for me, but I felt him trembling inside of me.

"I'm going to remain hopeful that our relationship can get to another level, Claudia!" He said as he began gripping me tightly. I wasn't about to answer that question. I sidelined his question, "Fuck me again Jasim since you're going to be gone for a while. Fuck me hard don't stop until I scream."

Jasim picked me up and carried me next door to our bed. He went to his toy box and returned with restraints and anal beads, which really was a big turn on for me. I shivered in excitement. I missed Kenji's skills, but I was afraid to mention it to Jasim, it would blow the control he thought he had on me. Bondage was my ultimate sexual pleasure, although Jasim had no idea how high my pain tolerance was. I craved the mastery of Kenji's practices. The tighter I was restrained the more extreme my climax became, and it had been a long time. Jasim had ended all BDSM practices and there wasn't any need for Kenji since my pregnancy. Was that part of my role over? If not, I needed to find a way out. But my need for the gratification I received from Kenji's flogging and the snapping his whips in all the right places was growing, even arousing Jasim's cruel actions wasn't enough anymore. Maybe focusing on those times now during the encounter Jasim was planning would help stimulate my deep desire for an extreme orgasm.

He began by stimulating my anus starting with one finger than working up to two thick fingers, before sliding the beads inside and then he anxiously began buckling me into the spreader bar and wristbands. I was ready; he couldn't know just how anxious and excited I was.

"Bring it on Jasim, show me what you have for me."

Shortly after I was extremely happy as Jasim walk out the door. He was flying to Dubai it couldn't have been a more perfect time. I would send most of the staff away and spend my time alone with Mik, but before I did that, I phoned the Four Seasons Hotel-Des-Bergues and enquired about Kelly: he still registered. Then making sure everything was okay with Mik's staff, I ran a delicious bath. I dressed down in a pair of jeans, a white silk blouse, and a navy hip length jacket. I phoned the hotel again and prayed Kelly would be in his room.

When I arrived at the hotel he was waiting for me in the lobby. "I'm surprised that you actually came Claudia, will you have dinner with me? I haven't eaten and it would be nice to have your company."

"Of course, I'd like that, but only if have they serve us in your room, that would be the only way, I'm sorry Kel, I will explain."

We took the elevator to his room and I did something I hoped I wouldn't regret: I kissed him, deep and deliberately because I thought this might be the one and only chance to make him believe it was still only him I loved. Kissing him was better each time, even better than England.

He grabbed my hands and pulled back, "You're confusing me, Claudia, what are you doing?"

We sat together on the bed and I began, Kelly six years ago in London you asked me 'When did I lose you, Claudia?'"

"I stayed true to you until I heard you married him so quickly after you met each other! He must have swept you off your feet huh Claudia?"

"It's not like that Kelly, not at all. You never lost me, I told you in London that you are my one and only love for always. I knew I couldn't let you go home this time without telling you my secret, why my life is the way it is. You have to swear to secrecy Kelly."

"Of course, Claudia, I really need an explanation, especially ever since London and the tidbit you dropped on me."

I took a deep breath, "When I went to the University of Bethlehem in 1973 I got involved with a militant group and was responsible and took part in a killing spree. There were only three of us who managed to escape and return to Jerusalem before being identified and caught. Kelly, I believed in the cause strongly, that helped my guilt dissipate.

I thought I was in the clear until I met Jasim, he used . . . " I stopped, I couldn't tell him what Jasim forced me to do. I didn't want him to find out my truth, at least not yet. Kelly reached over and placed his fingertips next to mine. I continued with the story, the part about my marriage, but nothing about the rape and pregnancy.

Kelly poured a scotch. It was such an ordeal going over it with him. "I will understand if you can't deal with this, I didn't understand until recently how Jasim got all those pictures and the proof, how anyone got pictures and documentation. I can only believe that he arranged it in order to blackmail me. There's more Kelly, much more, but this is not the time to share it all with you."

I couldn't be sure of what he was thinking. All I knew was that if he said anything, or confronted Jasim, my life and even his could be in jeopardy. If any of this got back to the government they would hunt me down and kill me.

Kelly stood up and walked around the room, swishing his scotch around the glass.

"I feel fucking helpless, all this time, what the hell Claudia? So, there is nothing I can do is there?" His one hand went to his hip while the other combed his hair. "Christ Claudia! What are you going to do? You can't continue like this." He kept his distance and I respected this man like none other.

"I have to continue to do what I'm doing now, wait, wait patiently until Mikhail grows up while I can still build on his trust. I think our son is the catalyst."

Kelly was now kneeling in front of me, "How am I going to be able to board that flight tomorrow and leave you behind, Claudia? That information was too much for me, I will worry about you."

I ran my fingers across his cheek, "I'll be just fine Kelly, and the worst is over. I promise you, I will be fine . . . you must never forget how much I love you, Kelly, I always have. I can handle anything he throws my way." I looked deep into his eyes. He held me gently like a dear friend would.

"Claudia, there has never been a time that I didn't love you, I will always no matter what." He squeezed my knee. "You need to know something Claudia, Cindy and I separated last year, she changed. Wants different things in life than me. But I think deep down inside she knew our secret. I kept your letters hidden and one day I found them, not exactly how I'd left them. I'm getting a divorce, it's the waiting period now.

"That gives me hope Kel. I have that as food to carry around and if times get unbearable I will remember your words."

"You need to come home more often. I need to know you're okay, I know you have a son to think about." His fingers were now weaving into mine. If I didn't leave now, it would only be harder as the time passed.

"I've got to go, it's getting late and I can't trust the staff, they will report to Jasim on my actions." I let go of his hands.

"I don't want you to go Claudia." He pulled my head to his chest while I wrapped my arms tightly around him.

"You can kiss me, Kelly, I would welcome your kiss." I rested my forehead against his.

"I'm afraid that if I start I won't be able to stop, I won't be able to let you walk out that door." He searched my face and I smiled. "It's okay my darling it will be okay." He walked to the door and wanted to walk me out. I deterred him before opening the door whispered to him. "I love you, only you Kel." I left and didn't turn around because it was ripping my heart out leaving him.

Chapter 10

SIX YEARS HAD PASSED . . . It was 1989 when Jasim moved us back to the United Arab Emirates, this time Abu Dhabi.

He had built a new home and was anxious to have us there with him. But, I knew it was mostly to keep an eye on me. I knew he was aware of everything and everyone in Canada, including Kelly. I had been able to travel back and forth to Canada a couple of times by myself and I decided it was time to go again because two years had passed since my last trip.

When I told Jasim of my plans he became colder than normal, no doubt he was suspicious. I had no difficulty convincing Daina to spend a week in Whistler with me and when I told him, Jasim gave me a look that made me swallow hard. I had to figure a way to appease him, so I waited until just the right time.

We often bathed together, so I arranged a beautiful evening for us filled with sex just the way he liked. I used clamps; I wore them for hours. I had our meal served on the patio looking over the city and we drank champagne and danced. Then, I excused myself long enough to change my clothes. I returned wearing the traditional costume for belly dancing. I seduced him, running my finger into my sex and applying it on my neck knowing he would pick up on the familiar fragrance eau de Claudia. Every part of my body was ready. I performed a belly dance for him so erotic that his eyes didn't leave my body. At the end of the dance, I sat on his lap, positioning my breasts close to his face while my rapid breathing allowed my chest to expand enough to entice his lips towards my hard-large erect nipples as I gyrated over him. I could feel him growing rock hard against my rectum. I did everything I was taught to use against him, for my own benefit. Jasim was caught up in everything I was doing . . . and took the bait.

Before I left I told him, "I want to make another baby with you Jasim, let's have another child. Mik needs siblings and I quit taking birth control." I lied, but it was something that would stay in his psyche.

"No, that's not a good idea. No more babies! When did you stop your birth control?" There was fear written all over his face.

"A few of days ago," I whispered and watched him twitch. It became evident he wasn't finished with my assignments.

It was difficult leaving Mik to go to Canada, but I relished leaving Jasim all worried that I may have conceived again. It was sweet revenge. I had more control over my life now than ever before. I was smiling for the first time since Mikhail was born and my evening with Kelly three years ago. Every detail of my plan was in motion, right down to the last detail, but the bitter ending was a short few years away wouldn't be the one I had hoped for.

I cleared customs in Vancouver and when I saw a pay phone; I wasn't waiting any longer to call Kelly. He picked it up on the third ring; I was delighted and unable to stop grinning. "Hi there, how are you? It's me Kel."

"Baby, where are you? Have you left. . . ?"

"I'm at the airport in Vancouver, I'm meeting Daina in Whistler later. It's so good hearing your voice. No baby, I haven't, not yet, but I have a week here. How are things with you?"

"At this very moment, I'm on top of the world. Would it be out of the question if I kinda just showed up in Whistler, like tomorrow? Do you think Daina would suspect anything?"

"I wouldn't put it past Jasim to have people here watching me. I don't think it would be a wise move, especially if you came on your own."

"Yes, I understand Claudia, I do, it's been difficult these past three years knowing what I know, and knowing how far away from me you are. I understand the situation, but I can't help but hope. If you change your mind and feel its okay for me to come, I will get the first Heli-flight out. I love you, baby, it is so nice to say those words."

"It's just as wonderful hearing about them too, especially from you . . . I will keep my eyes out for his people and if I feel safe I will find a way to get to you Kelly, but not Whistler. I will phone you soon. I love you, Kelly. Bye, for now, my darling.

I hung up the phone and found the silver limousine in front of the VIP exit and then I spotted her, she was obvious.

Oh, Jasim you're getting sloppy in your old age. It was obvious the younger woman reading a magazine at the entrance was assigned to watch me. I thought more about Kelly, concerned that he would come to Whistler, I needed to make sure that my instincts were right.

"Driver, if we could make a couple of detours I will make it more than worth your time!"

"Of course, Ma'am, where would you like to go?"

"Yaletown, please."

"Where am I taking you, Ma'am?"

"Please don't use ma'am, call me Claudia okay. Any place that makes great coffee."

"You got it, Claudia!"

Checking her appearance, her thoughts went to Mik, was he missing me? I hated not being able to bring him. I promised I'd call him at bedtime, ten o'clock, Pacific time, so no matter what I do, he's still my priority. I handed the driver a large bill and asked, "Would you mind getting me a double shot of espresso please?"

"Right ma . . . Claudia," he corrected himself and I watched for my stalker and sure enough, a light blue mid-range sedan type vehicle pulled up and my driver returned a few minutes later with a beautiful rich espresso.

"Thank you, it's very good and close to what I got in Geneva." I sat back and thought for a second.

"Is there somewhere else Claudia? Would you mind calling me Rob since were on a first name bases?"

"Yes, sure of course Rob. There is a little boutique on Robson Street, I can direct you, but for some reason, the name has slipped my mind." I tried to remember it. But it had been such a long time ago. I was looking for solid proof that the blue car was hired by Jasim.

As we drove through the city, I noticed all the changes in the since my last trip. Vancouver still had a wonderful energy, and I swore I would bring Mikhail here to make Vancouver our home. I ached for freedom, to have total control of my life and my body. I thought about the four years in Palestine and working with the organization, maybe there was a paid assassin in the PLO that would remember me. The memories of those times sent rushes of adrenalin to my brain. There had to be someone that could get to Jasim, I had no regrets about the killings. I grew to hate the Israeli Government just like my comrades. Suddenly I felt the hairs standing up on the back of my neck, maybe these eighteen years is God's punishment for my role in the ambush.

"Ms. Claudia, I think we're being followed. There is a blue sedan that keeps appearing. What would you like me to do?"

"I'm glad you are so observant, I am aware but let's just play her game for a while longer. I think the little boutique is right a block down on the left. I hope there is a spot for parking."

"No problem, I have ways to deal with that. I can turn around and drop you off right at the door if you'd like, and I will be right out front when you are ready."

It wasn't long before he let me off in front of the store and I walked in. I felt sure the woman of the blue sedan was taking notes. Daina was meeting me later in the afternoon, so I still had a few hours. I was looking forward to skiing Whistler again. I found a stunning natural wool wrap in shades of grays and silver . . . I had to have that and wear it with a pair of black jeans that Jasim would not allow me to wear in his presence, or let alone own a pair. Fuck you Jasim. I laughed at my own joke. I found the perfect pair to add to the ones I'd hidden back home, but what would I wear for shoes? I wanted a new pair of Christian Louboutin shoes, but where would I find them? Holt Renfrew, of course, next stop.

Rob was right in front of the store, he double-parked and jumped out to open the door when I exited the store. Right opposite, was the little blue sedan. "Okay, one more stop then Whistler Rob, Holt Renfrew please." I smiled, wondering if Jasim was getting the play-by-play on my where abouts. I almost laughed out loud when it came to mind I needed to find a maternity store, maybe I can find one in Whistler. I giggled quietly to myself; please, please lady report back to Jasim with that, he'll have a great week.

We arrived in Whistler at the Pan Pacific Whistler Village Centre. Before I got out of the car I handed Rob five hundred-dollar bills and thanked him again. I wasn't surprised when he passed me his business card. "If you need my services while you're in town I'd be happy to drive you around."

February seemed like the perfect time to ski in Whistler, and I would enjoy the time I spent on the mountain. I unpacked one of three ski suits and laughed thinking how fortunate for me I had the use of the jet especially with all the luggage I had brought.

I had brought way more than I needed for the week and I still planned on using Jasim's credit card. Daina and I were going to have some fun!

Now that I knew for sure I was being watched, I needed to get to a phone and discourage Kelly now even more. I left my room and wandered through the hotel looking for an inconspicuous place that had a pay phone to call Kelly. Caution was very important, she would probably be lurking at every corner.

Kelly's phone rang and rang until his recorded message clicked on. "Kel honey, you have to stay in Kelowna, you can't come here no matter what, Jasim has people watching me and I know that for sure. I have an idea, I will see you before I go home, I promise you. I will call you soon, love you!" I was relieved. I couldn't let one moment of weakness ruin everything.

It was the perfect time to phone Mikhail, I still had time to construct a lie, a lie that would allow me to get to Kelly but what would I use, he'd forbidden me to visit my parents and I never understood his reasons behind it. That was someplace I couldn't go this time. My soul ached for my parents, I wondered how one person could be so cruel, but Jasim had that title.

Daina would arrive shortly, and I decided to wait until I had all my eggs in a basket before calling Jasim. I didn't think Jasim would question Daina staying up at Whistler a couple days longer. . . . I realized that would be my only alibi, but the other problem was, I couldn't say a word about anything to Daina. I was taking the biggest chance of my life but nothing would stop me from trying.

Wine, dinner, more wine and careful conversation with Daina was how we spent our first evening. There were so many times when it was all I could do to stop myself from spilling everything to her.

I waited until 2200 here to call Mik before he went to school. I bit my lip and while Daina showered I placed the call.

"Jasim, by the sound of your voice I woke you! You're not often asleep this early. How's our Mik, doing? I miss him, can't wait to see him." I rattled along.

"Claudia darling, it's okay, it's okay, you know you can call me anytime sweetheart. Our bed is so empty without you, when are you coming home?" Jasim yawned as he spoke.

"Soon Jasim, when I do, you better be rested for me . . . I have plans for you okay? Can you send the jet for me on Tuesday? I'm keeping Daina here a couple days longer. Is that ok? Jasim I will be at the airport early." I held my cool calm reserve.

"Yes whatever you want, I could come too, Mik and I both will be there, to meet you, and would you like that?" He cooed.

"Oh, that would be incredible, yes, please," I responded, loathing the thought of him coming here to get me. But if that was what it took to sidetrack him, I would go along with it. "Oh, Jasim Whistler is so beautiful., I wish we had slopes like this in Dubai". I laughed. Just then Daina came out of the shower and mouthed" You talking to Jasim?" I nodded.

"Hey Jim, I'm having a great time here with my girl Claudia." Daina hollered in the background. That added more fuel for Jasim's inquisitiveness and should relieve and rest my case. "Okay my darling, we'll see you Tuesday morning."

"Tell Daina I say hello."

"Okay, see you soon, kiss, kiss!" I hung up. . . . You Fucker!

Everything had been put into place with the help of Rob. After saying our goodbyes and Daina was well on her way back down into town, Rob would make arrangements for my luggage and equipment to be stored until he brought me to the airport in Vancouver. My stomach was filled with butterflies. Rob drove to the Whistler Helipad; I was off to meet Kelly in Hedley.

"Did you see any signs of the blue sedan or anyone resembling her Rob?" I asked because I didn't sense there was anyone tracking me. I wondered if maybe he pulled off his detectives after their conversation and hearing Daina's voice. I prayed I was in the clear.

"It doesn't look like we are being followed, in fact, it's pretty quiet this morning. I have the pre-paid credit card here." He went to pass it back to me.

"No Rob you keep it, you have no idea how much you've done for me," I responded.

"I can't accept that much money Claudia, there's five g's left on it. That's too much." Rob argued.

I shook my head, "Rob that's coffee money for me. Please don't give me any grief." I tried to sound annoyed.

"If you say so, you are kind Ms. Claudia, thank you," Rob said shaking his head.

The helicopter's blades were whizzing and Rob carried my one piece of luggage to the pilot. Then, taking my elbow, he helped me into the seat. Smiling I thanked him. Rob nodded as he backed away from the large chopper. Seconds later I was on my way. The flight was breathtaking. It was just over twenty minutes before we are hovering over a field close to the Colonial Inn in the small historical mining town of Hedley BC. I'd known about this place ever since I was a child. My family used to travel to the Okanagan to camp and get fresh summer fruit. I loved my childhood and how I was missing my parents. How will they ever forgive me, they don't even know they have a grandson. One day I promise, I will make this up to them. One day everyone will know the truth, every bit of it.

It was a bit of a walk from the chopper to the inn, but I didn't mind, even the cold February wind was welcoming. I wondered when Kelly would be there, no sooner had I spoken those thoughts when I saw his arms waving. I eagerly waved back. My feet picked up and soon I was tightly wrapped in his arms.

We both stood apart long enough for the pilot to hand Kelly my bag. I thanked him, and he assured me he'd be returning Tuesday morning. Kelly dropped the bag on the ground and pulled me near him, "I have you all to myself for a couple of days that makes me very happy Claudia."

I placed a hand behind his head at the base of his neck, pulling him towards me. "I've been thinking about this since I left Abu Dhabi Kelly Mac Askill." I reached up to his lips, I never wanted our lips to part. We stayed close for a few moments longer. Then, taking my hand, we walked to the inn.

Everything was rich in the old English tradition. The stately house was still a serene reminder of the great gold mining days. The heavy antique furniture warmed the old mansion. We were in room number one and the decor was masculine with a feminine touch. The bed had an oak head and footboard encasing brown tufted leather with a matching settee. An oval crystal drop chandelier hung in the center of the room. While I took off my new wool wrap and sat at the edge of the bed, Kelly stood against the dresser without taking his eyes off of me. I released the clip that held my massive amount of hair in place letting it fall down onto my back.

"That's better! Yes, Claudia, that's beautiful, you are exquisite. I wasn't too sure this would come together, I'm sure glad you made it happen."

I smiled, "It's so good to be here with you, I can breathe now." I said as I exhaled gloriously.

"I brought a few bottles of wine from the local winery, shall I open a bottle?"

"Mm . . . oh yes for sure. I always look forward to good wine. Daina and I killed off a few bottles, I sure miss her Kelly. It's been tough without you guys, and I now understand the depth of that saying, 'You don't know what you've got until it's gone', it's tough."

"I know she's missed you too, we talk often, she has always been supportive, it was hard keeping what I knew to myself Claud, but Daina wouldn't have been able to keep it a secret."

I froze for a moment, panic set in. "Oh Kelly, please tell me you haven't told a soul?"

He shook his head, "No I wouldn't do that. You can trust me, honey. I wouldn't put you in danger." I let out a deep breath and watched him continue to open the wine bottle. He was more buff and muscular than when I'd seen him three years ago. The years were good to him and he still was a handsome man. He still had a combination of Robert Kennedy and Gerard Butler good looks, with his copper streaked brown hair and face covered in freckles. I wasn't ready to take my eyes off of him.

"I see a different Kelly, have you been working out or something? You look so good, Kelly!"

"Well, I guess you could say that I felt dead inside, so that's when I started bodybuilding." He poured us a glass of wine. "To us Claudia . . . " saluting me with his glass.

"For always, Kel." I held mine up and tipped it towards him then drew in a large mouthful of the lovely fresh wine from the estate. How perfect things were at that moment.

Taking his wine glass and setting them both down on the bedside table, I took both of his hands and brought them to my lips, closed my eyes and kissed his knuckles.

"How did you manage to do this? We don't have to worry about anyone finding us here do we?"

"No Kelly, we are safe here, don't worry. We can relax and enjoy this time together."

"I don't care if we have to hideout here, I'm going to enjoy every second with you Claudia." He reached for the strands of hair that hung down the front of me. "What would you like to do now babe?"

I smiled at "babe," his word of endearment, I liked it. "Just more of this Kel, drink, inhale and taste you. I don't want to share you with the world right now." I buried myself against his chest. "Do you have any idea how difficult it was that New Year's when for the first time I saw you with Cindy. It killed me, I believed I'd lost you to one of my friends Kelly. Acting, I am so good at acting, I don't want to do it anymore. It may have been puppy love when we were kids, but I loved you and have always loved you." I ran my finger up and down his back, not letting him escape. I couldn't say those words enough, I had gone too many years without the opportunity to express myself to him.

"Cindy and I finally ended our marriage Claudia, it should have happened years ago . . . she changed so drastically over the last few years. After seeing you in England I had to fight to keep sane and there was no saving our marriage. Claudia, I'm in love with you and I have always been in love with you too, this is not some cheap affair I would rather you be free because being just your lover is not good enough for me. I do know I could lay naked against your naked body and you can trust that I would honor you." He rested his head on mine.

"I'm glad that's how you feel Kelly, I want exactly that but my marriage is not the true definition of a marriage, I loathed him then and I loathe him now. So if you're worried about us breaking vows, there are no vows to break. I understand if you feel we should wait. I can do that." I pulled him down onto the bed, we rested our heads on pillows face to face, not really needing to speak, kissing and touching, playing with each other's fingers. I clung to him and wished I could climb inside of him and let him protect me for the rest of our lives.

"Claudia I'm not going to put my feeling or desires away, of course, I don't want to wait to be intimate with you, but if it's going to make your life difficult we won't. At least we have this and hopefully, we can meet each other more often, but I don't want another three years until I see you again." He said as his soft kisses trailed along my cheek. I moved my head under his chin and he began to recite words of a poem that was familiar to me.

> When we two parted, in silence and tears, Half broken-hearted, To sever for years, Pale grew thy cheeks and cold, Colder thy kiss; Truly that hour foretold Sorrow to this. The dew of the morning Sunk chill on my brow . . . It felt like the warning Of what I feel now. Thy vows are all broken, And the light is

thy fame: I hear thy name spoken, And share in its shame. Thy names thee before me, A knell to mine ear; A shudder comes o'er me—Why wert thou so dear? They know not I knew thee, Who knew thee too well: Long, long shall I rue thee, Too deeply to tell. In secret we met—In silence, I grieve, That thy heart could forget, Thy spirit deceive. If I should meet thee After long years, How should I greet thee? With silence and tears"

(LORD BYRON 1788–1824)

"How bittersweet is that Kel? Is that how you felt? How awful, I'm so sorry." I felt my emotions settling in.

"Claudia, you don't have anything to be sorry about." He wrapped me tightly in his arms. "I've memorized a poem of Elizabeth Barrett Browning . . .

How Do I Love Thee?

"Remember our days in the library together. We both were a couple of nerds weren't we?" I chuckled.

"Hey, I was no nerd, and neither were you, you were and still are the most beautiful girl in the school Claudia. I happen to think we were pretty cool even if the both of us are fond of literature and poetry. I have other fond memories of you standing in the front of our grade seven class reciting that bird poem, remember? I think it was Emily Dickenson."

"Wow, you have a great memory! A bird came down the walk: He did not know I saw; He bit an angle-worm in halves. And ate the fellow, raw." I sipped from my glass and grinned that he hadn't forgotten.

"I think I remember everything about us growing up. That must have been the tell tales of love huh?" Kelly twisted his glass between his palms. I've thought about what happened in Israel, and if I had have been around, would you have come to me when he blackmailed you?"

"If I had, what could you have done huh? I'd have kicked his smug face in Claudia, that's what I would have done, at least that's what I would have wanted to do and maybe still would like to do." Kelly's voice changed to a different octave.

"You would have gotten hurt Kelly, he's cruel and capable of murder, I know that for a fact, I know he killed Aswad!" I studied Kelly's face. I never had time to think about the consequences, it wasn't more than a day later when he forced me into marriage, then I was taken to France and my life took on a whole new meaning.

Kelly turned onto his back. "Come here, sweetie." I slid across him. His hand moved up and into my hair, "No more talking, we have a lot of kissing to catch up on Claudia." His forefinger ran up and down my cheek.

"We do, oh yes we do." I cooed joyfully. "Mm. . . , I just love kissing you Kel."

"Shh . . . my sweet girl, you are so easy to love!"

To me that was how being in love was meant to feel, I was grateful to be having this wonderful experience with him. I felt safe and special, but most of all I could be myself and that was what made it all worth the risk. Our kisses became hotter and the passion exploded inside of me. I knew I wouldn't have to prepare to be molested. It was like experiencing our young innocent love that had been short lived. Once again, I tucked myself under his chin, listened to his heart beating along with the warmth of his breath on my head, his fingers in my hair was mesmerizing and I must have dozed off.

What is a poet? Is he not that which wakens melody in the silent chords of the human heart? A light which arrays in splendor things and thoughts which else were dim in the shadow of their own significance. His soul is like one of the pools in the Ilex woods of the Maremma, it reflects the surrounding universe, but it beautifies, groups, and mellows their tints, making a little world within itself, the copy of the outer one; but more entire, more faultless. But above all, a poet's soul is Love; the desire of sympathy is the breath that inspires his lay, while he lavishes on the sentiment and its object, his whole treasure-house of resplendent imagery, burning emotion, and ardent enthusiasm. He is the mirror of nature, reflecting her back ten thousand times more lovely; what then must not his power be, when he adds beauty to the most perfect thing in nature—even Love.

When I awoke Kelly's, eyes were smiling just like his lips, "You know sweetie, you snore!" As he kissed the tip of my nose.

I shook my head, "I feel so relaxed right now, I don't ever remember feeling this good, and what do you mean I snore? "Then giggling I checked the time and it was late afternoon. The sky was changing to gray.

"Let's go for a walk Claudia and get some fresh air, there is something I want to do."

"Kelly, do you realize we haven't eaten anything since we got here," as I reached into his jacket pockets.

"I was very satisfied chewing on your lips and drinking you in my darling. But yes, now I'm famished! Kelly bent forward for a kiss.

We walked back to the inn and I suggested room service. I didn't want to share him. I needed to be alone with him for as long as possible because I knew it could be a long while before I would see him again.

"I like that idea sweetie, sharing you with other people, hell no! I've waited too long for this." He said rubbing his hands up and down my back.

We hurried back to our room and when Kelly opened the door the room was glowing in the candlelight. There was a bowl sitting on a table for two filled with pink and red roses and Somewhere Over the Rainbow sung by Faith Hill was playing.

"Kelly you've even remembered this." It was the first school play we had acted in together. I gasped in awe of him and what he had done. "When did you find time to do this?"

I wasn't so eager to go outside. I'd become content lying there next to Kelly. We both threw on warm sweaters and coats headed out. It was a little nippy outside and I slipped one hand in my jacket pocket that was when Kelly tucked our hands inside his warm jacket, walking close together we laughed at memories of the silly things we did as kids.

Across the road was a grove of pine trees. Kelly pulled a pocket-knife from his coat pocket. "I've always wanted to do this Claudia, this is tree number one, everywhere we travel together from today on we will leave a tree with our names on it. When he was finished, it read Kelly loves Claudia 71/97. I hooked my arm through his and traced his carving. He gently pushed me up against the tree and tenderly squeezed my bottom lip in between his.

"Kelly, do you realize we haven't eaten anything since we got here," as I reached into his jacket pockets.

"I was very satisfied chewing on your lips and drinking you in my darling. But yes, now I'm famished! Kelly bent forward for a kiss.

We walked back to the inn and I suggested room service. I didn't want to share him. I needed to be alone with him for as long as possible because I knew it could be a long while before I would see him again.

"I like that idea sweetie, sharing you with other people, hell no! I've waited too long for this." He said rubbing his hands up and down my back.

We hurried back to our room and when Kelly opened the door the room was glowing in the candlelight. There was a bowl sitting on a table for two filled with pink and red roses and Somewhere Over the Rainbow sung by Faith Hill was playing.

"Kelly you've even remembered this." It was the first school play we had acted in together. I gasped in awe of him and what he had done. "When did you find time to do this?"

I was able to drive out way ahead of you and arrange all this before you got here. I had time to explore. He pulled me into him. "Claudia, I promise you this is just the beginning. We are going to have many, many more times like this. I promise you."

I clutched him, and the tears flowed; allowing my emotions to take over. "I hope and pray you are right my darling. Oh, sweetheart, I don't know what to say."

"You're saying it with those tears, my dear." He took both thumbs and wiped the moisture from my face. "Come and see what I have for you."

Kelly changed the ambiance with laughter, his stories and his sense of humor made the mood lighter and we spent the rest of the evening reconnecting and getting close again. "I brought something with me, Claudia, I think it's one of your favorites, Kahlil Gibran's The Prophet." Kelly smiled as he retrieved the book from his bag.

We ate and later Kelly's beaming face would be the wonderful image to paste in my memory and I teased him, "Have you claimed your side of the bed?"

"Nope, if you prefer that side I'd be more than happy to switch." His altruistic attitude was one I was not familiar with.

I shook my head before speaking. "I am happy on either side of this bed, so read me something from The Prophet please." Crossing over the bed to slide in beside him, I nuzzled in and his arm slid around me finding that wonderful spot on his shoulder to rest my head on as he read,

> On Friendship Your friend is your needs answered. He is your field which you sow with love and reap with thanksgiving. And he is your board and your fireside. For you come to him with your hunger, and you seek him for peace.

"I got this copy when I heard you got married and looked into his words for insight about you because I knew I was the one you loved, but sadly this book didn't hold any answer, Claudia. I had to trust one day my answer would come back to me." His lips caressed my temple. "Should I continue?" I nodded and listened absorbing every word and every tone in his voice.

Awaking to the weight of Kelly's hand on my shoulder and the sound of his breathing against my ear made it even more hopeful in some way. I didn't understand, but it was as though this wasn't the last time. Unfortunately, the bittersweet situation would soon be coming to an end, today I would have to start preparing for inevitable: leaving the real essence of me, Claudia Samara, and return to the façade as Claudia Kassis al-Masri. Kelly's body shifted and his welcoming kiss heated the base of my neck.

"I worried that you were a dream that I was waking up from. But yes Claudia, it's real we have another wonderful day to make memories."

I rolled over and into my love's arms; my flesh had come alive at his touch. I was no longer satisfied just being near him. The beautiful February sunshine had found us and filled the room, beckoning us to come and play. After morning kisses and our bodies entwined in each other's, we knew the passion we had brewing inside of us needed to be reined in.

Kelly offered, "Sweetheart, you go ahead and shower first." But I encouraged him to go first, even the muscles in his back were buff and sculpted, this was a different looking Kelly than the years he was married to Cindy. I remembered his comments of how Cindy recreated her body and he hated it. I cringed, what would his reaction be to my surgery? I had to know. Entering the bathroom uninvited, I removed my nightwear and opened the shower curtain, he turned and the look in his eyes revealed what I took as sadness.

"Kelly, I have to know, does my body disgust you in any way? I hate these!" My hands moved to cover my breasts. "I never wanted them to be like this." I searched his face for clues to his thoughts at that moment.

"Come and join me in here Claudia." His invitation surprised me.

I stepped in and he released my hair from the constraints of the hair tie and the wet strands relaxed across my back. His hands took my shoulders and he bent his head to meet my eyes. "My darling, your body could never disgust me, not ever Claudia. It's not your body I love, it's the essence of you, okay?" He never took his eyes off mine. "I would like to wash your hair Claud; can I do that?" He had my face in his hands and his thumbs were stroking my bottom lip. "Oh, you have such a beautiful mouth, and lovely lips, lips that are begging me to devour them."

I nodded, "Yes please!" I sighed patiently waiting for his to reach mine. The water felt good on my skin. His lips moved across my jaw and I felt his erection.

"I'm not sorry Kelly, we don't know what tomorrow is going to bring, we have each other right now. Let's pretend we're on our honeymoon, I don't want to wait. We love each other Kelly that's all that matters." I was filled with the desire to familiarize myself with him. Soon my hair was full of rich fragrant lather and his fingers were making small circles in my scalp. He washed away all the lather and my jet-black hair shone. I had my answer; the backs of his fingers slowly ran along the sides of my neck, relaxing me even more. Finally, after sweet kisses along my neck, he had me in his arms. Our eyes locked, I knew his thoughts. "This is exactly how it's supposed to be isn't it Kelly?"

He winked, "You bet it is. It was always supposed to have been this way. I accept and you are really mine Claudia."

My insides fluttered as he placed me on my back amongst the pillows before sliding alongside me. He slowly and lovingly brought his lips to mine. I reached up to his face and traced the place behind his ear; our kisses were soft and sensuous without any harshness. It was a tenderness I had only known from the boy, who was a man and I had waited so long for him.

"Claudia, honey, are you okay?" Kelly whispered.

I nodded and kissed his chin while he found the little spots down the length of my neck to the valley between my breasts. Our bodies, damp from the shower, ignited at each other touch. I shuddered in desire before his fingers explored me. He inhaled, me lavished me, molded his hand over the sensitive place between my legs, his finger rubbed lightly over the place where my nerve endings gathered. I moaned and the moisture that had collected there in the warm entrance called for him. Drawing my hands into his, he positioned himself and with one long stroke he filled me, "Ohh . . . Kel, so good, you feel so good . . . " he sent goose bumps through me.

We rocked in rhythm and his mouth found my taunt nipples, rolling one around his tongue. I shifted as my vaginal muscles tightened around him, it wasn't long before my back was arched and my breathing accelerated, with one deep thrust my body trembled and he burst inside me. Kelly gathered my body tight against him and I panted, "Kelly I came, it's never been like this before."

He raised his head from between my breasts. "Is it a good thing?"

"Oh yes, it's definitely is a good thing."

I wrapped my arms around his neck. I couldn't tell him orgasms only happened with pain or abuse to my genitals. "I guess that's what happens when two people love each other." Kelly piped up. I was silent for a few moments.

"What happened, Claudia did I hurt you?" Kelly pulled out of me. I brought the back of my hand to my face, shaking my head.

"No, oh no Kelly it was wonderful, that's why." I sobbed. He must have sensed this was something I needed to do and wrapped me in his arms. "Baby if you want to talk about it I'm here, let it go honey."

I just hung on tight to my best friend, my love. After a few moments, I shifted. "Kelly, can we do that again?"

He kissed the tears off my face. "My lady wants more, of course, she can, how does she want me? Do you want me like this?" Kelly shifted onto his back and carefully took hold of my waist. "Slide on baby, take as much as you want." I found his mouth and sensuous kisses took over as his fingers slid inside me.

The next day we decided to have brunch downstairs and then investigate Hedley. We explored the vintage buildings and the second-hand stores, and of course wandered into the small-town library and found a special place on the floor in the back.

Kelly's next statement sent my head spinning. "When you're home with me, I intend to read to you often. Then you can wash my back and run to the door to greet me when I come home to you!"

"Kelly, how did you know?" I asked pressing tightly against him. He moved his thumb over my bottom lip. The experience was one of the most sensual, loving and erotic moments for me.

We sat there while Kelly reminisced about our first intimate time together at Porteau Cove, neither of us knew what we were doing, but we both knew we needed to connect in a way that would bond us together forever and we both knew that was what we had accomplished those eighteen years ago.

"Kelly, I thanked God every day that you were the one who took my virginity. Jasim was so smug thinking he had a virgin when he took me so unwillingly."

"I would rip him apart with my hands Claudia if I knew I could get away with it, but he's not worth the energy." His nostrils flared, that wasn't something I'd ever expects from him.

"You're right. He's not worth a second of your energy, let's pretend for the rest of our time together that he doesn't exist, all right?"

Claudia, I was so angry and hurt when I learned I'd lost you to Jasim. But I didn't have any intentions of marrying her Claudia; you have to believe me. I started drinking and feeling sorry for myself I let her in . . . and you know the rest."

I reached around and wrapped my arms around his neck. "It happened and I don't blame you, I understand how someone could be worn down, Cindy is lovely and knows a good thing when she sees it. I don't blame her for going after you. I just envy her for being the mother of your twins. I died inside when I thought she had your love. But now Kelly, I know you love me and you have wonderful children, I have something she will never ever have, you! The rest of it will work itself out." I didn't want to let him out of my embrace and it hurt knowing how the domino effect had taken its toll on us.

After a short while, we got up and headed down the street. "Oh, look Kel, ice cream! I think we should get a big sundae and split it. What do you think?"

"Sounds good, only if I get to feed it to you, missy!" He smiled brightly. Tilting his head back, he got a curious look on his face. "When was the last time I told you how much I love you, Claudia." He brought his hand and placed it at the base of my neck and his other at the base of my back.

"Every moment we're together, in everything you say and do. I feel it and I claim it." I replied softly. "Don't ever doubt my love for you, even in the challenging times and I don't doubt there will be a few."

Kelly squeezed me tightly. "Let's go get that ice cream."

"I have never doubted you and I know I never will. You have proved it over and over again. Kelly, I really know just how much you love me."

Our two days together was not what I had imagined, I wouldn't be ready when Tuesday arrived, but I was cautious about Kelly's questions. Kelly had become super protective of me, so if he got any hints of what Jasim did to me, I knew it would be difficult keeping him from flying to Dubai. I knew how volatile Jasim could be and how he didn't value me, or my life. I lived in fear of knowing when I no longer served his purposes that he could be capable of giving me to the Israeli government or simply dispose of me. Therefore, I savored every moment with Kelly.

I placed my belongings in my luggage, all except the few items I'd bought in Vancouver, which I folded and put in a shopping bag. "Kelly, I need you to keep this stuff for me, I can't take it back. Trust me it's kinda silly but I need you to do that for me." I rested it against his bag.

"Okay. I can do that. Only if you guarantee you'll be coming for them."

"You got it, one day I will come claim them, and you better have them, mister."

Kelly stroked my hair and pulled me into his arms, "I will think about our time here every day for the rest of my life sweetheart. Thank you for making it so special."

I told myself, stop it, stop it, Claudia, hold it in, and keep it together. "We had a great time, didn't we? They are special memories and they belong to only us Kel. Just remember, no matter what happens, you will always be my love." I kissed the space under his ear and made my way to his mouth. That kiss would have to carry me forward for a while. Kelly rocked with me and the silence was soon broken by the clicking sounds of a helicopter in the distance.

The helicopter pilot soon had me up in the air and on my way to the Langley Airport. Rob, the chauffeur, was meeting me at there and then we had a quick drive to Vancouver International Airport. In no time I would evolve back to being Mrs. Kassis al-Masri, and all my thoughts of Kelly had to stay in Hedley for now.

"How was your flight, Ms. Claudia?" Rob's chipper voice greeted as he escorted me to the limo.

"It was a beautiful flight; the scenery is so incredible."

"I'll get your bag and we'll be on our way to YVR."

I was looking forward to one thing and one person only. The feeling my little boy's arms around my neck and hearing him calling Mommy! Oh, Mikhail, Mommy can hardly wait to see you.

"Any stops you'd like to make along the way Ms. Claudia."

"I'm good; I promised my husband I'd be there as close to ten as possible. He gets a little anxious if I'm late." I said, checking the time, not needing to add any fuel to the fire.

The drive went too fast. The rush hour traffic diminished and soon we parked at VIP entrance. Rob got out to unload my bags and ski equipment onto a luggage dolly when an airport concierge greeted us. "Where are you departing from?"

"The Kassis al-Masri jet," I replied.

"One-moment Ma'am and I will find out what gate."

I turned to Rob, automatically reaching for a large bill and he waved me off, "Ma'am come on now, you've overdone it already."

She raised an eyebrow." Ma'am?"

He cleared his throat, "Claudia . . . " he said reaching out to shake my hand. "Thanks again for your help Rob. I will keep you in mind for the future."

"Any time you give me a call, I'll be at your service."

I walked into the terminal and the concierge smiled, "This way Madame."

Chapter 11

My eyes scoured inside the jet for my boy, but he was nowhere in sight. Only Jasim was seated reading something in a folder.

"My wife is on time! Hello, Claudia!" I recognized the tone, the coldness, the hairs at the back of my neck stood up.

"Where is Mikhail? I thought you were bringing him Jasim?" My heart sunk.

"It was better that he stayed at home Claudia. I want you all to myself right now." Jasim's expression was unreadable. This wasn't good, but I proceeded with my plan. Slade, our pilot, advised us we were authorized for takeoff. I buckled in and tried to study Jasim's expression. I knew something was up; my insides grew queasy. Did he know? He must have found out. When we reached out altitude, Jasim contacted the crew and barked, "No interruptions under any circumstances."

Christ, twenty-one hours to go, now what? His eyes were studying me and I could tell he sensed my discomfort, "My cock hurts Claudia, it hurts real bad, suck me off." He adjusted himself so I would need to get out of my seat. He nodded looking down at the floor. I knelt before him. He flicked a switch beside his seat. I licked my lips, in preparation for the worst and that was what I got. Jasim's hand moved around my throat, his fingers rested at the trachea, fuck, fuck . . . what does he know?

Jasim unzipped his zipper and grabbed my hair and pulled it as tight to my head as possible. He pushed my face down hard until his erection was at the very back of my mouth, then he let go of my hair and waited for my performance. I continued to perform precisely as he liked, and felt relieved when he climaxed. I waited to be excused, but he said, "You can do a better job than that, come on baby lick it clean, honey."

When I was finished I undressed down to my bra and panties. "Jasim touch me I have been waiting for you, please fuck my cunt Jasim. I stuck two fingers inside my panties, trying to arouse his interests. I was getting totally aroused and caught up in what I was doing. I almost forgot about him. He ripped my panties off. Replacing my fingers, he pulled me over his lap, and for the first time, I didn't know what he was about to do.

He inserted his thick thumb into my anus, I squirmed and he ordered, "Stay still Claudia." It was right after that his two middle fingers entered my vagina. Whatever he was doing, it was very painful and I didn't know what to do, he was squeezing the tissues together and it felt like my vaginal wall was going to tear. When his hand came down hard on my ass I thought I was going to pass out. He did it again and again, but I still didn't make a sound. I wouldn't give him the satisfaction. I could only pray it would end. When it finally did, I could barely walk. When I found my clothes, I had difficulty putting them on. He wouldn't see my pain. I finished dressing and got back into my seat.

"Jasim could I please have a glass of scotch?"

"You know where the bar is Claudia, go ahead help yourself." He picked up the folder and went back to his reading. He pressed the staff button, "I need you to bring my wife something to eat, perhaps a bowl of soup."

I was hungry, but food wasn't what I wanted. I wanted to know what he knew. After trying to eat a little soup, I drew my legs under me and tried to sleep. I was sick and scared. That was the first time I sensed that something really bad was about to happen.

Coming home to my child was my initiative to be strong. I was so excited walking through the doors. I headed straight to his room, knowing full well he would be sound asleep. "Mikhail," I whispered soft enough not to wake him. I noticed dark circles under his eyes and this was when I learned it was the beginning of the end. I lay beside him on his bed, being careful not to wake him. But he instinctively knew his mommy was there, "Sleep darling, I love you baby boy, your mommy is home now," and he snuggled into my neck. Yes, this is love, love so pure and I soon fell asleep holding him tightly.

The sound of Mik's door opening and his nanny entering woke me up.

"Oh I'm sorry, but it is time for Mikhail to get up for school."

"Yes, that's okay, I will get him ready myself. I pulled him into my arms and rocked him side to side. Kissing his head, I sang to him in Arabic. "I love you Mikhail, Mikhail, Mikhail my little one."

Mikhail giggled while I wiggled my finger gently into his neck. "Mommy, why were you gone for so long?" "Was I away from you too long Mik? I was only gone a week, If I was, I won't go away for so long again honey." His doe-like eyes didn't seem to have the liveliness that was there before I left.

"Mommy, can I stay home with you today?" He looked up at me eagerly. "Yes, Mik you can stay with me today . . . " Jasim was standing in the doorway.

"Mikhail, you know you have to go to school. Mommy will be here when you get home."

I turned around, made eye contact and shot him the, "How dare you" look, while Mik looked up at me. "I'm not going anywhere son, your daddy is correct, you should go to school. Come now darling, let's get you dressed and some food in that tummy." Turning to face Jasim I said, "Daddy, you can go to work now, Mik and I have it all under control." I glared at him.

I had breakfast with my son and kissed him as he went out the door with the nanny. I had to catch up with everything that went on with Mik while I was away. I opened the door to our bedroom and everything from my suitcases had been thrown around the room. Jasim must have been in quite a rage to do that. This was why he made Mik go to school. I was frightened. I heard the door close and there he stood.

"Why did you lie to me, Claudia?" Jasim was walking towards me.

"What are you talking about, I never lied to you? Jasim why did you do this?" I questioned him.

He stepped closer, "Where did you go when you left Whistler Claudia?" He was on my face. I didn't answer, "I asked, where you went when you left Whistler? I'm not going to repeat myself again." He said with condemnation in his voice. I stood my ground and said nothing. He struck me with the back of his hand. I swallowed. "Well?" He challenged.

I said nothing and he slapped me again. I looked down at my feet. This time his knee came up and I received a blow to my abdomen. Then his other knee found the same spot and I went down on my knees. He kicked me in the head, I felt woozy from the second blow to my abdomen, the kicks continued and I kept my silence and silently began to sing, "Somewhere over the rainbow, way up high, there's a land that I heard of once in a lullaby . . . "

I felt another blow above my kidney. I gasped to get air in my lungs. "Just kill me Jasim it's not worth it anymore!" Then I rolled into a ball and he left the room. I couldn't move because of the pain, all I could think of was my son, I didn't want to leave him behind.

When I awoke hours later, in so much pain I wanted to die, Jasim personal physician was taking my pulse. "Claudia, I have some pain medication here for you, I'm going to inject it into your hip, it should help right away."

I moaned so loud when he turned me onto my side. "Somewhere over the rainbow, way up high, there's a land that I heard of, once in a lullaby, somewhere over the rainbow skies are blue, and the dreams that you dare to dream really do come true ..." I tried losing myself in the song, repeating it over and over again. "Dr. Ali, my son, my son can't see me like this, but he will think I left him again." I began to cry. My eyes were swollen shut and my lips were split open.

"It's too late Claudia he burst into the room when you were sleeping, his nanny is with him now. He'll be okay, Claudia, you rest. I'll be back to check on you later. Jasim has hired nurses for you around the clock. I am going to set up some appointments for X-rays and blood work. Jasim has forbidden me from admitting you to the hospital, I will do my best Claudia; you need things I can't provide here. Just rest I will deal with him." And Dr. Ali left the room.

I wasn't sure how long I had slept, but I woke up to Mikhail's worried little face. "It's all right my son, Mommy will be okay, I promise." My son was rather insightful for such a young age. "You want to come and lay here beside me Mikhail?"

"If I won't hurt you," my young son asked.

"You won't hurt Mommy. You will help Mommy feel better." I said as he climbed ever so carefully beside me. I was in so much pain that I could hardly breathe, but I kept that at bay. Mikhail brought the book The Legend of the Wandering King, one of the novel's I had picked out for him in Canada. It was the only way I had to teach my child differently than how he was being trained with Jasim's traditions.

I focused the best I could as Mikhail read to me while praying the painkiller wouldn't wear off. I was trying so hard to hide the hurt from Mikhail when Jasim entered the room he was aghast that Mikhail was on the bed beside me.

"Mikhail your music teacher is waiting for you, and your mommy needs her rest, now go son." Jasim's stern parental ways kept Mikhail in line, just the way he wanted his son to be. I was alone with Jasim and once again I panicked, afraid he was going to interrogate me again and inflict another beating. He stood at the end of the bed.

"Claudia, I want to know where you went when you left Whistler." He tapped his fingers on his thigh.

"Do what. . . . what . . . " I gasped for air. "What you need to do Jasim, but this time, finish the job." I closed my eyes, believing and waiting for another round of blows.

"Is that what you think I'm going to do to you, Claudia? No, I'm going to keep you around, our son needs his mother Claudia, but I am going to find out where you went." Jasim moved around the side and sat on the bed his hand swept the strand of hair from my face before he pulled the covers back. My body began to shake uncontrollably. "Relax Claudia, I'm not going to hurt you, I just want to see if what Ali said was true."

He undid the buttons of my nightshirt and his eyes examined my naked body. "There is a medical taxi coming to take you to a private hospital. Claudia, damn it why did you have to ruin it, we were getting to a good place. I knew you were starting to love me, I could see it, I could feel it every time I made love to you the way you melted into me." Jasim's hand traveled over my naked skin across where those painful blows had occurred. Then once again his fingers closed the buttons and the covers were secured in place again.

My eyes stayed closed, during the ambulance ride I no longer wanted to look at the world around me, I contemplated which hurt the most, my body or my soul? Jasim got the job done, just short of killing me, breathing even was a chore. The biggest regret I carried through this experience was Mikhail seeing what his father had done. . . . not because I was his mother but because I am a woman. I couldn't bear the thought of my son growing into a person like his father.

Too soon I would learn my son would never get that opportunity, nor would he have the experiences of growing into the man that would make us proud.

I was still under the care of the hospital staff, healing naturally, Jasim denied me any type of surgery, maybe he'd hoped I would die, but when he told me it was because my body would be scarred, and he couldn't have that as I had to get back to work it had to heal on its own.

Jasim kept me in the dark about Mikhail, the month I spent hospitalized he forbid Mikhail to visit me. Instead of it breaking my spirit it helped me fight to get stronger, later I figured out that was Jasim's plan.

It would be one of those days that felt like rape all over again. Jasim made a visit to my hospital room and as soon as he shut the door and made sure no one could witness what he had in mind for himself. My spirit took flight, back over the rainbow. . . . It began again, the cruel violent acts he shamed my body. When it was all over, Jasim sat still beside me. "Claudia your evil nature is now going to be punished by God. See Claudia what happens when a wife betrays her husband. God is taking your son from you, Claudia... How do you like that?" His words were racing through my mind, "What do you mean by that Jasim, why would God take our son?" I stared at him waiting for a response. He is dying Claudia, he has maybe a year, maybe two. Your fault Claudia."

"I don't believe you Jasim, that's a lie. I want the doctors to tell me, do you hear me Jasim?" He did not reply, he left the room.

Was that why my son wasn't coming to visit? I wouldn't cry, I had no proof. I laid there in an agony I had not yet begun to experience.

The next morning my hospital room received a visitor, one of the specialists Jasim had sought out for Mik. It was the tone of the doctor's voice that drove it home. My Mikhail was diagnosed with a congenital heart disorder?

Chapter 12

I SUFFERED ALONE in that hospital room, I cried for my child, I cried because I was helpless and unable to save Mikhail, let alone be with him until Jasim decided. That decision came two weeks later when Jasim sent a car to bring me home. This prison would not get the best of me, I had only one option, getting strong, physically. That would help keep my mind from over thinking, I had to be strong for my son.

I refused to be separated from Mikhail, I slept on the floor beside him, waking up before he did, allowing as much normalcy as I could give him. There were some days that were better than others for him those days he'd continue with the routine Jasim had set for him. The days he was at his weakest I barely left his side, I would send Jasim's staff away. And then wait for repercussions, which thankfully never came. My happiness came when Jasim went on his trips, I knew I was under the staff scrutiny, but it didn't matter. I could smile and laugh and have happy times with my son he was my son in every way.

A year had come when out of the blue Jasim brought me another blow. My father was terminal, pancreatic cancer. Here I was just where Jasim wanted me to be, at his mercy. I had become a caged animal, unable to make any decisions. I had little hope to see my father alive let alone go home for his funeral. Not only was this situation horrific, but my own child was deteriorating rapidly. All I could do was beg Jasim to say goodbye to my papa.

I waited until Mikhail was asleep and Jasim had retired to his room before I made the decision. I knew only one way of getting Jasim to agree. I had to give myself to him willingly. I prepared my body, clamped my nipples and clitoris until I could no longer feel any sensations. The female staff oiled my skin and dressed me for him in reds and gold, his favorites.

When every last detail was in place, I found him lying on his bed reading, I\d seldom ever seen him with a novel, but this night it looked to me he was engrossed in it.. that was until he took a second glance and then I danced, seducing him, smiling at him as my hands raked his dark mass of hair. I attempted to straddle him, but Jasim grabbed my waist. "You don't have to do this Claudia, I have decided for you to go to your Canada and say goodbye to your papa. But you will go without Mikhail Claudia, the boy stays with me." Jasim guided me away from where he was lying. I was surprised, then I realized I would be away from my sick child. God had to understand and give me more time with my son.

As I turned to leave, I had taken merely a couple of steps when I felt a tug of the material I was wearing. The next tug had torn the material off and left me naked. I knew what was coming. I'd pay a hurtful price to travel.

Mik was having a difficult day and I believed by snuggling him close to me would heal us both. I had to get my child's approval, to know he would be okay for a few weeks while I went to say goodbye to my papa.

I drew my boy under my chin and massaged his back. "Mikhail there is something I need to discuss with you. You have a grandpa and grandmother who live in Canada. I am so sorry they never got to meet you, Mikhail. Grandpa is very sick and he doesn't have much time left. I need to go there, to see him and tell him about you...you mustn't tell your dad Mik. But there is something else I don't want to leave you Mik. I won't go if you don't want me to." I hated putting that burden on my son, but he had the right to ask me to stay.

"You go, Mom, I'll be alright until you get back...I'll be here when you get back." Mik chuckled. "I promise." My boy's smile did such good for my heart.

"You're sure son? I don't want to leave you. I owe my parents this much. I love you, my strong son. I will be back as quickly as I can. Kissing my son's now shallow cheeks I held him close. "My special child, you are Mikhail, how blessed am I? How come God gave me you?"

"Because you are a very special Mom!" Mik grinned. I laid beside him until he went to sleep then found Jasim.

When Jasim's private jet landed in Vancouver, it was a bittersweet time for me. I would finally have the opportunity to tell my folks about Mikhail and keep the rest of it to myself. They had the right to know of their grandson's existence.

My stomach was full of knots and the sick feeling was not about to leave, I wasn't sure how I was going to be received, maybe they wouldn't want to see me. Maybe they had written me out of their lives altogether. I wouldn't blame them if they had. I would make sure of one thing for sure they would see a picture of their only grandchild.

I walked through customs proud to show my Canadian passport if only I was coming home for good, I thought to myself. I had been lucky arriving at the time I had, the airport wasn't very busy. As I made my way to the car rental section I thought about the young chauffeur, Rob, I felt over-whelmed at what Jasim had done to him, the pictures were graphic in every detail. Jasim was proud when he tossed them in my face. If he was in the airport now, I wondered how I could ever face him, because of me he suffered at the hands of a lunatic.

This time I rented an SUV and headed into Burnaby not having any idea how I would be received by my mother. My parents were probably deeply hurt when they learned about my marriage, and I still couldn't confide in her. My legs almost ran to the phone booth,

I dialed the number and as soon as I heard Kelly's voice I fell apart.

"Claudia, it's you!" He sighed deeply into the phone. "Oh my God baby where are you. I'm coming to you, I won't take no either," and I wasn't about to stop him. I told him about my father in Burnaby General Hospital and that I was heading there as soon as we got off the phone.

"I'll be there as soon as I can get a flight Claudia, even if I have to charter a jet I promise I will get to you."

"I need you, Kelly." "Hang in there sweetheart, I'm coming." After we hung up I was able to release. . . .

The twenty or so steps from the nurse's station into papa's room were some of the heaviest my feet have ever felt. I had no idea what I was going to be faced with on entering the room. But Papa's smile took the weight off my shoulders and my feet, which were almost bouncing to get to his bedside.

"Oh Papa, you must be so disappointed in me, I don't deserve your forgiveness. I am so sorry, it was..." Claudia stopped herself in mid-sentence. I bent forward and placed my cheek against his and kiss both sides of his mouth. I felt his hands stroke the length of my hair just as he had always done when I was a child. "You're safe now Claudia, mama and I know your secret, we will keep it safe for you." He whispered before patting my hand. "Claudia, there is a deeper sadness about you, I can see such agony in your eyes." He tilted his head slightly, "My child you didn't need to suffer all this time, why didn't you trust your papa and mama to help you?" I could only lower my eyes feeling shame. No one but Kelly knew the truth and I was almost relieved that he had confided in my parents. But how much had Kelly told them? I sat beside him, scrutinizing him, how age had taken over and now his illness, he was skin and bone, not the sturdy strong man I had last seen over twenty years ago. It was painful thinking of what we'd missed out on as a family. Then in an instant, a cloud of tears burst. I tried to control it and push them back, it was having the freedom to cry and knowing I was loved that helped them pass. Papa became quiet and it was inevitable that he would doze off. I pulled a chair up close to the bed and made myself as comfortable as I could and then placed my hand on his cool one. I finally relaxed enough that sleep took over, I knew I had to be dreaming, how could I be here, my head was swimming. The warm soft kiss I felt on my forehead, was just like the ones I remembered as a child. How could that be? I need to check, something isn't right. I opened my eyes to see mama's smile and dancing eyes. Her arms opened and I filled them without a second thought.

"My girl is back, I knew one day you'd come home to us Claudia. Papa must have been thrilled to see his daughter home." She brushed the hair off my sweater. "When did you get here and how did you find out about Papa?" "I've been home a few hours, it doesn't matter how I found out, I am so thankful I got home in time. "Come sit down Claudia, we need to talk." I was prepared for the questions and I had selective answers, but first I needed to know about my papa, then we would discuss Kelly.

"Tell me about my papa...what is the diagnosis?" I kept her eyes connected to mine. She just shook her head, anytime Claudia, he has been fighting to stay alive for such a long time. I think he was willing you home. I don't know my daughter only God has his plan for your papa." Mama's eyes welled up.

"Somehow things manage to work out, in the end, don't they Claudia?"

I folded my arm over her shoulder and my nostrils were familiarized with the scent of orange blossoms, her fragrance. It was welcoming, oh how I loved that scent. I wondered how I could have forgotten that. 'You need to know something, Claudia, Kelly came to visit us, and he told us you would probably be angry with him for speaking about you. Papa and I know why you felt you couldn't come to us Claudia, he could have helped, with Uncle Ashif's connections, as well as Papa's in the Middle East, things wouldn't have gotten that awful for you. Claudia nothing you could have done would have changed us. We know we have our own ghosts." "There's a lot more Kelly doesn't know, he can never know. I was young and rebellious just as Uncle Ashif said. Bull-headed and strong…I was on a mission. Yes, it cost me everything that is dear to me and now I'm losing my. . . . " I stopped and caught my words, did Kelly tell them about Mikhail?" I wanted to tell them both at the same time, how they would love him. It was a fight keeping the tears back. I was relieved when I heard papa calling. "Jada, come here please Jada." I could hear the pain in his voice. "Yes, yes Galib I'm here my husband, what is it? Are you in pain?" "I saw Claudia, like an angel she came to visit me. Did you see her Jada?" "Yes, Galib our Claudia is home she is right here." He sighed. A smile curled up the left side of his mouth.

I opened my bag and found the picture of Mikhail. "This is a picture of your grandson Mikhail, he just turned thirteen. My wonderful son." Handing the picture to papa, with mama getting nearer to see it. They looked over at each other. "Yes, Jada we do have a grandchild, I knew we would." His tears were uncontrollable and so were his sobs. I felt ashamed and filled with hate, it had been easy for me to kill so long ago. Why hadn't I killed Jasim, there were many opportunities, and there was Aswad. It was too late for that now. I stumbled around my thoughts, do I share sadness about my son? I knew they needed to hear it from me.

"There is more sadness, we learned a while ago that Mik has a congenital heart disorder and he may not live too much longer. I wish I didn't have to bring bad news." I lowered my head…so ashamed of how I made my life.

Mama gasped, "Why are you not with your son Claudia? He needs you to be there." I nodded, "Yes I know, Mikhail to me it was right that I come here. He knows he is dying but he knows how important it is for me to be here. Mikhail is a bright young man. He is very perceptive and spiritual. He will be ok until I get back."

"Tell us more about him, our grandson." She asked. I felt relief once again and smiled, I felt so proud of the child I raised. I told them as much of everything I could about their grandson. Papa kept alert during the conversation.

"Can I keep this picture Claudia?" she asked quietly. "Of course." I nodded, "But you have to promise me you will keep it hidden from everyone. Jasim forbids me from telling you. Please, you have to keep the secret." "Of course, I will, Jasim is a very evil man. We should have had the chance to take matters into our own hands, Claudia. That man will rot in the dungeons of hell I promise you." Those type of words from my mama's mouth were foreign to me, and it told me of another side of her. Papa was still focused on Mikhail's picture.

"Have you eaten or drank anything daughter? You need to eat, you can't be strong for everyone unless you eat." I shook my head, "Not right now if I had a scotch it would be just the thing. They were against alcohol, but that they would have to get used to her drinking. I looked over and papa had finally fallen asleep, I ran my finger across his forehead and pushed back his thin hair. "I love you, papa…you sleep now." How I hated hospitals and I swore Mikhail would not die in a place like this. I wanted to whisk my parents away somewhere where it was serene and beautiful. If only. . . .

Looking over at mama who was now fussing over him. "He hasn't slept for more than an hour at a time, he's at peace now that you're home. Claudia, he told me you would come, that he would have the time to say goodbye and tell you how proud he is of you, that even what you did in Israel, you stood up for your beliefs. We know what war is Claudia, you were meant to survive."

"I know you must have many questions for me…I promise you before I leave you will know everything…but there will be things you won't like. I'm not the Claudia that left here in 1974. You are not going to like her very much." She glanced over, "Nothing you could ever say or do will ever change the love I have for you Claudia and don't you ever forget that. We know things . . . how could we not it is our heritage there are very few secrets." I shivered.

"Claudia... hi...I wish I could have gotten here sooner." Kelly reached for my hand. He shook his head, "You don't look well at all." I closed in and rested my head against his shoulder. "It will be ok. I am here where I belong if only Mik was with me." Kelly insisted we go out into the hall and mama encouraged us.

"I am worried about you, you are so thin. What the hell has happened to you?" Both of his hand grasping my face. "Right now, I have to focus on my dad...Kelly Mikhail is sick, we learned he has a congenital heart disease and is dying. I will be ok, especially now because you are here to keep me strong." Kelly pulled me close. "Always, I will be here always, you can count on that."

I pulled back and looked into his eyes. "I don't know whether to be choked with you or grateful. They told me you paid them a visit a long time ago. I only hope it didn't upset them any more than what they were at my disappearance."

"They deserved something, they have spent too many years not knowing your where bouts, if you were alive, Daina told them as much as she knew, but she didn't tell them when she saw you. I had to say something. I hope you can understand." Kelly ran his fingers through his hair. "Kelly, you overstepped, but I am glad you did. I need to tell her the whole story, I am grateful you refrained from telling them about my son. Thank you." I reached out and wrapped my arms around his neck. Feeling him against my skin was what I ached for.

"Could I go get you and your mom something to eat or drink? I bet you have eaten since you left home." Kelly stepped back to look at me. "I'm not hungry, but if you had a bottle of scotch I sure wouldn't refuse." I attempted to joke, little did he know. I'd probably drink the whole damn bottle. "Sorry, I didn't know you'd want scotch. I grabbed a cab and came here. Oh, Claudia, why did this have to be the reason to bring you back?" His hands were wrapped in my hair and soon he brought my lips to his. It was natural to part my lips to greet his. I got lost and let go, I felt weak and needy for the very first time. He must have felt my body weaken and those arms tightened around me. And a hand supported my face as my head rested against his chest. I don't know how long we stayed in that position, I wasn't about to let go.

"Do you want to go back into the room? I will get you something to drink, your mom needs you too Claudia." He kissed my forehead.

I returned to mama's place beside my papa's bed. "Claudia his breathing has become shallow, I don't think he'll be with us in the morning." I felt the tears forming and didn't hold then in. "Papa thank you for holding on . . . waiting for me... I love you, you don't have to hang on for me. Mikhail told me to tell you he will meet you in heaven. You look for him ok. I love you so much." I looked over at the woman who had been by his side for 60 years or more and knew it was her time to be with him. I found a chair in the hallway and slumped into it. I felt so cheated, enraged.

Mama Kelly and I left the hospital a few hours later, she said papa had left life content. She insisted we all go home together and try to get some sleep, although I knew sleep wasn't going to be easy. I was suddenly keyed up. Handing Kelly the car keys it was a solemn drive to the home I grew up in, the home I hadn't seen in twenty-three years.

The moment I walked up the front steps and through the door my heart was uplifted. It was home just like it had always been. The door opened and my eyes took stock of everything, very little had changed. I felt the love in this room, the laughter still echoed around me. "I think we could all use a good cup of tea, at least I could. Mama said as she started towards the kitchen. "Yes, that sounds wonderful Mama...I'm going to my room, I need to shower. Kelly carried my bags up to my room. "I guess you know I'm not going anywhere Claudia, I'll sleep on the floor beside your bed if necessary, but I won't be leaving you anytime soon." His expression was intense.

The next few days went by too quickly, like a whirlwind, Jada

Samara was calm and never once showed her emotions. She just went about preparing papas funeral with my aunts and their families. Something must have been mentioned to family members because not one of them brought up a single question to me regarding the last twenty-six years. I was so relieved, I didn't have the courage to discuss anything with anyone.

During the funeral Kelly kept his distance staying close to our longtime friends. We were careful when our eyes met that no one caught us. Every time he looked at me I was afraid he would see my angst. Time was nearing, I had to leave, I needed to be with Mikhail. There was no easy way to go, but I had to leave without Kelly knowing or it would be unbearable. Mama had arranged with one of my uncles to take him on an errand, that way I would slip out, without saying any goodbyes to anyone. But first I needed to catch his attention and direct him to my childhood bedroom. He caught on immediately.

I closed the door behind us, "I sure could use a hug right now, it's been a difficult day. You, Mr. Mac, have the perfect arms for that." I smiled up at the man that held my heart. Kelly buried his face in my neck while I memorized his being. I pressed my forehead against his. "I don't think I have told you recently how crazy in love with you I am, now have I?"

Kelly grinned "Oh it's obvious, every look you give me speaks those words. You are loved my dear, more than you could ever know. Now hurry up and kiss me!" There was no hesitation, it would be the kiss I would take with me to keep me strong.

The expected knock came at my door, it was Mama, "Claudia do you think Kelly would go with your Uncle Seif . . . he has forgotten his medicine?" "Of course I will Mrs. Samara, just give me a minute, I'll be right there."

I held on to Kelly and gently kissed the side of his jaw. "My love..." Then I gently pushed him out the door. I gathered the rest of my belongings and with Mama beside me, she guided me through the back door to the rental car. "I will come back, I promise you, Mama, I promise. I love you always." Her smile was bright and I saw that same love for me in her eyes she had given me as a child, she reached her hand out, holding her cherished Hamsa. "My child this time keep it with you at all times, it will keep you safe and will bring you home again." I placed the treasure around my neck.

Scotch made all the difference during the return flight to Dubai, having the privacy of the jet gave me the freedom to drink my face off and numb my brain enough to finally get long needed sleep. Images of Kelly cradling me while he slept and I stared into the blackness of my long-ago bedroom. The desire to give my body to him was traumatized by sadness and a pain I was unfamiliar with. Death, death was dancing all around me now, waiting to torchers my heart even more. I was broken, I finally had to admit it, I lost myself and my dignity, my strength had been severed the day Jasim nearly took my life. There was no more fight left. Having to be present for Mikhail as best I can is going to take a great deal of energy. It wouldn't be under the influence of scotch. I told myself as I guzzled the last inch of amber liquid in the glass and made my way to the cabin, scotch bottle in hand.

What seemed like hours later was only an hour since I'd passed out, I woke up to the buzzer from the cockpit, "Yes Slade what the hell time is it?"

"Well it is almost three AM and we're about to land in Montreal to refuel."

"Thanks, Slade I'm going to try to get some sleep. Wake me when we land in Madrid. Please."

"Will do Ms. Claudia. Have a good rest." I wondered who the co-pilot on this trip was. Jasim was very controlling, it would have to be someone he totally trusted. I attempted to sleep again.

Chapter 13

From the time of Mikhail's diagnosis, Jasim had a difficult time keeping his resentment of me to himself while in the presence of our son. We both took pleasure in making good memories with Mikhail. Having the yacht and the jet made travel much easier for Mik when he had his down times the yacht was comfortable and private. Mikhail seemed to get his strength while we sailed.

The scotch bottle became my best friend: it became my comfort and motivator to get me through every day. I avoided Jasim as best I could, other than the obligatory times with our son.

There's one day I will always remember. It was when Mikhail asked Jasim, "Why do you hurt Mom?"

Jasim's response was disgusting and unbelievable, "Because Mikhail, Mommy disrespects me and that is how we deal with disobedient women who don't do as their husbands' say." It was difficult for me to make eye contact with my son during that comment. I had to prevent him from seeing my disgust for his father.

Jasim and I never shared a bed, but on many occasions, he would still come and take what he believed was rightfully his.

This was one of a few occurrences Jasim would invade my cabin, this one incident after staying with Mikhail until he finally was sleeping comfortably. I retired to my cabin exhausted, and emotionally spent, on verge of tears when I found Jasim waiting. That familiar stomach wrenching grin was unmistaken, I responded the way I believed he expected and fell to my knees.

"Yes, my husband how can I serve you?" it was all I could do to get the words out.

"Get up off the floor Claudia, what are you doing?" He roared.

I found enough sarcastic enthusiasm to respond, regretfully that was the wrong reaction, and seconds later he had my ponytail wrapped around his fist. The anger in his eyes I had seen so often and I knew what was coming next. His hand connected once then on the right cheek. I closed my eyes and went limp, the foul language that came out of his mouth just added insult to injury. There would be something good coming from this the genital pain would give me the orgasmic release my body craved now. Returning to the kneeling position, I untied the strings around my neck and reached down to undo the row of buttons, before removing my skirt, I sat on the heels of my feet and folded my hands in my lap.

"On your knees, Claudia, bend over, spread your legs and grab your ankles." My libido was excited...Jasim's finger slid along the slit and I was ready. It was the sting of the strap repeatedly across my buttocks that jarred me. His rhythm was consistent over and over.

"You keep forgetting Claudia, I own you, I could kill you and nothing would happen to me...but I wouldn't Claudia... you still have a lot to work off." His words swirled through my mind, but there was only one thing on my mind, his hands massaging my buttocks and teasing my genitals that got me aroused, desperate to be penetrated. Jasim picked me up dropping me on my bed, he took me hard and mercilessly, exactly what my body responded to. Jasim ejaculated all over my face and breasts...then laughed as he pulled on his pants. I knew my title Jasim's wife whore.

We sailed the Mediterranean, Tyrrhenian, Ionian and Adriatic

Seas around Spain, France, and Italy and up to Croatia with Mikhail. Every time the helicopter took Jasim away, I celebrated. Often, he would be away for weeks at a time on business and it was only Mik and me. Those were the times I openly answered Mik's questions, the ones I knew he was reluctant to talk about with Jasim.

"Forgive him, Mikhail, your dad only knows his own definition of love. But honey he loves you to the depth of his being, that I'm sure of." I wanted Mik to know forgiveness, compassion and unconditional love. Loving his father was just as important as the feelings he had for me.

The last few months of Mikhail's sixteen years were filled with the sights, sounds, and scents of each new adventure. But this day God blessed me, it was the day I said goodbye to my child because Jasim was away.

Mikhail and I were curled up on the bow of the yacht in the master suite, Mik's room. The glass doors opened onto the deck; it was a wonderful place to fall asleep and wake up to. My son knew he was dying that beautiful spring morning.

"Mom, I just want to stay here today, I think I saw grandpa in my dream last night. He said that I would be coming to see him and he had a lot to tell me. Do you think so Mom?"

I plumped up a pillow, laid it on my lap and brought Mik's head onto it. "Yes, sweet boy I do, grandpa promised me he'd wait for you and be with you always." I stroked his curls and studied his features. Mik was so serene, it was difficult holding my emotion in check. I seldom played the flute anymore, only the times I was on my own, I would never share that with Jasim.

Mikhail's fingers stroked my hair then caressed my face, "I'm so tired Mom I just want to sleep for a while ok?" "Yes, baby it's good to sleep, you just sleep my son. I love you, Mikhail." "I love you too Mom." He whispered faintly just enough for me to hear his final beautiful words as he died in my arms.

If the silent screams could be heard from my insides they would have deafened the oceans habitants. The most horrendous time of my life and I didn't want to share it with Jasim who would be returning to the yacht shortly with the medics.

I resented the arrival of the helicopter when it came to take us back to Dubai. Jasim wanted an autopsy done, because of the congenital heart disorder. He was making sure he had answers to understand why his son died.

I grieved alone, I had lost all desire to go anywhere or do anything. Surviving the funeral was difficult, especially without my loved ones, my only solace was Pascha, I could trust him, but even though we were involved in the same terrorist group Jasim had managed to erase all evidence that Pascha was involved.

It was difficult now, living in the penthouse without Mik's presence, I only had memories now to comfort me in this prison. Having Pascha here was bittersweet his eyes saying the things he knew he couldn't vocalize. The yearning was inevitable but rekindling an intimate relationship was not what I wanted, I would wait for Kelly.

The late-night sky was full of stars and I was ready to leave the patio, I pulled the blanket tighter against me and just stared out to the last visible star. I felt a hand on my shoulder. "Claudia, seeing you like this is doing a number on me." Pascha squatted beside my lounging chair. "I wish you and Mikhail had gotten closer Pasch."

"Me too Claudia, he was a smart kid . . . you realize he could very well have been ours. It was in that time frame, that time we were together in Greece."

I shook my head, "I was six weeks pregnant then Pascha, but yes I get your point."

"I fell in love with you Claudia, the first time we met before the old man spoiled everything. I should have told you." He stared over at me.

"I know Pasch, but things don't always work out the way we want them to. I had to give up love and a life with I was working towards. I had a great life before coming to the Middle East Pascha, there is so much you don't know. You have no idea what I've lived through."

Pascha dropped his eyes to his hands and he stood up and sat on the other chair facing me. "I know Claudia, I know and I witnessed him. No one knew, I showed up in Morocco out of the blue and I watched you perform those gross indecent acts, and then I watched how he fucked you, Claudia. The old man is sick in the head. Why the hell do you stay, you can leave now, there's nothing to stop you. Come with me Claudia, I can take you out of here." His eyes were huge with desperation.

I shook my head, "Damn it, Pasch, you don't know anything, please just leave it alone, for the last time. I'm not in love with you. Stop!" I threw the blanket off of me and made my way to the liquor cabinet for my friend the scotch bottle. Pascha followed.

I had just brought the glass to my lips when I felt Pascha's arms tighten around me. "No, don't do this, let me go Pascha." I tried pushing him away.

"Not yet, Claudia, not until you tell me everything." He tightened his grip, exactly how Jasim would confine me. I slapped him hard across the face. "How dare you? I don't want you Pascha, leave me alone now." I sobbed, Pascha didn't go. His arms softened enough to let me move into him, it all surfaced, the pain and sorrow I was trying to fight off. Pascha let me release held me gently until there was silence again.

"If you're okay Clauds I'll go now." Pasch rubbed the sides of my upper arms.

"No Pascha, don't go." I poured us both a drink, "One more time Pascha, one last time." My eyes burned into his. Gentleness and Pascha body would be my quick fix.

He followed me to my suite, behind closed doors and peering eyes I pulled the t-shirt over his head and as fast as my hands could move undid his belt buckle and zipper, he was soon standing before me naked. His hand grasped the back of my neck as he pulled me to him while his lips found the space beneath my ear. "You don't need this dress do you Clauds." He whispered, I shook my head, then with one quick jerk, I heard the material crack. He snapped the flimsy material covering my buttocks and then my lacy bra. "Clauds. . . . I'm rock hard, touch me." His finger moved under my hair cradling my head. Pascha pressed the shaft between my legs. I shuttered as his tongue moved in and around my earlobe, down the length us my neck. "Open your eyes beautiful, look at me." I did as he asked. "Don't close your eyes while I'm kissing you, Claudia, when I make you cum I want you to look into my eyes. You'll see everything." Gently he pushed me up against a wall hoisting my legs around him, the excitement bubbling inside me.

My fingers finding his perineum I massaged it while his lips, tongue, and teeth were causing havoc to my nipples.

He sucked my upper lip so tightly then pulled my thighs apart with a quick fast motion Pascha was deep inside me, banging me rhythmically against the wall. He pressed his face into my neck his teeth grazing the muscle on the side of my neck, gently biting into it while his hardness pushing deeper into me. I felt myself tightening up, gently he bit into me. "Claudia look at me!" He ordered. It was all I could do my climax was growing, but I opened my eyes and together we shuddered I was filled with him...with the energy of a man who swore he loved me. I felt sad but not fulfilled it would take more to make me rock n roll and squeal in passion. But Pascha wasn't anywhere near finished with me and I could take everything and more that he was able to give me.

That night Pascha stayed in my bed, resting between sex acts, a little part of me was summoning Jasim. If he hadn't already witnessed us in an intimate situation she wanted to see the look in his eyes while Pascha pounded me.

Late morning found us in the shower, cleaning each other's

bodies. Dripping wet he carried me to my bed and started at my toes sucking the beads of water carrying up each part of my body until his tongue wiped under the clit hood and into my vagina. . . . I had been made love to and an unexpected orgasm shook my body... My eyes wide open.

Chapter 14

HAVING HEARD THE PHRASE 'God doesn't give us more than we can handle.' Well, that was definitely a test that I had been given and it was one extreme test. I never understood how come Jasim was privy to what was going on in Canada and how come he kept in contact with Daina? Did he have something on her, why did she contact him? Another devastation in my circle of friends had occurred. There had been a serious car crash and Cindy Kelly's ex-wife my friend isn't expected to survive and here was Jasim telling me to pack the jet is waiting to fly me to Canada.

He took me down the elevator to the waiting car, "I don't think you need to be reminded of the consequences Claudia. . . . remember I have eyes everywhere. I'm letting you go home…I'm being a kind husband and when you come back you will reward me, won't you Claudia?" The smug look on his face made me ill, I knew the price I would pay.

As I gripped onto the last thread of my fading strength I found out that I had more than Kelly to help me through the nightmare. During the flight over Slade, Jasim's pilot asked to speak with me. He revealed to me that he was expected to report everything he witnessed while in my presence. "Ma'am I want you to know I have great hearing a good eye sight and Mr. Jasim is cruel. Please, ma'am, make sure my back is turned and that I maybe out of earshot before you do anything I would have to report on." I smiled, "Slade out sight outta mind."

The jet landed in Kelowna and Kelly was there to meet me, it would be a natural thing for a friend to pick me up. I watched as Slade left the terminal, not even once did he look over in my direction.

One look at me Kelly knew I was distressed, I lost all control and allowed Kelly to hold me up and guide me to his SUV. Once we were seated safely in his vehicle I was greeted by the warm sensation of Kelly's hands supporting my face.

"Claudia what has happened to you, how come you are so frail and sullen looking? Tell me what has happened to you? Are you alright?" The concern was obvious, he was worried and I didn't know how to handle the situation.

"I look worse that what I really am Kel, honestly, don't worry."

"Don't worry! My God Claudia how could I not worry? Have you looked in a mirror lately?" He paused long enough to put two and two together. "I think I know why don't I?" He searched my eyes. "He's gone, isn't he? You've lost Mikhail, haven't you?"

I nodded and tears rolled down my cheeks. "I can't begin to know what you are dealing with Claudia and this is troubling seeing you like this. What can I do for you? I feel so God damn helpless."

"Let's just hold each other right now, I think it's going to be a long road these next few hours. Justine and Jason must be beside themselves, Kelly they need you and you must need them. I hugged him tighter.

"I'm all right honey, I made my peace with Cindy months ago and my kids know I'm here for them. Right now, you're all that matters to me. Oh, Christ, I'm glad you're here."

Having tried to make myself look refreshed before the jet landed seemed to have vanished. I couldn't go into the hospital looking like this, they'd check me into the psych ward for sure. I attempted to brush on some color on my face and concealer under my eyes. Brightened me up a bit and adding some lip gloss was the trick.

"I want to know, I want you to tell me everything? Claudia when you're ready, give me some of your pain... I think you are one remarkable woman. "Kelly moved across the seat and took my chin between his fingers, he found my lips and softly covered them with his. I moaned in relief, thankful I was here, close to him. When he broke the kiss and sat back behind the wheel I knew it was time to put my personal grief to the side and support Cindy's family and our friends. I studied him, his profile and even noticed the lines around his eyes, not remembering them being there the last time I'd seen him. He knew I was surveying him and reached for my hand curling his fingers over his, Kelly brought my fingers to his lips. Then after kissing them announced, "Next left turn sweetheart and we're there."

The waiting room was filled with Cindy's family and friends, I had to swallow hard, take a deep breath, and greet everyone. Daina and Sherry took one look at me and we three women embraced.

"How's she doing Daina? Has she regained consciousness?" I searched my best friends face.

"Off and on Claudia, she's not fighting, it's really bad." Jason Justine and her parents are with her right now."

"Have you been in with her, will they let me in?" I asked urgently. "I would like a few minutes with her. I looked over to where Kelly was sitting, he had his elbows resting on his knees and I could tell his attention was elsewhere.

Sherry excused herself, "I'll be right back." She said as she squeezed my hand leaving Daina and me alone.

"Excuse me Claudia, but you look terrible . . . why are you so fucking skinny? Something's up with you, I know it Claudia, and you need to spill it." Daina took hold of my hands. Fuck I thought to myself. How am I going to deal with that? I knew I couldn't keep my secret for too much longer, I would have to avoid times alone with her. "We'll talk, I promise Daina, soon, but right now it's not the right time. Don't worry, I'm okay." I did everything to keep my wits about me.

Sherry returned, "I just talked to the kids, they are so glad you made it and if you want to go in you better go now."

With that, I moved towards the hospital trauma room. Seeing my longtime friend in the condition she was in took me back, I had to bite my lip to keep my emotions intact. Sitting down beside her I was afraid to touch her. "Cindy, I hope you know it's me, oh girl what have you done to yourself? You need to fight Cindy, come on, we all need you. I'm coming home soon and you need to be here. We have some celebrating to do." I pleaded. "If you wake up I'll share a secret with you Cin. Come on Cindy wake up." I was begging. I wanted nothing more than to tell my longtime friend how much I loved Kelly and that they were in love as far back as primary school. Not to hurt my friend, but to help her understand why her marriage didn't work out. "Cindy I should let your family come in now, just know I love you girl and I'm pulling for you." I bent over and brushed my cheek against Cindy's.

I hate hospital waiting rooms. I had spent too much time in them. I found Cindy's mom, Mee, and went over to see if there was anything I could do for them. It was just plain awkward after all these years, everyone lived in their own world, and they were all so different from mine. I wondered if I could even fit in any longer.

"You look exhausted," Mee said. "Such a long flight for you I bet?"

"Yes Mee, it is a very long flight. How long have you been here? I know the accident happened a couple of days ago." I wrapped an arm around the elderly woman's shoulder.

Shortly after, Cindy passed away. It was all so unreal how death had been hovering around me. God was being cruel taking the wrong people. It was Sherry who suggested the three of us spend the night at Cindy's and celebrate her life. The only place I wanted to be was with Kelly, there was so much to explain and I knew he wanted answers; it was time to share everything.

Two days later we were standing around Cindy's grave telling stories about what we remembered and loved most about her. Kelly had a difficult time with his emotions, I didn't care what anyone thought, I reached out and took him in my arms like any good friend would do, but I wasn't just any good friend, this man was mine.

"Sweetheart, you are the most important person in my life and I sat back for all these years not knowing what was happening to you in between visits. I can't do it anymore Claudia. Jasim or not, you are taking a cell phone back with you, somehow some way we are going to find a way to conceal it. I need to hear that you're okay. Will you do that please, for me?" Kelly rubbed his finger across the base of my thumb.

"I'm coming home soon, I promise, I am just putting things in place. There is a medical examiner's report coming and I want to see it, I need to know what happened to my son, why he had a congenital heart problem. I have no problem bringing a cell phone back with me. Jasim has hurt me for the last time." I rattled on not looking at him as I spoke because I knew what and where his eyes were focused.

"When did he do that to you, Claudia? Why, what kind of reason did he have to do that to you? Please don't be afraid to talk to me Claudia, I love you and whatever affects you affects me. Please let me help take some of the pain away." Kelly brought my hand to his mouth, kissing each one of my fingers.

"I understand Kel, I just don't want you to take on my troubles, especially now." "Oh no you don't Claudia, you said we were now one, and you can't take that back. When things have settled down here I'm taking you somewhere even if it's just for a day and you are going to trust in me and let it all go, I need to be strong for you, I have stronger shoulders, Claudia. You have to promise me right now that you're not going back to Dubai until I know everything. Please give me that much." He stretched their enclosed hands and held them at his chest, pulling me closer.

It was time to finally let it go and allow Kelly to be my strength. I nodded in quick repetition.

"Claudia stay a day or two and give me some time alone with you."

"If I could stay here with you indefinitely I would, you know that Kelly, for sure I want to be alone with you. But I'm scared that the next person he will go against will be you, he owns me, Kelly. I don't want you getting hurt. He had some people beat up on my chauffeur when he couldn't tell him where the helicopter took me last time, that is why the scars and the broken bones because he didn't get the information he was after. He would kill you Kelly, and not think twice. Please, he will know were together, I think he already suspects."

"Honey you need to let me worry about that! I'm sure I can handle him, besides I don't think he would. So say yes, you and I are going to go and figure this out together right?"

"You're really sure you want to take on this kind of risk, really Kelly?" I sat back, looking sideways at him. "Yes, my darling, I am willing to risk it, I just don't want him hurting you, and I can't bear that thought. We'll be careful, I promise."

After the funeral I knew I had to contact Jasim, there was no way he would sit back and allow me any extra time away. The conversation was short, Jasim seemed preoccupied, "Claudia, you are going to have to fly home commercially, I have some important matters to take care of and I will be using the jet. You phone me when your flight is confirmed and I will have the car waiting at the airport at home for you. Don't forget that." I sighed, I could possibly miss a flight, and as long as he knows I'm booked home he shouldn't care. I couldn't hang up quick enough and make my way into Kelly's arms.

"I have an idea, there is this great little spot in Penticton on the

Naramata Bench called the Inn at Howling Bluff Winery. It's quiet and very romantic, are you up for it?"

I smiled at the thought and couldn't resist. "As long as we find a tree, I am happy anywhere you take me." I smiled.

"Okay let's go to Penticton, while we're driving Claudia, there is a notebook on the back seat in that blue box. I have a trusty pen right here. I need to be able to find you. If I don't hear from you within the next six months I will be coming to look for you. I want addresses, phone numbers, doctors, lawyers, whoever you can trust that will direct me to you. Baby, I've been on pins and needles, I saw those scars at your dad's funeral and I had to bite my tongue. Claudia honey, please humor me, or I'm going back to Dubai and not leaving until you are on the same airplane coming home with me."

"That's not an option, it would be a very bad idea, and you have to trust me I can handle this, I believe the worst is over." I wrote three words and closed the notebook.

"Cindy once made a comment, she pegged Jasim right when she said there was something cynical about him. Cindy tried numerous times to contact you and sensed trouble, but I brushed it off as the lifestyle you guys were living. She just shook her head and said 'that's not Claudia.' She read it correctly didn't she?

I nodded. "Okay you have questions Kelly, just ask me. I will tell you everything you want to know. Just be prepared for the worst of the worst Kelly." I said keeping my eyes on the road.

"Okay, tell me what you would classify as the worst?" You have to trust that anything you tell me won't change my love for you Claudia, I guarantee it."

"How do I describe it? What would be the very worst situation you could imagine a wife-whore would be ordered to do?" His eyes expanded wide. "I had a non-gender handler who awoke every sexual nerve in my body, from bondage, whips, canes, double penetration from the numerous men Jasim was making deals with. He watched as they had sex with me, then when they were finished, he took what he wanted, however, that was. Everything that a man could do to a woman, was done to me, my body was violated in every way possible. So any thoughts you are having, yes! That is what they did to me. I was exposed to Asian bondage, even Geisha training. I learned how to walk, how to dance. Kelly, I know you may find all this disgusting and maybe I will become that way too. You can still walk away." I spoke softly. Kelly put on his signal light and moved off to the side of the highway, I reached for my bag and was about to open my car door for sure he was disgusted with me.

"Claudia, honey you don't think I . . . oh my God you do! You think I pulled over to kick you out. Oh baby, oh no, not ever, I pulled over to hold you. Oh God Claudia, you can't believe I would ever do that to you. Honey, I love you." He turned off the ignition and slid over to me, it was wonderful being comforted, but I would wait and see if he'd change his mind.

We sat in silence for a few minutes before he started up the SUV again and by the time we reached Penticton there wasn't very much left to tell him. I shared all the humiliation and the violation with another human being. I just worried that it might be more than he could handle. I could tell that he was deeply moved by everything I told him, but when I told him of Jasim's actions with me, his demeanor changed and I saw his jaw clench and there was no doubt he was on fire. I knew that I had to find a way to talk him down, he would be Jasim's next target, and even now I was concerned that my husband had suspicions. I would wait until we were safely in a room at the winery. My hand had become a fixture in Kelly's, and I got close but not too close, I was near enough to run my finger across his jaw, and then into the hair. I thought about the twenty-two years, all the years we will never get back. The lives we were robbed of and the children we might have raised together. Kelly stayed quiet; every time he looked over at me his eyes spoke of pain. I couldn't go back to Dubai without making sure he was in an all right place. I knew Kelly but I didn't know what Jasim was capable of doing.

"Claudia, how do you feel about the intimacy we shared? Is love making difficult for you? Because I don't want it to be like everything else you have experienced."

I should have expected that, but I didn't. My thoughts were about his safety. I closed my eyes and reached inside myself to find the right words to convince him of my love as well. "There is a difference when you and I share ourselves with each other. I am giving freely and with love and joy and passion and such desire for you, my darling. Oh, we have so much to experience, you may think some of these acts are cruel and inhuman, but I leave my body and go someplace that there is a void. I'm not scarred from sex Kelly, I'm scarred from Jasim. I know that there is a difference because you were my first maybe if you hadn't, I might be broken sexually. I promise you, Kelly you will see, it was evident in Hedley, and everything was wonderful."

"I will make it all up to you, I promise."

The drive through the winding road towards Naramata was beyond beautiful. The sun was shimmering on the lake and I was in heaven. I felt in my heart this was where I belonged, this is where I wanted to spend my life with him. I stood beside Kelly as we checked in at the winery I felt like we were on our honeymoon for some reason, maybe it was the air that made the romance of it all so real. He handed me the bottle of wine he had just purchased and was told there were glasses in the room.

I stood in front of the window and the view of the lake and left me in complete awe. Kelly stood behind me, his chin on my shoulder and his breath warm against my cheek, "Claudia you have to promise me that if at any time I do something to you that makes you uncomfortable you will talk to me about it okay?" He moved his face slowly along mine, grazing my cheek with his lips.

“Yes, I promise, I promise . . . ” I was so intoxicated with what he was creating inside my soul. His voice against my ear spoke of honor and respect.

“I value you, Claudia. I will show you during our lives together, you’ll see.”

I couldn’t wait for the sensation of his mouth taking these waiting lips of mine, I inched my mouth closer to his. “Kelly, you are what kept me alive, you and Somewhere Over the Rainbow got me through the worst time of my life. God, I wouldn’t have made it without memories of us together.”

I squealed in desire as he pulled me into his arms and sat me on the edge of the bed, “I think this is a perfect time to open a bottle of wine. You in?”

I smiled and nodded, “Oh I’m so in you can believe that. I’m here for the long run.”

That first sip of wine was interrupted by Kelly’s mouth finding mine, his thumb at the corner of my mouth. “Are you really going to be okay with me? I’m a man who can be aggressive, and yeah controlling . . . but I won’t do anything you don’t want me to do . . . ever Claudia.” Kelly rubbed my cheek as his voice softened.

“I think you should let me convince you, let’s just take one step at a time Kelly, there’s no rush. My only rush is going back to Dubai and getting my freedom. But today we have this and look out there Kelly the valley. Oh, if I could stay here for the rest of my life, I would, I’m so enchanted.” I deserved his love and he deserved to be loved in return. I reached up to let my hair loose and I was longing to have him. I would show him. As my hair fell around my shoulders and across my face, I took a mouthful of wine and slowly ran my tongue along my upper lip, closed my eyes and took another small sip. With the other hand, I undid the first three buttons of my shirt. I lowered my eyes under my lashes and saw the expression in Kelly’s eyes. “It’s okay Kelly for you to want me if you do want me I’m just yours,” I said softly.

"Baby, you know how much I want you." His voice said as his fingers lightly roamed my neck.

"You can show me, sweetheart." My words of encouragement echoed inside my being. He turned me towards him and focused his eyes on my shirt as he slowly took over from where my fingers had left off. I rested my forehead against his tilted head. I helped release my arms from the sleeves of the shirt. He ran the back of his fingers up the sides of my arm and up my neck until they were cupping my face.

"I think I have died and gone to heaven at this very moment Claudia."

He found my upper lip and gently began sucking it, then releasing it to take full control of my mouth. The kiss was hot and so passionate. I felt the tips of his fingers stroking lightly up my spine until they unhooked the clasps of my bra. He let go of my lips long enough so I could pull his T-shirt over his head. His mouth leading me up onto my feet as his tongue swept my bottom lip before pulling it tightly between his lips. I undid the belt on his pants and fumbled with his zipper. With his hands firmly planted on my backside his face was now sliding slowly down my throat and slowly between the space at my breasts, Kelly was on his knees before me, hooking his fingers at the sides of my panties. My stomach did flips, and soon I stood naked in front of him. His mouth was approaching my navel as each soft kiss created a familiar sensation within me. I felt his lips move over the clear skin of my pelvis, gently parting my legs I thought I was going to a place of oblivion as his lips encountered the flap of nerve endings. I began to vibrate magically and excitedly at the erotic sensations he was creating within my body.

I stood there in awe of this experience. I was on fire and my passion screaming for more of his touch. He stood up, meeting my eyes. His hands reaching for my hair, Kelly brought it over my shoulders and watched as it cascaded softly covering both breasts.

"My Lord Claudia, I can't breathe at the sight of you. How

beautiful are you." He winked, bringing an inward glow from a place so locked away. I felt truly beautiful for the first time in my adult life because his seduction and possession of me left me in a place of satisfaction beyond my wildest imagination. He loved me, my body, and it was more than wonderful. Moving on our sides, Kelly kissed the palms of my hands.

"There is no doubt in my mind this is where I belong. Claudia, you can't leave me again! I swear I don't know what I'd do if you never came back to me. Each time you left I wasn't sure if you'd come back again."

" Kelly sweetheart, oh baby I will always come back to you, you have to know that within yourself. This time will be the last time Kelly I promise you! No matter what, I won't leave you again." I saw the concern in his eyes and the determination inside of me woke like a sleeping giant.

Kelly slid out from under the covers, "Stay there Claudia, don't go anywhere." He said as he filled my wine glass handing it to me and planted a sweet kiss on my waiting lips. He grabbed his bag and headed into the bathroom. I sat back against the headboard, sipping the wine and retracing the last hour, I decided from this day forward I was going to close the window on the past chapter of my life.

I felt his hands sweeping under me when I came back to reality, "I have a surprise for you and I'd like you to put yourself in my very competent hands and just enjoy what I have planned for you baby."

As I filled his arms, he moved into the bathroom where there was a fragrant bath drawn and soft pink candlelight flickered around the room. He placed me in the tub and handed me the glass of wine. He was careful not to get my hair wet so he placed it carefully at the back of my head where it hung around the edge of the tub. I closed my eyes and let my head relax as Kelly squeezed the sponge full of foam under my chin and as the foam slowly caressed my breasts he followed it rotating the sponge in soft circles starting at my shoulders and across to the other shoulder. All the time he was reciting, Robert Browning.

I had never had an experience like this one. Kelly was truly the most romantic man, one day I will show him how this has touched my heart. I would allow him this, this pleasure he was lavishing on me, but I didn't realize he wasn't quite finished. He wrapped me protectively in a large pink towel and ordered me to have a seat.

"Okay baby close your eyes." I followed his directions. Kelly was cleansing my face with a couple of soft cotton pads. I felt the movement and relished his touch, but when his finger moved so sensually across my bottom lip I let out a sigh, and his lips replaced the finger. He whispered onto my mouth "I love you."

"I love you, Kelly," I returned the words. I felt the sensation of the cool creamy substances, soothing my skin as he massaged each area on my face. Then my eyelids, it was sensual and I felt warm and adored. Then, once again he had me in his arms and he carried me back to the bed.

"Let's get you on your belly baby." He waited as I turned and I pulled a handful of my hair and lay to one side of my head. There wasn't an inch of my body that he left untouched. I was so on fire with passion for him; it was electric when he touched me. Kelly's hands lovingly followed the shape of my breasts and as his thumb pad rolled over my nipple my body shivered. He massaged lotion into my belly then my thighs and calves and into the arches of my feet, each toe was massaged and gently pulled.

When he completed this, he hovered over me, with his hands planted on the bed beside me. His mouth swept in and took possession, with his tongue sweeping my longing one. He continued a deep hungry kiss. As he pulled away he kept his eyes on mine. It was when his hand palmed the soles of my feet and he began his kisses all along the inside slowly up to my thighs then nipping the fleshy part. I squirmed as his mouth rested on my labia before repeating his actions along the other leg. I let the sensations fill me, every part of me. He stood up then brought my knees up placing them wide open, and I was in anticipation of what I desired. His tongue flat over the labia, and his arms under and supporting my thighs Kelly's tongue explored every crevice, flickering at the tip of the clitoris. I felt ripples forming inside my body, he sucked the labia into his mouth and I felt tides of ecstasy leaving my body. He moved and his one hand released my thigh as it positioned his manhood, Kelly filled me full of his strength and once again our rhythm began. I was complete and full again as we responded to desire and the love that flowed between us. Kelly was moving out of me.

I begged, "Please not yet!" I reached out to him as he stretched over me and weighed me down. I ran my hands through his hair and spread kisses over his eyes and brow. "I am so glad we didn't wait, we have lost so much precious time apart to deny ourselves this gift." I sighed, "I never ever thought I could be so full!"

On our walk down Three Mile Road towards the lake, I knew Kelly was searching out the perfect tree. "What do you think honey? Do you like this guy?" He grinned wide as he spoke. "I think he is perfect, perfect in every way!"

I replied, referring to the incredible man before me, "Yes the tree is pretty good as well!" I gushed. He began carving, Kelly forever with Claudia 2000. "Oh, I like that Kel, yes, it is true, forever!"

The scent of fresh cut grass wafted through the open window that I awoke to. Behind me, I felt the warmth of Kelly's breath washing the skin on my shoulder. His hand resting on my thigh. I rolled over and positioned myself into him. "Claudia! "He whispered. "I didn't mean to wake you," I said snuggling under his chin. Kelly's hand found a handful of my hair and pulled it through his fingers. "I'm glad you did, I have plenty of time to sleep I would rather be doing things like this." Kelly rolled me on top of him, "Mmmm good morning baby! His fingers returned to my hair, at the same time our lips found each others. Our bodies connecting once again in love.

While Kelly headed to the shower I contacted Royal Emirates Airlines and booked a flight out of Vancouver. Seated on the bed my mood changed, I felt sadness taking over replacing the joy I had been allowed to experience. I had to pull myself together, I didn't want Kelly to feel he had to make me feel better. This was going to be the most difficult departure.

The sight of Kelly coming out of the bathroom towel flying through his hair helped lift up my spirits. The grin his mouth was projecting woke something up inside of me. Being with him brought me back to life. "Well, I must say all this bedroom rugby has worked up my appetite, and I am now on a mission to get some food into that awesome body of yours, Ms. Samara." Kelly stopped abruptly. I smiled, "Ms. Samara, which sounds pretty good, especially hearing you say it." "Oh Ms. Samara, I am so hungry, I'm starving for more of you woman. I don't think I will ever get my fill of you."

I swallowed, and my brain went woozy and soon my breathing exhilarated, I loved him and now we were a part of each other once again. The towel dropped off his waist exposing his well-formed hard on. My mouthed water, I would pleasure him like I had never pleasured another man orally.

Making sure I collected all my belongings while Kelly was taking our baggage to his vehicle. I stood against the wall feeling content and fulfilled at what had transpired between in this room. I felt Kelly's eyes on me. "Tell you what, I'm going to bring you back here on our first wedding anniversary when you are Mrs. MacAskill, would you like that?" I think every part of my being smiled. "You have a deal Mr. MacAskill, and I promise to hold you to it. I swung around and grasped his neck with both hands, then pressed one kiss after another on his sexy mouth.

How quickly the scenery changed, from the desert type fauna, sage bush and pine trees to the tall grand cedars, spruce and oak the lined the highway coming into the city of Hope. The dry climate was now filled with damp air and soon less than three hours I would be returning to my disgusting reality. I pressed my hand on Kelly's left shoulder and rested my head on the other. He leaned his head against mine. "Kel, I like this feeling of calm, I don't remember when I've experienced this degree of peace. Thank you for this, the time you have given me has made such a difference from the person that arrived just over a week ago. I love you for that, for holding me up, giving me strength as well as holding your own family together." "I would do it all over again sweetheart, you mean too much to me." Kelly took his eyes off the road long enough to kiss my forehead.

The city of Richmond closed in and the evidence of the airport ahead was soaring above us, all sorts of aircraft heading in different directions. Kelly and I had to say our goodbyes at the Terminal entrance to International Departures that was when the lump in my stomach appeared again. We couldn't risk any intimate encounters, other than a quick hug goodbye, and I made sure my nostrils were full of his scent. But removing myself from his side was like ripping me from the claws of a hawk. I wasn't able to turn around, I couldn't watch him drive away.

Chapter 15

NEVER HAD I BEEN so unenthusiastic to have a plane land as I was when we touched down at Dubai International Airport. Of course, the driver was present and anxious to escort me to the car. This was not coming home, there was no Mikhail waiting with a huge grin for me. I walk into the penthouse like I had left, with a dead spirit. At least Jasim wasn't home but he was precise with the phone calls, checking up on me.

Jasim returned home shortly after me but didn't spend a lot of time at home, only to sleep. He didn't seem to be too interested in getting his needs met through me, which satisfied me all the more. I had my memories with Kelly to sleep on. I was becoming restless and anxious, being cooped up not knowing what was coming, now that our child was gone what things were Jasim planning for me. I craved Kenji, I needed to expel the pain and anxiety the best way I knew. If I asked Jasim that could trigger something not so positive.

I had been back three weeks when the medical examiner's office phoned. Their report was ready and we could come that afternoon. Jasim wasn't home, he was at his office in the city center. I called to tell him and he told me he would be home shortly.

I paced the penthouse waiting for him, anxious to find out what the coroner's report would reveal.

The car ride all the way to the coroner's was in silence until we were parked.

I was determined that I was would just leave, and take the risk. It was only me that would be hunted down. I had to plan carefully, my biggest challenge was not being able to access my passport. I assumed that was kept in a safe in Jasim's office.

"You look worried Claudia." Jasim's perusal of me was irritating, but I responded respectfully.

"I guess the months of waiting have gotten to me. It's been a very difficult time not having Mikhail here. I want answers Jasim, that's all." I never even looked at him as I spoke. I kept my eyes on the streets as we drove towards the hospital.

"Yes, it's taken far too long, I agree we need answers."

The chief medical examiner introduced himself and offered us seats to sit down. We both were anxious and I was surprised by his question, "Claudia your parents, were they your biological parents?"

"What does that have to do with my son's death?" I replied.

"Actually Mrs. Al-Masri it should all make sense." He responded dryly.

"I was adopted at birth." He nodded, "Do you have any knowledge of your biological father and mother?"

I was beginning to worry. "No none what so ever."

I felt nervous. "The blood trace marker shows a rare chromosomal trace. A duplication that occurred tells us that the deceased was a result of incest." He focused on me. How could that be? I felt a cloud of nausea sweep through me: incest. I looked over at Jasim, whose face was as white as the sheet of paper the medical examiner was holding. My head began to spin. My whole world was becoming out of whack.

Then Jasim spoke, "This can't be right, something dreadful is going on. I have another son, his name is Pascha, and I knew I had another child so long ago, but how could this be?"

"Mr. al-Masri, are you able to contact the woman you had the child with?" I felt woozy and light-headed, my father . . . could Jasim be my father? It all went black.

> Somewhere over the rainbow Way up high, There's a land that I heard of Once in a lullaby. Somewhere over the rainbow Skies are blue, And the dreams that you dare to dream Really do come true. Someday I'll wish upon a star And wake up where the clouds are far Behind me. Where troubles melt like lemon drops Away above the chimney tops That's where you'll find me. Somewhere over the rainbow Bluebirds fly. Birds fly over the rainbow. Why then, oh why can't I? If happy little bluebirds fly Beyond the rainbow Why, oh why can't I?

When I came to, I was in a hospital bed and I heard the words 'the death was a result of incest' in my mind. As I woke up, I started to gauge the context of the situation. Was he really my biological father? The man who was my rapist, my lover, my exploiter, my husband, the man that fathered my son, my abuser, my jailer, my blackmailer. The words kept swirling through my head. Oh my God, oh my God oh my God no, no, no, no . . . why oh why did this happen to me? I knew I was yelling inside but it was when the nursing staff came quickly into my room.

Mrs. Al Masri . . . its okay you're all right now."

"That's not who I am, don't call me that no, please, please don't call me that," I begged. I felt disgusted and even dirtier than I ever had, "I'm going to be sick." I said as I started heaving and covering my mouth with my hand. Oh, Mikhail, I'm so glad you will never know what disgusting thing your father, oh my God your grandfather, he was your grandfather too, oh what he did to you. I began moaning and couldn't control myself; my brain couldn't grasp it any longer. I don't remember anything after they sedated me. I was put into the psychiatric ward and kept under sedation until the psychiatrist was able to see me.

I knew that I couldn't go to the black place, the hole of despair where I had lived for all these years and survived. I knew I had to make it through this. I had a reason to . . . Kelly! I needed to know more, I needed to make sure this was the truth, that Jasim fathered me. I couldn't go back to that place. I knew I would have to find my biological mother. How would I find her? Jasim, Jasim would know and he has to tell me now! I needed to leave here. I needed to face him. He needed to look at me and see what he's done to me.

After a month the psychiatrist determined I was emotionally fit to be discharged and I went home. Everything was like it was the day I left.

One of the staff greeted me with, "Mrs. A . . . " she began,

I quickly interrupted, "Don't call me that. Claudia is my name, as long as I'm here you will now refer to me that way. Do you understand me?" I growled. I had become hard and angry. "Please make the rest of the staff aware. Where is Jasim?"

"He's not here Madame, he left earlier this morning before you arrived."

I went to his study and found an appointment book and scanned the page for any information as to where he might be, but found nothing. I telephoned his office and his secretary said he would be back later this afternoon. Jasim never carried a cell phone, but he always had a driver with him.

"Who is the driver with Jasim today? I need his cell number."

"Mr. al-Masri didn't use a driver ma'am, he went off on his own. He left a package for you, it was supposed to be delivered to you later today. What would you like me to do?"

"Please send it out with a courier. I will be home." I thanked her and hung up. I went to the kitchen where I knew I would find one of the staff. I saw the maid and told her, "Please have the staff pack up everything on the right-hand side of my closet, shoes, and everything and clean out and pack all my drawers. I will take care of my ensuite. There are things remaining in Mikhail's room that I want to be packed as well." It felt good taking control of my life and whatever threats Jasim has for me I would deal with them as well.

I received the package later in the afternoon and I wondered why Jasim hadn't just given it to me himself until I had the contents displayed on the desk in front of me. First was my passport, Then I noticed pictures taken in 1974–75 and all the documentation that he was using to blackmail me. Enclosed was a letter, my hands shook as I read.

> I am a despicable man Claudia, I know that but I did not know that you were the product of a short relationship I had with Clarissa, I knew she was pregnant; she also had convinced me that she would end the pregnancy and I took her at her word. I never saw her or heard from her again. This news has taken a toll of both of us, but for you, it must be excruciating Claudia. I'm sure by now you have perused through the remainder of the contents of the package. Everything I had regarding you is in the package; I promise you that, you are free to go, Claudia, free to make a life in Canada with Kelly. You will have nothing to fear from me ever again.
>
> Go in Peace, Jasim

Clarissa, her name was Clarissa, my biological mother. I looked through the rest of the pictures and there it was, I knew immediately who she was. On the back of the picture was her name Clarissa Brownlow 1954 / Vancouver in Stanley Park. I studied the picture for any resemblance to me and it was obvious I had her eyes. I needed to speak with Mom. I was taken aback by this, and then God spoke to my heart. I didn't forsake you, my child, I brought freedom through the death of your son. My son my wonderful child was brought to me to assure my freedom.

I could jump on a flight and be back in Canada in a couple of days.

I was dancing around Jasim's study. I didn't want to see Jasim's face ever again, the thought made me cringe. I still couldn't fathom it all.

I watched the pictures and documentation go up in smoke, there was nothing left. It was something that I had carried with me for so, so long. I thought about phoning Kelly, but I wanted to show up at his door and throw my arms around his neck. My heart was beating in happiness.

I had been so busy organizing that the day flew by and suddenly it was ten o'clock at night. I gathered Jasim was taking up a residence elsewhere, which I couldn't be more thankful for.

I ran a bath, poured a scotch and headed to my quarters for the night. It was eight o'clock in the morning Vancouver time, and I wanted to telephone my mom. It was going to be good news this time. I was just about to take a sip of scotch when I heard the voice I loved so much.

"Mom, it's Claudia . . . I'm coming home, I'm coming home for good. I'm free to go now."

"When Claudia? When can I expect you?"

"Very very soon, I will be there this week." I didn't want to discuss Clarissa or Jasim over the phone that was going to be difficult enough when I got there.

The excitement about going home was unimaginable. I had waited years for this moment. Suddenly, our doorman announced that the city police were on their way up to speak with me.

"Mrs. al-Masri, we are here to inform you that there has been a gun incident at Mr. al-Masri office, unfortunately, it was fatal. We have confirmed it was a self-inflicted shot to his head that killed him. His secretary found him this morning."

I stood there in shock and disbelief. "That can't be right officers,

Jasim wouldn't do that." Or would he? But I didn't care, I just didn't want anything to interfere with my plans, "Officers we just separated and I am going back home to Canada will that be a problem?"

"Shouldn't be Ma'am."

"His lawyers will have a contact number for me if you need any further information." I didn't feel any sympathy. All I felt was shock and disappointment that he wouldn't have to live with what he has done. I was angry because I would have to stay here awhile longer. I knew that I should contact Jasim's legal group for further advice. I was curious if he left a will and how he had delegated the rest of his estate. I wondered if the team became aware he was my father as well as my husband, wouldn't that flap their tongues. The police left me dazed and dismayed, only because I didn't know where to go with all this new responsibility.

Later that afternoon I showed up at the law offices of Martin, Bennett, Helm, and Roche, an American team he had been with for many years. I was escorted into one of the partner's office right away.

"Claudia . . . " Gabe Martin held out his hand. "We are all shocked at the news we received, my deepest sympathy to you Claudia." I remained cautious. I didn't have any idea what he might know about our situation.

"Jasim and I were separating before he died. I was planning on returning to Canada soon, will I be held up? I want to leave.

"No Claudia, you won't. Are you wondering if Jasim was forthcoming with the latest developments? Yes, we were aware of the situation and he left many instructions with us. In fact, Claudia, Jasim authorized us to transfer a large sum into an account for you. You need to think about investments Claudia. Go home if that's what you have planned, we will contact Jasim's son Pascha unfortunately, we aren't aware of any other family members. You will have access to whatever you need, the aircraft, yachts, they are yours." Gabe shook my hand. "Good luck Claudia." I placed my contact information on his desk and left. I am now in charge. I called up the crew and told them to get the jet ready to leave for Canada the following day. I left Dubai with Mikhail's ashes.

Chapter 16

2001 Age: 46

Seven months and three deaths later, 2001 had to hold some happiness for me I told myself that as I walked through the gates and out of customs. My feet felt like they were ready to skip along with the cartwheels I was imagining.

One look at the entrance of the terminal, it was deju vu there was Rob, standing beside a new white limo.

"Madame Claudia! Should I be looking over my shoulder now?" He questioned with quite a serious look on his face.

"Rob, I am deeply sorry for what happened to you, I didn't know. My husband was a very devious and cruel man Rob. Is there some way I can make it up to you?" I stood in front of him almost begging for forgiveness.

"No Ma'am, I mean Claudia ma'am," he grinned a cheeky grin at me. "I don't hold you responsible. You had no idea that was going to happen to me. Are we heading to Whistler?"

"No Rob, take me home, to Burnaby please." I must have hummed the address because it never sounded more beautiful.

Mom was on the watch for me, because the door flew open and my wonderful mom was standing on the porch arms wide open for me. "Claudia! My darling girl, oh how good it is to see you. You have really come home to stay?" She grabbed hold of me and hugged me so close and so good.

"Mom I need to pay the driver," I said knowing she didn't want to let me go. Rob had brought my luggage up onto the porch and I walked back to the limo with him. I gave him another rather large tip and watched as he shook his head. "Don't shake your head at me!" I joked.

The week I spent with Mom was not how I dreamt it would be, trying not to overwhelm her I shared what I felt she needed to know, being discreet with the rest, those things she didn't need to carry around. The most challenging part of the week was not contacting Kelly. I owed my mother my undivided attention. Since the death of my Papa the age was showing, she seemed so fragile.

Her responses to everything I shared with her were, "Oh Claudia your Papa would have been so mad, he would have killed Jasim with his bare hands."

Her hearing that Jasim was my biological father was too much. It made her gasp and I thought she was going into cardiac arrest. I promised her that I was working through it and that Jasim had no idea. He believed Clarissa had terminated the pregnancy. She was disgusted and upset. Being home with her gave me much-needed insight into her lifestyle. I could see she was struggling to be alone without my papa.

I hoped she would agree and allow me to hire someone to live in and take care of her. I knew she wanted me to stay, but my heart was desperate to get Kelly and I knew she would understand. Maybe in the future, she could come and live with us, but for now, I would make sure she was well cared for. I would be closer and have more time to spend with her. I loved her and I couldn't have had two better parents.

I was stunned when I heard those words coming from her. "Claudia you must find Clarissa, she needs to know about you and the life you had.",

"Mommy, I have no intention of doing that, I only have one mother and bringing a skeleton out of the closet won't benefit either of us. I think she did me well by giving me to you and papa, I'm grateful for that. So, no further discussion on that subject okay?" I wrapped my arms around her neck and hugged her close.

I hadn't had a BC driver's license for over twenty years so I was anxious and worried I would fail the exam, but I passed. Burnaby had changed so much since I grew up. I was quite pleased when the examiner announced I had aced the road test and said, "Welcome back to Canada."

I arranged care for Mom and after a week I couldn't wait any longer to see Kelly. Life for me was one big whirlwind and I didn't want Kelly hearing all about it over the phone, I wanted to look him in the eyes and be held when I fill him in with all the disgusting details. News like that was face to face only.

I had to go. I rented a luxury SUV and headed out early the next morning. I drove all the way praying to God that Kelly was at home and not on some business trip to who knows where. I arrived feeling a little sneaky leaving the vehicle parked on the street and sprinting up the long driveway I rang the doorbell and waited.

No answer, so I rang it again. Still no answer, so I rang it the third time.

"Go away, I'm sure you don't have anything I am interested in." Kelly hollered. I rang the doorbell again and heard, "For Christ sake would you go away! I'm not interested."

"Oh but sir, I beg to differ! I know you want what I have to offer!" The door flew open and I was off my feet being swirled around the entrance in his arms, his kisses were eager and so amazingly wonderful. He placed me back on my feet and looked at me then grinned.

"Oh yes, you definitely have everything and more that I want.

Does this mean . . . " "Yes Kelly, it's all over, I'm safe, I will tell you all about it later, but first we have a lot of kissing to make up for, and a whole lotta loving to get to."

"Oh, baby we can get right on it! Wow, I'm so surprised, you're here, really here. I could have come and got you. Oh, it doesn't matter just come here, and let me look at you, and kiss you, and never ever let you go again."

Tears filled my eyes, "I've been longing to hear those words for so long."

There wasn't any polite, 'Are you hungry or can I get you something to drink?' he hoisted me up and I wrapped my legs around his waist as the articles of clothing were dropping all the way into his bedroom.

Our appetites for each other couldn't be satisfied. Finally, I relaxed without any fearful thoughts in the back of my mind that someone was going to track me down. He asked, "When did you get back?"

I figured he was going to react, "I got here a week ago, I needed to be with my mom and share as much as I could without exposing the sadistic part of my life Kel. A lot has happened since we parted, and it was hard not contacting you when I arrived, but I really wanted to surprise you." I said apprehensively.

"Hey baby you came that's all that matters, I got you back, I totally understand your need to spend time with your mom, of course, it would have been selfish for me to have thought otherwise. I'm surprised she let you go this soon." He said lovingly. "You know babe I don't expect you to move in here and get on with your life. I am expecting nothing from you right now. I just want you to know that, where ever I am, you are welcome to be with me. I want you here all the time, but when you're ready. He stroked my arm. "I want more than just this Claudia, I hope one day you will agree to be my wife, but we will take that one day at a time, okay?"

Suddenly the words left my mouth, "Jasim killed himself!" I announced shocking Kelly and causing him to sit up in bed.

"You're kidding me because you left?" He questioned.

I shook my head. "You are not going to believe this Kelly. I still haven't quite grasped it. You are going to be shocked, and believe me when I say that.

Jasim was my biological father! He didn't have any knowledge until the medical examiner's report and Mikhail 's chromosomes were identical and that could only occur because of incest. I now know who both my biological parents are. It still feels surreal, as though this was all a dream, make believe."

"I'm surprised you are coping so well. Claudia, what is keeping you going?" He asked puzzled.

"You Kelly, you, along with my new-found freedom, and the opportunity of living again." Kelly sat back holding me and all of a sudden, I had verbal diarrhea. "I was so shocked when he gave me the file that contained all the proof of my participation in Israel. Kelly, he even had a video. I worry that there could still be other copies somewhere. I don't trust Jasim. I burned it and all the other evidence he had on me. I can't yet grasp the extent of all this . . . and I heard God speak Kelly. He told me that I was given Mikhail and his death that set me free. If it wasn't for my boy I would still be living in hell."

When I finally exhausted myself, I looked up at Kelly and he was looking very emotional. "I don't understand how one person could have been given this much to deal with. Why? Just listening to what you have said is too much even for me to comprehend baby. I am so incredibly proud and in awe of you Claudia. You are remarkable in every way." He found my mouth and brushed his lips over them. "Where would you like to be Claudia? Do you need time to just be by yourself right now?"

"Right now, this is exactly where I want to be. I desperately want to have you close by me. I'm happiest where ever you are, though, I have something I desperately want to do immediately."

"Okay, what would you like to do?" Kelly asked as he played with my hair. I pulled back the covers and sat up facing him. "I need to get rid of these . . . I want my own real breasts back. I hate them, I've always hated them, please help me find a plastic surgeon."

"Of course, I will." Kelly pulled me back into those strong protective arms of his again. "Your breasts are wonderful however you choose them to be."

We were now 46 years old and finally, I was so blessed to have Kelly in my life. His lifestyle was strange and different environment for me. There was no one to wait, cook or clean or do my laundry.

Budgeting my money was not a concern Jasim's lawyers had moved the money to the Cayman Islands. I would reveal that piece of info to Kelly another time.

Even though I needed time alone, but I panicked if there was too much time away from Kelly. He laughed at my homemaking skills, but he was right there to help or teach me. I could say anything to him and he wouldn't jump to conclusions. I, on the other hand, had lived such a dysfunctional life.

He was wise and aware of how traumatized I was, so he'd encouraged me to find a therapist and get professional help. Kelly believed I have the symptoms of Post-Traumatic Stress Disorder because of the nightmares which were traumatizing for him as well. After a month of settling in and just unwinding with Kelly, I had my breast implants removed. When the physician suggested I replace them with a smaller size: I lost it in his office. It was like Jasim all over again, pushing me to do something.

Kelly heard the commotion and insisted on being in the room with me. I believed as long as Kelly was with me I would be heard. Kelly encouraged me to get some therapy. He believed I'd learn how to take back my power and distinguish authority from self.

"I'd really like you to consider the therapist route. I'm not pushing you. I think if you have a chat with a professional, you will see you can get the help you need baby. You've been trapped for so long. I will stand behind you and support you all the way." His eyes deepened with so much love for me.

Kelly was having difficulty keeping me hidden from his children Jason and Justine, and their families. That was when I decided to find a place for myself. Kelly was not enthusiastic about it, but he stood behind my decision.

After a week, I was eager to get the bandages off and see my true self again: these were the breasts I was comfortable with. At the surgeon's office, I refused to go in without Kelly, I wanted his eyes to see the results with me. I was aware that the doctor was not too impressed with me, but Kelly was there and I knew he was smiling because of my expression. My breasts were now in proportion to my body, I touched them, they were firm but pliable I was so anxious to have him feel them too, but I had to wait until we got home.

"We have a problem, Ms. Samara," Kelly announced.

"We do? Oh no, what's wrong?" I asked cautiously.

He carefully walked his fingers up my front and stopped at the side of my breast. "I think you need to go shopping for lingerie, hmm?" He wiggled his eyebrows and smirked.

I took his hand, "I guess we do, don't we?" I was so excited about my new shape that buying new lingerie was not on my agenda. "I don't want to go into any stores right now, I will do that soon Kelly, but not today, okay?"

"Hey, you don't have to do anything you don't want to Babe!" Kelly's reassurance spoke volumes.

I waited until Kelly went for his morning run and after I showered, I stood in front of the bathroom mirror and an erotic feeling overcame me. I let the towel drop to my feet and I began posing. I pushed my chest out and then relaxed. I was watching how my new sexy breasts responded. I brought my waist long hair over my shoulders so the wet strands covered them and suddenly wanted to do something with my hair. I flung it back over my shoulders again and took my plump perfect breasts into both hands. I liked what I was feeling and soon my fingers were rolling my nipples gently. I was becoming aroused and not aware that Kelly came back for his water bottle and was watching me.

"Ohh . . . you are hot Claudia!" He said sexily. I stopped and became a little shy. "Ohh . . . don't stop, wet your finger and roll it over your nipple baby, feel the coolness, does it feel good? Yeah, Claudia, gently baby gently, Claudia masturbate for me, let me watch you, fuck you've given me a big boner! I'm going to have to do something about it."

I gasped. My sudden shyness returned to the extroversion I was a natural with, something inside of me let go and I found the performer that was once forced to act. But this was different; this was Kelly, would I turn him on or ruin the moment? I danced, spread my legs wide apart and bent forward, raising my rear in the air exposing my now swollen and moist vagina. I turned my head to the side just enough to make eye contact with him before biting down on my lower lip and slowly closing my eyes.

Kelly was standing there drooling at the sight of me. I continued, creating heat before using my index finger I slowly ran it inside the lips of my vagina and slid it in my mouth. That spurred him into action. Coming behind me, he knelt down and rested his hands on the front of my thighs and with his flattened tongue on my open vaginal lips, he began trailing his tongue all the way up my backside, then down again until he felt me squirm, his teeth nibbling gently in all the right places. We found ourselves hot and sweaty and sexed out.

Kelly looked over at me., You can do that anytime girl that was incredibly hot!" He said while his finger moved delicately all over my vibrating body.

Three months with Kelly, one day out of the blue I had a major meltdown. I withdrew into myself. There was no way I could move about Kelowna in case our friends and Kelly's family members would run into me. Kelly was caught in the middle. His life with his family was getting cut off because of me.

Kelly decided because of my mental health and the sensitivity I felt towards my situation he needed time away from the winery and Daniel was very capable without him there. Kelly had a quarter investment with Young Ranchers Estate, but Daniel treated him as an equal.

Having a man like Kelly prepared to stand behind me no matter what was difficult for me. There was a part of me that wanted to be independent to make my own choices, but the other part of me was desperate to have him make the decisions for me. I felt getting my own place would be healthy while we were getting to know each other as a couple and while I was dealing with the residual effects of the twenty-eight years being a wife-whore. Kelly got angry with me every time he heard me refer to myself in that perspective.

Throughout my search for a place to live, I felt such a connection to Penticton up on the Naramata Bench where we had been before. Eventually, Kelly and I found a cabin owned by one of the smaller wineries in the area and signed a one-year lease. The cabin overlooked the lake and the orchards, everything I desired was there.

It was convenient because Penticton was only 40 minutes from Kelowna. I thought I was ready to explore new possibilities for myself that would give Kelly the space he needed with his family.

It was a natural thing for me to want to share everything with Kelly and that included my financial portfolio. Myself being secure in my relationship with him, what belonged to me I wanted to share with him. I asked him to come to the bank with me and we met with a financial advisor. I suggested that Kelly be added on the account.

When he saw the financial statement he was flabbergasted, "Claudia, that's an obscene amount of money, whoa that's crazy. I can't sign my name, fuck Claudia that belongs to you! Excuse me for my foul language! But you should have given me some idea about this." My advisor took a moment to step out of her office to give us a few minutes of privacy.

Kelly pointed his fingers inward at his chest, "This is the bread winner Claudia, I look after my needs and I was hoping that would include you too. I really want to have that role. You are entitled to all of that. We will discuss this further honey, but not here. But you definitely can afford a vehicle." He chuckled.

"Kelly that's very unfair, this is retribution for both of us, no one other than us needs to know. If you don't want an equal share then at least let's talk about a figure that you would see as reasonable. Besides, I intend on being your wife one day, and I refuse to sign any prenuptial agreement. I love you beyond the beyond."

"Honey, we'll talk about it at home, I promise I will give it some thought okay? I also love you more than beyond the beyond!"

We drove into Kelowna and I bought an ice white Audi Q7. The following day I spent an afternoon in Penticton getting familiar with the community while Kelly went to meet with Daniel at their winery. We decided it would be logical for Daniel to know about our situation and have some idea of what happened during the past twenty-eight years.

At the cabin, we needed everything from cutlery to towels as well as appliances and furniture. So, my mission that afternoon was to scope out furniture. I was pleased with my choices and hoped he would be as well. I was looking forward to creating our home together. The next few days we headed into Penticton again and I soon found out we didn't exactly share the same tastes in décor, but we learned to compromise and soon we had pretty much had the basics for the cabin.

We finished unloading the parcels and I was looking forward to expanding on my cooking skills with all the kitchen goodies Kelly was keen on purchasing. I was not familiar with the emotions I was experiencing; it was all new to me. I never had any say in my previous environment with Jasim.

Then, Kelly handed a gift to me and I almost fell over when I tore the wrapping paper off. Kelly had found a portrait of Mikhail and me and had it framed. I was missing my son even more at that moment.

"Where am I going to hang it? '

"If I was making the decision," he said, "I think over the fireplace where it can pretty much be viewed from all angles of the house."

"Yes, of course, Kelly it is the perfect place!" Handing it to him I asked, "Would you hang it up for me? Thank you, you did this for me Kel, it's the best gift you could have given me. Oh, Kelly, it makes it seem so much more like home to have that picture there. I knew there was a reason why I loved you so much."

"Only one huh? Hmm . . . guess I better get on my game Claudia. Come let's get our bed made." He wiggled his eyebrows when he spoke.

I stood for a few moments longer looking at the photograph and remembered how he smelled when he was a baby, how good he felt against my breast. "I was blessed to have Mikhail."

Kelly was making the bed and I went to help him. "Mmm . . . I can't wait to get you under these sheets my darling."

I tilted my head to the side and dragged my teeth across my bottom lip. "Sweetheart that's gonna get you in trouble if you keep that up! Claudia, we'll never get things arranged if you keep that up, and stop looking at me like that with those eyes." "Yep, okay baby!" I replied.

We finished unpacking dishes and Kelly opened a bottle of wine. "Oh, I don't believe it, Claudia, we forgot wine glasses, of all things." Kelly shook his head.

"Well, we do have regular glasses. I said as I found my iPod and scrolled through my song list to find the song that saved my sanity: Faith Hill, with her version of Somewhere Over the Rainbow. I took a sip of my wine and said, "Come dance with me, baby." My arms moved around his back and I buried my nose in the crease of his neck.

Even though Kelly wasn't doing any work at the winery, he and Daniel had meetings from time to time, so, this was one of those meetings and he was off to Kelowna bright and early in the following morning. There were so many things I envisioned myself doing. I was looking forward to getting familiar with the communities of Naramata and Penticton, for me they would be exciting and so different than my life in the Middle East and Europe. I didn't have any constrictions. I was now free to come and go as I chose and I did just that, but I didn't have a clue of just how damaged I had become. I thought I was strong and resistant to everything that twenty-eight years had engulfed me was the biggest façade I believed about myself.

The wardrobe I had brought with me was not appropriate for the lifestyle I was now living and I was eager to check out the local boutiques. I loved shopping for clothes and dressing to the nines whenever Jasim had some place he needed to show me off, I dripped in gold jewelry and gowns costing thousands of dollars. I wore designs created exclusively for me for those occasions and on those occasions, I knew my next assignment was about to begin. Now, I despised it and promised myself I would never wear gold again.

"You have been a difficult person to get a hold of today, my dear. You must be busy?"

"Oh, you've been trying to call, I'm sorry Kel, I'm finally getting the things I've put aside done. It's been a great day though. How about you and your day, how is your day going so far?"

It was so good to hear his voice, "Then," he asked, "are you up to spending some overnight time alone?"

Even though we had discussed taking time alone and I felt it would be good for both of us, at that moment I wasn't so sure any longer. "I guess so, I know we said we needed to. Is everything okay?" I figured it would be a perfect time for him to spend time with his family, but that's when panic set in. I couldn't understand why though. I was shaking inside and out, Oh come on Claudia! Get a grip I scolded myself. I began sobbing profusely and he returned home: that is what it took to get me to see a therapist.

Chapter 17

"ARE YOU SURE?" Kelly asked? "Yes," I said.

"Really Claud?" he asked.

"Really, and seriously yes!" I answered.

"I'm not sure I can do it to you!" Kelly said toying with me.

"It's just hair! Come on baby buck it off!" I got anxious because I thought he was teasing me.

"I'm gonna close my eyes, I can't look!"

"Kelly!" I exclaimed.

"Oh, baby I can't cut that beautiful hair of yours! Really Claudia." He twisted his lips.

"Yes, you can." I was getting flustered. "Honey just cut it at the end of the elastic band."

He scooped me off the stool, threw me over his shoulder and into his vehicle, then off into Penticton we headed. "You want it cut, we'll get it cut, but I'm not going to do it, oh no, no, no sweetie pie!" He responded.

On one of my trips into town, I had seen a salon on Front Street and Kelly headed in the direction. "So you're seriously going to cut it off, honey?"

He commented. "I'm not going to cut it all off, I promise, I showed you, two inches below my breasts, that's all. It is just too long and it's a part of the life I want to leave behind. I have my body back and this is another extension of me," I explained, knowing full well he had intuitively recognized that.

"I was waiting to hear if you were aware of your reasons behind these changes. This is a great thing Claudia, and as you know, I died and went to heaven when you removed the implants, but honey, I wouldn't care how you looked. I have everything I have ever wanted: you Claudia."

I knew I excited and pleased him, that proved I had a sexual hold on him, and that was obvious, and him with me. Kelly's hands were always ready and wanting to touch and caress my body. So feeling his fingers moving inside my bra, sent chills all over me. "Mm . . . Claudia, I really need to get you home so I can remove this." He whispered as his nose inched into my hair. "I better stop or these poor people on the sidewalk will be envious of my beautiful sexy woman. Let's get you to the salon."

"Oh Kel, I still have nightmares, is this all a dream? Oh, honey, I love you." I said watching him get out of the vehicle.

He paused, "Ditto baby, ditto!"

Kelly and I flirted during my haircut. The stylist flushed as Kelly explained exactly where we decided the length should fall, and it was obvious his thumbs had connected with my nipples. It was so freeing for me when the length had been removed, it cut off years of unwanted luggage. The fullness hung in big waves and fell at the perfect places.

Slowly, I was willing to get out in public more and suggesting that we have dinner in town somewhere quiet and private surprised Kelly.

"So my sweetheart, are you saying you are ready to go public now?" he said surprised.

"Here yes, because the chances of us being recognized are less likely than if we were in Kelowna." There was no rhyme or reason for us not to be in public, but that was part of the PTSD, and my Kelly was aware of my disorder. Now that we had five months together and I had been in therapy for three of them, he saw me slowly coming into my own. Before therapy he asked, "Honey, does he think you're ready to spend more time in public? Or, honey what do you think he'll be working on with you this week?" Kelly was in tune with the issues plaguing me and so patient as my insecurities reflected on his lifestyle.

When Kelly reminded me that his twins Justine and Jason were celebrating their twenty-second birthdays the dilemma began, and it would take everything he had to deal with me. An elaborate party was planned and Kelly had every intention of being part of coordinating the event which meant he would need to be in Kelowna for a few days.

"Wouldn't this be a great time for you and me to make an appearance as a couple?" He asked calmly and hopefully.

"I, I can't, I can't Kelly I'm not ready." I blurted out in complete panic.

"Okay Claud, I understand, but you are aware I will be in Kelowna for a few days, are you going to be okay here on your own?" He asked, taking hold of my shoulders.

"A few days Kelly, how many is a few?" My eyes widened and my heart pounded. "Two days at least sweetheart, it is their thirtieth, right? I'm going. I have too, I intend to, so you have to make a choice honey."

I had less than a week to make that huge decision and even after seeing the therapist I was nowhere prepared to make that kind of a decision. Neither one of us doubted the love we felt for each other, we both knew we would spend the rest of our lives together, but they would expect explanations and I wasn't willing to explain. I chose to stay home in Penticton.

The morning that he was leaving, I didn't act in a very mature manner. I was waiting for him when he returned from the shower. I was wearing a snug T-shirt and panties. My hair was exactly as he liked it, wavy and hanging down at my front. I got the response I was after his eyes, his mouth.

"Yes, my beauty you have my attention, my full attention." He stood against the wall and I walked provocatively towards him. I knelt, undid his zipper and exposed his manhood. "Claudia you're going to make me late." He growled.

I had his growing erection in my fingers and my tongue was playing, doing what I knew so well. I took my sweet time lavishing his beautiful long hard penis. I was tasting pre-cum and I knew he was worked up. I slowed down, my tongue swirled down his underside. His hands reached into my hair, gripping it tightly. I didn't want him climaxing, not yet, he couldn't. "No Kelly not yet," I ordered. But I didn't get the reaction I was hoping for.

He got control of himself and reached down taking my chin in his fingers. "That was nice Claudia, but you can't play games like this. Yes you've got my attention and yes we are going to finish this, but then I have to go. Please don't do that to me because I know you have ulterior motives. I love you and that was unfair Claudia."

He disciplined me with love and did it respectfully. He kicked off his jeans and boxers and T-shirt. I was tight against him as he removed my clothing. I took his mouth in desperation, kissing him hard and passionately. "Claudia," his whispered at my mouth, "Oh Claudia, yes, I want you so bad. He set me on my feet and his hand held my arm above me; he slid his tongue all the way down my inner arm and into my armpit driving me wild. He spun me around and propped me against the wall, he entered me slowly and determinately. I squealed in an immediate orgasm. Kelly's effect on me was like nothing I had ever experienced, not even Pascha. Keeping himself fully engulfed inside of me, he brought me into our bed and continued to please me like he always did. Then kissing and comforting me he said, "I will be lonely without you Claudia, I will call you often, I promise. You will be okay." Kelly left me in our bed, got dressed before returning to leave me with a tender loving kiss. "I will be home soon. I love you!" He winked.

"I love you." I pouted.

It was going to be a challenge for me with Kelly away, I knew that I could always contact Dr. Bloom, my psychologist and he would talk to me. I knew I had to snap out of this, whatever it was. I changed into a pair of shorts and a tank top and decided to start running again. After the attack and rape all those years ago I was full of fear, but this was a different life now.

It was a challenging run, hilly and all, but it felt good. When I got down to the beach, I sat on a rock for a while and felt such a calm rush over me. I hadn't felt this serene since Mikhail was alive during all those times we spent investigating the world together. I was his mom; his teacher and we learned together.

When I got home to the cabin, I noticed that Kelly had phoned several times while I was on my run. I wasn't in the mood to talk, I was sure he was going to try to convince me to come to Kelowna and reveal our relationship, I just wasn't ready, I was afraid of the questions and it would be too much. It was going to be a long night without him beside me. I found the scotch bottle and made a big dent, it helped get me through the first night. Making a phone call to Kelly should be such a simple exciting event, why wouldn't I want to talk to the dearest man in my life? I couldn't for the life of me answer that, all this caring was a little to un-natural, but everything I had ever wanted. When I drank enough of the liquid courage and picked up my phone, it was dead, I had forgotten to charge the battery, so for sure now Kelly would be busy with his family and now wasn't the best time to call. I would be all right. I had a bottle of scotch. I'd call him in the morning.

In the morning I made a snap decision to drive to the coast to spend a few days with my mom. I couldn't handle being alone in the cabin another day. Leaving a note for Kelly on the bed, letting him know where I was, that I would be home in a few days. Inadvertently I left my cell phone charging, not used to having one I never gave it a second thought and headed out.

The weather was fabulous as drove towards the coast. I stopped in Keremeos at the fruit stands to bring some fresh early summer fruit for Mom, she and I both loved fresh cherries and early plums.

I was looking forward to spending this time with her, there were things we needed to discuss. I had decisions to make and talking this through with her would help me put everything in perspective, Clarissa and the right choices for me. It was then my mind wandered back to Kelly, it was obvious, I was making things difficult in the relationship. Being confined to the lifestyle I had been trapped in for all those years added more confusion even in the healthy relationship I had with Kelly. I never knew how a healthy relationship would evolve. Maybe if I had something to occupy my time. Would it be possible to actually get my Ph.D. in Arabic Studies, what would I do with it here in Penticton?

Maybe it would be best if we lived apart for now, and date, besides I thought, eventually he has to return to Kelowna and participate in the everyday activities at the winery.

The drive seemed to go by quickly and I was pulling up in front of my childhood home. I had spent so many wonderful years running up the steps. Life was good here.

After retrieving my luggage from the back of the SUV I walked the pathway into a very quiet house.

I sensed an uncomfortable energy in the air as I walked in the door and wandered towards the kitchen where my cheerful mother would have her hands either in flour or preparing meals.

"Mom I'm home," I called out, expecting to find her either in the kitchen or doing some crafty thing, but I was greeted by a caregiver.

"You must be Claudia. My name is Jasmine and I am one of the daytime staff. "Nice to meet you, Jasmine, where is my mother?" I asked confused.

"Jada is resting she hasn't been quite her normal self the last couple of days, she insists that she just needs to take it easy."

"I don't understand I just spoke with her a couple of days ago and she sounded happy and full of energy. Has she seen a doctor?" Something inside of me panicked, and then I reminded myself she was not a young woman anymore and allowed to have down days.

As I jogged up each step the good memories touched my heart. I was so free and home where I longed to be.

She was sleeping, but I thought her skin looked a little ashy, she should be seen by a doctor, I didn't like what I was seeing. I wasn't going to wake her, but I was going to contact her doctor. I returned to the office where Papa's den used to be. Jasmine was logging her report when I interrupted.

"Jasmine is it me or does my mom look ashy? To the touch, she felt clammy. I think we need to get her to the hospital or speak to the doctor. I don't think we should leave her like this." Jasmine quickly headed up the stairs with me right behind.

"Jada, Claudia is here sweetheart can you wake up and say hi!' Jasmine's voice sounded of concern. "I stroked her hand,

"Hi Mom, I thought it was about time we had a visit." Jada's eyes opened and her smile brightened her face.

"Yes darling girl, I know you have been busy."

"Well that is going to change, maybe you should come to Penticton and spend time with me, what do you think?" I knew what her answer would be even before she spoke. At eighty-six she would never leave her home, here she was close to Papa and it was obvious she still hadn't gone through his clothes and belongings. I studied her and made the decision. "Mom you don't look like you're feeling like yourself and I think we should take you to the hospital.

She shook her head, "I'll be fine Claudia. "

"Jasmine I think we need to have an ambulance."

"I agree, this must have just come on when you got here. I was just upstairs before you arrived she looked good." Jasmine took her cell phone out of her pocket and left the room.

I sat beside her on the bed, stroked her forehead as she had when I was under the weather. "How long have you been feeling like this? I'm concerned, and there is an ambulance coming I am not about to take any chances with your health. I love you and I'm here now, not going anywhere until you're back to your old self."

Mom became a little agitated, "No hospital Claudia, please." "I understand your concerns, it will be for a short time and then I intend to bring you home. I promise. I hate hospitals just as much, please humor me, just once ok?"

Jada dropped her eyes and stayed silent, I knew she was upset, but if she is on the verge of a stroke or heart attack it is going to be somewhere that she will be looked after.

I was surprised how quickly the ambulance arrived, and just as I thought they felt she was possibly on the verge of a heart attack. The moved quickly getting machines hooked up and she was on a stretcher in a matter of minutes.

I followed the ambulance, as I held the steering wheel of my car, I felt my hands shake my insides were twisting, I knew the outcome wouldn't be good.

Waiting was excruciating, a few hours had past and her doctor arrived.

I'm Dr. Rawlings your parents have been patients of mine for ten years. It was unfortunate that I was away when your father passed. It must have been difficult for you being in The United Arab Emirates for many years. I heard a lot about you from them both." I nodded, not wanting to share, let alone think about those years. "I'm glad I came when I did, I just knew to come, and it is strange. Is this just recent health concerns?"

"Claudia, I've only had her in my office once since your dad passed, the agency had concerns, I'm sure you are aware?" I shook my head, "No I was never told anything like that, I'm going to have to find out why I was kept in the dark, instinctively I bet, Mom didn't want me to know I bet she threatened the staff."

"There is something you need to be aware of, she has signed a

DNR (do not resuscitate) order, so all we can do is get her stable and keep her comfortable. She was very specific on the DNR. I'm sorry Claudia. She has deteriorated rapidly since I last saw her." I folded my arms tight in front of me. "When can I be with her? This is too soon, too quick, I just arrived.

I wished Kelly was here, I didn't know what to do, and she was going to be extremely agitated if she stayed hospitalized. I promised her I would bring her home. I felt a sharp pain shoot across my forehead, a headache was coming. When I was finally allowed in ICU I thought I was going to be sick to my stomach. I was angry at myself for leaving the cell phone behind. At that instant, my mind wouldn't present me with Kelly's cell number or his home phone. I used directory assistance for the winery to contact Daniel. It took quite a few rings before his deep rich voice answered. "Daniel, how good it is to hear your voice, it's Claudia. How are you doing?" A smile crept across my lips. His calm voice seemed to soothe me somewhat. "Well Ms. Claudia, it's been too long, and there have been some changes in your life I hear." I paused momentarily, "Yes there sure has, and for you to my friend. I was sad to learn you and Sherry ended your marriage. I'm not surprised though, Daina mentioned a few things several years ago."

"Well people change Claudia, and it was coming for a long time, so how are things with you?" He changed the subject and I didn't want to linger on that topic there would be other times to get the goods on that situation. Right now, I needed Kelly.

"Listen, Daniel, I'm here in Burnaby at the hospital with Mom and forgot my cell at home and like an idiot, I didn't memorize Kel's cell. Can you give it to me?" I asked trying to sound calmer than what I was feeling.

"You happen to be in luck, Kelly is right outside, I can actually see him, just a minute. Claudia is everything ok with your Mom, you said hospital?"

"It's not good Daniel, just keep her in your thoughts OK?" "Of course, I will hang in there, here's Kelly." "Thanks, Daniel, I hope to see you soon."

It was within seconds Kelly's voice was on the other end. "Hey Claudia, I've been trying to reach you for a while, where are you? Are you ok?"

"I'm at the hospital in Burnaby with Mom, still waiting for the doctor, it doesn't look good. I don't have a good feeling about the diagnosis. I needed to hear your voice and let you know where I was." I felt ashamed, for not contacting him before leaving home.

"Claudia I'm not going to let you deal with this alone, I'll be there as soon as I can. I'm sure I can grab a flight. Okay? I love you, sweetheart, hang in there." I felt tears welling up, "I love you too, thanks for doing this, see you soon." I returned to ICU and after too much time Dr. Rawlings exited. I was never one to try to read another person's expression, but I knew by instinct what he was had to say I wasn't going to like it.

"Claudia, Jada has had a series of small heart attacks and she is very reluctant for treatment. I know this is going to be difficult for you, but we can be hopeful with rest and no stress she could very well have fewer, but that is being hopeful. She has been desperate to see you. I insisted she rest, but she was determined to see you." I swallowed hard and felt my stomach turn. "Thank you, Dr. Rawlings. I need to be with her." I turned and rang the buzzer for access.

Mama looked peaceful, but not well, I had to find a way to convince her to let the doctors treat her, but I knew in my heart she was not the same since papa died and she never wanted to be without him. "Hi, Mom, did you get some rest? I kissed the side of her mouth. "Claudia there is no time for sleep, there is something I think you should hear from me. Papa wanted me to tell you many years ago, but I couldn't. Clarissa Brownlow wrote to us when you were a teenager and wanted to meet you. I hid her letter, you were our daughter Claudia, I'm just so sorry I didn't tell you before . . . you would never have married that monster Claudia, and he would never have taken you away from Papa and me." I could see her tearing up, I didn't want her to cry.

"If I didn't meet that monster I wouldn't have had Mikhail and 16 wonderful years with him . . . it's okay Mom, it was supposed to be that way."

"Darling girl . . . " she always called me. "That letter is behind our wedding photo in our bedroom. It is important Claudia, you must read it. Promise me, daughter, you will?" I froze I wasn't ready, she was my Mom and there was no room for another.

"Ok Mom, I will get it later. Right now, I just want to talk with you. I heard Auntie Maysam and Nasrin and the rest of our family have been coming to see you. You are so loved Mom, I love you, and I hope you always knew that." I said gently, she reached out and took a strand of my hair. "You have such pretty hair Claudia, and always a good girl for Papa and me. We are very proud of you." Her voice was becoming labored.

"You should rest now, is it all right, I'm staying right here I pulled the chair closer and laid my head on her shoulder. How I wished I could rest my head on her breast like I had when I was a child. Mom began to hum an old Arabic song, the same one I sang to my son. I hummed silently along with her. It was serene and comfortable being next to her. I stayed until I knew she had fallen back to sleep. I must have dozed off as well because when I opened my eyes I expected to see Mikhail, he was so real and I felt dismayed when I realized that he really wasn't here. My son was smiling and so happy, "Mommy, I'm going to see Grandma and Grandpa really soon. I will help them adjust here, it is so much fun. She will see Mommy!" I heard my child's voice. My head popped up and I knew immediately she was willing herself to go. It was the monitor that had woken me. . . . the loud buzzing told me what I didn't want to hear. The nursing staff was in the room and there was nothing I could do no convincing them to resuscitate. The machines were turned off and soon I was left alone with her. I could hold on to what was coming, so many years lost. I should have killed Jasim, I should have freed Mik and me a long time ago. I don't know how long I sat there, the nursing staff came in asking me if I was ready to let them prepare her body, all I could do was shake my head.

Hearing Kelly's voice caught the place inside of me that controlled my emotions.

"She's gone isn't she sweetheart?" He stood in his spot. I left her and found his arms and held on to him. I felt too overwhelmed to cry and probably angrier at myself for not being nearer her and Papa for so many years.

"Claudia, what can I do?" He kissed the top of my head as he asked.

"Just stay right where you are, please? I'm not ready to move. I'm so glad you're here."

"Claudia what can I do?" he asked as he kissed the top of my head. "Just please stay here with me . . . Oh, Kelly, I'm not ready to say good-bye to her. We didn't have enough time." "I know sweetheart, but you were with her, she must have been happy, right?" I pulled out of his arms. "She didn't want to live, it was all my fault for not being here, spending time with her."

"Claudia, you don't really believe that, do you? I don't believe for one moment she wouldn't want you to be happy. She knew how horrendous your life was honey. She asked me to always be there for you, I told her always, I will always be here for you Claudia. I think she missed your papa." Kelly rubbed both my shoulders. I nodded, "Yes I know she did…they had a special love. I am happy they will be together, now they will be with Mikhail." I sobbed.

"Come on sweetheart, let's get you home… home to the house you grew up in, where love is everywhere." Kelly took my hand, but I needed to touch her one last time. Her skin was cooling and her essence was gone, but there was a slight smile on her lips…had she saw Papa while she was dying?

"Farewell Mama…I'm so so sorry. I love you."

Kelly hand on the small of my back guided me out of the hospital, "What have you eaten today? I think I know you, would I be right if I guessed nothing?" He took hold of my hand. I knew he could read my mind. "Baby please, forget the scotch right now and we'll go grab something to eat, something light. Please let me take care of you, trust me, I'm worried about you and scotch isn't what you need, it's your enemy." His eyes pleaded with me.

I became perturbed, "You have to appreciate that after all these years I know what's best for me Kelly. Yes, I hear you, I'm tired of being told when to breathe, how to walk, how to talk, how to be Claudia. Yeah, you may be totally right, but if I want a scotch I'm going to have a scotch. You can join me, or not, it's your call." I pushed his hands away. "Please Kelly let's go back to the house, you can eat there." I reached in my bag for the car keys and handed them over. I was aware of a bottle of scotch I'd left there. My mind began wandering to the events of the day, I realized she had waited for me to get home, she had it all planned.

Oh, what have I missed all these years! I thought about photographs and family holidays. Oh shit, I must notify the rest of the family, they are going to think I kept everyone away. "Fuck and double fuck!" I said out loud. Kelly turned to look at me.

"What is it, honey?" He questioned. "I need to notify the family, Christ they're going to think I kept them from her." I rubbed my forehead, "Claudia why do you think that?" "Because Kelly I didn't phone anyone to tell them she'd been hospitalized. Once we get home I'll call Aunt Maysam I know she will notify the rest of the family." I reached over for Kelly's free hand and watched as the vehicle approached our street.

Dropping my bag and sweater on the chair beside the front door, I continued to the dining room where I knew that bottle of scotch was. "What would you like to eat Claud? I'll cook, you choose." The sound of the fridge door opening addressed his need for food. The bottle was right where I'd left it. Making my way into the kitchen I took a glass tumbler out of the cupboard.

"Are you going to join me? "I caught his eyes, and saw his reply, he shook his head. I poured and then located the phone where it rested in its cradle. I looked for Maysam's number and hit the talk button. "Aunty, Hi it's Claudia, I have some sad news, Mom passed away this evening. I'm sorry I didn't have the time to call you or anyone." I responded while waiting to be lashed out at. Surprised at her response. "We're you there with her? Because she told us all to leave her house, she wanted to be by herself. Claudia, I didn't have a way of contacting you, she said she wanted to die in peace. We all saw such a change after your papa died. Claudia, I know you are going to have a lot to deal with and we are here for you. Would you like me to phone the rest of the family?"

"Yes, please auntie," I answered. We chatted a little more and then hung up. I finished the last mouthful and poured another, I carried the bottle and glass then headed upstairs to her room.

I noticed mom's sweater resting over the back of a chair, so I slipped it on and felt her comfort and warmth. Crawled on top of the bed and placed her pillow against my chest. Their wedding picture was displayed in the same place it had been since I'd been a child. I just stared at it, aware of what was waiting for me inside at the back of the frame.

"No Clarissa, not today, you're going to have to wait." It didn't take long for me to drink half the bottle and when Kelly knocked on the door I knew he would have a comment or two to make.

"I just need to be by myself right now Kelly, please? It's been a rough day, I know you understand. Good night Kelly." I was surprised when there was no reply. I figured he may have gone to my old room and gone to bed. Now it was me and my half-empty bottle of scotch.

The following morning, I found a note on the kitchen table from

Kelly, *I came to support you because I love you, and I gather you don't need my support. I'll be in Kelowna, call me when you get home. I love you. . . .* Kelly

It's probably better this way, I didn't need a dad. I had one harsh headache and I was ravished. I hoped there was something in the cupboard or the fridge. "Oh Christ, what I would give for coffee strong black and espresso." I fell onto the chair, now what do I do? What would she want me to do?

I phoned Maysam again, "Auntie, I really need your help. I'm sorry I don't know what to do." I began to cry.

"Don't cry now, we are here to help you, we'll come really soon. Okay, Claudia?"

"Of course, Auntie, I'll be here."

Then I went to the local Starbucks and left with two double shots of espresso and a pastry. The fog was clearing and for a moment I felt bad about Kelly leaving, I was conflicted, why did he go back to Kelowna. I really messed things up this time. Maybe I'm more of a headache than he needs, but I still couldn't believe he walked out on me.

My aunts arrived shortly and it was a whirlwind, they knew where my mom left instructions for her funeral. I felt such a relief. I was overcome with grief and it was a lot worse than I realized. I didn't have the strength to bring it all together. I leaned on my family and trusted they would make Mom's service as special as she was.

A few days later, after the funeral, I had to pull myself together. I didn't understand why all my friends showed up, but Kelly didn't. I figured he had given up and couldn't handle this fragile, drunk of a woman. It hurt more than I could have imagined, I could only imagine how he was feeling. He wanted so much for me to reach out to him, only I couldn't, I didn't deserve to have him.

I slowly began organizing all their valuables, giving my aunts the go ahead to take what they wanted, having the sentimental items; like their wedding rings and her jewelry especially the large Hamsa pendant. I believe that now my protection would be coming through her. Papa had some first edition books of Arabic and English literature that I wanted and their wedding picture that hung on the wall.

A few weeks later I chose not to return to Penticton, nor to phone Kelly, I hadn't heard from him so I decided to have the jet brought to Vancouver, I put the Audi in storage. Maybe this was the answer to everything.

Chapter 18

I FLEW TO SPAIN, to the coastal province of Malaga and the Costa del Sol. All I did was lay in the sun, shop, go for massages and spa treatments . . . and party. I was pleased with how well I still looked in a bikini at 46. My now perfect breasts complimented my body and I felt extremely sexy and that was my biggest mistake. Being unknown and in a strange country gave me a different kind of freedom. I became "Stella" in the evening. I explored every nightclub in the city, but it was the pubs on the beach and the wine and the music that won me over.

One afternoon I chose to wear a skimpy white bikini and sarong that I tied just under my navel. At an open-air bar, the lively Spanish band triggered my soul and my body began to move to the rhythm. I was joined by a very handsome, dark–haired man who must have been in his early thirties. I studied him as he studied me; his eyes were on my eyes as we moved to the beat. He moved like a professional dancer; he stood behind me with his hands on my hips and controlled my movements.

He was smooth. He pressed me tight up against him and put his hand flat on my stomach while the fingers on his other hand wove into mine. He led me around the sandy dance floor and as he moved each time our cheeks pressed against the others. I was on fire, and unsure if it was the alcohol or those old seductive ways had come alive again. I didn't have any inhibitions. I knew I was being seduced and was enjoying every bit of it, but I wasn't going to make it easy on him. I decided I was going to seduce him, probably like he has never been seduced before. He was going to have to hunt me down.

I intentionally let his leg connect with my labia and my almost naked breast at his naked and hairless chest. He was a looker. After the dance I excused myself and walked away, leaving him to wonder if I would return. I didn't. He didn't even ask my name, we didn't even exchange words only an unspoken body language.

After that, I went to the spa and chose a little tapas bar to have a meal. Then, I saw him walk into the bar. I turned knowing he hadn't seen me yet, my short white tunic dress was not as revealing as my bikini, but my athletic long legs would definitely be the bait. Even with my back to the entrance I felt him close and didn't jump when his hand twisted in my long curls.

"You're absolutely stunning!" He whispered against my cheek.

I smiled, "You dance well!"

"There are many more steps I'm sure could teach you." He replied ordering himself a drink and pointing to mine. "I hope you don't mind me buying you a drink?" He stared at my mouth as he spoke.

"I don't mind at all," I answered back.

"Are you alone here in Costa del Sol?"

I nodded, "You?" He nodded. I smiled; I was in my game. We still hadn't exchanged names. A song started up, he pulled me to him, and across the floor, we went. But this time it wasn't as sexual, as it was romantic and sensual. He pulled me tight against his chest, moved one leg between mine and moved me like I had never been moved on the dance floor before. I felt incompetent, but my body it obeyed his lead. I felt myself heating up, but tonight wasn't going to be the night. There was one instance that I felt his lips near mine, then he jerked away. He was seducing me and I liked it.

He said, "Excuse me, and don't go anywhere." It was a perfect time. I left the bar and got into a waiting taxi.

For the next couple of days, I kept a low profile. I didn't even leave the hotel. I ordered room service, swam, and drank fresh fruit juice and finally left the booze alone. I had spent enough time here and felt ready to fly on to a new country, but not before finishing what I started.

I waited until it got cooler and wearing just the white bikini and sarong, I walked the beach knowing I was going to be the honey the bee he would sniff out. I must have walked ten or fifteen minutes when my radar detected him. He saw me immediately and jogged down to meet me. He had the widest smile and his perfect white teeth added to his sexiness.

"You shattered my feeble heart." He said as he walked backward ahead of me.

"I did, how did I do that?" I toyed with him

"You left without telling me your name." He frowned.

"It's Stella." I murmured.

"My name is Miguel." He replied, throwing me another beautiful grin. Miguel, I thought, of course, a common Spanish name, touché' I giggled. He frowned and looked at me. Then, he grabbed me and explored my mouth as his tongue was searching for mine. I was playing catch-me-if-you-can with mine. He had his hands caught up in my hair, pulling it out of the mound on the top of my head. I gave no thoughts to having spectators and decided it was probably not an issue. The sun was almost setting and the water was sparkling from the moon. After his lips parted from mine, I undid the strings at the neck of my bikini top, allowing it to fall in front of me.

He took a deep breath and pulled me into him while his one hand manipulated my breast and soon his fingers were rolling the nipple in them. "Come I know a place!" He took my hand as we jogged up the beach towards what looked like a rock cliff. It was the place to be seduced, and then fucked. He murmured something in Spanish, as he took my nipples in his fingers and squeezed them hard enough to make me moan softly. I closed my eyes and again he tweaked every nerve ending in me.

Finding my mouth, he pulled wildly at my bottom lip, tugging gently and then biting it carefully. I moaned again. He was skilled at kissing and I was soon caught up in an incredible passion. The sensation of his index finger plunging into my vagina surprised me and I felt my body release its moisture and the trembling began. He whispered how wonderful he was feeling, his breath, warm against my ear.

"You are one horny girl, one fucking hot woman!" His fingers were now hard against my pelvis tapping inside the wall of my vagina. I quivered and pushed myself into his fingers as hard as I could. I came again: it was like a thunderbolt entered my body. As I came, he caught the tip of the clit between his nails and pinched it enough to send my head back in delight.

He showed me a condom package and I nodded, "Yes!" with a gurgle in my throat. His quick movements had me up against the flat wall face of the rock, he pulled my legs around his waist and handed me the unopened condom. I quickly ripped it open and took hold of his manhood, not too big and not too small and I was confident he knew what to do with it. I slowly rolled the condom over his head, grinning and flipping my eyes up and back down on him.

"What do you like?" He asked. "What don't I . . . everything!" I whispered. He had my body's attention at every bit of movement. "Oh . . . fuck. . . !" I screamed as the waves of pleasure burst. I was having multiple orgasms. He had struck gold within me. I was panting so hard, as my body vibrated, and he kept pounding and moving to exactly the right place. "Stop . . . please. . . . please!" I begged, "Holy fuck, how did you do that?"

"Are you done already?" He whispered against my mouth. I searched for his tongue and capturing it, I sucked hard. He banged himself hard into me again and again. I kept responding to his hard thrusts. He let my legs down and removed the condom as I waited, my body still vibrating; this time he put another condom on.

"Show me beautiful, show me what you have." I knew immediately what he meant, so I did my dance. I dropped my head slightly to the side, moved slowly with my back against him. I flung my head back slowly and I heard him moan when I gyrated my hips, "Oh . . . yes, show me beautiful."

I rotated my hips the other way before slowly moving forward, inching my feet apart with each movement, until I was in perfect position. Then, I pushed myself up on tiptoes and raised my ass up, before bending over, he groaned. Reaching underneath myself I dragged my index finger slowly back to front. Then back again before inserting it into myself. I continued masturbating, feeling my body fluids leaving my insides. I pulled my finger out and stuck it in my mouth.

"Wow . . . wow, that was nice." He moved closer to me. I arched my back, just in time to be impaled by two fingers, moving in me from the front while the fingers on his other hand began massaging my anus. I gyrated against him and he moved inside me slowly spreading his fingers apart applying pressure. I felt the tip of his penis moving carefully against the opening of my anus, he eased himself inside slowly until he had me fully enclosed around him. He pushed, I groaned, he pushed harder, I groaned louder, while he still fingered my vagina, pushing deep into both places. This man was giving me everything I needed, I felt the pinching of my one nipple between his fingernails sending me over the edge. Then a finger connected with my g-spot; I was beyond orgasmic explosion. I gushed, squirting into his hand. I convulsed all the while he was pumping inside my anus. He wowed me, and he knew it.

Then it was over. I was breathless and hot all over. I pressed myself into him, tracing his lips with my wet tongue. I pressed mine hard against his, taking one more long hot kiss. "Thank you for that, it was hot . . . goodnight Miguel." This was my way of saying goodbye. I stepped into my bikini bottoms and jogged down the beach, the cool breeze felt wonderful against my naked breasts. I worried that he would follow me, I turned scouring behind me, he wasn't anywhere in sight. I stopped to tie up the neck strings of my bikini top and continued the run. I returned safely to my suite and thought about the hot Spaniard; what he had done to me was so very delicious.

It was very late when I called the pilot and requested he get ready to fly out tonight. Still, in my bikini, I packed the rest of my belongings and called a limo. I checked out and left Miguel and the beautiful Spanish seaside. I hoped he was craving more of me.

Chapter 19

KENJI WAS WHAT I WANTED and after some effort, I found out, was working in a seaside community called Portol, on the island of Mallorca. It was going to be perfect. I needed only what Kenji could give me. We landed, but I stayed aboard the jet and slept until noon, showered and found a new bikini and skirt with a netted wrap. I was soon ready to meet with Kenji again after all these years.

We had arranged to meet at a small café. Kenji arrived before I engaged in and looked up at me unexpectedly.

"Sorry Claudia, sorry! Good read."

"I see that Kenji, how are you?" I smiled at the familiar face of my former trainer. "You are different Claudia, I like what you have done to your hair and there is something else different about you, still the exquisite Claudia!"

I undid my bikini top and exposed my smaller breasts. Kenji nodded. "I preferred your big tits Claudia, but hey."

I retied the strings. "Yes, the men do."

"So, tell me, what are you looking for Claudia, I can only think of one thing," Kenji said with a raised his eyebrow.

"Yes, how soon can you arrange it? "

"Soon, I have the equipment and there is someone I'd like to introduce you to, a student, I think you will both enjoy each other." Kenji looked very self-assured.

I looked out at the ocean and had an idea. "Do you get seasick Kenji?" Kenji looked at me inquisitively.

"No, why?"

"I'm going to charter a small yacht for a few days."

"A few days?"

"Yes, but not to spend the whole time with you Kenji, an afternoon is good for that." I chuckled. I savored the rich black coffee. "I will make the arrangements and call you soon." I was feeling the moisture developing outside of me. It's has been so long, it was an internal calling.

The yacht, with a discreet crew, could be ready to launch within a couple of hours. I contacted my pilot and had my small weekend bag taxied to the marina. I called Kenji; who would be there as soon as he was organized. I thought about the student and because Kenji knew my tolerance level for pain, I was apprehensive.

The marina operator was quick to understand what I wanted. I needed a chef and personal staff to be able to come and go. I wanted a massage therapist, my body was not like it had been before. While I waited for everything to come together I was able to relax on a lounge chair until Kenji and the student arrived with everything I had requested.

I studied the man Kenji introduced to me. Peter was a black, tall, attractive and from the West Indies. My eyes went directly to his hands, they looked strong and so did his long fingers. I saw his thick muscular arms and chest. There was a lot of power behind this man. I shuddered at the thought of what I could experience from those hands. I was anxious and ready for them to set up the room. I tried relaxing on the deck, but my body wouldn't respect my commands. It was wonderful looking out at the ocean as I consumed some very expensive scotch and that was when my mind took me to Kelly.

I knew he was angry with me and probably finished with me now. I knew I was incapable of giving him the type of relationship he wanted. It was nice to have that experience with him, knowing what love could really be, but I knew that would never be enough for me. I needed this dark side of sexuality. It was ingrained in my being from the time I was a very young woman.

Kenji came and joined me on deck. "Claudia, what all are you prepared for? We can keep it at a mild pain level, it has been awhile Claudia."

I looked over, and reminded Kenji of my safe word, "fire". There was no middle word, "Exactly what you know Kenji, just do it! I'm vibrating. Please, are you ready?"

"Peter is well trained in inner stimulation, fisting with anal stimulation; that is something you can think about."

Kenji led me into the blacked-out room with spotlights ready to be focused on my eager body. I removed my clothing, Kenji blindfolded me and prepared my body. Those hands attached the nipple and clit clamps extending the nipple clamp at the start of the areola, I winced, realizing since surgery my breasts were much tenderer than before.

The pinch on my clit sent little shock waves through me. I was vibrating inside and outside with anticipation. When the hot oil splattered on my skin it perked up my other senses, fingers slid all over me from my head downwards slowly and deliberately in each erotic spot. Peter came in the room and Kenji told him to attach the leg restraints. I felt my legs parting widely. I began to pant.

Kenji's familiar fingers slid inside me vaginally, massaging the inside wall then lightly flicking the now blood-filled nob of my clit. I moaned softly. Those movements increased in a quickened movement I had grown so familiar with, I knew an orgasm was not far away and so did Kenji as he saw my body tighten. Kenji flicked my clit harder jolting me, I gasped. It was sensational. My moans increased. Kenji's other hand was now slowly fingering my anus. Then I felt the clamps being tightened around my now throbbing nipples.

I moved my attention to the enjoyment my vagina was having. It was the click of the whip that hit the tip of the clit that brought my attention back, I groaned and breathed deeply, pulling air into me.

I heard it whizzing around my ears expecting it to once again reach its target. Nothing was happening except Kenji's stimulating fingers, it was when I felt some apparatus being pushed inside my rectum that the sting of the whip met each nipple in sequence. I tried to arch my back, I couldn't move.

I heard the beat of the thunder playing in the background then the snap of the whip got more frequent each time the intensity increased. I thought I was on the brink of orgasmic tides when the nipple clamps were removed and they stung, the pain sharp and overpowering as a hard-brisk snap greeted each one. I exploded, my body convulsing. Kenji's fingers were gone and so was the clit clamp. I felt my legs being spread further apart until I thought they were going to snap. They were released slightly. Then snap across my clit again, another snap over my nipples I felt strange fingers at first just massaging my clitoris, as the tip of the whip met my throbbing nipples I climaxed, feeling the creamy substance oozing out of me.

Peter continued massaging me; my instincts were sharp, as I felt the sensation of knuckles rotating at my opening. It was deliciously painful as he slowly pushed his fist against me, and then I felt the awkwardness of his knuckles rolling back and forth inside of me it was beyond anything I had experienced. I was unable to move any part of my body as the restraints held me snug in the air.

My orgasms were multiple and the whips had stopped, but the sensations in my nipples were electric as I felt a strange metal teethed object rolling around them. The pain jolted inside, it was almost to the point I needed to stop. Each sensation my body was producing exactly what I had been wanting, the erotic pain-saturated the places I was so familiar with.

Peter asked Kenji if I wanted penal penetration, "I want to see your size first." I demanded. My blindfold was removed. He was extremely long and thick, much thicker than Jasim. Yes, that would be the perfect finish to a delicious afternoon.

"Oh yes," I said looking directly at Kenji, and with my eyes, I directed Kenji to the door. With a nod, I was left at this man's discretion. I was very aware he was not fully erect, and I wanted the pleasure of creating that with my mouth. "

Peter, you need to release one of my wrist restraints. I would like to make you hard in my mouth. Are you okay with that?"

His eyes were dancing at the thought. He did as I requested and he moved to where I had the perfect access. I felt the weight and the girth in my hand as he slid himself into my mouth. All the while his fingers working my vagina, it was crazy and wonderfully pleasurable. As saliva filled my mouth I took over, he wasn't resisting and I didn't have the complete pleasure I would have liked before he was too much for my mouth.

He asked, "Should I remove the apparatus in your rectum?"

I shook my head. I was ready as I let him slide slowly from my lips. He placed a condom on and before I knew it, he wasn't taking it easy, he slammed into me pounding me harder and harder until I exploded. I immediately came with a rush, but the pain was jolting through my body I whimpered, "Fire!" He pulled out. I'd had enough. I was in severe pain. I thought I was going to pass out.

Soon, Kenji was back in the room. "Damn it, Claudia, your bleeding severely, you waited too long. Shit, what the hell Claudia? You need a doctor." Kenji made a call and alerted the crew. Kenji assured me it would be kept confidential and discreet. The look on Peter's face was of horror. He was extremely apologetic.

I stopped him. "No, don't, it was everything I wanted and needed. God, you were so good, don't blame yourself. Thank you. I'm all right."

"I pushed myself into you to hard and fast Claudia."

I shook my head, "Please just go now."

I stayed on the yacht for another two weeks and sailed around the coast and I felt the completion of this sexual journey, knowing full well it would surface again in the future.

Chapter 20

HAVING LANDED once again at Vancouver International Airport, I retrieved the Audi and the rest of my parent's belongings. I was ready to go back to the world I created in Penticton. Being gone for six weeks I had no idea if Kelly would be all too happy to see me. I took my time as I drove through the winding roads and searching my mind for the different scenarios I might encounter on arrival. Being back in the Okanagan was right, and everything smelled of sage and pine, it resonated in my belly...... what was I really experiencing inside my being. All I knew as I was completely satisfied by the sexual encounters I had. But inside me, there was a gnawing feeling. I really love Kelly, I did. Why am I so incapable of proving it?

I pulled the Audi into the organic market and stocked up on the foods I might need, not knowing what I would have at home to eat, that much I knew, as for Kelly eventually I would have to face him. I asked myself how could I have done what I did and expect to have him waiting for me. Damn it, Kelly you chose to leave, you didn't even try to talk to me, I grieved alone, like always. He insisted that he loved me and would always be there for me.

It was obvious that Kelly had been home, the cabin was clean and the air smelled fresh, not lifeless.

After showering and changing clothes, I waited while the gas fireplace heated up the room and found my eyes on the portrait of Mikhail and me, time was passing, the anniversary of his death was approaching. Would I ever stop grieving him? Would all this ache ever subside?

Feeling hungry, I made myself something easy to eat and opened a bottle of wine Kelly and I had brought from Kelowna. I curled up on the sofa with a plate of food, a glass of wine and a book. I could see the snow drifting outside and was content not to leave over the next couple of days

I heard the door open on the third morning. I was awake but in deep thought. I got myself up, wrapped a robe around me and there he stood. My heart dived into my stomach at the sight of him. God I thought, he sets my heart on fire.

"It's good to see you, Claudia, you've been gone awhile." His eyes kept me frozen to my spot. "Is this how it's going to be with us, Claudia? You leave me and there isn't any communication of any kind?"

"Excuse me Kelly, who left who? As far as I'm concerned you ended it. Should I find a place of my own? I can be out of here in no time." I walked past him into the kitchen.

"I won't deal with a drunk Claudia, I won't live with it. Cindy became a lush, it was ugly and I won't put myself through it again. You have access to all the help anyone could want and you chose the bottle." Kelly stated as he threw his truck keys on the counter. "I waited for a call, I deserve an apology, Claudia. I would never do what Jasim did to you. To be put in that category, telling you what to do, how dare you."

"I was at the end of my rope and needed to escape, for just a little while. I deserved to pickle my pain, Kelly. Just go, just leave!" I took my glass of juice and walked to the patio doors. I was falling apart inside. I knew he was too good to be true. I was not worthy of love, anyone's love.

"I thought we had more going than that. But one of us is afraid, and it's not me Claudia. You want me to go, all right Claudia, I will do that. If you want my support you know how to reach me. I'll be in Kelowna." He retrieved his keys. I listened to the door close behind him. He was gone.

I panicked, what have I done? He has to have his cell phone on please God! It went right over to voicemail. "Kelly, it's me, you're right, please come back let's talk. If you are back in Kelowna before you get this message I will come to you." I paced, back and forth. What have I done? I couldn't wait for a response I had to find Kelly. I quickly dressed in a pair of jeans and a sweater, ran a brush through my hair and a toothbrush over my teeth. I dashed out of the bathroom and I felt the biggest relief come over me.

Kelly stood in the doorway with his hands in his pant pockets. "Kelly, oh, I was just about to come after you!"

"Why Claudia?" He spoke so calmly.

"Because I don't want to spend my life without you, I couldn't stand it if there was the slightest chance you'd walk away. Please, we need to talk."

"What does this mean Claudia?" Kelly crossed his arms over the other.

"You are my love, my only love. I came from a jailor to a new kind of jailer, please honey hear me out. Jasim created me to benefit himself. I had no control over my being or my body. I've broken Kelly and maybe I'm too old to fix." I reached my hand out and walked towards him. "I know you want me to be healthy and a certain way. I don't know how to be any other way than what I am. I do know what I want Kel, I want you, I want what we had, but there is a sexual part of me that has needs you can't fulfill."

"Clauds I don't ever want you to feel like you've come from one prison into another. I would never do that to you. I respect you and everything about you, your needs. I have my boundaries too, ones where I'm not willing to bend. I do have one question, Claudia after your experiences of doing whatever you do sexually are over, how does your soul feel?"

I couldn't reply. I didn't know the answer. I stood there dumbfounded. He stepped towards me, slid his arm over my shoulder and he drew me to him. "I ask only two things of you. Turn to me for comfort, not the scotch bottle. I don't care what you need it for I can and will handle your darkest times with you if you give me a chance." Kelly's fingers rested beside each side of my jaw.

"Ok Kelly I promise you, I will lay off the scotch . . . at least not over indulge. I will try Kelly I will.

"Do I satisfy you? I'm sure we both stimulate each other's minds, we always have especially because our interests are similar. I want nothing more than to satisfy your body, Claudia?" He looked away from me when he spoke. I reached over and took his chin and raised it to meet my eyes.

"Yes, of course, you do, that and more Kelly. I'm fulfilled completely, in more ways than you could imagine, because I know I'm loved. But you need to understand, I have other needs. I like disciplined pain and liked to be hurt. I like the pain I need it." I I stood back and waited.

"Is that's what he did to you? That demented bastard really fucked with your sexuality Claudia. Tell me what did you do when you were away? I need to know." He scrutinized me and every word I was saying. I watched his face, I read his pain and there was no way he could ever digest what I needed to satisfy the void inside of me. I shook my head. "It's not the kind of information you need to hear Kelly. I'm not willing to go there with you either."

"What if I'm willing to accept that you do what you need to do? But when you decide you need to go, I need to know your leaving, not where you're going, or for how long, just don't let me come home and not find you there. My second request is non-negotiable Claudia. I want you to move forward and consider getting intense therapy. I won't make things easy for you Claudia. I intend to work on helping you restore the truth of who you are. You took the first step, you had the breast implants removed. What would be the next thing to make a difference sweetheart?"

"Seriously Kelly, do you figure a therapist will make it all go away?"

He reached for my hand. "Claudia just gives it a chance, please, that's all I ask of you." Without any warning, he scooped me into his arms and took me into our bedroom. I grabbed his face and pulled his mouth to mine. I needed him to know I only belonged to him. "I love you Kelly this is why you and I are together."

Kelly slipped my sweater over my head. "Come and look Claudia." He brought me into the bathroom in front of the mirror. "Baby look at how beautiful these breasts are they are perfect. Touch them, Claudia, take hold of them in both of your hands. You rescued that part of yourself. Now, what is next?"

Kelly reached his hands around me and pushed them inside my jeans, moving down to my pelvis he rested his hands. "You gave life from here to your son, that's another beautiful gift, this body is amazing. You pleasure me and fulfill my needs with a deeper love than I could have imagined." He kissed my neck as I turned around and undid the buttons of his shirt, all the while he had his hands running up and down my sides. The sensuous energy between us exploded into a passion.

"I'm going to make love to you Claudia, is that all right?"

Of course, it was, I wondered why he was asking me. I swept my fingers into his hair, bringing him to my breast. "God Kelly, of course, you don't ever have to ask me, my body is yours."

His eyes found mine, "No, Claudia your body isn't mine alone, I have to share you."

I lowered my head in shame, which was something I hadn't felt since my wedding night with Jasim. I reached for my robe and I left the bedroom to sit at the kitchen table. Kelly's words cut through me like a knife.

I felt his hand on my shoulder. "Honey, this is important for you to know if we are going to make this relationship work."

I shrunk, "I'm embarrassed and I'm hurt. Kelly this has been my life for so many years, there is nothing more I can say or do, and either you believe me when I say I love you, don't you." I looked into his eyes as I spoke.

"I understand Claudia, I know you love me. Not once have I doubted that. It's up to you honey."

I spent the time to myself while Kelly was in Kelowna working with Daniel at the winery. There was a rift growing between us. I knew he was in protection mode, keeping himself safe from me and it gave me time to think about his requests.

And thinking was exactly what I did, and I found that worked best when I played my flute and even more tranquil as I looked over the lake. The emotion from my music set the tone to my memories and I wondered why and how Jasim chose me for his target. Finally, I knew exactly what I needed to do. The three months I'd been home was still awkward, I wasn't emotionally or spiritually in a good place. Maybe this journey would expedite my healing.

Jasim's lawyers must have information somewhere. I was blind to his everyday activities as well as his business; however, now as his widow, I had access to his personal effects. I needed to go back to Dubai, visit the lawyers and uncover who the real Jasim Kassis al-Masri really was. I still had to decide about all the property, it needed to be sold. Did he have other children than Pascha?

Pascha . . . the thought of him made me queasy, but sad. I hadn't spoken with him since finding out he was my half-brother. He went ballistic. He refused to speak to me and now I presumed he wasn't able to face me. We both had to heal.

However, having said that, if I was to be true to myself and Kelly I needed to clean Jasim's matters up before getting into deeper therapy, as Kelly called it. In fact, this would be a part of my therapy. I decided to go back to Dubai and deal with the past and the memories and all the horror that went with it.

I needed the closeness and the connection with Kelly, but his words 'I have to share you' would destroy us if I didn't get the help he insisted on. I dialed his cell and waited, he didn't take long to answer.

"Hi Baby, is everything okay?"

"Yes, sweetheart everything is fine, I miss you but that's okay. I promised you that I would never go away without talking to you first. This is why I am phoning you.

"Claudia, can you wait until I get there, I'll be back later this afternoon? Please don't leave yet?" Kelly sounded distressed.

"Of course, I will wait, I want to tell you what I'm doing. I'll be here. Kelly, I love you!"

"I love you desperately Claudia."

I spent the rest of my afternoon writing down the names of people and places Jasim took me, maybe they knew things that he kept from me. We had friends in Cairo that Jasim was extremely close to; after Dubai, I would go visit them. I was so caught up in making plans that I didn't even realize the time until Kelly walked in the door. He threw his keys on the counter and removed his leather jacket and shoes. He looked worried and it was obvious he was frustrated.

"Kelly, I'm not going away to do that, I really have other reasons and I want to share them with you. But first I need you to know, we are going to be all right?"

"I don't understand Claudia, what do you mean?"

"Kel, I agree with you, you're right I need to open up and be straight with a therapist and not pussy foot around the issues anymore. I promise you have my word I will get the help. Before I can do that, I need to clear everything out of my past. Settling the issues around Jasim, getting everything solved, liquefying his assets and deleting all traces of the Jasim Kassis al-Masri name. I have to go to the United Arab Emirates and Egypt. Please trust me." He said nothing, he just listened and studied me.

"All right Kelly, I guess I am going to have to show you." I walked towards him and he stopped in his tracks with a questioning look. My hand found him and I pulled his fingers to my lips and kissed the tips of each one before placing his hand at my throat. I tilted my head back and waited for him to make his move, it didn't take long before his mouth was near mine with his hand pinching my chin. Our lips were touching and my heart was racing, he had to know I was his in every way that was important.

I spent the rest of my afternoon writing down the names of people and places Jasim took me, maybe they knew things that he kept from me. We had friends in Cairo that Jasim was extremely close to; after Dubai, I may go visit them. I was so caught up in making plans that I didn't even realize the time until Kelly walked in the door. He threw his keys on the counter and removed his leather jacket and shoes. He looked worried and it was obvious he was frustrated.

"Kelly, I'm not going away to do that, I really have other reasons and I want to share them with you. But first I need you to know, we are going to be all right?"

"I don't understand Claudia, what do you mean?"

"Kel, I agree with you, you're right I need to open up and be straight with a therapist and not pussy foot around the issues anymore. I promise you have my word I will get the help. Before I can do that, I need to clear everything out of my past. Settling the issues around Jasim, getting everything solved, liquefying his assets and deleting all traces of the Jasim Kassis al-Masri name. I have to go to the United Arab Emirates and Egypt. Please trust me." He said nothing, he just listened and studied me.

"All right Kelly, I guess I am going to have to show you." I walked towards him and he stopped in his tracks with a questioning look. My hand found him and I pulled his fingers to my lips and kissed the tips of each one before placing his hand at my throat. I tilted my head back and waited for him to make his move, it didn't take long before his mouth was near mine with his hand pinching my chin. Our lips were touching and my heart was racing, he had to know I was his in every way that was important.

Chapter 21

I NEVER IMAGINED how soon I would be stepping back into the penthouse I shared with Jasim and Mikhail, but here I was, over a year now, and without any staff peering around corners. The atmosphere was filled with sadness and gloom and it gave me shivers thinking about my life here, but it would only be for a couple of days a week at the most.

I knew Jasim had a safe in every home we lived in. I had to find them and get a locksmith to open all of them. It was time to pack up, send everything to an auction house and hire a realtor to get this place and all the other properties sold. I wasn't attached to anything, other than what might be in Mikhail's room. I sprawled across Mikhail's bed remembering all those nights he and I curled up together.

I started my search for Jasim's safe; the first place would be his dressing room and then his office. I wondered if he had secret walls that could hide a safe and wondered if I should find out who built the apartment. I continued to search and then it clicked: the torture chamber where Kenji worked. He had it redecorated into a guestroom after Mikhail was born. No one would ever guess, Jasim was smart and that would be somewhere his sick mind would go. I opened every drawer and door and wondered about the floor. That's when I decided to leave it until I met with the legal team.

I showed up at the law offices of Martin, Bennett Helm & Roche and was just about to take a seat in one of the luxurious leather chairs in the waiting room when Paul Bennett appeared, "Well

Claudia, my goodness, I thought you were back in Canada? What brings you back?" Paul, the firm's elder, reached out and took both my hands in his.

"Well Paul, it is great to see you. I could use your help and expertise." Paul held a special place for me over the years and he made it well known. He knew what Jasim had used me for, so if anyone could give me the information I needed it was him.

He directed me to his office and I felt his hand at the base of my spine. He had the typical elder litigators' office with a deep rich cherry wood desk and wall unit. The view from his office was over the Persian Gulf, and it was quite a stunning view.

"So how can I help you, I gather it has to do with Jasim." He picked up his pen and shifted a notepad.

"Yes, it is about Jasim. Paul, I want every piece of information he had, I know he had safes many places where he kept his secrets hidden. Someone knows where they are and I believe it's you or one of the partners he dealt with here. I need to locate the safes and combinations can you help me?"

Paul twirled his pen from end to end before he spoke, "We have a conflict of interest here Claudia. Jasim's orders stipulated that everything remain confidential even after his demise. What are you looking for exactly Claudia?" He leered at me in a very uncomfortable way.

"I'm not sure I quite understand how confidentiality plays into my request, I am his widow and I am also listed in his will as his only beneficiary. What really is the problem here Paul? What else has Jasim done?" My intuition was on alert. Paul put his pen down and excused himself and left the office. He returned with a four-inch-thick file.

"Claudia, I can give you this file, it isn't everything that you're looking for, but I believe you'll get a sense of what I think you are looking for. I am going to meet with my associates and discuss your request further. The locations and safe combinations are in this file, we also have all the locations of the properties he owned. The keys are in his safe at your penthouse." Paul put the file in a big brown envelope and handed it to me.

"I would like you to press the issue with your associates Paul. Jasim has hurt a lot of people and I want to know. I also want to know what happened to Aswad, I'm sure he kept records and there was something quite substantial for Aswad's retaliation."

I stood up to leave and about to shake his hand. "Have dinner with me tonight Claudia, I think I can fill you in with some of the information you really want. I will pick you up at 7:30 at the penthouse." Paul's show of confidence was a real concern to me, but if he knew something, it may be my only chance to find out.

I looked over and nodded, "All right Paul, sure, I will have dinner with you."

I soon had the file opened and spread out across Jasim's desk. His expensive scotch tasted so smooth as it flowed down my throat. How interesting after all these years to see the properties, the hotels and resorts he owned, there were even corporations that I didn't have any clue about. There was so much in front of me and with Jasim dead, this could all be compromised. I had to trust that Jasim had good people working for him. I was stunned at the homes he owned, I suspected he had more than the ones he'd taken me too. There were sixteen properties spread throughout various countries. He even had another suite here in Dubai.

"What the hell? I looked through the file and found the suite number, which was on the forty-ninth floor. Hm... no time is better than the present to check this one out. I called Salid, our old driver, and asked him to take me there. I had my suspicion as to who lived who lived in this suite.

I studied our old driver and I knew he was faithful to Jasim. "Do you know who lives there Salid?"

"Yes, Mr. Jasim and Miss Borg ." He frowned. Borg I thought, that is definitely a Scandinavian name, was that the beautiful blonde of so many years ago?

I knocked on the door, but no one answered so I let myself in. The apartment was very contemporary, it was beautiful and I was aware there was someone living here. I walked into the living room and the first thing I saw were pictures of Jasim and her, the blonde woman from 18 years ago.

I headed towards the hall and greeted by a stunned blonde woman. She scowled, "What are you doing here? How did you get in here?"

"I have a key." I held it up to her. "So we finally meet after all these years, I remember you and how upset you seemed that night while Jasim and I were dancing. Wow, you've been with him all this time. My suspicions were correct, he did that to hurt you, didn't he, to prove a point? You must have wanted something from him, to take my place, am I right?"

She was silent. I held out my hand, "I'm Claudia," and smiled.

She hesitated and then slowly extended her hand. "I'm Tova, and yes Claudia I spent many years with Jasim and I resented you because he wouldn't leave you. He said that would never happen."

She lit a cigarette, "He really loved you."

I shook my head, "No Tova, he held me prisoner for over twenty-eight years. I detested him, I gladly would have divorced him for you. Was he kind to you? Did he . . . " She looked surprised, so I stopped in mid-sentence.

"He was wonderful to me, I would have done anything for Jasim . . . I did that and more, but he only wanted you and told me that over and over again."

It was strange to hear that especially with all the pictures of them around the apartment. I picked one up and Jasim looked incredibly handsome I knew that was our earlier years when I was fulfilling all his assignments.

"Tova you are very beautiful, why did you waste all those years with him? He was an evil man, but I won't tarnish your memories with that knowledge. He bought this place for you, didn't he? And I bet he supported you as well?"

She nodded. " Yes, and now my bank account is almost empty. Why did he commit suicide Claudia, he didn't even say goodbye to me. I loved him you know, I really miss him."

If she only knew my truth, I felt bad for her and knew that kicking her out and selling the apartment would be something she didn't deserve. "I know what it's like to love someone and not be able to be with them. Tova, I will make sure you are looked after and have the lawyer put your name on this place. What did he have set up for you financially?" I walked around the room, getting a feel for the place.

"A credit card, but it expired I've taken the maximum amount. His lawyers told me they couldn't do anything for me. I was going to go back to Sweden, which is probably the smartest thing for me now. I have nothing here anymore."

How ironic, she had happiness with him and he didn't want that. He could have been a happy man. He looked so happy in each one of the pictures. I could only shake my head. "I'll have the lawyer call you and you can make arrangements with them. It was nice meeting you, Tova." I left without hearing her response.

Paul arrived at precisely 7:30 PM and we had a drink before we left for dinner. I chose to wear a white halter top and white matching wide leg trousers and my hair was styled in a knot at the base of my neck. The moment Paul saw me a bulge in his pants gave him away. His salt and pepper hair was groomed and styled to match the dark Armani suit he was wearing. Paul was close to Jasim's age and a very attractive man, he stood over six feet and on the leaner side, with pale blue eyes.

"Excuse the appearance around here. I gather no one has been here since I left. What can I offer you to drink?"

I was aware how Paul's eyes moved over my body. "Well if I remember correctly Jasim has the best scotch. So, tell me did you find anything in the file?"

I poured two shots in the Swartzsky crystal tumblers. "I actually made a visit to see Tova today. What a stupid fuck Jasim was, he had a woman who would have walked on water for him, Christ. Listen, Paul, that apartment belongs to her and she needs the financial support he was giving her. Continue with what he was giving her for the year and I want to know if she sells and goes back to Sweden if she does then we'll terminate it at that time." I sat down across from him.

"Why do you care so much about his mistress?" Paul twisted the glass in the palm of his hand.

"She spent 20 years or more with him. She deserves it, besides she loved him. Paul, I don't want her to find out anything about the dark side of Jasim and me, ever. You got that?"

"Of course, Claudia, I just bet old Jasim is laughing right now. What figure do you want to be deposited?" His eyes moved up to meet mine.

"Five hundred thousand should be enough. Not sure, maybe that's more than enough, especially since she has minimal expenses. I don't care."

"I'll take care of it tomorrow. But I am curious Claudia, we heard many, many rumors of what Jasim was using as leverage and I'd like to know if it's true? There were pictures of you in various explicit poses if I can put it politely."

"Where is this leading Paul? Are you absolutely positive it was me? How can you be sure, besides whatever it was you saw, how would that be leverage for Jasim?" I wondered, for fuck sakes how could Jasim have let that happen? Christ, what else is out there?

He answered, "Jasim made a lot of enemies and those enemies had voices, he could only silence people for a while."

"Look, Paul, my private life was just that, private. Now, are we ready for dinner?" "Ready if you are Claudia? Please don't expect to hear any more about that tonight, I would like to have a nice evening with you. I apologize if I have overstepped in any way." I smiled and motioned at the elevator.

The evening turned out to be extremely pleasant and I enjoyed Paul's company, he was an interesting man with incredible stories.

"You know Claudia, I have envied Jasim since he brought you to Dubai, I'm not a shy man, too old for that nonsense . . . I was, and still very smitten by you. I would like to spend time getting to know you." He reached across the table and traced my fingers with his.

"I know Paul and I am flattered." I shook my head. "You and many other men, besides I live in Canada and intend to remain there."

Paul grinned, "It was obvious? Well, I'm not going to apologize either, you are a beautiful woman. I'm hoping this evening doesn't have to end with dinner do you like the Blue Bar? I know there is going to be some great sounds tonight."

"I would prefer an early night Paul, it's been a lovely evening. I will give Salid a call to pick me up." I was aware of this man's charm and I didn't want a confrontation, I sensed what was coming. He sat back in his chair and I read his expression.

"Claudia, I have a proposition for you. It's one I know you would be stupid to turn down. Jasim gave me a flash drive and trusted me with it. I know it's what you are looking for. It has some sensitive information on it that could expose a lot of people."

I knew how to keep a straight face, could it be what I thought it was. If so, Jasim had lied to me. "What do you want Paul?" As if I didn't already know.

"You Claudia, I want one night with you, either your bed or mine. I promise you, you won't be disappointed." My mind was going in circles, was he bluffing? Could I do this?

"I will give you a preview of what is on the flash drive if you don't think I'm on the up and up." I've got to call his bluff. "I don't think so Paul, I've got to pass." He shook his head, "Bad call Claudia, bad call. There is a very interesting document about a terrorist bombing in the Middle East, hmm, does that ring a bell?

I froze, "If I agree to your demands you had better guarantee me there aren't any more copies." I stayed calm on the outside but so agitated on the inside. "You can meet me at the penthouse I expect you to have that information with you." I excused myself and left the restaurant.

Everything was on that flash drive. I thought I was going to be sick. "I promise you Claudia this is the only copy, I know his dirty secrets and how he ended up with you, I have no intention of seeing you hurt anymore, you have my word and more if you ever decide you could be interested in me."

I was seeing some interesting information and my interest was piqued at the next file, but before I could get a better look, Paul clicked it off. There wasn't one iota of sexual interest in me at this moment, I could only think about being with Kelly. Paul's hands were resting on my shoulders and moving into the knot at the back of my head undoing it.

"Let's find someplace comfortable Claudia. Where is your bed?" Paul asked as he strategically placed the flash drive on Jasim's desk.

I led the way, removing my shoes and earrings on the way. I knew how to get myself through this. I needed music, I turned it on and then checked my closet for some condoms. This felt like Jasim all over again. I returned to the bedroom and Paul had already removed his jacket and shoes. I scanned his body and threw the packages on top of the bed. I was about to undo the buttons on my trousers when Paul stopped me.

"Don't, I want that pleasure, come here, please Claudia."

I surrendered and stood before him. "I really wish this could have been mutually agreed on Claudia. Christ, I'm excited, touch it, please touch me." It was nothing I wasn't already used to. My fingers unzipped his trousers and reached inside his boxers at his swollen manhood. I stroked it and did exactly what I knew he was going to request. I pushed his trousers and boxers to the floor, then getting on my knees I took him into my mouth and did exactly what Jasim would have expected of me. From that moment on, I shut myself off.

When he ejaculated and I licked the traces of him from my lips he reached down and took my face in his hands, gently pulling me up onto my feet.

"That was wonderful Claudia!"

Now his hands were removing my trousers and I was left standing in my panties. Paul rested his forehead against mine as he untied the sash at the front of my top, then unbuttoned each button leaving my breasts exposed fully in front of him. He didn't touch them, but his fingers hooked the sides of my panties and soon they were skimming down my legs. Paul got on his knees and kissed my belly while I waited, knowing what to expect. Paul pressed me up against the bed with his arms hoisting me up over his upper arms. The faint sensation of his tongue at the clit hood caught my attention, his tongue now flicking quickly in and out I sucked in the air. Paul moved my body onto the bed firmly keeping my legs spread apart and continued with assault.

Still holding my legs up onto his shoulders, his hands pushed upwards and found my taunt nipples, I felt them being squeezed between his fingers like scissors. Then, my attention was immediately drawn to what his mouth was doing; it was like a vacuum sucking my genitals as deep as he was able to. He licked me just as though I was an ice cream cone. This was not the pleasure I shared with Kelly, it was dead, his fingers rolled my nipples between them while his tongue was desperate to create and conquer his male desire.

"Yeah, that's perfect Claudia, come on baby let go . . . " he moved his fingers down, sliding two inside of me, finding that spot, he was consistent, I was not about to give him that pleasure. Then, pulling out, he massaged the opening for a few seconds before repeating his internal actions.

"Oh, you're so beautiful Claudia, just like I imagined you would be. I'm going to fuck you now, God you make me hard." I felt him reaching for a package and heard the foil rip. I waited for his next move as his fingers massaged my whole outer area. I didn't feel any desire. I didn't have any natural aroused responses to his fingers as they desperately prepared me for his entrance. As he slid himself inside me his mouth and tongue moved up the center of my body until his lips possessed mine. There was nothing large or long about Paul but he did what he intended on doing he had me. He was only fucking me.

As soon as he finished with me, I left the bed I once shared with Jasim. It wasn't any different than what the man who called himself "my husband" had done before. I put my robe on and went back to Jasim office and retrieved the flash drive and put it in a safe place.

Paul joined me, "Please forgive me, Claudia, I know you must think I'm like the other dogs that took advantage of you. I guess I am, Claudia I had to have you. Forgive me?"

"Yes you're in that group Paul, you and I both have what we want so please will you leave me now?" I smiled confidently and kept eye contact with him. "Oh Paul, I expect you to release any and all of whatever documentation you and your associates have by tomorrow." I wondered by his expression if he regretted what he demanded of me because if he gives it some thought, he will realize he may have jeopardized a multi-million-dollar client. If they want my money, there had better be something in it for me. It would all be scrutinized once I got everything home and with Kelly, understood all the legalities.

This March morning was quite warm for such an early hour, I hadn't slept very well and I desperately wanted to talk to Kelly. I and wanted to be up front and tell him what had happened and the reason why I did it. The more I thought about it; perhaps it would be best if it stayed here. He already had too much to forgive me for. I knew I wasn't capable of stopping, I yearned to fulfill the dark side of my sexual appetite, so I was lying to both of us.

I had to put that out of my mind, there were things to be sorted out before I left. My dressing room was full of designer clothing worth thousands of dollars, clothing I would never wear again and it was time to have a consultant come in, appraise them and either put them on consignment or purchase them. This was the perfect time to go through my wardrobe and really make the right decisions.

I also spent hours going through Jasim's files and boxing them up. I wouldn't part with them yet; there could be information in them that I might need. Paul's assistant telephoned to notify me that a package was being couriered and wanted to make sure I am home to receive it. I was relieved, yet cautious and hoped the firm wouldn't do anything underhanded by keeping important documents.

The next few days I spent with consultants and the realtor deciding how the sale would proceed. The documents were prepared and signed and the remainder of Jasim's belongings would be auctioned off and the money to be given to the poor.

Then, I received a phone call from Pascha. "Claudia I have just arrived in Dubai, I talked to the old man's lawyer, they contacted me to let me know you are disposing his properties and the majority of his portfolio. We need to talk Claud, can I come over?"

I was a little hesitant because he was so angry when he learned the dirty truth of it all. "It depends, Pascha, what kind of attitude you'll be bringing with you. I was planning on sending you a document stating what was being done."

"I know Claudia, I was an asshole, and I've had time to examine my behavior. I'll be good, I promise."

Both Pasch and I had been raped in the most deplorable ways, the years we had intimate relations and the chances we took without having any inkling that we were siblings. It took a harder toll on him than on me. Pascha had always proclaimed his love for me and believed that one day we would become a couple. It didn't matter what I said and did to convince him otherwise.

When he stepped off the elevator; it was awkward. His cockiness had disappeared and a more serious Pascha manifested. I soon realized how much I adored the former personification of him.

He wrapped me in a warm hug, “Claudia, how do I say I’m sorry for being such an ass, but not sorry for loving you?”

“You don’t have to be sorry, you just have to let go now, once and for all. Let’s figure out how we can be siblings and share that kind of love.”

“Hey wait a minute, something is different with you Claud.” His sexy grin returned and his eyes reached my chest. “They’re gone, those big beautiful tits of yours are gone. What did ya do that for?”

“Tit fucking envy or what Pasch, yes thank God they’re gone.” I shook my head. “Suppose you wouldn’t share these ones with your bro huh?” Pasch teased.

I turned towards the bar to find a bottle of wine. “No, I suppose I won’t share.” The words were a little more sarcastic than I had intended.

“All right Clauds. I’ll give it up, and get to the subject. What are you planning to do with all the assets? I have an idea if you are interested in listening?” Pascha opened and poured the wine.

“Let me hear it, I’m curious.” “Our organization Claudia needs support and we still have much work to do, if you don’t agree or meet me half way, I’m going to sue the estate for my share Claud. I just want to give you the opportunity to continue our fight.” Pasch wore that determined expression I had seen so long ago while we worked side by side with the organization

“How much Pasch, what do we need to do to support the people? I’m in you know that?”

“You don’t know this, but Jasim pumped a million dollars into the cause, at least that’s the figure he gave me. We need that and more Claudia, not only for the cause but we need to build houses, and there is so much to do. I’m so glad you’re in . . . ”

The excitement filled me like it had when Pasch introduced her to the cause. "I will donate the proceeds from the sale of the penthouse and everything else that gets auctioned."

"You're kidding Claudia, seriously you're willing to part with that much cash?" Pasch drew a mouthful of air as he whipped his head back to look at me. "Money is not an issue, we need to use it to benefit others. Trust me, this is a drop in the bucket of our father's wealth." Suddenly changing the topic, I asked him, "I'm hungry, want to order something in?"

"Yeah sure. Come back to the Middle East Claudia and continue what you started with us. You remember how exciting our lives were, how entrenched in the work you'd become."

Pasch moved to the sofa I was sitting on and faced me. "Those days are over for me, I have the life I'd dreamed about, for so many long years, I have it now in Canada and with Kelly."

"Who is Kelly?" he asked.

"A man I've known all my life . . . anyway, it's become your journey, you have to continue now for both of us. I still can't trust the Israeli's they could know who I am."

I moved off the sofa to refill our glasses and he followed me. I felt his breath on the side of my face. "Claudia, I think you are in denial about us. No one needs to know that we're half-siblings, we've been lovers for years and do you really want that to change?" His hand moved over my upper chest. He pulled me back against him. His lips moved along the side of my ear.

I mumbled, "Please . . . stop . . . Pasch!" With no fight in me, I said the words, while that same hand hunted for an entrance through the fabric of my top. His kisses tantalized me, I wasn't even sure when his finger had slid beneath my skirt resting at the top of the crease.

"Nothing can come between us now Claudia, baby." I stood there feeling the hardness of him at my backside and as he familiarized himself with my smaller breasts, he aroused me like he did all the other times. I couldn't breathe, I weakened to the comfort and familiarity of him. The familiar awareness building inside as my body exploded.

"How I love you, Claudia!"

I heard those words and alarm bells went off in my head, "Do you know how evil we are? Fucking each other now especially after we know we're half-siblings! Pascha, what's the matter with you?"

He released me, "Does it really matter? I've always loved you." Pascha trailed his fingers around my breast.

"Yes, it does! You're as sick as I am . . . I'm never going to see you again Pascha, Stay out of my life!" I slapped his hand away. "You will have all the capital you need for the cause. I will make sure it's available. Goodbye Pascha!"

Chapter 22

THE SECOND WEEK OF MAY had come by the time I returned home to Kelly. It was obvious from the dust and the lack of food in the fridge. I was sure he left the day I did. I called his cell and it went directly to voice mail. I phoned the winery and hearing his voice sent a relief through me.

Kelly, Hi, honey, how are things?"

"Sweetie, hey hi, where are you?" He asked calmly.

"Home, at our place, when you're able to come, I'll be here. I've really missed you and I'm glad to be home." I replied as thoughtfully as I could.

"You might want to congratulate our friends here. Daniel and Daina have gotten engaged and there will be a wedding early September."

"Kelly is Daina in the room? You promised me, you'd keep us a secret." I panicked.

"No neither her or Daniel is in the room, they're up at the main house. Claudia, don't you think we can finally share our situation? We're a couple, and unless you have something to be ashamed of, enough is enough. I'm tired of hiding. What is it that prevents us from sharing our love with them? They're our old and dear friends." He asked in an agitated tone.

"Because I'd have to share with the world that Jasim shot himself . . . because we had a son that died and that my dead husband was actually my father." I shuddered.

"Claudia, you don't need to explain anything to anyone. Jasim passed away, that's all they need to know. They love you, Claudia, I understand, they will too. Or are you ashamed to be seen with me in public?"

"Kelly MacAskill, you don't really think that, do you? Oh my God Kelly! I am proud to be by your side. One day at a time please." I said on the verge of tears. I knew I needed to make a decision.

"This is not how we should be having this conversation, I'm finishing up here, I have to stop at the house, then I'll be home, we'll talk, we need to figure this out, Claudia. I love you honey and I'll be home soon." He was hasty.

After we hung up, so many thoughts filled my head. I didn't want to expose the embarrassment and shame that I felt. I didn't want the pity I knew I would hear. All I wanted was to be free from the past from the suffocating memories that were choking me. The flute . . . finding a position in front of the fireplace, I sat cross-legged, looking up to Mikhail's photograph, I closed my eyes and let the peaceful sound of the flute fill my senses.

Kelly came up from behind and hung his arms over my shoulders, "Baby you have sexy ears, and you know that?" He said sweetly.

I turned to face him, tilted my head up and back for a kiss. Kelly pulled back and looked at me with a smirk. He slid his hand under my hair before joining me on the floor. "There isn't any joy in your music today, it's so mournful. I have a tiny understanding of what you have been through Claudia, I can't even begin to imagine the pain you have locked up for so long. All I know is our friends care about you, you don't have to go into great detail. They will accept and understand whatever you tell them, sweetheart." I

I looked up at the man I adored. He had so much wisdom and compassion. He bent forward and pretended that he was about to kiss me, but then he stopped.

"Yes Kelly, I'll talk to Daina, especially since Daniel already knows about us, you're right I miss and need our friends too. I will call her, but first I need to feel my man's arms around me and his tender love-filled kisses."

"I would like it if you started seeing the psychologist again Claudia."

"I have been contemplating it, Kelly, all the while I was away and especially since there were a couple of events in Dubai." My gut was turning because I knew this information might not go over well, but I needed to be open and honest with him. I had shared everything from my past, everything except Pascha, so this can't be any different. "I have a brother, when I first went to Palestine I began tutoring this young man who was only a few years younger than me. Anyway, his name is Pascha and he introduced me to the organization, Pascha knew nothing about Jasim's part in the organization and how he set it all up to blackmail me.

It was Pascha I turned to for comfort . . . " I kept my eyes focused on Kelly waiting, anticipating his reaction.

When he realized it, his reaction was even worse than I had anticipated. His expression changed, as did his body language, I knew he was sickened by what he'd just heard. "You had sex with him even after you knew he was your brother? Are you kidding me? I don't get it, Claudia, I really don't. How could you?" For the first time ever, Kelly backed away from me. "I need some space, I can't do this right now." He turned and went outside.

I stood frozen on the spot. I wanted to run. I wanted to collapse. I wanted to scream. How could he forgive this? I've lost him, I know it, it's over. Suddenly, I thought, I will turn myself over to the Israeli's. I can't live with myself any longer.

I've got to go. Slade had taken the jet back to Dubai so I would have to fly commercial. I had to rush and leave. I could never face him ever again.

I had just started packing when Kelly appeared in the doorway, "Why are you packing Claudia? You're going to run from me again, aren't you? I'm pissed off because you find it so easy to run."

I couldn't look at him. "I think it's best this way, for you, I'm not worth it. You don't deserve a broken woman." I continued to pull items from the drawer.

"I wish you would allow me to make the choice about what I deserve. I don't know how to explain what happens inside of me every time you share these horrific experiences. Claudia, you've been exposed to things no human being should ever have to. Damn it, don't you get it? The love I have for you doesn't stop because of situations, I need to process this information, and it is so fucked up! I'm a grown man and I can't grasp it."

He shook his head. "Please don't leave Claudia." He headed to the shower.

I fell onto our bed, my whole being exhausted. I dozed off and then the sensation of Kelly's hand caressing my hair aroused me.

"I bet you haven't eaten anything have you, Claudia? I know I'm starving."

I lay there not knowing what to say. He brushed his lips across mine in a quick motion and left the room. Perhaps he didn't want to touch me, was I tarnished? I had to find out. Removing my robe, I chose a thong and a body fitting T-shirt, I tied my hair in a side ponytail and headed into the kitchen. I was going in for the kill. I knelt in front of him and made my way into the elastic of his jogging pants. I never got to first base before his arms hoisted me up onto the kitchen counter. He bent forward in front of me, placing his hand's palms down on each side of me and kissed each side of my mouth.

"I love it that I turn you on, make you moist between those beautiful legs, I like how uninhibited you are, you are a turn on in every way Claudia, I know something else, there is much more to you Claudia, you are intelligent, educated and Jasim stifled that part of you. Using sex is not going to work because you're afraid or unable to articulate your feelings or thoughts. As I see it, you think by using your body to deflect insecurities is the solution." He stared directly into my eyes. He knew my psychological make-up, all I knew is that was what my body told me what to do. "There are some things I can't grasp, I'm not in your head, and I don't know how to deal with your reality. I'm trying to understand sweetheart. Am I going to wake up tomorrow morning or maybe the next week from now to find a note saying you're gone again? Just because you can, because you can't deal with things that are simplistic. I want to ground the jet and all your other escape routes and force you to be still and look as well as reach inside to find your answers Claudia, you have them!" I knew it was a risky thing he had just done.

All of a sudden, I felt stifled, and I wanted desperately to run. "Kelly I need to flee, right at this moment . . . why are you doing this?" I questioned.

"What are you fleeing from? Me? Or is your inner locked up self is trying to get out, and you don't know her anymore, the innocent young light-hearted Claudia?" Kelly's face moved closer to mine.

"Since when did you become Dr. Freud Kelly?" I tried to push his arms away, but he stayed bolted to the counter preventing my escape.

"That's not funny Claudia. I've spent nearly ten years working with a therapist to learn about myself and how to cope with my feelings and how you have affected me. I am willing to do anything it takes to be a healthy emotional example for you. Does anything I say resonate in you, Claudia?"

I took a breath and swallowed? Who is it that needs to escape? It definitely wasn't the woman deeply in love with this man. I knew he nailed it, something triggered me. "I will be here in the morning and the next morning I promise. And I will make appointments to see Dr. Bloom, please take it easy on me. This is all I know." I began to cry. Kelly didn't take me in his arms he just remained in the same spot watching, allowing me to release the unfamiliar.

"I need a tissue, Kelly." I took it for granted he would let me out of his hold. He just shook his head. I had snot and tears running down my neck. He never moved an inch. I used my hand as a tissue, and the sobbing escaped from somewhere deep inside. He waited. I don't know how long he waited, it seemed all afternoon.

Then he broke his silence with a nod, "I bet that was a new experience for you. We can get through this. I'm here for the long haul if you are? You are worth it to me. This is the depth of the love I have for you Claudia." Kelly spoke lovingly. His hand was at the back of my head and the other around my back, he pulled me to him, I buried my snotty wet face into his shoulder and held on to him. Then he gently lifted me off the counter and carried me to our bed. "Now I am going to make love to you Claudia."

Chapter 23

IT WAS WONDERFUL seeing Daina looking so happy, she absolutely glowed and so did Daniel. Back in elementary school, they had a crush on each other, just like Kelly and I, but it never seemed to work out. Now, after 40 some years, they were about to be married.

Daina's mouth dropped open when Kelly and I entered the house hand in hand. "You can close your mouth, my friend." I grinned wide.

"Oh my God Claudia, look at you, your hair, I love it!" Daina gasped in delight. "Oh, I am so glad to see you, Claudia!" Daina said as we grabbed each other in a hug. Then I hugged and kissed Daniel on the cheek. "I'm so happy for you, about time."

"Oh . . . Claudia, what have I missed, it must be enormous for you and Kelly to be together too. I want to know everything!"

Kelly kissed the side of my head. "Take it easy on her Dai, okay?" Kelly intercepted.

"Of course, Kel, I am just so taken back, she's my best friend in the world, other than this guy, of course, I will take it easy on her."

I was so happy to see Daina and I felt a sense of relief now that she knew about Kelly and me. This was the first step to the rest of the world. I knew Daina wouldn't rest until she knew the story and if I could tell anyone it was her. Maybe if I had confided in her from the beginning things wouldn't have gone the way they did.

"Daniel I'm dragging your soon-to-be-wife away with a bottle of wine, so you two men can have some bonding time!" Daina went in the direction of the kitchen and returned with two glasses and a bottle of red wine. “Come on my friend, let’s go upstairs out on the deck.”

It was an incredibly hot summer night, but the cool breeze off of Okanagan Lake was as refreshing as the red wine I had just swallowed.

“Claudia, I’m sorry for acting so insensitive, I love you, and you mean the world to me. What ever happened to your marriage is between you and Jasim? I won’t intrude, I just want to know you’re okay.”

I trod slowly, “My nightmare began in Cairo I got involved with a terrorist organization . . . ” Several times Daina’s eyes widened like golf balls, and I thought to myself if she’s reacting like this when I’ve barely touched the surface, she couldn’t handle my reality. But what concerned me the most, was telling her about Mikhail she would be hurt that I never told her about Mik.

“I don’t understand! A son Claudia, you had a son! How could you keep it from us?” Daina was hurt and disappointed.

“Jasim was powerful and I was his prisoner. No one in my family, even my parents knew about Mikhail until my papa died. It wasn’t what I wanted Daina, you have to believe that . . . oh, this is why I wanted to keep my past in the past Daina, it’s too difficult to talk about. The only reason Kelly learned about my boy was a chance meeting in Geneva when Mikhail was three. That was when our relationship began again.”

“What do you mean again? You and Kelly again? When was the first time? “Daina, it’s been a very long journey for us . . . school Daina, just like you and Daniel, except his dad saw to it that we ended our relationship. Poor Daina I thought, she is so disheartened with me. I was okay telling the story but when I had to elaborate with details it got difficult. I wondered how Kelly had shared my tragedy with Daniel, maybe he should be up here enlightening Daina about the incest.

"What? Are you fucking kidding me, that's deplorable! Did he know?"

"No Dai, he was just as shocked as me. That's the reason Jasim killed himself Daina." I stated it as simplistic as I could. Daniel and Kelly must have been in the doorway when Daina broke into tears. "It's okay Daina if I hadn't had my son, his death wouldn't have set me free from Jasim. God gave me a gift, even if it was a short time. I had a wonderful child. I will show you pictures when you come to Penticton to visit us." I tried comforting her the best way I knew how, until Daniel took over. "I'm sorry Dai, this was not the evening you thought it would be right?"

"God Claudia, it wasn't me that lived through it, I'm just upset because of what my best friend endured. I'm angry because you carried this for so long. That son of a bitch!" Daina bellowed.

"Daina I'm here, I'm so happy, I am with the man I have loved all my life. So let's bury this for now and be happy. Life is good." I acknowledged.

Daniel and Kelly were able to change the energy and soon we were all laughing and the wine kept coming. After all these years, it was the first time the four of us were together as couples. It all seemed so expected and something that we'd done for years. It was an evening of catching up and reacquainting ourselves again after years of separation.

A few days later I was perched on one of the pub chairs at our table surrounded by stacks of papers when Kelly got home. After dissolving the Kassis Al-Masri companies, the legal team had been anxious for me to re-organize and decide on a new company name. I didn't have any idea, but Kelly convinced me that the Samara Group was a fitting name, and I had to agree, it did have a nice ring. I never, and still didn't have any interest in making or dealing in any financial decisions, and that was something else Kelly got on my case about. He warned me that if I didn't watch the portfolios carefully it could be an open invitation for someone to manipulate funds. Who better than Kelly to teach and guide me with this new task, his business degree and intelligence was exactly what I needed.

It was a logical and practical decision to keep the jet in Penticton for it could benefit both our company's needs. It would be available for Kelly and Daniel to run the winery business as well as my new project. So, that meant hiring a new pilot or keeping Slade and buying an apartment for him. I knew him well, and over the years he had been loyal to me in so many ways. He did what he could to protect me as much as he could from Jasim's cruelty.

"Well don't you look overwhelmed amongst all those papers, Claudia?" Kelly said as he approached and placed a quick peck on my lips. "What are you working on?" He scanned the table.

"Oh, jet stuff."

"What's the plan for that?" Kelly asked

"If Penticton is going to be home base for the jet, then what do we do about Slade? Keep him here, or give him up, that thought bothers me. He's so loyal and a good pilot, the best. Christ, he's been with Jasim since before me . . . what to do."

"If it were me, I would keep him, put him on a salary and find a place for him to live, he shouldn't have any trouble working around the valley to keep busy, but that might conflict with our needs."

"Thanks, honey, that's an idea, but Slade will have to weigh it, he might not want to live in this environment. As for living arrangements, I think we should purchase a condo for him."

"Baby?" Kelly said. "I have something I'd like to talk to you about. I've listed my house with a realtor and when it's sold I plan on buying some acreage here on the Bench, we both love it here, and we could build something we both would love." He was staring and I knew he was reading my reaction.

I was thrilled. "Kelly there's the matter of the winery. You'll be doing the drive every day back and forth to Kelowna." I reminded him.

"I know, been doing it for a while, now haven't I? Daniel and I have thrown some ideas around and I've been talking with Daniel and we plan to grow more grapes. I have actually spotted the perfect location, just up the road on 17 acres, with lake access and over 500 feet of private beach where we could build our house. There is an existing vineyard, we'd have to investigate what is growing, but that something Daniel and I would look later. Would you like to go take a look at it?"

It could not have been more perfect, it was a remarkable piece of property, secluded from the road, "Do you love it, Kel, I think it's a stunning setting. I can picture us living here!"

"I hoped you would honey. Oh, Clauds I can picture everything in my mind. Let's go home and I'll show you some ideas."

"Kelly we're buying it and we're not waiting for your house to sell, we don't want to risk losing it. I have the cash." I knew by his hesitation he didn't like that idea, but I knew I could convince him, if not I would just buy it and he knew I would.

"On one condition Claudia, when my house sells, that money goes into your bank account."

"Babe, it doesn't matter, that's fine, we can use it to build the new house right? And besides, money is money and I have way too much, I still insist this money belongs to both of us"

He answered, "Can we discuss that another time?"

I threw my arms around his neck, but Kelly shook his head and squeezed me tightly against him.

"We're doing it first thing in the morning, Kelly," I stated firmly. "Besides, when or if we get married this is a partnership in every aspect. I know you have investments and are in a good place, but I have so many liquid funds available it's disgusting, and if I remember correctly wasn't that the same word you used? So please! Please!" I pleaded my case.

Kelly wrapped his arm around my shoulder, "Let's go buy some property!"

Within no time we had blueprints for our new house. We were eager to start the build, but the design was challenging because Kelly and I both wanted the house to be as environmentally friendly as possible and have all the special touches we'd been dreaming about. Kelly promised me it was doable. So, I left it all in his hands and the concentrated on the jet and other business matters.

It wasn't long before I was up to my neck in making some big decisions. I wanted to help displaced, exploited and underprivileged women around the world to find a way to support themselves and their children. Fortunately, I was blessed to find organizations and staff that had the same vision and were dedicated to making that vision a reality.

Once I had hired my staff, they researched the poorest communities throughout the developing world. I wanted to create a co-op where they become self-sustainable. I needed to follow up with the staff on the ground and that meant several weeks of travel. I was concerned how Kelly would react, but I had been dedicating myself to healing and working hard with Dr. Bloom. And I believed one day I would become strong enough to let that part of my life go.

We were both delighted with our architect, he most definitely had been listening to us and our concerns. Meanwhile, Slade would be arriving in Penticton within the week. I had a schedule in place and anxious to get going. The trip consisted of meeting my teams in Egypt, Sudan, Nigeria, and India. Kelly came to the airport with me and we said goodbye. It was a mature, healthy "see you soon" farewell without any drama.

Chapter 24

My first stop was in Tobago. I needed to face my demons for the last time: I was meeting Kenji's student Peter. He was now on his own and I knew this would be the solution. I never had to use my safe word until Peter. I planned a week on the island and I wanted it to be the last time I traveled without Kelly.

Peter was at the airport when I arrived and I could tell he was uneasy in my presence. Peter had arranged a guesthouse for me and as we drove through town, my body was doing the dance: I felt and recognized my old excitement and anticipation surface. I wanted to get onto the beach. I was pleased that my door from the guesthouse took me directly onto the beach. I wished at that moment Kelly was with me. He was filling my mind and I desired him.

"Peter, please have seat I said as I opened my bag and searched for a bikini. I didn't have any inhibitions; this man would have full access to everywhere on my body. I stepped out of my skirt and panties, my top and bra were next. Naked, I sat down on the chair next to him and rested one leg over the other.

"Ok Peter, I feel your uneasiness, what's going on with you?" I knew my body was not turning him on sexually.

"Last time I hurt you pretty bad, bad enough to call the doctor. It concerns me, Claudia. I know what my job is, but not to do that."

"If I thought in any way you got off on it, or it was intentional, I wouldn't be here. I like your touch. Peter, I am interested in taking it to the extreme. Are you going to be okay with this now?" I asked as I bent over to pick up my bikini. I was curious to see his reaction.

If he was like Kenji he wouldn't be stimulated by me. He did look a little curious, but that's okay. I can handle that. "Electrical play this time Peter and I know you are well trained in it. No nipple or clit clamps this time, or penis penetration. So, I'm going for a swim, and hopefully, have a couple of drinks, will you be set up for me when I return?"

"Yes, Claudia that gives me plenty of time. So, just restraints, a mask, whips, and the violet wand? Enjoy your swim!"

I grinned as my body trembled in anticipation.

There were more than enough heads turning when I cruised along the beach, I noticed a lot of men, more men than women. I had no interest in them. Kelly was home waiting for me. What I was doing wasn't sex: this was sensational play. Of course, it is erotic when you challenge your body. My vagina was getting moist and throbbing as I entered the water. It was cool and soothing against the hot sun. I untied the strings that held my bikini top up letting it fall into the water, and my nipples automatically reacted to the chill and became hard and erect. It was erotic and I was excited at what was coming. I swam for a good twenty minutes and headed in for something potent to drink. I found a bar on the beach and an empty lounge chair. I unclipped my waterproof case from my bikini bottoms and put on my shades and ordered a scotch neat. I stretched out on a lounge chair and pointed my face to the warm sun, It was relaxing and I knew instinctively I would be disturbed.

I was surprised by the audacity of one very black Trinidad native who sat right down beside me. I didn't flinch, I kept my focus on the sensation the sun had on my face.

"Where you from beautiful lady?" He finally asked.

I smiled, "Do you use that same line on all women?" I asked not moving my body. "Ah .. I won't bother you any more beautiful lady, enjoy Tobago!" He commented and was on his way. I hoped any other man watching got the hint. I wasn't hit on again that afternoon. After my third scotch, my body was telling me it was ready now, let's go. I hustled down the beach anxious now to experience electro stimulation.

"Peter!" I said softly, "Are you ready for me?"

"Yes, Claudia." And he extended his hand to the door. After we entered it was closed and locked, the music this time was the lapping of waves as they hit the shore. How appropriate I thought. Removing my bikini, I slid up on the massage table and waited for Peter.

He started by taking my hair off my face and letting it hang. It was so sensual feeling his fingers massaging my temples and my face all through my body. His hands were amazing as they massaged me, then, his fingers entered me vaginally and something happened that I had only ever experienced once before: shame.

His fingers moved deep inside massaging the wall of my vagina. No, no, no, my head screamed out. "Peter, Peter, you must stop. I'm sorry, I just can't do this today." I swung my legs over the table and exhaled. I left the room and found my bag, I doubled his fee and thanked him.

I changed into another bikini and went back to the beach. I walked for what I thought was hours; all I could feel was the memory of Kelly's arms holding me. I knew the weeks away from him were going to be difficult and drag out. I prayed I would be extremely busy and the time would fly by. I wanted my vision to take shape and I reasoned that the more time I gave now, the sooner it will be running on its own and the need for me will subside.

My skin had absorbed the massage oil and I wished that my mind could forget where Peter's hand had gone. I would change my plans and fly to Egypt in the morning, but today I would enjoy the sights and sounds of Tobago. I had another 20-minute swim and then jogged down the beach to the guesthouse where every trace of Peter was gone. I ran a bath and soaked for a while. I wanted to phone Kelly so desperately, but Tobago was not on my itinerary.

I chose a bright red, sundress and a pair of red flats and walked towards a restaurant. I thought I would browse the stores and maybe find something special for our house and then I stopped in my tracks. I can't do that, now I feel guilty. Okay Claudia, let's go get something to eat and go, maybe to the jet. I felt so restless.

I stopped at the first bar on the beach. I had just ordered some Jamaican rum punch and a variety of seafood on a skewer when I felt a hand on my shoulder and a voice from my past. "Stella, it really is you. I saw you on the beach earlier, wow you look great."

"Miguel," I replied, "imagine running into you again!" He was still handsome and very charming. I had my work cut out for me now. He very brazenly ran his finger up my leg and near the top of my thigh before I crossed my leg over.

"Oh Stella, I would love to play that game we played on the rocks again. "Hmm," He grinned. "I play one time and I'm not into it," I replied very bluntly. I could tell he was not going to take me at my word. I was thankful I had my cell with me.

Turning my back to Miguel I contacted Slade, "Hi, I have a situation here at the Tango Beach House Bar, I need accompaniment. Also, I'll be ready for take off." "Claudia, are you needing a heavy hand?" Slade was intuitive.

"That's a good possibility," I replied as quietly as I could, thankfully the music would drown out my conversation.

"I'm on the way."

I casually finished what I had ordered and took a few mouthfuls of the country's drink, rum punch, which was killer good. I got up to go to the washroom, saw Slade and jumped in the limo.

"Thanks for being so quick, I need to make a quick stop at the guesthouse." It didn't take me long to gather my few items up and get back in the car. We left that evening for Egypt. It felt so good not to fall and have sex with Miguel, I was being true to Kelly.

Jasim and I spent many vacations in Egypt. I loved Egypt especially Alexandria, but my destination was Cairo where I was going to be working with a group of women. After I got settled in my hotel, I called Kelly. His cell rang and rang and he answered on the first ring.

"Baby girl, they've started digging honey, this is our last chance if you want to make changes!" Kelly sounded excited.

"It's perfect Kelly. We made a perfect choice and is building about to start?" "Pretty soon honey, everything has been approved by the building inspector. There aren't any issues of any kind."

"You and I have to come to Egypt one-day honey, I spent quite a bit of time here during my early marriage. Alexandria is so amazing as well as Luxor. Kelly, I need to tell you something. Please remember always that you are my love, my only love. I belong to you my darling." I said hoping he understood what message I was trying to get across without coming out with the words.

"I adore you, Claudia, as much as I love you. Be safe, sweetheart, I'm waiting for you." He replied. I felt that he understood. "I needed to hear that Kel, I should go, but I will call you again. Later Sweetheart!" That was the magic I needed to get past my head.

The following morning, I had meetings with my local team and aid agencies. It would be a day of brainstorming and I immersed myself in the work. The days began to fly by and I looked forward to meeting my team in Nigeria.

The low status of Nigerian women hit home to me. It broke my heart to hear their stories of violence from the hands of their husbands. Marital rape must be suffered in silence and the fear of more beatings and rapes keeps many women from questioning their husbands' sexual escapades. For unmarried girls, the situation is even worse. If a rape is reported, it is the girl who suffers the shame and all chance of a future marriage. Under such circumstances, women's ability to protect themselves is minimal.

The amount of pain and suffering I witnessed while being invited to tour the Lagos slums with my team was eye-opening in more ways than one.

I was invited to take a tour with a group of Aid workers and my team took us into the Lagos slums and surrounding areas. We traveled for three days and I saw so many sights that I will never forget. It was a village outside of Abuja where a team of Canadian and American doctors had set up a clinic and it was then, during an introduction to the doctors that I heard the name Dr. Brownlow and my ears perked up.

"Dr. Brownlow I'm Claudia Samara, it's nice to meet you."

I knew immediately who she was and by the expression on her face, she knew who I was as well. I studied her, my heart began to race, it was so unbelievable "Please call me Clarissa. It's very nice meeting you, Claudia."

Clarissa appeared much younger than her age of 61, she was fifteen or sixteen when she gave birth to me. It was obvious she was my birth mother we looked so much alike. I continued shaking hands with the professionals and I was sure it was going to be an interesting evening.

As a courtesy to the clinic, we provided the meal that evening and I helped with preparing the food. I was slicing fresh vegetables when she appeared in the doorway. She came and sat down across the table from me, picked up a knife and began to slice. She looked over at me, "Claudia, you know who I am?"

I nodded. "Of all places to finally find you, Claudia, here in Africa, I've looked forward to this day for 46 years. A day hasn't passed that I didn't wake up thinking about my child, my daughter. I knew one day we would meet Claudia.

My insides did several flips, why didn't she look for me, I wanted to ask.

"Claudia there are things I need you to know, but this is not the right place or time."

"Yes, Clarissa we have so much to talk about and many questions that need answers." My eyes focused on hers as we spoke, they were soft warm eyes that oozed compassion. I felt her warmth immediately, and wondered if I would be dishonoring my mama's memory?"

"Tell me, where do you live?" She asked as her eyes moved across my face.

"Well after many years abroad I have returned to Canada, and I live in Penticton, near Naramata. Do you know the area?"

Clarissa nodded, "Yes, my dear child, I spent a time or two in that part of the country, my practice is in Vancouver, so we are not all that far away from each other. Claudia, I am finishing my rotation here in six weeks, then I'm returning to Canada. Please, I would like to meet with you. I would come to you if that would work, would that be okay?" She asked as she handed me a business card.

"Yes, that would be okay. I will call you when I get back."

"Please do call me Claudia?" she insisted. Her words warmed my inside. The rest of the evening I studied her. I had so many questions. Do I have siblings? The questions added up in my head. Then, I remembered the letter Mom had told me about, the letter in the back of their wedding picture. I would find it when I got home.

The next morning when we said our goodbyes, I was unable to refrain from reaching my arms out to hug her, to know what it felt like to be held by her. In my emotional state, it was difficult to hold the tears, I didn't intend to like her. But I immediately felt the connection.

"Claudia my child, you don't know how happy you have made me." She hugged me close. "Please come visit soon, I will be waiting for you."

My heart was smiling, "I will Clarissa, I will call you soon."

I left Africa with a new-found hope, I had wonderful parents, and now I had a second opportunity to be someone else's daughter.

"Be well Claudia!" She smiled at me.

It was now nearly two months since I left home and India was my last stop. Before arriving, I learned about the city of Vrindavan, where the widows go to die. With a population of nearly 60,000 people, Vrindavan in Uttar Pradesh is home to an estimated 20,000 widows. In many Indian societies, if a husband passes away, the wife bears the blame for her husband's death, which is considered a manifestation of the wife's past sins. From newly-weds to middle-aged mothers to elderly women who can barely walk, almost all are dressed in white. Considered a bad omen, widows are often abandoned by their families, left destitute, and forced to beg for daily survival.

From the start, I did not want was my staff to know of my profile. They knew that I was financing the projects, but I wanted to keep my life private. At the end of each tour, I hosted a dinner and spoke to them about inspiring these people to look after themselves and have the basic necessities of life.

I was fortunate to have Jasim's legal team to oversee this. When I spoke with them originally, to discuss my mission, I was surprised how proactive they were. Of course, I had a plan in place to track any misappropriation of funds and every movement was monitored, I prayed I had an honest team.

Chapter 25

THE 21-HOUR FLIGHT from Delhi to Penticton gave me time look at the proposals and feasibility reports from each team. We landed to re-fuel in Tokyo and I sat with anticipation of seeing Kelly and all the excitement that was going on with the new house.

We hadn't been able to speak all that much over the past few weeks due to the time changes and challenges with technology in the developing world. I thought about Tobago, do I tell him what happened? I knew I couldn't. He just needed to know it was finally all behind me. One day I would shock him and wear nipple and a clit clamps . . . but I would have to weigh it out. I must have fallen asleep because Slade was calling to alert me we were less than 15 minutes out of Vancouver. I yawned and prepared for customs as we waited for landing instructions.

Within the hour I was on my way home, saying the word "home" made me feel warm inside. I was about to be somewhere I wanted to be, I had never felt like this since I left home at 17.

It was early afternoon when we arrived in Penticton and the chance of Kelly being home wasn't great, so I expected an empty house. As I drove up the Bench I saw our new property and the changes to the landscape. I really wanted to stop in and see what was happening, but I decided I would wait until Kelly and I could go together.

I was right, the house was empty and I wanted to phone him desperately and tell him I was home, but I thought it would be romantic to have him walk in the door and find me here waiting for him in something seductive and alluring. I knew exactly what I would wear. I applied a pheromone body lotion everywhere on my body; a small amount of eye makeup; and swept my hair up off my face into a big knot at the back of my head held in by a diamond clip. Then I put on a beautiful handcrafted red silk corset. It felt so good against my skin. I tightened the strings at the back and had all the clasps in place, I felt so sensuous and anxious for Kelly. All I needed now, beside him, was a deep red lipstick to complete the look.

While I was waiting, I picked up the few items Kelly had left lying around. I went through my mail and checked the Internet for new incoming email. I was soon engrossed in my work and time was passing quickly. Then, I heard a vehicle pull up in the driveway.

I quickly refreshed my lipstick and was lighting candles when he walked in the door. "Well . . . isn't this a beautiful sight to come home to?" Kelly stopped in his spot. "Oh, Claudia you have my heart in my throat, wow," He elaborated. "Oh, you have no idea what you are doing to me right now."

He dropped his suit jacket on the floor while I remained in the same spot, waiting for him to reach me. When he did, I gasped in anticipation of his touch. His hand found a place at the base of the back of my neck, his thumb raised my mouth to meet his, and I felt my body shake.

"Oh yes, baby." He whispered as he swept my lips into his. I was eager and anxious, nothing slow paced, no seduction, just us getting inside the other.

"I hated being without you Kelly, I can't do it anymore," I said in between our hot passionate kisses. "I know what I have and I'm in it for as long as you want me," I said loud enough for him to hear. I felt his hands on my upper thighs, massaging my flesh, then his lips wandering along my neck.

"I want you for eternity Claudia," Kelly replied. His hands moved up the silky covered cheeks of my ass. "You look so amazing wearing this honey, but I really like you without it. I really have to remove it you know." He spoke as his lips just touched mine.

"I know, I think you better hurry Kelly. I want you, I want you to make me feel alive again." I t was seconds before I was naked in front of the man I love. I was undoing his zipper as his hands removed the clip that held my hair against my head, I felt it wash over my breasts, and then I was in his arms being carried to our bed.

There wasn't a place on my body that Kelly hadn't explored with either his hand or lips. I groaned at the sensation I was feeling as his lips kissed my vagina and his tongue snuck inside my clit hood. "Oh Kelly, yes, you, you!" I moaned. I knew I was secreting body juices and his little flicker of his tongue was building up the heat. I waited eagerly anticipating his entrance, and when it finally came, it was like a bolt of lightning striking its target. I exploded around him immediately.

"Oh, baby you liked that didn't you?" He growled. "Ugh . . . oh, yes Kelly, I like it . . . " I replied still moving in his rhythm, our eyes open as we watched the intensity of our act displayed in the others face. I felt my body peak and began to quake; Kelly's movement increased and I couldn't contain the sounds that were coming out from my insides. I knew I surrendered totally to love, to Kelly. My body vibrated magnificent and serene emotional sensations.

"You more than meet my needs, you've conquered my demons. I love you, only you Kel." I felt tears welling in my eyes and even through the blur, his tears were visible as well. Our noses met and our eyes connected. He reached both arms under me and pulled me up.

"I have waited a lifetime to know that Claudia, I am now, what I have needed to be, the man at your side." He sealed those words with the most loving and consuming kiss I had ever experienced. My heart was racing, yet my soul was rested.

We dressed and kissed and kissed some more. I had white wine chilling and Kelly poured us a glass. We talked about the things that had happened, his house had sold, and he had purchased a new pick-up truck. He smiled every time his eyes met mine. "Kiss me, Claudia." He whispered, "That's the only way I will be sure this isn't a dream."

I walked my fingers down the side of his mouth to his chin, bent forward and ran my tongue across his bottom lip, before taking it between mine, then I did the same to his upper one. His lips soon took control of mine.

"Yes, my dream came true." He giggled, we giggled together. "Isn't reality wonderful? I came face to face with another reality in Nigeria, I met her, my biological mother. She's a doctor, doing a rotation with Doctors without Borders. Kelly, she is younger than I imagined her to be. She is warm and likable." I said swirling the wine in my glass with one hand, and the other holding Kelly's.

He was massaging the space between my thumb and forefinger: it was a very erotic sensation. "I have her business card and agreed to give her a call in a few weeks. Kelly, this is so strange, everything is moving so quickly. I'm so thankful I have you to keep me in balance."

"I think that's what you do for me too, I'm at my best now then I have ever been because I have us to look forward to."

"There is one thing Kel, I can no longer be away from you for any length of time, it was almost unbearable this time. Maybe two or three days max, or I'm going to have to take you with me."

Kelly's hand cupped my cheek, "I'm glad you've come to this realization, it's fucking miserable being here without you Claudia. You have made my day." He sighed after he spoke. Kelly and I prepared dinner together and cleared the dishes away and crawled back into bed, making up for lost hours without each other.

I was wide awake when the sun found us. Kelly was nestled in beside me sleeping peacefully. I couldn't stop my heart from racing; his firm tanned muscular arms were the arms I couldn't wait to be safely wrapped in. I was so tempted to trace his pouting lips with my fingertips, but it was early and I was satisfied just watching him sleep. I reveled in his love for me.

I had just closed my eyes for a moment, when he whispered, "I like sensing your eyes on me, what a way to start a day." He flipped over onto his back, bringing me with him. I straddled him. With our palms flat against each other's, I fell into him and searched for his lips. Our first-morning kiss was just as hot. He slid his palms down the sides of my breasts all the way to my waist before hoisting me up over him, Kelly was directing his erect long penis slowly and precisely into me. I gasped at the awareness.

I was feeling as he made contact and with each thrust, I was dancing with pleasure. We both collapsed in pure bliss. "This is what a good morning is like!" Kelly said grinning. "For an old couple I'd say we're doing mighty good, wouldn't you say woman?" He turned to me then placed his palm in the space between my breasts, "Oh yes my girl is definitely satisfied."

He commented and my eyes followed his that were now resting on my very erect nipples. He leaned in and I saw his tongue close in onto my nipple, closing my eyes I welcomed the shivers he was creating with the flick of his tongue. Then, his tongue, slick and wet, he roamed over the area and soon had my nipple and areola filling his mouth: he sucked and pulled it. I was feeling the tingling through to my clit.

He found my vagina and his fingers massaged it as they entered in and out of me. His teeth were grazing me just enough to feel a sharp jolt, he bit down carefully and I climaxed immediately making me woozy and on fire. He didn't let up, the intensity was building again, but this time he was banging himself into me.

"Oh, that feels so good . . . " I said throaty, he kept his pace moving harder and trying to get deeper. I was lost in ecstasy, little explosions went off all through me until I reached my peak again, and climaxed. I heard Kelly's sigh and he too was in the same land of ecstasy. I lay there, eyes closed, concentrating on what was happening inside my body. I never experienced or ever wanted to acknowledge the sensations.

It was Kelly's hands stroking my face and hair that brought me to the present moment. "Where were you sweetheart that was such a sensual look on your face?" He whispered.

"I was with my body taking stock on every sensation I could reach, Kelly my senses have come to life. Can we do that again?" I sounded serious. His head bobbed back.

"Right now!" he exclaimed.

I smirked, "Got yeah . . . I laughed. "No honey, I'll wait until later." Then it became a tickle session, we almost fell out of bed laughing so hard. I became short of breath and couldn't stop panting, It all felt so magical.

"Shower time!" he announced.

"Oh, I think I'll pass, I want to take the heady smell of our sex with me everywhere I go today."

"Really?" he asked.

I nodded. "Yes, there's not better fragrance than you and me!" I kept a straight poker face. It was only seconds later did he realize I was teasing him. I was over his shoulder being escorted into the shower.

"Now I get to do this . . . " and his hands moved the soap around my body and his fingers slick as they grazed my swollen clit. I followed his lead; the heat between us was like an inferno, inextinguishable. So, finally, now, all of this because I had surrendered to love.

Over breakfast, I asked him if he had time to take me over to our new house. "Oh honey I don't think this morning would be a good time, could it wait until this evening? I have a meeting with Daniel in Kelowna before our big meeting at Big White. Why don't you come into Kelowna with me for the day? You could do some shopping or whatever while I meet with Daniel then we'll go up to Big White, there is a wine event happening today. You can sample while we work. What do you say?"

"Why I'd like that, yes sweetheart I'd love to do that. Let's see . . . what should I wear?" I said as I tapped my chin and bottom lip, "Oh I know, that little red number you quickly removed from me last night." I teased.

"Oh you are so full of it, what am I going to do with you, Ms. Samara?" He growled.

"Exactly what you've been doing, fucking me good, and loving me immensely!" I replied earnestly.

"Anytime and always my dear, and that's a promise." We dressed and dragged ourselves out to meet up with the rest of the world.

I was feeling rather tipsy; a happiness that I had no idea was possible. My day in Kelowna had been premium, now it was okay for the world to see me. I found a couple of dresses and a pair of shoes, but I really wasn't all that interested in shopping. Daina had gone to the coast to visit with her family so she wasn't around.

On the drive home, it was nice to be seated beside Kelly and just relax. I could see he was in deep thought, probably business. I cranked up the volume, Kelly had some good rock on his player. I couldn't contain myself, I was in the mood to sing and Kelly joined in.

We pulled into our new driveway and got out of the truck. We stood side-by-side and Kelly said, "I like saying I love you, Claudia! I would say it over and over again until the cows come home because it's so much a part of me. So, Claudia, my darling Claudia I love you! That's all I want to say for now." He kissed me deeply and tenderly I thought I was in heaven.

I pulled away slightly to look into his eyes. "I will never tire hearing those words Kelly, they are words that feed my soul. My sweet, sweet, patient, patient, Kelly. I love you, I'm in love. I love you with every proton and ion in my being. I have the best now that I have you." I stated passionately. I was soon off my feet being twirled and my face was being covered in his kisses.

Then he rested me on my feet, "So my love, shall we go see our house?" He glowed.

"Yes, yes, yes, yes!" Kelly took my hand and I was so excited. I was about to see our house for the first time.

"Honey, close your eyes and don't open them until I place you down, I am going to carry you okay?" Kelly insisted. "I want you to experience the view in a certain spot before you see the rest."

"Okay, but I've seen the view before," I replied.

"Not like this," Kelly said as he carried me for what seemed to take forever.

"Okay babe, I'm going to set you down. Okay, Claudia, you can open those beautiful eyes."

I opened my eyes and couldn't believe what I was seeing. It was the most exquisite view of the lake and Penticton—and a table with two glasses and a bottle of champagne. "Kelly I'm utterly speechless. Look at this! We're going to be looking at this for the rest of our lives!" I said enthusiastically.

"Yes baby, we are going to have this for the rest of our lives." Then I watched him drop to one knee, I was puzzled until I clued in. "Claudia, I have waited 36 years for this moment and today I can finally make that promise and commitment to you if you will accept my proposal. Claudia please, will you marry me?" Kelly glowed as he spoke.

I started to quiver and my heart was in my throat. "Oh my, yes, yes darling I will marry you!"

Kelly reached into his pocket and held out a ring. "I chose this, it's a ruby and titanium band. If you're not comfortable, we can go together and choose something you would be comfortable with.

I just shook my head, "How perfect, it is the most perfect ring, I already love it. But not as much as I love you!" I said as the tears streamed down my cheeks.

"You can wear it now or wait until we say our vows honey it's up to you." Kelly kissed my fingers.

"I'll wait for our vows."

His arms were soon embracing me. My ears perked up at the familiar sound of a single flute, it was Beloved by Elias Rahbani, a Lebanese composer and the music that inspired Mikhail and me.

"I don't want to wait to marry you Claudia and I hope you feel the same way as me?" He alluded.

"I don't want to wait either," I said shaking my head. "I'm so sure about us Kelly. There is no reason to wait. Hell, I'd marry you on the beach in a bikini."

With the end of the music Kelly escorted me to the table, the sun was setting and the crimson and peach colored sky was the backdrop. A server appeared and uncorked the champagne.

Kelly said, "To my cherished one!"

We toasted and I looked across the water to the sparkling lights and whispered to Kelly as I held up my glass, "To my love my only love!" We sipped again and then sat together on a swinging patio loveseat.

Kelly chuckled, "Is this rocking the beginning of our golden years my dear?" Then he made a request, "If it is all right with you, I would like Jason and Justine to witness our vows." Kelly looked at me. "Really, they would want to?" I questioned curiously.

"Yes honey, I was sure you'd accept my proposal, so I discussed it with them and Claudia they think like I do, if you are my happiness then they are happy to."

"Of course, having them witness our vows is more than all right with me. There couldn't be anything more special than the ones who love you the most being there on our wedding day." I was honored. When Kelly said he didn't want to wait, I thought I would have at least a month, but he meant within the week. I didn't need a fancy dress or all the expensive details, but I wondered where the ceremony would be.

Back home I took a long bath while Kelly made some phone calls. I felt the calmest and most at peace with my life and the world around me. My life with Kelly has been like breathing, it just happens, easy, and natural in every way. I knew right then where I wanted to marry this man. I scrambled out of the tub and wrapping a towel around myself I found Kelly with a stack of papers.

"Did you have a good bath?" He asked as I rested my elbow on his shoulder and stood beside him.

"I know where and how I would like to become your wife Kelly. At dawn, on the top of Apex Mountain, amongst the wildflowers, closer to heaven so Mikhail, Papa, and Mom will be closer." I rested my chin on my elbow as I looked into his face, that loving face.

"I think that's a wonderful place to get married, so now we need to get a marriage license and someone that likes to get up before dawn. Just as long as I marry you, Claudia."

"There is one last thing, a flute player, you've always been so aware that it's important to me."

"We need to find out if the lodge is open this early in May. I think we should plan to bring everyone up the night before and that would give us the time we need to search out the right spot." Kelly suggested.

"The challenge is finding a marriage commissioner on short notice."

"No, we'll find one. I like the idea of a Sunday morning, the first day of the week at dawn." He suggested.

I smiled, "Yes I like that idea. So then, let's make this coming Sunday our wedding day May 23, 2002. The excitement was setting in. "To change the subject, I think we need to get rid of this!" Kelly said as he unfolded the end of my towel. "I think I'd like a little nibble starting right here." Kelly's teeth grazed along my jaw, then into my neck. "You know a towel is not much protection against your horny fiancé', and right now he is extremely bothered."

Kelly's hands were moving over my breasts. Then he hoisted me up off my feet, as he stood up and carried me towards our bedroom and I rested my head against him. "I'm going to be Claudia MacAskill," I whispered in his ear.

"You bet you are, Mrs. Claudia MacAskill, that sounds pretty awesome to me baby," Kelly added.

I watched as he undressed, he looked magnificent naked. Not very many men I knew at his age were in that shape. "Honey, flex those muscles for me, that is so hot." He posed, grinning from ear to ear, "There's another muscle wanting attention you know."

"Oh yes, I have been watching that with great interest," I said appreciatively of his manhood. I pulled back the covers for him, and as always, I couldn't wait to feel his nakedness against mine.

Sunday arrived and there we were on top of a mountain, about to get married. Kelly and I chose black and white: I in a white fitted pantsuit and him in a black casual suit with a black body shirt underneath. There wasn't any marching down any imaginary isle, just the six of us, Justine, Jason, Marjorie who played the flute the marriage commissioner and the two of us. We walked to the spot Kelly and I found amongst a carpet of wild mountain flowers.

Kelly and I faced each other. Kelly took both my hands and we said the traditional vows. It was special, yet simple and the sound of the flute was so peacefully: for me it was perfect. My emotions took over when Kelly placed the wedding band on my finger. And he the same as I placed his brushed titanium band on his finger. Kelly took my hands to his mouth and kissed my fingers before the marriage commissioner pronounced us husband and wife.

She didn't need to tell him he could kiss his wife, he was a bit ahead of her. "Oh Claudia we made it, we did it." To everyone he announced, "I am such a happy man!"

"Kelly, there was years when we were apart and yet you were always so close. The picture I had of you in my mind got me through some awful times, you were always close to me. Today as we watched the sunrise, every sunrise will remind me of today. You are my love, my only love! I am a very happy wife." I glowed from inside

The decision to keep the wedding intimate was something that was right for us, even though our friends and Kelly's grandchildren and his parents didn't attend was because there was a lot of healing that needed to be done. We had each other and felt that was all we needed.

Justine and Jason both commented to me that their dad became alive again when we found each other. Justine said something that I didn't expect, "I believe that Mom loved you Claudia and she is smiling right now. How could she not? Knowing two of her best friends are finally where they belong, together."

I was so touched and I did feel that. Cindy always wanted the best for everyone. As our limousine whisked away from the mountain, Jason surprised his father, "Dad your offer, is it still on the table? I would really like to work with you and Daniel especially knowing that I would be the head of marketing."

"That's fantastic son, Daniel will be thrilled that you accepted too."

Then Justine asked, "You are taking Claudia on honeymoon, right?"

I answered for Kelly, "Yes we are going to take some time away, but right now with the construction of the new house and the plans for the vineyard, it's not the right time. But as I told your dad, I am on a honeymoon every day with him, so going away is not necessary." I stroked his cheek.

"See why I rushed her into marrying me! I wasn't about to let her get away again." "We are going to the Lakeside Resort for a celebratory breakfast,"

I had planned our honeymoon and I hoped my plan would work, but I still hadn't figured out how I would get him to the airport. Then occurred to me, I could get my stepdaughter to help out. I nodded towards the washroom we excused ourselves from the table.

"Justine, I have a surprise for your dad, I need to get him to the Penticton Airport. The jet is ready to take us to Venice for a few days, so I need you to insist that you really want to see the jet. I pleaded.

"Really Claudia? Oh, that is so romantic and he has no idea?"

I shook my head.

"I am so in, and I will figure a way to clue Jason too. We'll get him there. Oh, I'm so excited for you both, he deserves that Claudia. I always suspected something wasn't right, and I can see the lighter version of my dad. Okay, Claudia let's go do this." She said excitedly.

Her arms were quickly wrapped around me. "You are so good for him!"

"It's mutual, believe me, he's dealt with a lot a lot more than he'll ever say when it comes to me. He definitely is one special man and I intend to make him feel that way for the rest of my life. I adore him, Justine. I really need you to know that." I pleaded.

"It's obvious Claudia, you don't need to convince me, just be happy together."

Justine waited a perfect amount of time, "Claudia was explaining a little a bit about the foundation and the vision she has for all the mission. I think it's an awesome idea having an office right in the jet. I know it's your special day, but we don't often get out to Penticton and if you guys have the time could we take a quick look. I promise to take only 10 minutes of your time and then you guys can go home or do what you were planning. Please, Claudia, I know Jason would be into, right Jas?"

I watched her; she was good. "Sounds okay with me," I answered. "Kelly honey you don't have any pressing plans, do you?" I said trying not to meet his eyes for too long because I knew my smile would make him curious.

"Sure, I guess. Then I want my wife to myself! Deal?" Kelly stated.

"Yes Dad, besides I must get back to Kelowna, both kids have activities that need both of us, you know opposite directions almost at the same time. Life as a parent." Justine remarked.

Kelly placed his napkin on his plate and bent over kissing my cheek. "Okay, I'm going to handle the bill and then are we all ready to head out?"

Kelly knew something was going on because the jet was out of the hanger and as we pulled up Justine commented, "You have a good time, you lucky devil!"

Kelly looked at me and tilted his head, "Claudia what's going on here?"

"You'll have to wait and see my darling. I think you might like it. We've got to go, Slade is waiting."

Jason and Justine both hugged us and I took my husband by the hand and headed to the waiting jet.

Slade came out of the cockpit and announced, "Mr. and Mrs. Mac Askill, we will be taking off as soon as you two are settled."

"Thanks, Slade," I replied. Soon the engines were whining and we were moving down the runway.

"Claudia, you . . . he tipped my chin and kissed me softly. You are such a brat, and I love that about you., It's difficult having a wife who is super rich. I know it will take some time to get accustomed to it, but I'm not going to deny it, sweetheart, this is awesome. But where are you taking us?" Kelly turned his head to the side as he spoke.

I smiled, "You are going to have to wait for a little over eight hour's darling." I replied feeling a little smug. "That's not too bad now, is it? We even have time to . . . well, we can use that time to consummate our marriage, we can't put that on hold for much longer husband, now can we?" I cooed and moved towards him, sliding my tongue over my lips as I kept my eyes on him.

"Claudia, we haven't even reached our altitude were still climbing," Kelly said as he fidgeted. I knew I was arousing him and I continued to do so by undoing his jacket, rubbing my hand over his chest.

"Just being near you makes my panties wet, Kelly," I said as I focused my eyes on his chest; now rising and falling at a more rapid pace. I bent over nestling at his chin far enough away to kiss and gently suck his jaw before his hands brought my chin up to meet his mouth. I heard a "ping", the signal that we had reached altitude and I didn't waste any time undoing our seat belts.

I reached over him and placed my hands firmly on his knees. "This is my gig while I have you in the jet, you hear me Mr. Mac Askill?" I said dominantly.

He nodded "Yes, I hear you Mrs. Mac Askill ma'am." Kelly swallowed and grinned.

"Mr. Mac Askill sir, it is necessary for you to undo this," I said calmly as I pulled at my jacket lapel.

"It's my pleasure, Mrs. Mac."

Kelly's fingers began at the bottom of my jacket and making his way up, he threw it open. I saw his hand reaching for my breast. I held up my hand and slowly shook my head.

"I didn't say go yet. No baby! Not yet." I sat on his lap. "My turn now."

I finished removing the buttons from their holes then pulled his arms through the sleeves. His black body shirt was like a second skin, tight against his body. "Oh . . . so sexy baby, you make me drool. But it has, it has to go."

I wrinkled my nose and pierced my lips. Kelly's eyes were filled with passion. I was melting and having a difficult time completing my dominant role. I pulled his shirt off and dropped it to the floor. I stood up, about to move back slightly but Kelly was too quick, he grabbed the waistband of my trousers, undid my zipper and clasp. His eyes were focused at my belly as he moved his flat palm between my skin and panties, he moved across my bare skin a few times before his index finger contacted my sweet spot.

I moved in closer and pulled his hair through my fingers as his forehead rested on my belly. My trousers and panties fell to the floor. He pulled me closer as he covered my pelvis with kisses. I melt at his touch, I thanked God for this man and the gentleness of what perfect lovemaking can be.

"So, Mrs. Mac, I think you still have way too many clothes on, I really like my wife's breasts, they are perfect just like her." Kelly's hands moved under the cups of my bra and he enclosed my breast in each hand tenderly squeezing them. I moaned in pleasure. I knew I would never get enough of his touch, I also knew there was so much love inside of me to give this man and this man only.

"Let's get this off of you," he said reaching his arms around me to unhook my bra, I took the moment to run my face up his chest even the hairs on his chest turned me on. My body felt like jelly from his touch. With our fingers at our sides, we entwined them as our mouths were exploring each other's hungrily before we came together intimately as husband and wife.

I lay with my head on his chest and his arm wrapped around me, there was a real sense of completion of the long 28-year journey bringing us to this day. Kelly pulled back up against the pillow. I was not ready to let him release me.

"Welcome to the mile-high club, Mr. Mac." I chuckled.

"Oh, hey yeah, nice club to be in baby," Kelly replied. "A question Claudia, what about my passport, am I not going to need it?" He asked.

"Yes, I've got it all covered." I moved on top of him propping my elbows on a pillow while we talked.

"I could stay right here in the cabin with you Claudia and it would be a perfect honeymoon. But I guess anywhere I am with you is all that matters."

“Oh . . . honey, yes . . . that is so true.” I left him alone in the bed and wrapped a sarong around me to get the bottle of champagne sitting in ice.

We toasted and without knowing how long we would be in the air, he asked, “Do we have time to catch a nap?”

I knew he was exhausted. He had been going steady and traveling back and forth from Kelowna to Penticton. He was determined to get us into our house before winter.

I checked the time. “Yes honey there is time for you to sleep, I’ll call the cockpit and have them buzz us an hour before we land.”

“When we land where?” Kelly thought he could trick me.

“Nice try husband.” I scolded lovingly and wandered up to the cockpit and stuck my head in.

“Hi, Slade.”

You look really happy Claudia, I’m glad for you.”

“Slade you are like family to me. I just came up to ask you to give us a buzz an hour before we land.”

“Of course.”

A few hours later he awoke and asked, “So now Mrs. Mac, are you going to tell me where you have brought me?” Kelly winked.

I shook my head and smiled at the very curious Kelly. “No!”

Then, as we prepared for landing I suggested, “Let’s look and see where we are. What is the name on the Terminal Kel, can you read it?”

It read Marco Polo International Airport. “I guess, Venice?”

“Yes we are in Venice darling, are you excited?” I asked.

“How could I not be, just seeing your face is exciting Claudia, anywhere with you would be just fine with me. Venice is going to be pretty special for us. I’ve never been.” Kelly grabbed me and pulled me into his arms. “Look out Venice here come the MacAskill’s!” His mouth took mine in a very long deep erotic kiss.

“God how I love you, Mr. Mac.”

“Ditto darling!”

"Kel, I have your passport in my bag along with mine. You ready?" I heard Slade unlocking the door and the customs officers were meeting the jet.

Once we cleared customs and left the main terminal, a white limo was waiting to take us to the glamorous Hotel Danieli. I stood beside Kelly as the reservations were being confirmed at the reception desk. He almost gagged. The 9900 Euros per night took him completely off guard. The look on his face was priceless!

The Doge Dandolo Royal Suite was exactly as the name said, it was "royal" in every way. The suite overlooked the Venice lagoon with 180-degree views of the Grand Canal and San Giorgio Maggiore Island. The walls were covered in antique portraits and a bookcase showcased rare silver pieces. The central lounge suite featured ornate gilded Baroque armchairs in gold damask and marble Carrara coffee table. The bedroom ceiling was graced with an original eighteenth-century fresco, antique carpets covered heritage Venetian terrazzo floors, and floor-to-ceiling gold tinged silk curtains.

Kelly remarked, "Claudia, look down there, let's go for a gondola ride, it's a beautiful night and maybe we could have something to eat." Kelly had definitely gotten caught up in the magic of Venice.

We rode on the gondola to the Bridge of Sigh's which the story tells that if a couple kisses under the bridge while drifting below on a gondola at sunset, they will enjoy eternal love. Thus the 'sighs' are said to come from lovers who are overwhelmed by the romance of the whole scene. Originally it was built in the 16th century, and it was the last view prisoners would see as they walked from the prison and interrogation rooms in Doge's Palace to their execution.

Kelly reminded me of Lord Byron's writing "I stood in Venice on the Bridge of Sighs, a palace and a prison on each hand." I thought about that writing, what a great souvenir of our wedding if we could find a copy here in Venice.

The next morning, we got up before seven o'clock, had a romantic breakfast on the terrace and welcomed the beautiful sunny day. We took in as much sightseeing as possible starting on the Canal Grande with the Basilica di Santa Maria Gloriosa dei Frari and St Mark's Basilica; we went to bookstores where we happened to stumble on Lord Byron's writings. There was so much to see. Plus, I wanted desperately to find fabrics and was directed to Rubelli, and Chiarastella Cattana.

We were back at the hotel by six o'clock for massages and spa treatments. Kelly had no idea he'd be getting a head to toe Italian overhaul! I got the "what's going on now" look from my husband and I just smiled.

"Oh you wait and see, I'll see you upstairs later honey, enjoy." I kissed my husband and we parted for our treatments.

I felt like the bride I'd always hoped I would be, for Kelly's eyes. My desire was to "wow" him. Feeling as beautiful as I knew Kelly would find me, created an urgency to see him in his black suit. I walked onto the terrace and I saw the restaurant below was booked just for us.

The glimmering hurricane table lamps reflected a gold light into the dark blue evening sky. Kelly had his back to me, he stood staring out to San Giorgio Maggiore Island. I knew he sensed my presence and turned around.

"Oh Claudia, oh wow, you are so beautiful." He said with a loving look on his face and then smiled so bright my stomach did their flips. The sight of Kelly was the most delicious image I could have imagined. I was soon in the arms of my one and only love, and a quartet was playing the Italian wedding song.

> Only for you in every way, my whole life through, love will be yours, all that I have, to give and every day I live, only for you so love for me you always be the sunshine your kiss a sweet a grape on a vine on this our wedding day come taste the wine
>
> All that I am all that I do come what may until eternity my love will always be from me to you.

I had no idea that the hotel would provide us with music such beautiful romantic music.

The quartet continued to play Italian love songs all through the meal that was created especially for Kelly and I. We drank Krug Rosé Brut champagne, we fed each other, kissed, ate more, kissed again, danced, and drank champagne.

Chapter 26

LIFE COULDN'T GET ANY BETTER. The honeymoon was over and back home and Kelly was working in our vineyard while construction on our house was coming to an end. This was definitely the life I was meant to live. I really liked wearing blue jeans and tank tops, and dressing down was allowing me to get back to my roots. I loved getting out in the vineyard with Kelly and the crew, knowing that my hands would also be part of the success was so rewarding

The quiet and peacefulness in the valley were wonderful, but my thoughts of Clarissa came to the front and I knew I owed her that phone call as well as to myself. I knew it was time, time to face the fear and move forward. I was safe and secure in every aspect of my life. I would call Clarissa this evening.

I got the chicken in a marinade ready to go, the rest could wait until Kelly came home. I showered, changed and then decided to read the letter that I had been putting off for such a long time. It was addressed to Mr. and Mrs. Samara . . . I took a deep breath and opened it.

> August 7,1956
>
> Dear Mr. & Mrs. Samara,
>
> I am Clarissa Brownlow, we have never formally met. I am writing to you because I am the mother of the little girl you adopted. I was not permitted to make my own choices and

because I was only 15 my parents made that decision for me. I want my baby back. I know that without you being in agreement that won't happen. I love my daughter and I think about her every day. I am living with my auntie now who is willing to help me raise her while I attend school and university where I will be studying to become a doctor. I know it will be very hard work, but I am prepared to do that. Please reconsider. You can contact me at the address posted above.

Thank you, Clarissa Brownlow

I must have read the letter four or five times before putting it down. I knew my folks would never have complied with her wishes because they had tried for many years to have children of their own and failed. I knew they must have panicked after reading this letter. But she loved me: Clarissa Brownlow loved me and didn't want to give me up.

I felt relief: I wasn't rejected. However, the rest of her story was still too much of a mystery. I needed and wanted more details. It was the right time to call. I wasn't going to hesitate any longer. I dialed the number and waited.

"This is Dr. Brownlow speaking." Her soft pleasant voice came across the line. "Hello, Clarissa this is Clau . . . " I started to say when she interrupted.

"Claudia, yes I recognize your voice, it is so good to hear from you. I'm sorry for interrupting dear. I have been waiting patiently to hear from you." Clarissa's nervousness was obvious under her gentle voice.

"I understand. I know it has taken me awhile to contact you and I apologize. I am hoping we could meet soon, maybe in the next few days. I am going to be in Vancouver the day after tomorrow would you have time to meet with me?" I lied, I had no plans, but I was now desperate for answers.

"Claudia, I will make time, what time would be best for you? I could arrange for lunch here at my office. We could eat on my private balcony." Clarissa sounded as eager as me. Shit, I haven't even discussed this with Kelly, here I am planning to take off again, but it wouldn't be for more than a day, gone first thing in the morning and fly back that afternoon, maybe even in time for dinner.

"Thursday would work well for me Clarissa, what time do you think?"

"12:30, I will be done with my last patient and you have my undivided attention for the rest of the afternoon. Do you eat sushi, Claudia?"

All that ran through my mind was her gentleness. She was kind and I liked her strangely enough. "Yes, 12:30 works for me Clarissa and yes sushi would be just fine. So I will see you then." I wanted to keep it short, there were so many questions and I didn't want to get too much into a conversation. We said our goodbyes and once again I picked up the letter and read it. I needed to show this to Clarissa.

I thought about Kelly, now, I had to break it to him. I didn't think he would have any problem with me leaving, especially under the circumstances. I thought to myself, I have an idea . . . I went to our closet and found one of his white dress shirts and a black tie. I also had a pair of black silk stockings, the "stay up" kind. Oh yeah baby, this will turn your crank! I figured he'd be home before six, so I phoned to be sure.

"Hi babe, everything okay?" Kelly asked.

"I hope so, I just talked with Clarissa and I ended up making a date with her on Thursday, is that okay, did you need me for anything?" I knew his answer, but this would be my reason to find out when he would be home so I could be ready.

"Of course, it's okay sweetheart, when are you planning this for?" Kelly's cheerful voice responded.

"Thursday, I'll fly there and be back in time for dinner okay? Oh, that reminds me, I have chicken marinating are you barbecuing, or am I?" I had a good lead in.

"No babe I'll do the cooking, I shouldn't be too much longer, within the hour. Okay?" He replied.

"Great you're much better at it than me. Love you, babe!" I replied.

"I love you, Claudia, see you shortly."

Oh good, I quickly slipped into his shirt, rolled up the silk stockings, which felt so smooth and added to my sensual frame of mind. My eyes caught a pair of sexy red stilettoes . . . yep perfect. I undid the braid and my soft curls released around me. I knew how much he loved my hair and getting his fingers caught in it. I fluffed it up perfect, perfect, then a bit of lipstick, a shade of deep pink and finally, a little eye make-up and I was set.

As I waited for the sound of Kelly's truck, I chopped vegetables for a salad and got the skews in place and everything was ready to go. I poured myself a glass of wine, turned on the iPod and sang along with some of my favorites. A few minutes later my husband was coming through the door and I was in position.

"Hi honey, look at you, oh my, what do I have here?" Kelly whistled.

"Hi sweetheart, hey could you give me a hand here?" I asked as I stretched reaching up to the top cupboard revealing only my long brown legs as they met my hips and then his shirt was riding over the cheeks of my ass. Turning to face him, my naked mound was exposed and Kelly stood and grinned. He headed in my direction and his eyes scanned my naked thighs.

He suggested, "Honey, I think if you stand on your tiptoes and try again you should be successful."

"Well, that's a good idea honey, Oh my!" I remarked as Kelly's shirt rose even higher this time. My husband's fingers slowly moved up the side of my knee over my hip and back down to where the stocking met. His breath was warm against my hair, while his other hand held my reaching arm up.

"You're looking awfully hot in my shirt Mrs. Mac. I'd like to check and see what the temperature is like between those thighs

Claudia, but I really need to shower." Kelly teased, knowing that I would be on the edge. He ran his finger along my bottom lip, kissing me slowly and softly. I was ready to crush his mouth when he pulled away. "Be right back babe, I really need a shower."

He winked and left me stunned, craving his touch. I sighed, just a little and thought about joining him in the shower. Then, I pouted because I didn't get my way. That was when I decided to light the barbecue and start cooking. I kicked off my stilettoes and pulled off my silk stockings and got rid of the black tie. I gathered my hair and braided it once again. I put all thoughts of seduction out of my mind and pulled out the food processor to make one of my favorite dressings for the salad, with the music and the loud processor I wasn't aware of Kelly coming in behind me.

But then, the sensation of his hands running up and down my ass cheeks surprised me. I attempted to turn and face him. "Stay right where you are!" Kelly ordered pressing his cheek against mine. He ran his tongue along my earlobe and gently nibbled on it pulling so gently with his teeth. "This is nice finding you in nothing else but my shirt, you're so hot, so beautiful my darling." Kelly then continued his kisses all the way down my neck and into the hollow. I attempted to turn. "No Claudia, stay right here." He said ordering me. I was becoming excited at his touch.

"Kelly the chicken is cooking on the barbecue! It's going to burn if I don't get to it." I responded.

"No way, I thought I was going to do the cooking? Wow talk about bursting my bubble, I had plans for you, my sexy woman, but I guess the barbecue is going to get my undivided attention. Sorry honey if you only knew what I had in mind for you." Kelly was now heading to the patio. I smiled and basted the skewers with an olive oil, lemon and dill coating.

Over dinner, Kelly had things on his mind and I knew something was up, but I knew he would talk about it eventually.

"So, you spoke with Clarissa today, how did it go? Other than you are going to see her and all." Kelly lifted his fork in the air and reached over for a piece of chicken.

"We had a good conversation, she was happy to hear from me. I like her, there is something about her that puts me at ease. I am actually looking forward to meeting with her on Thursday." I said before stuffing a mushroom in my mouth.

"That's good honey, ask all the questions you have for her."

"Yes, it's not so much my questions, it's what I have to tell her that is going to be hard." I picked at my chicken, then I got up from the table and returned with the bottle of wine and refilled our glasses.

"Honey, up in that cupboard there is a bowl, would you go get it for me?" Kelly said seriously.

"Nice try Kel, you had your chance." I smiled wide and watched as he winked.

"Have you spoken with Daina lately?" Kelly asked. No, not for a couple of weeks since we've come back, but I did get her a phone message and I was planning on giving her a callback, why?"

"Daniel was curious if we would be coming for dinner next week?" He announced with a cheeky expression, leaving me to wonder if I should know something, or if he was scheming.

Knowing him, I decided he was scheming. "Should I call her right now?"

"No, I accepted the dinner invitation honey, you can call her tomorrow or whenever.

I got up from the table and Kelly snuck up quietly behind me. I felt his finger slide up the crease of my cheeks, slowly, as he pushed his foot under me and rested it against mine.

"You don't think I'm going to let my pretty wife's hard work go to waste do you, sweetheart?" His body was tight against mine and his tongue was finding all the little spots at the nape of my neck that sent shivers down my spine. "Let's get these buttons undone!" as he unfastened all but the middle button. "Yes, that should work, yes much better, what's going on here?"

The sensation of his fingers, as they ran up my belly, contacted my nipple with his forefinger was adding to my arousal. "Very nice and soft and hard, yes that's what I like Claudia, feeling how your nipples become erect at my touch. Turn around baby."

I did as he asked. My husband rested his forehead against mine. "I love how you surprise me like this, you know how to turn your husband on." Kiss after kiss covered my eyes and my nose all around the corners of my lips until his tongue slid along the crease at my lips. Slowly he entered my mouth, our tongues dancing, while his hands took mine and held them up even with my shoulders. The kiss extended down my chin and the arousal between my legs was tingling. I closed my eyes and inhaled each sensation. His hands placed mine on my breasts.

"Feel how hard your nipples are Claudia, roll them in between your fingers for me baby. Yes, that's my girl keep them hard and erect for me." I was so focused on my nipples and the sensations going through my body I was brought back by his wet tongue sliding from one opening to the other and all around the labia, inside the clit hood, he darted his tongue in and out quickly slapping the clit.

"Oh yes . . . " I moaned.

Kelly had both his hands gripping my calves keeping my legs apart. He continued his routine, I knew my clit was swollen it was throbbing in response to his teasing. Quickly he pushed his tongue into me and I tried to arch my back, unsuccessfully, I moaned when two fingers entered and fucked me in and out, the wet moist natural lube was slick as his pace increased. I could feel my orgasm building and I began to quiver. Kelly stopped. "No Claudia, wait . . . I want you to suck me now please."

I dropped to my knees to meet him. Kelly was removing his jeans and his length was hard and thick waiting for my lips to bring it in. I licked my lips as I stared into Kelly's eyes, then, I took this beautiful part of my man slowly into my mouth until only the ridge was inside. My tongue moved in and around over and under, then it covered the tip licking the tiny hole. I sucked him in deep and pulled my lips hard and quick up and down sucking him tighter. Kelly breaths were deeper and he pushed against the back of my throat, I almost lost my breath. Once more he pushed and the next time, the warmth of his cum was filling my throat. He groaned as he unloaded his orgasm. I swallowed as he released himself from my lips. I smiled at the sight of my serene husband's face.

He was beaded with perspiration and when his eyes opened. I reached down and pulled a now softer piece of him, my finger massaging the head. Kelly pulled away and laid me on the floor on my back, he cupped the back of my head as a support.

"Honey bring your legs up over my shoulders, as I did, he pulled my bottom up onto his upper legs, as he knelt in front of me. "Good just a little bit more." I wiggled up my opening was at face level, there was no hesitation, Kelly resumed his attack on my genitals, licking and sucking and tongue fucking me. I pushed against his face and knew I was on the edge, the familiar sounds of my moans alerted Kelly. Retrieving his hands and letting my head gently rest on the floor, he brought my legs forward and then directed them under his arms. Still kneeling, he pulled me up on top of him, his hands on my waist as he directed me so he could enter me, and he plunged deep and I squealed at the sensation that was rippling through me. His strokes were religious, and I succumbed to the desires of my orgasm and quivered in delight.

Kelly lifted me off and we untangled our bodies and knelt in front of each other, our mouths searching deeply harder Kelly's finger sliding in between me until they were deep inside, "Cum again Claudia, cum all over my hand I want to lick you off my fingers". He continued fucking me, pushing his fingers deep as deep as he could get, while his thumb tapped my clit. Then a sharp slap as his hand connected with my bare ass. I gasped and climaxed all at the same time, screaming out his name.

"Oh, Christ Kelly ooh shit!" I was convulsing I could feel the juices leaving my body. He continued massaging the entrance.

"Good girl, yes that's nice." He stuck his two fingers in his mouth. "Mm . . . you taste good." Kelly's glowing blue eyes expressed his satisfaction. I stood up in front of him, spreading my legs and taking my breasts in my hands. "I'm oozing still baby." I moaned, he pulled his face against my pelvis and lapped up the remainder.

The jet cleared the Penticton runway and soared over Skaha Lake before turning to the west. We would be landing at Vancouver International Airport in less than 20 minutes. Rob, with his limo, would be waiting. I pulled Clarissa's letter out of my bag and read it again looking at the date August 1956, I was just a year old when she sent this. I knew how heartbreaking it was when my son died, but it must have been brutal knowing your child wasn't far away, yet you couldn't see her.

The ice-cold water ran down my chin, as I missed connecting the bottle mouth to my lips, because my thoughts were elsewhere, elsewhere with my biological mother.

"Shit, good one Claudia!" I scolded myself.

Slade buzzed from the cockpit. "Hi, Slade."

"I have just been notified we are third in line for landing."

"That's fine, I've plenty of time." I sent a text message to Kelly Husband, wish your fingers were here inside my panties, no lube needed! I wanted to tease him so that when I got home tonight he would be hot and bothered. I laughed to myself, we are a couple of nymphos and at our age. Cripes I could have an orgasm just because he is looking at me. I felt the jet descending and got ready for landing. I waited but there was no response, darn he must be caught up in something important.

Clarissa's office was walking distance from Granville Island and the view was breathtaking. She was on the twentieth floor. I was greeted by her receptionist who asked, "Do you have an appointment with Dr. Brownlow?"

"Yes I do, I am Claudia Samara." I wanted to say MacAskill, but Clarissa only knows me by Samara.

"Oh, yes, please follow me."

As we walked to the end of the hall, it was obvious she traveled a lot because of the artwork around her office.

"I am so glad you came Claudia, I have waited for this moment for 42 years. Please have a seat, I do have a bottle of wine if you would like a glass?" She offered. "Oh yes that would be great, I will admit it Clarissa I am a little nervous, it's not every day you meet the woman who gave birth to you when you're in your fifty's." I pulled her letter out. "I read this for the first time two days ago, I've had it since my mom died but I couldn't bring myself to reading it, I was afraid of what I would find."

"What did you feel when you read Claudia?" She asked as I reach across and handed it to her.

"I was relieved Clarissa, you just didn't give me up because you were too young, you never wanted to give me up. To try to get me back must have been heartbreaking for you. What happened after you sent this letter?" I asked watching her facial expressions as she read the letter she had written so long ago.

"I heard nothing from them, your parents contacted the lawyers and they had placed a restraining order against me. That was the last letter I wrote to your parents, but I was given one more opportunity to see you, Claudia, you were five years old and it was Christmas time. You were visiting Santa at the Woodward's downtown store. I was 22 and a store clerk working my way through university. I had the most difficult time keeping myself from scooping you up and running out of the store with you.

"Did you have any other children, your husband what does he do, is he a doctor as well?" I questioned, realizing I was intruding, but I wanted to know who this woman was and if I have siblings.

"No, you are the only child I ever had. I never married I guess my career and my goals took over my personal life. But now I see this beautiful woman and I am full. Claudia your parents did well with you."

Just then her receptionist appeared through the door. "I have your lunch ladies! I could set it up here, would that work?"

"Thank you, Lesley."

The conversation swayed while Lesley was in the room, but if she couldn't see the resemblance between Clarissa and me she was blind. We studied each other and I even recognized some of her mannerisms in me. It seemed so strange being here with her, surreal in every way. We had eaten more than half of the sushi when Clarissa wanted to hear about my life growing up. I thought to myself, how she will really feel when she hears the whole story.

I started to tell her and when I reached my university years she asked,

"What did you major in Claudia?"

"Arabic studies, I went to Cairo where my life changed forever. I got caught up in a terrorist organization and it was very alluring to me and I wanted to be part of the dynamics well my innocence caused my demise. I was responsible, along with my group of assassinating innocent people. I learned how to kill, and maybe I was brain-washed, I believed I was doing the right thing.

I taught English and attended University, just when I was finished my education and ready to return to Canada I was approached by a man. This man convinced me to help him with the task of telling my protégé Pascha that he was his father. He made it worth my while financially and being a student, I had expenses to look after so I agreed.

This man kept pursuing me and . . . "I continued to tell my story and finally I got to the really dark part, "Clarissa, my husband's name was Jasim Kassis al-Masri and the medical reported stated that Mikhail and I had duplicate chromosomes . . . "

She gasped. "My husband's name was Jasim Kassis al-Masri."

I continued, I didn't want to stop, "I learned that day he was my biological father. I thought I was going to lose my mind, I ended up in the psychiatric ward in a hospital in Dubai without any emotional support, no family and the loss of my son."

I could see she was in shock, her hand hadn't left her mouth, and I saw tears. Her head was shaking. "No, no Claudia, that should have never have happened to you, it's deplorable there are no words to express how much this hurts my soul, my child, I brought you into this world to experience that. I can never forgive myself." She sobbed.

"Please don't blame yourself, how could you have known?" I asked, her answer tore my heart out. Finally, I was to hear her story.

"I met Jasim here in Vancouver at the home of my parents' friends, it was summertime and they were celebrating a wedding anniversary. Jasim was older than me, but not a lot. He was handsome and debonair. We went out for dinner but when my parents found out they were angry, they forbid me from going, but I went anyway. Claudia, I was 15, he was 25. He was kind and respectful, but he was evil Claudia. He raped me so badly I couldn't walk. That was how I conceived you, Claudia, you had a bad start, and then it got worse."

We hugged and I felt an immediate connection to her, my mother, she was my mother. She loved and wanted me, but she allowed me to be raised and loved by my adoptive parents.

The time came and it was time to leave. We both had to process everything. I learned and so did Clarissa. I left knowing she would be a part of my life because I wanted her to be. I liked her I really liked her a lot.

Chapter 27

I WALKED THROUGH Granville Island trying to get my thoughts together. I now had the whole story and all I could do was wonder what made Jasim the way he was. He was pure evil and he used innocence to get him what he wanted. He destroyed so many lives, but karma got him back. And I had to admit, he adored Mikhail, he was a wonderful father that much I can credit him for.

I wondered now about Pascha and how he came to be, but that was not something I would search out. I knew this would be a chance to heal with my mother. I needed Kelly right at that moment. All I wanted to do was home.

At last, I was pulling up alongside Kelly's big black pickup. I had so much to share with him and I couldn't wait to crawl into his arms. He was stretched out on the sofa in his robe, poor baby, I thought, he must have had a bad day.

"Glad you're finally home darling." Kelly sat up, pulling the robe tightly around him, which I thought was an odd thing for him to do.

"Yes it has been quite the day Kel, I'm so glad to be home." I moved closer to get a kiss, but he darted over to the fireplace and turned the iPod on. I thought was strange until he ripped off his robe when the music began! It was Bing Crosby's Singing in the Rain.

My mouth popped open as Kelly began to dance and dance he did. He was only wearing a bow tie and a thong. My insides were doing things they hadn't done before. Kelly ripped off the thong and as the chorus began, his version was Swinging in the Rain.

I watched my husband grab hold of his penis and swinging it around and around as he headed towards me. I stood unable to move and unable to take my eyes off my sexy husband. I was so turned on at the sight of the bow tie and his muscles . . . I couldn't help but lick my lips in anticipation of him. I had plans for that erection.

I had my dress off and everything else off in seconds. I stood waiting for him to make the next move and what a move did he make. Our mouths and tongues, now hungry and eager, just danced while our fingers finding each other's special places.

Kelly backed me hard against a wall with my hands splayed. "Claudia, I want to fuck your ass, are you okay with me fucking your ass?" He said in a commanding voice. I went giddy and aroused to the point I knew I was becoming wet. "Yes! Kelly yes, fuck my ass."

He was quick to turn me around, and facing the wall his fingers plunged inside my throbbing body.

"Yes, you are creamy and ready."

He spread my excretion all around the puckered entrance of my rectum while his other fingers were thrusting in and out of me so quickly I was building up. My breathing was heavy, once more he wiped residuals of my liquid around the opening and then gently slid his middle finger carefully to the first knuckle. Kelly slowly moved it in and out with the other hand rubbing my clit. I was ready to explode. His finger moved hard and fast into me, and as he pushed deeper, I felt everything explode.

My movement was the perfect exposure for his hard cock to penetrate my anus. He was careful as he slid in slowly, his thrusts began, he pumped in and almost all the way out while his fingers moved around the sticky creamy substance. I moaned with the burning sensation. I rocked and he pumped. Kelly's breathing slowed down and I felt him explode inside me. He was trembling and I exploded with him. We stayed, our bodies still connected. He was firm up against me.

"That was so good baby, you make it so good." Kelly wrapped his arms around my stomach and then slowly released himself from within me. Then I was in his arms being carried into the shower.

Each long stroke was thorough and smooth as Kelly's hand brought the brush down each section of my hair. My husband was becoming more and more tactile when each opportunity presented him. I had to discourage him on some occasions, especially with a situation like tonight when we were getting ready for Daniel and Daina's dinner party.

Kelly came home and found me draped only in a towel and insisted that he apply the moisturizing cream. There was no way I could let him, his hands created too much sexual arousing in me which would not be a good thing tonight. But Kelly promised to behave and stuck to my shoulders and back.

"No chest play honey, I promise I'll leave that to you." Kelly grinned mischievously. I loved it when he brushed my hair especially when I was upset or anxious Kelly had always brought out the brush.

Tonight, he said, "Brushing your hair is an aphrodisiac for me. It gives me such pleasure, next to watching your eyes when I make you climax."

I shook my head, "This must be residuals from our teenage years." I giggled. "Is our sexual appetite ever going to be satiated?"

Kelly handed me the brush. "God, I hope not, I have never been satisfied until you. I only hope you don't get tired of my hunger for the beautiful Claudia MacAskill."

"Of course not, I can't see that ever happening. I have had too many years without you. We have a lot of fucking to make up for." I knew Kelly's libido spiked when I talked like that. I knew I better stop.

He raised his eyebrow. "Woman you best be careful. The bed is right around the corner." I continued with brushing all my hair back and then rolling it into a tight knot. I finished applying my eye make-up and joined Kelly in the bedroom to dress. I chose a fire red knee length chiffon halter dress by Halston. I slipped into a thong and was about to step into my dress when I felt Kelly's hand on my behind.

"If this is all you're wearing under your dress, baby this is definitely going to be an early night."

I pretended his hand wasn't there, even though it was burning into my flesh. I could only turn and look at him. I dropped my eyes, "Foreplay baby, this is all for you. You can't touch, not now, much, much later honey."

I slipped the shoulder strap over my head and my naked breasts filled the front. His eyes didn't leave my body as he watched my fingers tying the sash in the front. There are times in a woman's life when she knows she looks sexy and feels it, and this was another one of those times.

Kelly poured a glass of wine and was taking a sip when I joined him. "Claudia, I better keep my eyes on you all night, that's definitely going to be an attention getter. Fuck your hot!" Kelly shook his head, I took the wine glass from him and took a sip keeping my eyes low and meeting his gaze from under my lashes.

We managed to arrive at Young Rancher's Estate fashionably late. As we pulled up to the gate Kelly's comment concerned me. "You know, you are going to be the center of attention, there isn't going to be a man in the room able to keep their eyes off of you Claudia." His voice sounded a little agitated.

"Are you worried that I'm going to be affected by their looks?" I retorted.

"I guess I am, I know what I have, Claudia, it has nothing to do with trust, you know I trust you and I'm not jealous. I just know how men think." Kelly took my hand and kissed my fingers.

"You should know me and how I deal with situations, I have had years of it. Hey, enjoy knowing what I'm going to be doing to you at the end of the night Mr. Mac." I traced his lips with my finger.

"Yes Mrs. Mac, I'm going to keep you at your word." Kelly reached in behind the material of my dress and caressed my breast. I savored his touch and his fingers sent sensations between my legs.

There were a great number of vehicles parked in the driveway so Kelly parked the truck down near the office and we walked up to the house. We were greeted by a doorman and escorted to the grand room. Kelly had his hand protectively on my waist. I knew he was going to be on edge, I couldn't prevent that. I dressed for him and didn't care who ogled at me.

Kelly was dead right and I must have ruffled a few of the female guest's feathers because I got the looks. I was relieved when Daniel and Daina greeted us.

Daniel looked at Daina and she looked at me. "That is one incredible dress you're wearing Claudia and you look beautiful."

Then Daniel did the natural thing, he too reached in for a hug and a peck on my cheek. "Your Kelly, my friend, keeps telling me what a lucky man he is, and I definitely agree with him. Claudia, you are definitely one knockout." He commented before Daina grabbed my hand and pulled me out of her husband's grip.

"Daniel has a surprise for Kelly, his brothers Sebastian and Samuel are here. Daniel received the call from Sebastian months ago out of the blue and he was disappointed that Kelly hadn't told them about the two of you getting married. So, they both showed up because they want to mend fences."

Daina handed me a glass of red wine. "So then that is why the dinner party? I assumed.

"No, this is everyone's way of getting on. Besides, the rest of the world needs to congratulate the new Mr. and Mrs. MacAskill!"

"I should have known, this is not good. Kelly's parents would now be finding out if they haven't already."

Daina quickly changed the subject, "Okay Claudia about your dress, oh my God it is hot, and where did you get it? I wish I looked as good as you do!"

"Oh Daina, you do, whether you believe it or not. My dress well, this is a Halston and I got it in Geneva many years ago. It's one I saved, this is the first time I've worn it, I used to buy clothes that I dreamed of wearing for Kelly and put them away hoping one day I would still be able to wear it. Girlfriend I got to go find my husband, come with me please." I urged my friend and hooked my arm in hers, I loved my friend dearly and it is so good being much closer now.

I found Kelly standing talking with his brother Samuel. He was deep in a tense conversation and I wasn't sure whether I should join them. I wished he would glance up and motion me or something. Daina whispered I think your husband is trying to get your attention." She nudged me, oh thank goodness I thought. He smiled and winked and I pulled Daina with me to join him and his brothers.

Kelly's arm found its place at my waist and he kissed my temple. Samuel was eying me up and down before commenting. "Kelly, you have one hot woman there, I don't remember you looking like this when we were in school!" He teased and I kept a straight face. I waited for Kelly's input.

"You're such a liar Sam, geez you always said she was pretty. Remember how I threatened to kick your ass if you got smart with her." Kelly remarked.

"Congratulations Kelly, you too Claudia. I really mean it, I think you've got a great woman there, and don't worry about our parents, they'll get over it. Hell, what can they do?" Sam questioned.

Chapter 28

OCTOBER 2002, Finally, it was our move in day. Everything had been cleared out of the cabin and I was waiting for the cleaning crew to arrive. Kelly was at the new house when I reached him to advise him that the movers had just left.

After taking care of everything at the old place, I arrived and the movers had already come and gone. Kelly greeted me, "Welcome home Mrs. Mac!" Kelly had lit the fireplace and disappeared.

I gazed around me and I had everything right now. I was married to the most loving and supportive man and we had a home that was a home in every way I could have imagined.

Kelly had reappeared carrying a bottle of Krug Rosé Brut champagne and two flutes.

"Oh, Kelly honey, you haven't forgotten anything have you?" I announced and stroked his shoulder before reaching for a kiss.

"I hope not and I hope this is where we will spend the rest of our lives together Claudia," Kelly answered as he filled both glasses to the perfect level.

"Here's to the rest of our lives together Kelly! I love you only you!" We clinked glasses and took a sip.

"Darling here's many, many more days of love and laughter together," Kelly said before stroking my cheek. The two of us curled up together on the sofa and drank our champagne and enjoyed our view across Okanagan Lake.

My days were filled with familiarizing myself with the new house. We had been in constant contact and Clarissa wanted me to meet her grandparents and aunts and uncles: and I was ready to welcome my biological family into my life.

Clarissa greeted us with warm hugs as we arrived at her beautiful Kitsilano home.

It was a moderate size, open and airy, and decorated in bright and bold colors that showed the other side of Clarissa. We were the first to arrive at Clarissa's request.

When my mother opened the door, I wrapped her in my arms without any hesitation. "Mom it's so good to be here!"

Kelly looked on in complete surprise, but Clarissa knew within her heart one day her daughter would return to her in the truest form and hearing those words validated her belief.

Pulling Claudia to face her, "Thank you for coming my darling you have no idea how happy this has made me." Clarissa glowed.

"Yes Mom, I do because I feel like I belong. Now I have the chance to meet the rest of my family. Even though the Samara's were also my family, but in a different way. I loved them and I still do."

After that initial meeting, Kelly and I invited everyone to our new home for the Christmas holidays. December arrived and the background sound of Christmas music was sweeping throughout the MacAskill household as our staff was preparing the meal. Everyone was coming, my mother, my grandparents, Kelly's Twins Jason and Justine and their children.

Before they all arrived, I looked around our home and the decorations were spectacular. Kelly insisted that we have a 12-foot tree and yet with all that, my heart longed for Mikhail. Kelly knew I was dealing with something and he wasn't able to erase my sadness.

"I'm so sorry sweetheart, this holiday must be extremely difficult for you." Kelly wrapped his arms around me. "Are you going to be okay?"

"I'll be okay . . . " I promised him.

It was Christmas day, Clarissa and family arrived and her beautiful smile and open arms were one of the best gifts I could have received. After everyone was settled we opened our gifts and our grandchildren were over the moon. It was such fun watching them open each gift. After the gifts were opened Kelly made his way to the baby grand piano and began playing Christmas carols and I joined in with my flute.

The voices singing along with us were soulful and surprisingly in harmony. Justine's youngest daughter was fascinated by the flute and sat right in front of me as I played. Her little four-year-old face was filled with curiosity.

"Kaila play?" She asked. But Justine jumped in right away and diverted her attention.

"When you get big like Cameron, you can learn to play too." I could only smile, as I thought about Mikhail learning at her age and I would sway Justine into getting her lessons. Music was what kept me sane all those years.

We got the signal that we could be seated for a very extravagant traditional Christmas meal. Clarissa's father asked to say a prayer and he gave thanks for what had transpired over the year. This was one of the most blessed Christmases I had ever experienced and it brought tears to my eyes. I had everyone I loved sharing the season with me: except of course my son.

The following day, after the twins and their families left and Kelly drove my family to the airport, I had one more Christmas present for my husband that he would only be able to open with me.

When Kelly arrived back home I was waiting for him all curled up on the sofa in front of the fireplace. I poured us both a shot of cognac and underneath the covered dishes were a variety of tasty aphrodisiacs waited for us.

"Honey, we haven't finished our celebration yet!" I announced as my husband joined me on the sofa and accepted the cognac I handed him. I could see his eyes move from me to the table with curiosity.

"Ok Mrs. Mac what's going on here?" Kelly questioned. My movement towards him loosened the sash of my emerald brocade kimono and he got a glimpse of what was underneath. His quick wit and movement had me feeling his breath against my ear. "I really think I'm going to love opening this present Mrs. Mac!" He whispered as he loosened the sash fully and his finger traced up my knee towards my thigh. The silky material of the kimono fell to my sides revealing green bowed pasties.

Kelly inhaled before circling the outline of where the pasties rested. "Mrs. Mac . . . " he growled. "You just made me hard, what am I going to do with you?" he said, grinning from ear to ear. My devilish and now very horny husband continued roaming over my body before pulling me up onto my feet and completely removing the kimono.

"Yes, you're hot Claudia, your perfect breasts, but let's see what else you have here." He roamed from between my breasts down my belly past my navel stopping long enough to find my mouth with his. He tasted sweet like cognac and as his tongue moved over and under mine before licking my bottom lip. Then Kelly proceeded further down, slowly and enticing my libido to respond and that was exactly what it was doing. The heat inside of me was beginning to burn while the palm of his hand rested on my mound.

He kneaded me, I jerked, and in preparation, he moved back up. I whimpered desperately for the sensations his fingers gave my opening. Kelly teased and returned his hands to my sides. His kiss deepened as his hands kneaded my pastie-covered breasts. He continued roaming my body squeezing the cheeks of my ass considerably harder than he had ever done before. I winced, and he found the entrance to my anxious wet vagina. "Oh… do we have here, crotch less panties?"

He continued moving deep into me, harder and harder, I felt the surge come over my body and began breathy gasps. "What is on the table under the cover? Kelly questioned while moving me in that direction.

"A present for me." I gasped in desperation for an orgasm. He continued his deep hard movements in and out of me while he took off the cover from the item.

"Okay Claudia, double penetration, I can do that." Kelly took the glass dildo and put it to my lips. "Suck it, babe." He said as I pulled it between my lips and made it slick with my saliva. He had my back against him and removed my panties. Kelly rubbed my ass cheeks and then gave them a sharp slap. I winced and yelped. He began rubbing them, repeating the process again and I could feel my natural creamy lubricant forming at my opening and his fingers pulled the lubricant to the opening between my ass cheeks.

As his hard cock moved into me, he gently inserted the dildo vaginally. I gasped in ecstasy and as soon as the vaginal stroking began, his penis slid deeper and deeper until I growled loudly and I built a climax so quickly it took Kelly by surprise. He pounded me from behind, I shuddered and gyrated and came over and over unable to stop myself from loud whimpers.

"Are you all right baby?" Kelly asked sounding concerned. "Should I stop?" "No . . . deeper Kelly . . . " I begged, "Harder . . . oh shit, yes, yes . . . "

He complied with my requests until he began vibrating and I felt his warmth fill me anally. "Oh God Claudia I'm not done . . . oh . . . " he continued to spurt his sperm. My body was still convulsing in pleasure. He freed my body and pulled me into his arms. "God, I think I've been satisfied thoroughly by you Claudia, then you do this. Wow, how many more surprises can a woman have for her husband? I really, really like this."

Kelly ran kisses down my neck as he pulled my hair off to the side. "This is so important for me to please you, I need good hard sex, and you are very good at it husband," I remarked feeling the deep swallow he had just done.

I felt his two fingers press into me again. He didn't thrust; he just rested as his thumb flicked against my clit. He kissed me deeper and rather rough, I gasped. It was his other hand stripping the pastie from one nipple, he twisted and pulled and pinched while he continued working on my clit. I felt my body heating up again. Kelly stopped everything he was doing and swept me into his arms.

"We need a shower because I'm far from finished with you, my darling," Kelly announced. I swallowed and felt my clit throb at that thought.

It was a quick shower and I was eager for the rest of his offer. I quickly braided my wet hair while Kelly headed into the bedroom. I soon joined him and my eyes must have danced when I saw what he was holding, two of his neckties. I started shuddering at the thought of bondage, it wasn't something he was into, but I became totally excited. I dropped my towel and began twisting my nipples pinching as hard as I could. I didn't realize where this was going to take me. Kelly ordered me to the bed.

"Does this excite you Kel? Does it make you hard, the thought of tying me uptight and having control? Oh . . . Kelly, I want to feel your dick." I toyed with a now very flustered Kelly.

He pulled my right foot and arm and tied them together before tying the left ones securing them as tight as possible and careful not to cut off my circulation. That brought my feet up behind me. He propped a pillow under my lower back arching me upwards. "Are you comfortable honey?" He bent over staring into my eyes. "God I'm so in love with you Claudia, pleasing you pleases me."

I cooed, "You have taken the words right out of my mouth, we are so good together and we fit perfectly."

His soft kiss rested on my mouth as he lightly moved his fingers over my breasts, softly he blew on each nipple making them erect, it was when his fingernails flicked the tip that I stirred and alerted my whole body. He did it again, then his teeth nipping them I groaned and stirred. Each nip was firmer than the last, arousing me to the fullest. Kelly kept a tight grip on them and moved in on my throbbing clit then dragging his tongue from my anus to the top of my labia. Kelly licked, sucked and bit until I thought I was going to explode.

I didn't know what to expect when he pushed himself into me, I screamed as I burned. But the excitement of it all triggered a climax; it was not what I expected. Kelly carried me into our room and I scooted out of his arms and into the bathroom and ran a bath for two. I sensed his unexpected assault was his way of proving he was open to filling my needs if I would allow him.

In the tub, Kelly positioned his body behind mine and his fingers sensuously braided my hair. His lips kissed my ear lobe. My tender loving husband massaged lotion into every possible place on my body. It was wonderful and loving and I couldn't love him any more than I did at that moment.

Chapter 29

SPRING 2003 ARRIVED and there was so much going on around the winery and Kelly was gone until it got dark. I was becoming restless, restless to the point I knew I had to get involved with the foundation and that meant traveling again.

That would also cause some concern for Kelly and I was so aware of what my body was experiencing. If I didn't go, I knew what would happen. I needed to be busy so I chose to go to India to check on the foundation's progress.

I knew Kelly was exhausted when he came to bed at night and intimacy was challenging at times. Tonight, I would spoon him, caress him in a non-sexual way before breaking the news. I knew he was awake and having a hard time staying awake.

"Honey I need to talk to you, it's urgent that I go to India. I haven't been doing my due diligence. It is a perfect time since things are so crazy here for you. I want to go next week, please understand?" I kissed the top of his shoulder.

Kelly turned over to face me. "Are you sure you really need to go? I thought you had a good team?"

I was very aware of the alarm in his voice. "Yes, I think it is perfect that I go, if anything, a surprise visit will reveal any unethical situations. I won't be gone long, two weeks at the most, I promise. I will miss you too much to be away from you for any longer than that." I wrapped my arms tight around him and buried my face into his hard chest.

"I don't want you to go Claudia, but I won't stop you, I love you and you need to do what you need to do."

We landed in Delhi, where I was introduced to Simi the team leader in the area. I toured the offices and met with a small group of women and they had arranged a meal for me which was traditional foods Paranthas, Chaat, Butter Chicken Kebabs, Biryani, Momos, then we drove through the city. Delhi is one of the oldest continually inhabited cities in the world. Having been the capital of several empires in ancient India, Delhi was a major city in the old trade routes from northwest India to the Gangetic Plains and 160 kilometers south to Vrindavan which took just over two hours.

My time in India was not as fruitful as I had hoped it would be. There were too many things not completed and I intended to change that. The widows of Vrindavan did not trust our intentions and it was difficult reaching out to them. I needed to find someone they could trust. I thought my team leader was on top of it. I turned to the hospitals and was hoping to involve a head nurse or someone in a management position for insight and entice them to work for my foundation. I hoped that would be the key to moving things along.

I walked the streets of Vrindavan with Simi, my team leader, and met some of the women we were working with. I was touched to find that there were women in their twenties and thirties that were widowed. Vrindavan is also the center for various Vaishnava groups. In a centuries-old tradition Hindu widows have been coming to live out the rest of their lives in Vrindavan. They are expected to shed all physical adornments, including long hair, wear only white cotton saris and lead an austere lifestyle. In Vrindavan, there are thousands of widows coming mostly from Bengal. They begin their day by bathing in the Yamuna and congregate at ashrams to sing bhajans (devotional songs). In return, they get a daily ration of rice and pulses and some cash. Subsisting on charitable donations made by wealthy traders, the widows pass their life in devotion to Krishna, the Supreme Lord. These women eyes looked dead inside, I had to find a way to help make their lives worth living. I found myself reaching out to these women in any way that I could, there just had to be a way.

Then we traveled 12 km to the city of Mathura, located in the western part of the state of Uttar Pradesh, in the north of India. There are no direct flights or trains or buses are available between Vrindavan to Mathura. The convenient, fastest and cheapest way to reach from Vrindavan to Mathura is to take a taxi from Vrindavan to Mathura. It is a part of the great northern plains and is situated on the west bank of the river Yamuna. Vrindavan and Mathura are the most important places of pilgrimage for devotees of Krishna. Krishna was born in Mathura and spent his childhood in Vrindavan. There are over 5,000 temples in Vrindavan. It is a very interesting city to explore but unfortunately, the tour was quick and I was busy noting information and putting ideas on paper. This was a fact-finding mission and with Simi's knowledge, there was definitely a real promise to get my ideas in motion.

On the drive back to Delhi I learned all about Simi's journey and how she ended up living in Delhi

After an eight-hour flight from Delhi, the jet landed in Tokyo to refuel, which was when a familiar excitement developed in my chest. This was Kenji's territory and there was no chance of containing my needs at that precise moment. The flow of excitement traveled through my body to my genitals and my brain clicked in.

Giving instructions to Slade in the event we would be laid over for a few days pending my ability to make contact with a certain party. Slade would be on call and available to leave on short notice. There was no need to search any journals for Kenji's phone number. It was burned in my memory, and once I was through customs

I placed the call. I wasn't able to contain my excitement and Kenji recognized the tone in my voice. "Claudia, it's been awhile since we've worked together, actually you're lucky I have availability for you. I know the cost is no problem for you, is that right?" Kenji monotone chant soothed and energized me at the same time. "No problem at all Kenji, I will arrange a bank transfer. Are you still at the same location?"

"Yes Claudia, I will send a car for you." Kenji was all business and that was how I liked it. I was nearly jumping out of my skin with excitement all I could do to keep my finger away from my genitals. I pushed thoughts of my marriage and the desire to live a normal healthy married life with Kelly the man I deeply loved. I knew it would never be enough and Kelly would never accept this lifestyle. I knew he felt it was deplorable and I left out many details during our conversations. I craved it and like oxygen I needed it.

Electro stimulation was on my mind and creating a stir between my legs. It was so bad that my panties were soaking wet. The driver got me to Kenji's within half an hour after arrival, and I was ready. I left my wedding ring on the jet. I couldn't have any reminders of Kelly. I knew I would have to go home and tell him. I couldn't lie or pretend, he loved me and I knew he would forgive me.

The draw was too strong and I was vibrating inside when Kenji opened the door. I was already undoing the buttons on my dress.

Kenji's expression was like always emotion free, I often wondered what Kenji's true personality was like away from the business of pain.

"Claudia, thank you for your payment, very generous and I'm sure you will be pleased with the services I am providing today." Kenji motioned with a nod towards a heavy looking teak door. I entered into a room that was not inviting, no warmth or soft music playing in the background. It was dark with a metal décor, reminding me of a place where animal hides would be carved up. My eyes scanned the room, the familiar tools of the trade hung from the ceiling a body harness. The anticipation was sending pulsating energy through me. I stood in the middle of the room naked, slowly braiding my hair. When I was finished I blindfold was placed across my eyes right after Kenji entered. I sensed each movement each step that was being taken from me, I knew those eyes were scanning my body while the words were directing me. Kenji fingers examining my breasts. "You've had them reduced, good, good." With a firm grip of my nipples Kenji stretched them, twisted each one roughly and I winched, it had been awhile but both nipples responded and hardened I felt heat burning. Clamps were being attached, they felt like the blades of a saw gripping my tender flesh. I felt a slight rush and remembered the pain and, the adrenaline was kicking in.

"Claudia, I have a student, a woman this time, are you interested?"

I was curious, I knew a woman could be gentle, or lethal, I knew this would be very different. "Oh, of course, I'm interested Kenji. This was exactly what I had come for and the unknown would bring me to that eternal place as people call it Nirvana.

I was guided to a spot in the room and soon a leather collar was buckled around my neck, my wrist, and ankles. A pony bit gag was fitted at my mouth. I could hear the clanking of the chains and my mind zoomed to the beginning when I experienced this for the first time as a young woman, so frightened and filled with shame. But now my breath was exhilarated in expectancy. I was being lifted up, now my arms and legs were spread open, taut but not enough to cause trauma to my joints. I don't know how long I remained in this position. A chilling sensation jolted me an icy cold substance was being spread over my genitals, this was nothing I'd experienced, just before something metal was inserted vaginally and anally. I tried to determine what it was, whatever it was, filled me. I had no idea what was happening, I was getting extremely cold in my lower extremities, it was followed by a large masses of ice massaging me in four different location. I shuddered while fans blew cold air on me. When the ice massage was finished someone's, fingers were tugging my clit hood, I tried to wiggle, I couldn't, I felt a catheter being inserted into my urethra as the instrument in my anus was being replaced by a smaller rod. I sensed that both Kenji and the female were involved. Her fingers rolled over my clit, she flicked the end over and over again. I heard a click and then their electrical impulses were traveling along the nerve fibers in both orifices. I was squirming unable to move, the impulses were raised. The cheeks of my ass were being flogged I felt a deep pressure vaginally and deep hard thrusts in quick repetitive motions. I had not realized the nipple clamps were gone until harsh lashing across them brought my attention. The foreign sensation was getting more and more aggressive to the point I thought I had reached my pain tolerance, almost immediately everything stopped, the tools were removed from my body while a volcanic eruption took over internally, it felt like someone's hard cock was being plunged into me, the pain was excruciating I disappeared to the black.

Kelly wasn't at home when I arrived. I was somewhat relieved. I felt so conflicted about my duality: being the person I knew I was, and being the wife and lover, I wanted to be for Kelly. He made sure that the house was spotless and everything in its place.

Although it was spring, it was not the best of weather that day, very windy without the sunshine, but that didn't stop my urge to go for a run. For me, running has always been the best way to deal with anxiety. I laced up my runners and jogged up the long driveway from the side of the house. I had thought about contacting the psychologist again, but I wasn't in agreement with the suggestion he made the last time I saw him. He wanted me to see a psychiatrist was out of the question. I couldn't see how this was a mental condition. Or was it? Hell, I know I am fucked up, but if I'm so fucked up why does it feel right for me? The pain feels so good, I really craved it when it wasn't available. Jasim never knew the extent of my erotic pleasures and what his handler had introduced me to. Should I thank you or curse you Jasim? Both, I decided.

My feet were taking me south along Naramata Road and not even the scenery attracted my attention, it was only the sound of a horn from an oncoming vehicle. I didn't understand why they were honking I was off to the side and shouldn't be interfering with traffic. When I looked up, it was Kelly's big black pick up. He pulled off to the side of the road, and I ran over to him.

The expression on his face was questioning, I believed he sensed intuitively what I had done, and I knew I had to confirm his suspicions.

"Hi, there!" I tried to sound as cheerful as possible, while my mind ran all over the place. I won't be surprised if he asks me for a divorce. He doesn't deserve me, he is too wonderful to be treated the way I have treated him.

"Claudia, hi, hop in!" Kelly studied my face as he spoke. I was so happy to see this man and wanted to pretend nothing happened during my trip. "It's been awful without you here Claudia. I still have difficulty with you being away from me." He said as his fingers reached across the seat for mine. I swallowed hard and the tears formed in my eyes. "Hey, honey please don't cry, I just missed my wife more than I imagined." His soften eyes met my guilty ones.

"That's not what's making me cry Kel, not at all. Just hearing how much you miss me touched my heart." I replied sadly, knowing what I had to tell him would only give him more discomfort.

Kelly turned into our driveway and pushed the switch and I watched as the automatic doors opened. We hadn't been in the elevator for more than a few seconds before his mouth met mine seeking, probing for my response. Kelly's kisses continued as we exited from the elevator and he backed me towards our bedroom.

I desired him desperately and didn't refuse as his fingers quickly removed each article of my clothing. Our hands shuffled between each other's, eagerly tugging, pushing undoing, while our mouths desperately searching and connecting. My head was woozy; my heart was aching. Kelly's fingers burned everywhere he touched me, filling me with desire. He attempted to say something, I slid my finger over his lips. "Shhh." I covered those wonderful lips with mine, then rolling over top of him I slid down him onto my knees. I could please him before destroying us.

Satisfied thoroughly and throbbing from the sexual workout my husband gave me, he though was insatiable and surprisingly erect. I needed to catch my breath and find a way to direct his needs temporarily. We lay on our backs side by side; our bodies moist with perspiration as we caught our breath.

I felt his fingers move upward towards my nipples and even before he reached them I winced. I knew how significant the bruises were and his eyes would convey that. It was as painful as I anticipated it would be. I closed my eyes and didn't acknowledge the raw pain he was unknowingly inflicting on me, but as soon as his lips connected and grazed over the erect spot. I arched my back, Kelly was quick to respond and check his game.

"Claudia, what did you do, you're bruised, bruises all around your areola." He froze, those eyes of his filled with surprise and a realization of my reality. He pulled me into him, kissing my face. "What happened to push you back there? "

I clung to him, sobbing desperately. "I don't know, I don't, I just need the pain, I'm wrong for you Kelly, I can't stop myself I have no fight when it comes to this part of me. Kelly, you should divorce me and find someone who deserves you." I was shaking in shame. Kelly just pulled me closer.

"No Claudia, no, that's not the answer, don't ever mention divorce. I wish I knew what the answer was. I hate seeing you hurt or in pain. God Claudia, what do I do?" Kelly expressed with his voice and his hands and his body consoling me in a way that he could only do.

"You're the one who is being hurt Kelly, not me! I don't hurt the way you think I do. For Christ sake's Kelly get mad at me or something, please! How, why do you do this?" I attempted to push myself from his hold, but he just held me tighter.

"When are you going to get it, Claudia? I love you nothing you do or say could ever change that. You ought to know that by now, I'm here for you always!" He replied as he ran his fingers over my cheeks moving my hair from my face. What could I say? All I could do was meet those striking blue eyes of his.

"It's not your fault! Claudia, it's not your fault, this should not have happened to you baby. Christ, I need to know how to get you past this."

I ran the back of my hand over his cheeks lovingly, wanting to erase the cause of his sadness. "What do I say to you, Kelly? There is no justifying my actions." I whimpered.

"Just tell me you love me that is all I need to know." He folded me tight to himself once again.

"I do love you, Kelly, I love you so much you will never know how much." I needed to show him in every way possible, but first with my body. I wiggled down to position him where my body could consume his length. Showing him was the way I knew best.

"That's my girl. I don't think I can hear those words enough." Kelly growled his words as he accepted my body anxiously.

I whispered again and as often as I could, "I love you, only you Kelly!"

Chapter 30

SPRING ARRIVED and my eyes roamed over Kelly as he sat across from me, he was describing the new building plans and Daniel's ideas. I could tell how excited he was having his son Jason on their team and soon he would be taking on some of the duties around here.

I was hearing every word he spoke, but admiring his features. His hair was a little longer than normal and the soft waves were now a deeper bronze, his skin was drinking up the sun and that was highlighted by his white polo shirt. I ran my finger down his arm sensuously, drawing a curious look from him.

He looked up at me, through the rim of his reading glasses and grinned. "I hope my wife likes what she sees." He responded then winking.

"She sure does, oh yes very much." My eyes were now resting on his.

"I hope that never changes sweetheart." Kelly squeezed my arm.

"How could it Kel? My heart thumps harder every time I see you." I smiled before asking more questions about the buildings.

"Babe, it's all coming together all the buildings have been mapped out on the property. We've selected the strain of hops that are going to be planted next year. The grapes are producing well, Claudia we made the best decision when we purchased this property. I still am a little overwhelmed on what is left to do."

I was having urges, and on the other side of the scale feeling very comfortable in this lifestyle, being adored. It was so foreign to me being in a conflict like this one. I needed to escape and I had the means as well as the perfect alibi when I got the annoying email.

Once more my foundation faced problems and I needed to spend some time in visiting the countries to sort out the bribes and criminal intent that had gone undetected in both Algeria and Nigeria.

I had to leave and Kelly played the understanding game. It was obvious he had angst about my travels. This time I would return home late May. The opportunity for communication was minimal between Kelly and me due to our obligations. I found myself in turmoil at times struggling without Kelly there to keep me in his positive frame of mind set. My strength and will fell apart during a stopover in Egypt. After visiting the Foundation site, I created in my head the need for a break and relaxation, so I ended up in El Gouna on the Red Sea.

While exploring the shops in the Marina, I met a couple of Canadian women close to my age who were having a blast and they insisted I joined them for dinner. Well, dinner led to daytime activities and nightclubbing. Well, we all looked hot and one evening it wasn't long before the drinks were being sent over.

I was into the scotch, not the cheap stuff either, and they kept coming. I asked the server who was sending them, but he was held to secrecy. The other two women were just as curious as I was and set out to find the person responsible. I giggled at their determination and watched as they wandered through the club. It couldn't have been more than two minutes before I was approached by a very handsome black man. There was no pickup line.

"I recognized you right away, you're the model of some of the most incredible sculptures I have ever seen. I knew you had to exist somewhere in this world." He announced in a smooth French accent, his hand extended to shake mine. I knew immediately he had seen Sofie's pieces somewhere in Europe.

"Where are you from Jacob? Your French accent is apparent. Tell me about you?" I shifted my head to the side and waited for an answer.

"My family is from Martinique where I was raised until I went to study and I did my psych degree in Paris, loved France and decided to set up a practice early on in my career." I was looking for clues about the sculpture.

"Have you ever lived in Geneva? Maybe even Dubai or Abu Dhabi?" I looked down at my drink instead of greeting his eyes with the question.

"No, although I have visited those places, I have traveled extensively, just like you, at least I am assuming you are well traveled." He brought his forefingers together and rested them against his lips.

I was curious. " You have a good eye, where did you come across these sculptures?" I took back my hand, releasing the heat I felt from his touch.

"Geneva, about a year ago. It took a lot of negotiation to get the artist to part with one, lucky for me I have memorized your beautiful face and excuse me . . . your incredible body." It was obvious he was much younger than me. He was very attractive; he glowed and I was immediately taken with him.

"My name is Jacob, Jacob Samuels." He reached into his jacket pocket for a business card. I didn't even glance at it. I just tucked it into my bag.

"Claudia, my name is Claudia, please join me. I'm curious which piece did you purchase?" I brought the scotch glass to my lips, drew in a large mouthful as I waited for a description because intuitively I knew exactly which one.

"Claudia, my name is Claudia, please join me. I'm curious which piece did you purchase?" I brought the scotch glass to my lips, drew in a large mouthful as I waited for a description because intuitively I knew exactly which one.

He brushed my cheek, "Ah . . . yes, this definitely was the

profile, your lovely face resting on your knee while . . . " I stopped him. Damn her, she made a duplicate. Jasim guaranteed me he had cleaned up the mess.

"I know that piece very well. I will pay you to double what you purchased it for. That piece should not have been released. Write a figure and I will have your money tomorrow."

I studied him while he shook his head. "It's not for sale Claudia, I assure you, I have kept the piece away from public eyes. I don't share my possessions, especially ones as stunning as that." Jacob took a drink and placed his glass beside mine.

"I insist, give me a number I want that piece. I am serious." I remained cool.

He shook his head. "I'm not parting with it, that's final." He was bold. His finger was now tracing the shape of my face; starting at my ear he slowly moved to the end of my chin. I had one more card to play. A card I knew could work against me, but I had to get the piece no matter what. I reached up and placed my fingers on his, and gently moved his from my face.

"I would like to see you again Claudia, I'll be at The Three Corners Hotel if you're interested. It's late and I will say goodnight." Jacob ran his finger across my lips then turned and walked away. He left me vibrating and curious.

I looked around the club but my Canadian friends had disappeared, I guess they figured I was busy. That was okay I had had too much to drink and I needed to return to my room: at The Three Corner Hotel.

I woke up with a terrible headache. I knew I need a spa day and a juice cleanse, a couple of days vetoing all alcohol. I stood in the hot shower for longer than normal and of course, Jacob crossed my mind. He has had a very intimate insight of me, I didn't like that one bit. Again, my mind searched for a way of getting that piece away from him. I would do anything, anything to get it and have it disposed of. But today was not the day, I needed a clear mind and find a course of action.

I desperately needed to talk to Kelly. Right now, I wanted my husband. It was after ten a.m. here so it was eight pm at home.

I called his cell and it went to voicemail. I left a message, "Sweet man of mine, I am missing you desperately and coming home soon. Please call me, I love you."

I spent the whole day in the spa and it was exactly what my body and soul needed. I was feeling a little off, similar to other times when my hormone levels were off not taking any chances of slipping into menopause I needed to check things out. I was doing what I could to keep my body and bones and every part of me healthier. I decided that I needed to get to Geneva and see the medical group there before I went back to Penticton.

After the spa, I found the patio and pool area rather quiet. It was wonderful to relax in the sun. I closed my eyes and let the shade of my sunglasses soothe me into further relaxation. Today and tomorrow I would treat my body and then I would head to Geneva.

Being in a meditative state, I didn't hear the waiter's question, until he raised his tone and brought me to reality. "Ma'am is there something I can bring you?" He asked.

"Oh yes, yes, please, carrot and beet juice please and some water with a slice of lemon as well, thank you."

"Right away ma'am." My mind wandered off to foundation's business and I was brought back to reality by the icy cold sensation against my shoulder. It was Jacob. I wasn't in any way ready to see him.

"I see you are enjoying the sunshine, Claudia." Jacob handed me both glasses. "Yes, you can set them on the table, thank you." I took my shades off and met his eyes.

"I have to say, Claudia, I am a little disappointed. I was almost positive I'd be hearing from you today. I thought a debate might be the next tool for you getting my sculpture. I can't see you giving up this quickly." Jacob sat on the other side of the table.

"So now you are trying to analyze me are you Jacob? Hm . . . I see." I took a sip of my juice.

"No, not at all, I'm just hoping to find a way to capture your attention. Did you happen to take a look at my business card?" Jacob asked calmly.

"Actually no, I haven't, should I have?" I replied self-assuredly.

"I think you should have Claudia. I know you could use my knowledge, I know I can help you! I knew that when I set eyes on your sculpture and saw what your eyes were holding. I'm going to take a guess here, you are sexually broken, and your spirit has been destroyed and disconnected from your soul. Hasn't it Claudia?" Jacob words caused my head to snap and turn in his direction. I was speechless but unwilling to give him the benefit of a positive response. "The way your body spoke was another giveaway, I can only guess what has been done to your body. I wondered if you'd search me out." Jacob took a sip of the fruity looking beverage he was holding while I rested my head on the back of the lounge chair.

Oh my God what have I gotten myself into now? The man had definitely spiked my curiosity. I looked at my shining wedding ring. "So, tell me, Jacob, how can you help me? And what's in it for you?" I continued looking ahead of me.

"I have an intense background in sexuality and abuse. I am a psychologist, sexologist. I incorporate different spectrums and methods for healing trauma besides body psychotherapy, eye movement desensitization and reprocessing. I go as far as using Kama Sutra techniques. I have been written up in the American Journal of Medicine Practices and if you are interested, I can provide the article for you to read." Jacob spoke confidently.

That caught my interest. My first thought was, could Kelly have sent him? I knew that was preposterous, he didn't even know where I was. I wondered if anyone was able to help me, or if I really needed help. Of course, you do, you fucked up fool!

"About the Sculpture Jacob, that was done fraudulently. My former husband paid thousands of dollars to keep it out of the public's reach. I am considering a lawsuit against the artist and I won't think twice about drawing you into the suit either." I was annoyed and he was aware.

Then he handed me another business card. "I would like you to give what I have said some thought, and read up on me. If you try my techniques and you're successful, I will give you the sculpture."

Once again, he snapped me to attention, "Are you for real? Where did you come from?" I turned and faced him.

"Yes Claudia I am for real and I've heard about you and how you were exploited by Jasim. One day I will tell you more, but I am hoping you will do your research about me and let me help. I believe in what I do. Give me six months without any outside contact and you will be well on your way to emotional, spiritual and mental well-being, as far as physical, it is obvious you are very aware of that by looking at you."

I was absolutely speechless, could this be real, and could he save my marriage and possibly my life?

"Jacob, you are being sincere, aren't you? What is in it for you? Why?"

"I am sincere Claudia, very, what's in it for me? Revenge, and besides you can afford my services." Jacob grinned. He managed to get a chuckle out of me. I would pay whatever it takes to get my life back.

"One thing Jacob how old are you, you seem awfully young to be doing that kind of work?" I must have caught him off guard.

"Does not knowing my age bother you, Claudia? Well if you're worried that my age might conflict with my qualification then will you feel better if I told you I am in my late forties. He smiled as he spoke. "Are you more comfortable now?"

I grinned, "I'll have to think on that."

"Claudia, I have a flight to catch in a few hours, I trust I will be hearing from you soon. I'm looking forward to working with you." Jacob squeezed my hand.

"Jacob, I will do my due diligence where you're concerned. Have a safe trip." My eyes found his and I allowed him a half a smile. I watched him walk away and then I got up and went back to my room. He had my full attention and this could be the answer, yes please God I need to control that dark part of my life not just for myself, but for Kelly most of all.

On my return to my room, I was disappointed to see Kelly had called and I missed it. Oh, why didn't I take my phone with me? I quickly dialed my voice mail. "Hi honey, I'm sorry I missed you, I'm here waiting, come home soon. Love you too baby girl. Bye."

Then I phoned the clinic in Geneva and if I could be there tomorrow afternoon, they could see me at 3:15. I made the flight arrangements with Slade and then I dialed our home number and relief fell over me at the sound of his voice.

"Hi sweetheart, I'm sorry we've been missing each other's phone calls, oh I miss you." Not giving him the chance to say anything other than hello.

Kelly laughed. "I miss you too, so you're coming home soon?"

"Yes, darling yes, I am first stopping in Geneva at the clinic I go to all the time, I need a checkup to make sure my hormones are level. I'll be a couple of days at the most. They do the testing right there and I'm on my way home. Kelly . . . I've stayed away from the darkness, I promise you I am trying. I love you so much, Kelly."

"Thank you for telling me that, I try not to think that you have gone there. You're brave and strong Claudia and I love you for that. Things are crazy here, I haven't had much time to even breathe, but I need my wife Claudia."

"I know you do and I need you badly, you better be getting some rest I don't want you sick, are you eating properly?" I knew the answer to that, even before he answered. "Yes, I'm trying honey. I will tell you one thing, I'm awfully glad Jason is on board. Honey, he is brilliant."

We spent a few more minutes chatting and neither one of us wanted to hang up. I wanted to share what I had learned about Jacob Samuels, but it was premature. I decided that I would start to research the moment I got on board the jet.

Then, I made one more phone call: I called Sofie, but the line was disconnected. Where had she gone? It had been years since I had last seen her, she could be anywhere in Europe. Damn you, Sofie, you must have done that sculpture after Jasim died because you knew he would have destroyed you. I needed to find out if there were any more out there. After a lot of thinking, I decided to leave it to my team of lawyers and not go looking for her myself.

Chapter 31

THAT LATE MAY EVENING when the jet arrived home with me as soon as I exited the plane I could still smell the blossoms and the cooler night air greeted me. I was quick to get in my Audi, drive home and quietly let myself in. Then, I put on a delectable Egyptian silk nightdress and crawled in beside him.

I had researched Jacob Samuel's successes and I had contacted some of is colleagues who sang his praises. I wasn't prepared to tell Kelly because if I didn't get the results, both of us would be let down and I couldn't put Kelly through that. If I was to do it, I would have to do it underhandedly and what would the consequences be after six months? But I couldn't think about all the details right now.

His beautiful stretched out the body was naked and relaxed, so peaceful. I carefully adjusted my body and nuzzled against his loin, resting my nose in the soft mass of his genital hair. Slowly, I let my tongue swirl around the head, over and under as slow as possible. I heard him whisper my name.

"Mm . . . mm . . . Claudia, I'm dreaming!" he mumbled and became still. I wrapped my lips around a growing shaft and with a quick movement I took all my mouth could hold and sucked him deep. "Oh, you're here I'm not dreaming, oh Claudia," he moaned after each thrust of my mouth, in and out until he moved in sequence, his breathing was signaling the explosion about to fill my throat. His body trembled as his semen filled the back of my throat. The familiar taste of my husband was welcome, I kept my lips tight against as he slid out of my mouth, swallowing the remainder.

Then, I raised my head up and made eye contact. "Honey I'm home." I giggled, his hands were already clasped into my hair.

"Yes, you sure are, that was no dream, thank you, God. I think you better get up here woman." Kelly ordered. I was on it immediately, blanketing him with my body. He smelled wonderful, and the coolness of his body against mine was soon heating up as his hands moved around me.

"What a beautiful sight to wake up to Claudia, my beautiful wife." He took my hand and placed it on his heart. "Feel this Baby, it only beats like this when you're here with me." I drank him in before his hands gripped my face and brought it to his. Our lips were melting together in desperation, lovingly consuming the others. I needed this. I needed him and every nerve ending was begging for his attention. And his attention I got, there wasn't an inch of my body that wasn't washed in kisses and his breath. I fell apart tears flooding my face. "

What did I do?" He gasped.

"No, no, Kelly you didn't hurt me, you just love me so much, I've been too long without you." I buried myself into him. "Please don't let go, you can't let go. Hold me tight Kelly." I begged sounding so desperate, and desperate I was. How could I be without him for another six months?

"Hey, hey honey it's okay. I'm not going anywhere and neither are you, I've got you, honey, I've got you." He rested his face against my neck. I felt his lips nibbling along the length of it. "You're safe Claudia, you're safe here with me. You are so loved sweetheart, just know that always, no matter what." He tightened his arms around me.

The house phone was ringing off the wall and when we checked the time it was after ten o'clock

"Jason, yes I slept in, don't expect me in for the next few days. You can handle it just fine on your own. If you can't, then it'll have to wait until I get back . . . " Kelly stroked my cheek. His eyes planted on mine as he continued his conversation; his thumb extending slowly along my jawline. I couldn't take my eyes off his. I felt the flat palm brush slow to the top of my chest. "Don't do anything about them, they have an outstanding bill, just keep an eye out for any payment." The heel of his palm reached my nipple and I shivered under his touch as he continued, "That's all been taken care of, you will need to make a trip here, there is paperwork on my desk, check the supplies while you're at it. Listen, son, I'm going to let you go, do your best, I'm out for a while."

Kelly nuzzled at my ear. I heard my name mentioned. "Yes, Claudia's home, we're home but unavailable to anyone, okay thanks, Jason and tell Daniel for me. Got to go. Talk to you in a couple of days." Kelly reached over and unplugged the phone.

"I'll get the other ones later, but right now this little rosebud needs my attention," Kelly smirked, while his fingers worked a firm grip on each nipple.

We spent three days totally alone without even leaving the house. There wasn't any reason to go anywhere and I was more than happy just being at home. One evening Kelly was insisting on preparing the meal while I sat back and watched.

"I think there is something under our bed you should check out Claudia. Tell me what you think, okay?" He said with an unreadable expression.

"What, what is it?" I asked as I squinted.

"Go see." Kelly nodded to his left. I put my wine glass down on the table and hurried to our bedroom to find a square package.

"What could this be?" I spoke as I returned with it to the kitchen.

"Aren't you going to open it?" Kelly asked eagerly.

"Oh, Oh, Oh Kelly!"

It was us in front of a rising sun the morning we got married. It was taken right after we were pronounced man and wife. I sat it against the wall.

A few weeks had passed by and I knew I needed to decide, the longer I waited the longer it would take me to do what I knew I needed to do to have a full life with Kelly. I made the call and said I would be at the Marseilles address he gave me by the end of the week.

This trip had to be a secret because if it didn't work and I didn't get the results I desperately wanted, I knew I could live in this body any longer. The days of my need for black pain were reoccurring more frequently and it was a struggle not following through.

If this didn't work I made the decision to disappear, I knew Kelly would never agree to a divorce, but being free of me would give him the chance to move on in a happier life.

I decided that it was best for everyone that it was on a day I knew Kelly was out of town in Kelowna for the day and that came sooner than I could have imagined when he mentioned a meeting Thursday. The hardest part would be making Slade lie about having any knowledge of my whereabouts. I couldn't even tell my mother I was going and that would be upsetting for her as well.

That Thursday morning my stomach was in knots and I thought I was going to puke my guts out. I had to be cool, the need to keep him near me, touching, skin next to skin was urgent for me. My last words to Kelly as the elevator door closed were, "You are my love, my only love forever sweetheart, you have a spectacular day." I blew him a kiss and Kelly's face glowed.

I left my wedding band because I wanted to fully be dedicated and committed to a sexual relationship with only him, my husband. I slipped on a pair of jeans and a sweater then phoned Slade and advised him I would be on time. My last task was writing him a note.

I Love You, Baby!

I wrote it in red lipstick on the bathroom mirror above his sink. Then, I placed a note on a magnet and stuck it on the refrigerator. Those were the two places he would look at every day. As I rode the elevator, I had to believe I'd be coming home a whole person. I hadn't any trust that this process would work or what was ahead of me during the next six months.

That June morning when the jet ascended the skies over Penticton I wanted nothing more than to run back home. The only thing I knew was I had to take the plunge and do this. If I didn't I would be falling back into the black side.

I knew I had to contact with my mother and it would have to be the same sort of message I left Kelly. I turned on the laptop and set her a very short message. Don't be concerned by my absence, I will explain in time. Claudia.

The trip to Marseille seemed to drag, I had nothing to occupy my mind with, no business issues, things were moving along. I did think of a side trip but knew it would defeat this purpose. Anxiety was building. I paced through the cabin. I thought happy thoughts of Kelly would calm my angst. It only made me yearn more, I sang quietly, read, slept finally came a short time before landing. My mind and soul were exhausted.

I arrived at Jacobs I arrived at Jacob's and it was like an oasis. It was a very modern design. I was greeted by Jacob who was very professional in his mannerisms. I appreciated it and I trusted him explicitly. I was curious where he was keeping the sculpture, I didn't see it, so I asked and he promised when the right time came he would show me.

The first few days Jacob reviewed the terms of my stay, which included no alcohol of any kind, no drugs, and no painkillers. I would remain here in the confines of the property, with no outside contact. This allowed me to focus and acquaint myself with my being and my soul without any interruptions.

He started by doing a full assessment; starting with my childhood. The second day Jacob explained that while I was here, I would be wearing silks and satins and lace. That was when Madame Louisa was introduced to me. I was measured, she asked questions regarding my preference for colors. I had my own questions, how many of us were here for treatment? Jacob assured me there were five other women each working with their own specialist. It was kept confidential no one intermingled but I was assured the practice was legal and licensed.

The next day Madame Louisa returned with several items of luxurious clothing almost identical to the choices I made when we cruised the Greek Islands and Cypress. The fabrics were the same quality as I had been accustomed to.

Jacob began with psychotherapy and that continued throughout the course of treatment. The sessions eventually worked into psycho-sexual therapy centering on Kama Sutra beliefs. He had also trained in Mumbai, India as a sexologist, while he also held a doctorate in psychiatry.

I let down my guard with him. I was an open book. I released everything I had bottled up and protected myself from. Jacob encouraged me to write at least an hour before bed and again when I woke up in the morning before my day began.

My body was doing unexpected things. My hormones had been perfectly balanced after my Geneva visit, but one important aspect was overlooked. The absence of birth control, I quit using it when sex acts stopped with the men Jasim had me seduce.

Because my body had never been allowed to go into menopause, I was still very fertile. Here I was 48 and possibly pregnant. Neither Kelly nor I even thought about protection, I honestly thought my black side may have damaged any possibilities of conceiving. This wasn't the right time to have a pregnancy happen, or was it? What was Kelly going to say, or do? He has grandchildren.

Jacob asked me, "Are you concerned that this will interfere with therapy Claudia?"

"Isn't that the question I should be asking you?"

"Possibly, tell me, Claudia, how do you feel about being pregnant especially now, at this time of your life?" Jacob sat back and watched me.

"Blessed Jacob, very blessed. I am also concerned for my child, will there be any issues? My husband, well, I'm not sure how he will feel about this but if I know him the way I think I do he will be over the moon."

"You're going to want to share this news with him I'm sure. Once you see a gynecologist, this puts a bit of a twist on the process. All we can do is proceed one step at a time Claudia."

"My husband has no idea where I am, I didn't. I couldn't disclose this with him, I had made some decisions before leaving. I want him to know, but this news has to keep until the therapy is done."

Jacob nodded, "This is something we need to go over in a session Claudia. But right now a pregnancy confirmation is a priority.

"Do you have any objections to me contacting the clinic in Geneva? I need to confer with my doctors there, and they should be able to refer me to someone here. I have to look out for the health of this child. Or should we discontinue the therapy?"

"I really want to return to my husband as healthy as possible, even more so now."

Jacob was silent, I assumed in thought. "Claudia this is how I would like to proceed, you're physical well-being needs to be established and from what you have told me so far I have minor concerns about the trauma you are holding. It could be problematic during the pregnancy. Does sound like the direction you would like to take?" I nodded throughout his conversation. "Yes, I'm hopeful this will work for me."

Jacob had given me the privacy I needed and I started to journal. What I wanted more than anything was to contact Kelly, I knew he should be part of this too. I had only been here a month and the pregnancy would have taken place during the three weeks I was home. I calculated and realized I missed a period. I had to be six weeks along. If able to continue this therapy, I would go home with a bit of a tummy.

Because of my history, the doctors felt that there shouldn't be any abnormalities or birth defects but recommended that I be tested after the first trimester. That meant the amniotic fluid would be analyzed. I would consent to that being done here as soon as possible. I needed the assurance my baby would be normal. The doctors here in France decided that I could proceed cautiously with Jacobs's therapy and keep being monitored. I couldn't have been happier, I wanted to reclaim my identity and I was ready to do the work.

The relationship that developed between Jacob and I was different than any relationship I had ever experienced, void of anything of a sexual nature. The rough road began and I was taken back to that day I learned who Jasim really was and Jacob guided me through the emotions. The weeks flew by and it was during a meditation that I felt the presence of my child. He fluttered and I was absolutely positive I was having a son, I was sure but that I would wait to find out with Kelly. I knew God had gifted me once again. How blessed I am, I had another opportunity at motherhood.

The doctors decided it was a safe time to extract enough amniotic fluid to test and now the wait for the results was a difficult time. Jacob was aware of my anxiety and decided it was a good time to re-introduce me to my body. How I incorporated the now-sexual and erotic part of me would come to play when my body gave me the signals. He started with "Inner Child" work and gradually the part of me that held the lost innocence had surfaced and we worked carefully through it. Jacob did exercises in self-touching with me that I was to do in privacy. That was when the raw and self-destructive traits were exposed: we were getting to the root.

The long-awaited telephone call came from the physician the test results were ready and they couldn't have given me any better news. Our baby was perfect, without any birth defects, there wasn't anything out of the normal. They were prepared to share the baby's sex, but I stopped them. Kelly would be the one to tell me the results.

I thought I had done the worst of the work until Jacob brought me to the room where the sculpture was kept. I was face to face with my own image and I fell apart when I saw how Sofie had captured my weaknesses my strengths my beauty and my flaws, my bold sexuality and the softness of my sensuality. The tortured body throbbing in hurt and loathing, but there was the mother that shone through, in the fine lines that once were stretch marks from a pregnancy so long ago.

Jacob was right; he knew how affected I would be. I collapsed against my image and Jacob kept his awareness on me. Shortly after, Jacob left the room and came back with a sledge-hammer.

"This is your opportunity to destroy the image of that Claudia, the one you were forced to become." I stared at the sledge-hammer and knew what Jacob was offering. I grabbed it and swung the hammer and connected it to the huge breasts. The grieving process began and Jacob verbalized his concerns. "We need to tread very carefully now Claudia, I fear you will be experiencing nightmares from this point on. I think I need to bring a cot into your bedroom and sleep at a safe distance. I can't let you be alone especially with the baby, we can't risk a miscarriage. Are you going to be okay with me sleeping in the same room with you?"

I was in total agreement. I knew changes were occurring. Boy did I have nightmares and then night terrors, everything I had buried was coming alive and I was afraid to go to sleep at night. It got to the point where I slept during the day. I became violently sick and vomited to the point where Jacob was ready to admit me to the hospital.

"You must have one strong willed little one in there Claudia, he's hanging on, and you can get past this as long as you keep reminding yourself that you are safe. Nothing can hurt you any longer you come through it now."

This was the first time there had been any physical contact between Jacob and me. "Do you need to be touched in a safe manner, Claudia? Would you be able to let me hug you? If you feel uncomfortable at any time just say the word and I will let go."

I absolutely did not know if I wanted to be touched or not. I knew within me the desire to be held was lurking, but would there be any after effects? I was scared to death, what would his touch be like now? I stood up and walked in his direction cautiously. As soon as I felt his energy, I knew the difference in myself. I would soon be able to go home in somewhat of a healthier mind, but I had work ahead of me and I expected Jacob would be in my life for quite a while after I had this baby.

This pregnancy was totally different than with Mikhail. I was showing quicker and my belly was more noticeable this time. My last examination in France went well. The ultrasound confirmed that everything was progressing at the normal rate. My blood pressure was good and I was exceptionally healthy.

Six months had passed and I was ready to go home and face Kelly I took care of myself from head to foot, went shopping for a stunning maternity outfit. It was a beautiful red and white trimmed tunic with a pair of leather boots along with a white cashmere full-length coat which would be perfect for the Penticton winter.

Christmas was nearing and I have so much to be thankful for.

The warm greeting, I received from Slade when he heard my voice. "Come get me Slade I'm almost ready to come home. I will have things in place by the time your flight hours are secure." I announced with giddiness.

"Sure, thing Claudia, I will be seeing you in a few days.

I knew it was going to be awkward, extremely awkward seeing

Kelly. But worst of all did I have a home and a husband to go home too? I held on to his promise, his words kept me believing in what I was doing all these months. My only concerns would he be able to move forward with a child we would now be raising a child in our 60s and 70s, so much for retirement. I was afraid of what his reaction was going to be, but I was more hopeful that we had a product of our special love and commitment to each other and a child to share that love with.

I must have dozed off because the buzzing sound alarmed me. I quickly realized where I was and picked up the cabin phone.

"We will be landing shortly Claudia, we've just flown over Kelowna, how are you and that baby doing back there?" He sounded thrilled.

"We are both good Slade, can you drive me home this time?"

"Yes ma'am, I mean yes Claudia, I would be happy to take you home. Over and out, we are approaching Penticton airport, seat belt on."

"Yes sir, over and out." I giggled. Hey, little one you will soon be hearing your daddy's voice and feeling the warmth of his hands. He's a going to be a wonderful daddy you wait and see.

The jet came to a full stop and I felt anxiety sweeping over me. Oh, please God don't let it be too late. Please, please give me the chance to share my true self with you again. I waited anxiously for Slade to drive the jet into the hanger and lock up. I felt myself shaking.

He asked, "When was the last time you have spoken with Kelly?"

"I haven't spoken to him at all . . . I hope this time I have a husband to come home to. Between you and me Slade I don't deserve that man. I have been a rotten partner. I hope I have one last chance to make it right." My voice cracked.

"He knows what a lucky man he is, and if I know that, he does too, you've been pretty open with me and I know what you've faced. He loves you Claudia that is so apparent to anyone who sees the two of you together. I think it will all work out just fine." Slade turned left into the driveway and it was quiet just like it had been the day I left. "I've got your bag. I will make sure you have it in the elevator." Slade opened my door and was about to help me out.

I shook my head, "Hey, I'm not helpless, just pregnant. I unlocked the garage door with my key and to my surprise, Kelly was home, or at least his truck was home. I took a deep breath and called up the elevator and waved to Slade as he drove out. Okay, Claudia, it's now or never.

Chapter 32

THE ELEVATOR DOOR opened to the sounds of a sports game on television, I wasn't quite sure if it was hockey or football. Kelly liked watching both. I pulled my white cashmere full-length coat around me, careful to keep my pregnancy from his view and took the twelve steps towards the family room and stopped.

He felt my presence before he saw me and was up on his feet. He said nothing, but the look in his eyes said it all: the sign of relief. Still, he said nothing. I was at a loss for words, I was looking for a sign to give me direction. Do I run into your arms? What do I need to do? I did the first thing that came to my mind and took slow steps towards him. He waited, and I reached out for him, he didn't take his eyes off of mine. I fell into him, and his arms fell into place.

"Claudia . . . " He whispered. "I'm worn out."

"Yes, Kel I bet you are. You haven't gone through what you did or nothing Kelly, the running is all over because now I know why I punished my body for the pleasure I got from the abuse. I've been in treatment all this time. There is a doctor in France who developed a therapy. I lived in a compound with his staff, there were no outside interferences to allow me to keep focused on myself"

My hands found his face and I held it. I needed him to see my sincerity, "Kelly only time will prove it, and you will see, but I do need to warn you, I still have nightmares and often night terrors."

"Oh Claudia, it took a lot of courage for you to do what you did. I just felt separate from you and that was the most difficult thing, not knowing where my wife was and if she was okay."

"Kelly, I am so sorry, you're the one person I love with all my heart and you're the person I've hurt the most. I knew every time I came back home how you must have felt, wondering where had I been what was I doing to myself. I knew if I didn't get the help I would have had to walk out of your life because it hurt me seeing you' hurt."

I sat beside him wishing he would hold me. I wanted to open my coat so he could see what was happening to my body. "I really love you Kelly and I knew I needed to do whatever it took to conquer that nightmare I lived for so many years."

I waited for him to say something, but his eyes just darted back and forth over mine until his fingers stroked my cheek and his lips reached out for mine. It was when he buried his face in my hair, against my neck, that I knew with time we would be in the best place we have ever been.

"You smell as wonderful as you feel Claudia, I'm so glad you're home darling. "His kisses were hitting all the right spots and my insides were filling even fuller with the love I have for him. I wasn't at all surprised at his next statement.

"What was hard for me, was you doing this without my support, not giving me the chance to work through it with you. Are you sure this was the answer? I don't want you to leave me like that again." He whispered.

He was being ever so cautious. I took both his hands. "Yes sweetheart, I'm sure, this time I took something with me when I left." I brought his hand inside my coat to my belly and let them rest. The look on his face was a look of disbelief.

"A baby, how is that possible? I don't understand how? Aren't we too old to be making babies?" He said distraughtly. I shook my head.

"Does it really look that way? I've kept my body out of menopause, you should be aware I have always had my period with all the emotional stuff going on. It happened the first week I was home those three days we spent mostly in our bed." I grinned widely.

"I am almost seven months Kelly, I've been well looked after, we been tested, the baby and I are both very healthy and no birth defects or missing chromosomes," I said calmly.

Kelly pulled away from me and that was something he had never done before. My body tensed up as he walked away and left the room. I was crumbling inside, I couldn't move, but I figured I had better try. I'd lost him. I pulled my coat around me again and attempted to take the twelve steps towards the elevator and just as I got there so did he.

"You're not leaving me again Claudia, no way. I want you to put this back on and promise me you won't ever take it off again." Kelly held out my wedding ring. I let out one hell of a sigh.

"It not too late, you're saying it's not over?" I couldn't control my emotion any longer.

"My darling, oh Claudia, of course, it's not too late, it could never be too late, I love you and this time if I have to tie you down I will."

I opened my coat, "Looks like you have done that already, don't you think?"

We grinned and I snorted. "Yep, it does kinda look that way, doesn't it?"

I didn't hesitate to slip my ring back where it belonged. It was a bit tight on my somewhat swollen finger. My arms went around his neck and as I drew him to me, our foreheads met and our eyes rested once again on the others.

"Forgive me Kelly for the way I left you, it was a big gamble for me to take, I couldn't live in a body controlled by two desires. But worst of all, seeing what it was doing to you that made me move on the opportunity."

It was obvious Kelly has been stressed and his eyes were tired and there were dark shadows deep underneath those striking topaz eyes. His lips moved slowly and expertly greeting mine with the fire and desire I was so familiar with. Our moans so audible and my heart exploded in joy. Not much was said as the passion took over us. His hands, now at the small of my back, drew my body to his and the little life growing inside of me responded to his mother's emotion made his presence known.

"I felt that." Kelly hesitated, "This is mind boggling! We're pregnant. Wow, you and me after all this time." He gently rested his fingers at the sides of a well-formed baby bump. I knew it was going to take him some time for all of this to sink in, I had all those months adapting to the changes. He knelt down in front of me, I felt his face against my belly through my dress as his hands pulled the fabric up over my belly to expose the tight firm flesh extending out of me.

I melted, as he placed multiples of kisses over me. "I want you in our bed, Claudia, is it okay to make love to my wife again?" He questioned.

"Of course, it is, it's exactly what we both need right now, skin to skin." I grabbed hold of my husband's hand and directed him to our bed; to consummate once more my commitment to us, and our marriage.

I succumbed to his every move. I gave him complete control, the access he needed to have me the way he needed me: naked and at his mercy. I watched how his hands followed his eyes as they moved over every inch of my changing body. My now swollen breasts were so tender and aching for his roaming hands.

"Claudia this is wonderful, seeing you like this filled with our child." Kelly had both my hands together at the top of my head, he was positioned over me and carefully after placing my legs over his shoulders, he took me gently and lovingly as we entered into the abyss of joy.

My fingers were finally free weaving through his soft wavy hair, while my heart beat hard and grateful to be where I was always meant to be. Kelly's touch and intimate connections were the only sensations my body would ever need again.

I preferred to wait until Christmas Day to share our wonderful news when all of our extended family would be together. Clarissa and the rest of her family, as well as our friends, were all flown in: everyone other than Kelly's parents. Having everyone in one place made it much easier to explain the details of our pregnancy than repeating it individually.

When our family and friends got over the shock and amazement of the miracle pregnancy as they insisted it was, there were tears of joy and of course questions of our baby's sex. Kelly and I both decided to leave that envelope sealed and wait until the moment of birth.

Clarissa revealed that her father made her cradle all those years ago and she asked if we would like to see it. There wasn't any Antique Bentwood Cradle hesitation in our voices, we both jumped at the idea. Even though my grandparents had pressured Clarissa into giving me up for adoption, I understood, they knew how much their own daughter had suffered at Jasim's hands. They believed I would have been a daily reminder of his brutality, they trusted it would be better for me to be placed in a loving home. I knew they had made the right choice for all of us, and I loved them even more.

"So many more blessing is all around us now. Claudia having you and Kelly in our lives and now a new grandbaby, our Lord knows what he's doing." Clarissa announced as she hugged me and kissed my forehead.

After Christmas dinner, Clarissa made an offer. "I have something I'd like you to think about Claudia, even though I have no idea what your birthing plans are, I have delivered a few babies in my time, and could you and Kelly give me the honor of letting me assist you with the birth of my, my grandchild?"

"I really don't have to think about it, but Kelly and I need to talk it over first. I really want to have a home birth especially since my first delivery went well and he came quickly. Mom, I would love it, it would make the delivery even more special."

The holidays came and went I was so at peace within myself. I was loved like I haven't felt for such a long time. Winter had with a full blast and I stayed pretty much at home while Kelly worked from home, not wanting to stray far from me.

Then on February 14, 2005, Kobe Ryan MacAskill, our healthy boy, surprised us both when he arrived early that morning at home with the help of a very proud Grandma Clarissa as the attending physician. Kelly held his baby boy before laying him across my chest. It was the picture-perfect moment for me seeing what I thought had passed us by, my husband holding his son against his chest. My heart had never felt so much joy at one time. I was triple blessed surrounded by the people that meant the most to me.

Spring came and went and summer arrived. The winery was buzzing and I was able to be a support for Kelly and devote the remainder of my time with Kobe. Our sex life was just like food, a necessity and to keep it that way our health had to be taken care of. That meant keeping my hormone level balanced and using birth control regularly.

Now every decision I made came with Kelly's input and unless both of us were was on board it never happened. We were a team now a solid team and with the ongoing support of Jacob's therapy, I was healing in a healthy way.

Kobe was definitely a combination of Kelly and me, it was obvious he has my skin tones and a head of dark curls and blessed with Daddy's striking topaz eyes. I had to work extra hard to keep as much intimacy with Kelly as we had before Kobe came into our lives. My body needed that just as much as Kelly's did. I slept when Kobe slept, so when my husband reached out in the middle of the night for intimacy, I was a willing partner.

Then, I made one last decision without his knowing: to pay an unexpected visit to Kelly's parents. This would be the only time I would go behind my husband back again, they had the right to meet Kobe and if they chose not to accept him then Kobe would have no memory of them other than stories. But my hope was to encourage them to get to know me as the woman that loves their son and their son's choice as a wife.

Clarissa supported me and on one of my trips to Vancouver we took the chance that they would be home. I set out on my own and rang the doorbell, to be greeted by Kelly's dad; the person I dreaded the most. I was hoping Mrs. MacAskill would be a gentler touch.

Wallace MacAskill stood in the doorway and appeared to be taken back by my presence. I held out my hand, "I'm Claudia Samara, do you remember me?" I asked as I wanted for a handshake and I wasn't about to withdraw my hand until I got the response I was waiting for.

His stern domineering expression hadn't changed, but there was a hint of softness behind the stare. "I remember you, Claudia." He said as his eyes moved to my extended hand.

Before he could respond Alison appeared at the door, "Who is it Wally?" she called out.

"Claudia Samara has come by Alison." He stated and his eyes moved to where she was now standing.

"Claudia, this is such a surprise, please come in?" She quickly took over for Wallace. She was as warm as I remembered her to be, especially when I was a youngster running in and out of this house with Kelly.

I walked in slowly between her and Wallace followed. It was awkward, to say the least, but promising.

He stayed silent, "Please sit Claudia, what brings you here?"

Alison reached over and took a hold of my hand between both of hers.

"Your son and grandson, I trust you know Kelly and I married and have a miracle child." I opened the conversation.

She dropped her eyes to her hands while he spoke, "Yes Claudia, my wife and I are very aware of these things. But our son hasn't been man enough to step up and talk to us. His brothers have kept us up on what's been happening. Is Kelly with you?"

"No Kelly has no idea I came here today, I came to make peace with you sir. I know you don't approve, but I would like the opportunity to get to know you better, and your grandson should have the opportunity to grow up knowing who his grandparents are and where he comes from. I would give anything to see my husband with one of your arms around him. I welcome you to come to Penticton and see the type of man he is and what kind of life he has created for us."

He asked, "Do you have our grandson with you?" I tried not to react and smile. I nodded. "Yes he's in the car with Clarissa, my biological mother, we found each other a few years back. Would you like to meet her and Kobe?"

Alison spoke up, but not before turning her attention to her husband. "Why yes my dear, Wally and I would like nothing more, wouldn't we Wally?"

"I think that would be fine Claudia." He said as he stood up and walked to stand beside the fireplace.

Alison wrapped her arms around my neck before whispering. "He's not the same person anymore Claudia, he's changed."

I squeezed her in return. "I will be right back." I smiled at them and went to the car. I drew my son into my arms and walked hand in hand with Clarissa back to the house.

Alison was at the door and she extended her hand to Clarissa. "Please come in, I'm Alison and this is my husband Wally, I mean Wallace."

"Would you like to hold him, Alison?" I asked before kissing his sweet little head. "Yes, may I please?" She beamed with happiness.

After letting Alison take Kobe, I sat down beside my mother and glanced over at Wally. He looked uncomfortable as he ran his finger across his forehead. I wouldn't push him into doing something he wasn't ready to do, but there was one thing left. I had placed one of our brochures in my jacket pocket in case an appropriate situation arose, and I had to believe this was the one.

"Wally if you want to take some time to think it over, here is one of our brochures, one of us is always around or not far away, please come for a visit, you don't even have to call. The directions are on the back."

Wally MacAskill surprised me like no one else had ever before. "Mistakes and unforgivable words have been said Claudia, I am ashamed of the things I've said to you."

Kobe began to fuss and the doting mother that I am was anxious to take him, but I caught the look in Clarissa eyes, the slight shake. I knew Kobe was all right and I couldn't lose this opportunity with Wally.

"Thank you for giving me this opportunity, I have forgiven you a long time ago. I had hoped that the time would come when you Kelly and I could mend this. Your son loves you Wally, and whether or not he will ever admit it, he misses you both. I'm not going to tell him I was here. I will let you decide when the right time is to come to him." A different Wallace MacAskill emerged and squeezed my shoulder. I didn't need any words to understand his actions.

I flew back to Penticton, my husband familiar's frame was standing with his hands in his jean pockets and the wind blowing through his hair.

"Hey little man, did you take good care of Mommy for Daddy?" He glanced over at me protectively.

"It was a good trip, but our little one needs a nap and so does Mommy and Daddy." I took my husband's hand. As we settled Kobe in the back of the Audi, and ourselves next to each other, I still couldn't believe how happy and settled I felt.

I knew there was a circle that eventually connected everything perfectly together and anything that was put in front of us now, I believed Kelly and I could face it together and deal with it successfully.

As we drove Kelly covered my hand with his and asked, "Hey can I check something?" He grinned and I knew where his mind was at . . . he checked our sleeping boy before pulling over to the side of the road.

"Kobe's going to wake up soon and I want you to nurse him. I want you and need you right now." He motioned me to slide over. Kelly hiked up my skirt and yanked my panties down. I was ready after one or two swipes of his finger over my opening. Holding my knees against his sides Kelly moved into me, "Don't move Claudia. Just kiss me, sweetheart, I just want to be inside of you for now." I was eager for his mouth, but someone else in the backseat woke up and was beginning to fuss. My breasts started reacting to his little sounds. "I'm leaking Kel, I wish you could drive with me in this position. Maybe I should feed him right here."

"Mm . . . if only I could keep you like this as you feed him." Kelly slowly pulled out of me, doing his jeans up then he took Kobe out of his seat while I readied my breast for him.

I nursed while Kelly's fingers replaced his hard on. I wasn't sure reaching an orgasm was the best thing to do while nursing, but I wasn't about to stop him and watching Kobe at my breast furthered our arousal. My fingers and toes were curling. "You're going to cum aren't you, let go, cum all over my fingers, I want to taste you. Now, Claudia let go."

I was pulsating and Kobe wasn't latched on and starting crying.

It was all I could do to keep my focus on putting him back on my breast; my eager boy didn't hesitate once he found it. Kelly found a baby wipe and wiped the traces of my orgasm. We were so close to home we decided to risk it and break the law. Kelly was driving while I fed him. I was satisfied.

A few days later Kelly's cell phone rang. Kelly's face went white. I got scared and grabbed Kelly's arm.

He stared at me, "My parents are on their way here for some reason."

I sighed in relief. I touched his arm. "Kelly it's all right." I was so surprised they had taken my offer so soon. I took his hand and walked beside him. "Honey, please don't be mad at me, Clarissa and I stopped in and had a visit with them, I invited them. Please hear them out?".

"I should be really pissed off with you, how the hell did you make this happen?" he took a strong grip on my shoulders. "Claudia, what aren't you telling me?"

"Come and see what they have to say, I promise you it will be okay." I grabbed his bum and tried to change his mood, but Kelly was not about to cooperate.

"I don't like this Claudia, I wish you had of warned me." Kelly scolded.

"I didn't know they were coming, I gave them an open invitation, Kelly they have a new grandson, let him explain. Please?"

They pulled into the driveway and we met them at the entrance way. Kelly looked like a mad bull ready to strike out at the red cape. "I would like to speak to my parents in privacy, so please excuse us."

Kobe and I retreated to the bedroom and had some mommy and Kobe time. I still couldn't take my eyes off my baby, still, he seemed so surreal, I began singing to him in Arabic the song I used to sing to Mikhail and wondered if his brother's spirit was watching over us.

"Oh, Kobe your brother would have loved you so much." I dozed off, it was the sensation of my baby being taken from me that aroused me. It was Kelly reaching in carefully not to disturb him.

"I'm going to put him in his bed." I hadn't moved, I didn't want Kelly taking him. "Why did you do that? He was fine, I was fine, we were having some quiet moments alone Kelly." I felt sadness, it came on like a blanket covering me. Kelly knelt in front of me.

"Oh honey, I didn't mean to upset you, you both looked so peaceful. Are you okay?"

"Just a feeling a little melancholy, I sang the song I used to sing to Mikhail and it made me think about him."

Kelly pulled me into his arms.

"I guess I made a mistake trying to make amends with you and your folks. I'm sorry for interfering." I buried my face in his neck.

"Honey you did the right thing, I'm so glad you took Kobe to my parents, my dad realizes the mistakes he made. Thank you, Claudia, that took a lot of courage for you to face that man. These are the times when I can't believe you're my wife." His hands gripped my face, he kissed me and I collapsed into him, I felt so needy and hungry for him.

When our mouths separated, he spoke first, "They're waiting for us to join them."

I checked my sleeping boy before washing my face and changing into something dressier. With the baby monitor in hand, I joined my in-laws.

Wally greeted me first, "Claudia, I would like a few minutes to talk to you, I'm the biggest ass, and if I could take all those nasty words back I would eat them. You took a big step thank you for bringing my son back to me."

"I did it because of our son, he was the reason. Don't give me any credit, you're still the one who chose to come and work it out with Kelly. So let's forget the past and there is so much to look forward to." I responded before giving him a cautious hug. What I would have given for a glass of wine right that moment, but I needed to keep a clean diet for Kobe's best health.

Kelly seemed on top of things and a big smile fell across his lips. "It looks like you have things under control my darling."

My hand touched his back, "I think everything is under control." "We are blessed, we have so much you and I, I have so much gratitude and am so proud of you."

"You were worth it, you did the hard work I had to sit on the sidelines and wait, but patience can be so sweet." Kelly took a kiss before adding, "I must say you are looking lighter, it's good you have Jacob as a therapist. I owe him for whatever he did to get you back to me."

"It's all good Jacob has been well looked after financially I promise you, and he's earned every cent . . . oh, I hear our waking baby! I'll be back."

Kelly's parents came and went, the deep wound was now in the process of being healed and even though we knew there would always be issues and challenges; we also knew that was the norm for every family.

We were now 50 years old and we felt blessed and grateful for all we had. It had been one hell of a ride. Thinking back to our Burnaby high school days, our innocence, our youth, encountering life's challenges, losing loved ones, friends and family . . . in my darkest days I never imagined I would survive, but with love and support, I did it. I met my demons, I asked for forgiveness and forgave others: I survived.

Now, for me, it's about not allowing my past to determine my future and to rise to be the best I can be. I also want to be there for others and inspire them to see they can do the same as well . . . maybe, just maybe, I'll write a book.

About the Author

D.H. Wright relocated from a small farming community in Manitoba to the West Coast of BC at the age of four. As a young girl she dreamt about being a successful writer and that dream led her to creative writing courses in the Okanagan, as well as pursuing her counselling education. She delights in being able to work in the social service field that led her on her journey.

It was on this journey that she found her inspiration for *That Quote was how it Began*, the first novel in a series. *Claudia Returns* is the third in the series.

Now D.H. Wright longs for a time when she can simply spend her days as a writer.

97613303R00217

Made in the USA
Columbia, SC
17 June 2018